THE MASK OF THE HOLY SPIRIT

ALAN SCARFE

SMART HOUSE BOOKS

Heidi von Palleske/Smart House Books
100 Bain Ave, 35 The Oaks, Toronto, M4K 1E8
www.smarthousebooks.com

Publisher's Note: This is a work of fiction. Although many of the people and events described were real, the entirety is a work of the author's imagination.

Book Layout © 2018 Smart House Books
Cover design - Aaron Rachel Brown
Cover concept - Barbara March

The Mask of the Holy Spirit/ Alan Scarfe -- 1st ed.
ISBN — 978-1-988980-09-6

This is a revised edition of the novel previously published as Vampires of the Holy Spirit by Clanash Farjeon (Trafford Books, 2011).
It is now the only author-approved version.

Also by the same author:
The Revelation of Jack the Ripper
The Vampires of Juarez
The Demons of 9/11

Praise for The Carnivore Trilogy

Book One – The Vampires of Juarez

"Scarfe's vampires are nothing like the classic literary and cinematic archetypes. They are neither romantic nor troubled spirits. They are pitiless, arrogant and vulgar, without immortality and unafraid of the sun."
- **Vito Tripi**, *Word Shelter*

"This book is a masterpiece. To write such a magnificent, bloodchilling work one has to plunge into the bottomless abyss of pure evil. Alan Scarfe is 'The Abyss' for he terrifies the living daylights even out of me."
- **Christopher Berry-Dee**,
former Director of the Criminology Research Institute,
Portsmouth, UK

"Fast moving, eloquent and funny and at the same time profoundly violent and distressing . . irony saves it from insupportable sadness and instead creates a fresh and captivating story."
- **Susanna Raule**, *Cut-up*

"This book is simply stupendous . . a beautifully told punch in the stomach." - **Valerio Bonante**, *Ca' delle Ombre*

"Witty and hilarious throughout thanks to the liveliness of its central character yet so disturbing it makes your hair stand on end . . an eloquent indictment of the corruption of power."
- **Giovanni Scalambra**, *Stradanove*

"Scarfe asks us to consider the extent to which we are all culpable for the endless saga of bloodletting that is the dark side of our legacy as a species. But he tells stories, he does not lecture."
- **Eric Ross Green**, *Awash with Blood*

Book Two – The Demons of 9/11

"Macabre and enjoyable as Doctor Strangelove . . political horror fiction at its best." - **Maurizio Crispi**, *Italia Informazioni*

"Getting to the truth of 9/11 has been consistently and successfully avoided. Scarfe's savage satire exposes the infamy."
        - **Eric Ross Green**, *Awash with Blood*

"A subject taboo within the cocoon of mainstream media can be accessed outside that cocoon through the art of the novel. This book is the real McCoy. Stieg Larsson would approve."
        - **Barrie Zwicker**, author of *Towers of Deception, the Media Cover-Up of 9/11*

"It opens the door to a world of darkness even more terrifying than the daily news." - **Stefania Auci**, *Diario di Pensiero Persi*

"The spiral of the story captivates the reader in a disturbing alternate reality." - **Igor de Amicis**, *Thriller magazine*

"The narrative rhythm is exemplary with stunning scenes that are effective and credible. The ethical thrust is sharpened by the horror and creates a perfect balance of denunciation and entertainment."
        - **Sergio Riotino**, *L'informazione*

"Scarfe convinces and thrills with his rapid-fire invention. He never lets you forget the leitmotiv ever-present in all his books which pushes one to ask - is everything truly as it seems?"
        - **Susanna Raule**, *Cut-up*

"A book to read, reflect on and understand the perversity of power. But also to enjoy the lively and amusing style of an author unafraid to call George Bush a degenerate war criminal."
        - **Simone Scataglini**, *Horror.it*

for Jon and Tosia
all those they love and all
that may come after them

"Howl, howl, howl, howl! O, you are men of stones!
Had I your tongues and eyes I'd use them so
that heaven's vault should crack."

King Lear
Act 5, Scene 3, 257-259

Circles, Cycles and Circumlocution

"We will all be lost in the mists of time though time itself is an illusion."
- Michael Edward Davenport (1449 - 1527)

§

Michael knew his Davenport ancestors originated in Cheshire. The name was recorded as 'Deneport' in the Great Domesday Book of 1086 and seems to have referred to an obscure harbor or perhaps a mere wharf on the river Dane or Dauen, Devenn or Dann, a pre-Roman nomination probably connected to the Middle Welsh *'dafn'*, a trickling stream. Many linguistic forms now thought almost god-given were far less standardized then. Even five hundred years later William Shakespeare spelled his name in a variety of charming ways.

Like many an innocent victim of Secondary Modern history schoolmasters Michael still immediately heard 'doomsday' when he saw the word Domesday and the Old English root *'dom'* is the same for both.

The harsh 'accounting' or *'recknynge'* of taxable wealth set down by the Norman conquerors of what is now England in the Little Domesday and Great Domesday Books created widespread resentment among the Angle and Saxon property owners of those far off days. In the twenty years following the Battle of Hastings on October 14th, 1066, William of Falaise the second duke of Normandy's, or more familiarly William the Bastard's, conquest of the easily accessible countryside south of Hadrian's Wall was virtually complete and he was understandably anxious to hear some good news about the value of the green and pleasant land he had overrun at such enormous cost and horrific loss of life.

To put a smile on his face his zealous assessors exaggerated their numbers and then refused any appeal or repeal of their excess. It was a heavy yoke to bear for the vanquished and it was doubtless of scant consolation that the shoe had been squarely on the other foot six hundred years previously when, after the collapse of the Western Roman Empire, they had migrated out of Germany across the *Oceanus Britannicus* and ruthlessly displaced the ancient *'Brythons'*. Yet for those who were doggedly argumentative or perhaps groveling enough to maintain or even better their older standing within the new social order life was evidently not so bad.

Sometime in the next eighty years the Norman feudal lords known as the Venables of Kinderton reinstated Ormus de Dauenporte in his old manorial seat at Astbury near Congleton. In the Pipe Rolls of Cheshire of 1162 his son Richard was recorded as 'de Daveneport' and in 1166 as having become the Chief Forester of Leek and some years thereafter the family was granted a Coat of Arms and the hereditary status of Magistrate Sergeants of Macclesfield Forest. The office held the power of life and death over poaching felons and the crest reflects it. A silver shield with a chevron between three crosses and above them the head of a knight fully encased in shining black armor and at the apex a small woebegone bearded face upon bare shoulders tied with a golden rope around his neck.

The descendants of Vivian de Davenport who died in 1257 have lived in Capesthorne Hall near Bromley continuously for the last seven hundred and fifty years. Other branches of the family established comparable estates in Calveley, Wheltrough, Woodford and, the grandest of all, Bramhall. This magnificent black and white timber manor dates back to the 14th century and, though the surrounding park and woodland now belongs to the Stockport Metropolitan Borough Council and the great house is open for public viewing, Michael's direct ancestor John, of the Wheltrough Davenports, wed Alice de Bromale there in 1366 and it was occupied by their offspring for the next half millennium.

In 1631 an illustrious scion named Humphrey rose to become Lord Chief Baron of the Exchequer and was knighted by Charles I, happily several years prior to the latter's beheading in front of Inigo Jones' Palladian Banqueting Palace in Whitehall, but Michael's forebears split from the main Davenport line long before then. Indeed the only point of interest to Michael about Bramhall was that his old acquaintance, Jeremy Brett, had filmed part of a double episode of his series The Adventures of Sherlock Holmes in the boudoir and Victorian kitchen there in the autumn of 1992. It amused him that its title was The Last Vampyre.

It was based on Conan Doyle's short story The Adventure of the Sussex Vampire which intrigued Michael because the location of the tale 'just south of Horsham' was less than twenty miles from his boyhood home in Worthing. Though he knew about the Cheshire Davenports he had never bothered to trace by what circuitous route nor in what era his kinfolk trickled down from the Midlands and arrived on the south coast.

An added element in the television adaptation that had special resonance as he watched a rerun in the safety and comfort of his study in Chalk Farm more than a dozen years after its first airing on January 27th, 1993, was that one of the characters, the disabled son Jack, actually believed he was a vampire whereas in Conan Doyle there was nothing of the kind. It reminded Michael of Juarez and his kidnapping by a vicious family of drug lords who were suffering under the same delusion.

Michael wrote the occasional article for a magazine called Enigma. A very small circulation offering dedicated to the rational examination of any and all inexplicable phenomena. His pigheaded curiosity in the pursuit of such elusive matters had more than once landed him in serious hot water.

Shortly after the tragedy of 9/11 he went on assignment to New York and Washington to investigate some extraordinary occurrences that came under the broad rubric 'transhuman'. He was invited to the White House by Condoleezza Rice and the vampirish Dick Cheney and for one brief shining moment even allowed himself to imagine he had changed the course of history but, much to his lasting disappointment, it did not turn out to be the case.

He was still in reasonably frequent contact with a remarkable gentleman he met during that visit. Louis Lamy, a semi-retired billionaire, who, in April, 2004, sent him a genealogical surmise by a distant relative, Sonja La Franche, an archivist at the university of Rouen who at the age of eighty-eight was still able to maintain a 16th Century manor house and farm near the village of Beaumont-en-Auge in Lamy's native Normandy, claiming the great-grandfather of Ormus de Dauenporte had, in all probability, met the Norman invader Radulphus de Quesnay, a credible ancestor of the aforementioned vice-president, broadsword to broadsword at the Battle of Stamford Bridge on September 25th, 1066. A particularly ghastly bloodbath that was hailed as a victory by the Anglo-Saxon king, Harold Godwinson, but whose boast proved barren as, three weeks later, he was slain at Hastings.

Mlle La Franche did not speculate whether either combatant survived this undoubtedly ferocious encounter because it was obvious that, if not, they had already been successful in the implantation of their seed.

Michael and his sister Helen's mirth at *Mlle* La Franche's anecdote was due to the fact that Helen, with whom Michael shared the small flat in Chalk Farm, had accompanied him to the White House and been partly responsible for what appeared at the time to be the vice-president's sudden death.

Richard de Casper Wyoming, as they now jokingly referred to him, had collapsed on the carpet in the Yellow Oval Room while attempting to shoot both Michael and the president in the back. Helen leapt upon him from behind and clawed at his eyeballs, forestalling his intent, and he succumbed, despite his recently implanted defibrillator, to an apparent massive coronary thrombosis.

What goes around comes around, they say, even if the shrouded aspect of the repetition may be invisible to the participants.

Shuffle One

"When there were not so many books religion grew more quickly than it
has since."
- Fra Girolamo Savonarola (1452 - 1498)

§

On the morning of February 7th, 1497, the last day of Carnival, a grand
mass was celebrated in Florence by an idealistic and reform-minded
Dominican monk. Brother Girolamo had been the *de facto* ruler of the
Tuscan capital since Charles VIII of France assisted the citizen overthrow
of the Medici three years previously. He proclaimed the city and its
flourishing environs to be a Christian Republic and immediately began
urging that sodomites be stoned or burned or driven away.

The faithful that Shrove Tuesday, men, women and children, received
communion from his hands and in the evening, after returning to their
homes for a frugal meal, gathered in a solemn procession which passed
through the narrow streets of the city with growing fervor to the Piazza
della Signoria where a memorable bonfire of the vanities took place.

First into the piazza came Donatello's beautiful carved figure of the
Infant Jesus borne up by four angels with his left hand pointing to a crown
of thorns, carried on the shoulders of six chanting stalwarts clothed in
white. They were closely followed by hundreds more similarly clad holding
aloft large red crosses and singing solemn hymns of praise. Alms-
collectors went everywhere among them with silver trays. It was said they
obtained more money that day than the whole remainder of the year
combined.

At the center of the square a gigantic octagonal pyramid towered sixty
feet above the heads of the celebrants. The entire structure was stuffed
with faggots and on the seven tiers leading up to the monstrous figure of
King Carnival a myriad of 'vanities' were piled high. Books and
manuscripts of secular songs, mirrors, cosmetics, playing cards, jewels,
silken gowns and feathered finery of every description, musical
instruments, paintings of all classical subjects, even items of sculpture,
anything and everything that might in any way be construed as immoral,

lewd or lascivious.

The children had been congregated under the Loggia de' Lanzi outside the Palazzo and were led in a continuous back and forth of lauds for the Lord Jesus and decrials of the evil nature of humankind.

With the piazza packed to bursting the guardians of the pile fired it at four corners, the trumpeters of the Signory blasted forth, the bells of the Palace rang and as the flames rose to consume the offending baubles everyone shouted for sheer joy. The uninterrupted cacophony lasted a full quarter of an hour and one and all imagined Satan himself suffering a final immolation.

§

On that very same afternoon another man named Michael Davenport, of whom the contemporary Michael was as yet completely unaware, was relieved of his post as an occasional tutor of Latin at Eton College because of a growing rumor he was not the devout he pretended to be but an heretical freethinker.

§

On April Fool's Day, 2005, Fox News jumped the gun by twenty-four hours and reported that the ailing pontiff, John Paul II, had died and Michael received an unexpected phone call from Louis Lamy.

It was only a few minutes before midnight and Michael had just crept in the door of his flat with a sometime lover named Gillian, an assistant casting director at the National Theater who wheedled him to accompany her to the second last performance of the revival of Philip Pullman's His Dark Materials at the Olivier. He hadn't enjoyed it very much despite his admiration for the trilogy of novels from which it was adapted.

He was quietly hanging up their coats in the tiny vestibule and leapt for the phone on the kitchen wall in order to stifle it at the first ring because Helen was asleep and he didn't want her to wake and find he had company.

"Hello," he whispered.

"Is that you, Bartholomew, old boy?" Lamy asked amicably.

"Good lord, where are you?"

"Cat got your tongue or has someone slit your throat?"

"No, no. Helen's in bed. Where are you? It's been a long time."

Michael was gesturing his already slightly tipsy companion to a cupboard where she could find glasses and to make herself comfortable in his study and that an almost full bottle of scotch was perched high on one of the cluttered dusty shelves.

"One year exactly."

"Yes, yes, that's right. Good lord."

"What are you doing for supper tomorrow?"

"Um, ah, nothing whatever. Are you here in England?"

"Not yet. Listen, I've got a proposition for you."

"I'm not sure I like the sound of that."

Lamy chuckled.

"Oh, I think you will. Can you find your way to Earl's Court?"

"I'm sure I can manage."

Lamy knew it was a silly question. Michael had lived in London since he was nineteen.

"There's a fabulous little fish restaurant called Stratford's. Same name as the street it's on. Meet me there at eight o'clock. Bring Helen. How is she by the way? And how the hell are you?"

"Fine. We're both . . "

"Good. Look, I know it's late. We'll talk tomorrow. *Ciao*."

The line went dead and Michael smiled in anticipation of their meeting as he tiptoed into the study and ever so softly closed the door.

§

Michael's middle name was Anderson not Bartholomew.

In Mexico in the spring of 1997, following a woefully misguided attempt to retrieve some precious video footage of a white Siberian tiger, Michael fell into the clutches of Amado Portillo, the vampire-wannabe *patron* of the Juarez cartel. But the drug lord spared his life, at least temporarily, and, to Michael's undying chagrin, dressed him up in an expensive Italian suit and colored his graying hair and forced him to play the part of a mysterious *eminence grise* named 'Bartolomeo Vespucci' at a clandestine meeting with two high-ranking members of the Russian Mafia.

Portillo discovered that Michael had a fleeting acquaintance with the stage and with malicious irony suggested he prepare for his role by imagining himself as the pope, notwithstanding that he was to remain absolutely silent throughout the meeting except to say *'si'* and nod in agreement if Portillo looked at him, and, to his wild amaze, the *mafiosi* scraped as obsequiously before him as if he had been the re-embodiment of Uncle Joe Stalin.

The meeting concluded with an arrangement to secrete a large quantity of contraband weapons-grade plutonium in the Samalayuca desert south of Juarez and presumably hold it there for sale to the highest bidder.

The Russians were guzzling vodka and at the culmination of the meeting Michael had to watch a sexual ritual of blood between them, Amado's ravishing younger sister Cecilia and a black woman who was there to interpret and closely resembled Condoleezza Rice. At the end they made a toast, *'Bessmertnaja smert' nash vladelec!'* which, in the days after Michael's return to London, his Hungarian wife, Marta, translated as 'Immortal Death, Our Master!'

Ever since his extraordinarily lucky escape Michael had tried to discover the identity of 'Bartolomeo Vespucci' but had never been able to turn up any satisfying contemporary suspect. All he could find were a few brief references to an obscure professor of astronomy at Padua in Renaissance Italy, a relatively unimportant member of a wealthy Florentine family intimately intertwined with the affairs of that city, who had once written a letter to Niccolò Machiavelli concerning the influence of the stars on free will and whose sometime explorer uncle Amerigo shortly thereafter politicked himself an eponymous connection with two newly discovered continents.

However, much to Michael's astonishment four and a half years after the horrors in Juarez, in the weeks following 9/11, it became apparent some very powerful people in Washington also believed he was this impeccably shrouded phantom.

Not only Ms. Rice and the vice-president but the beleaguered ex-Secretary of State, Henry Kissinger, and even the frequently confused president, when they discovered Michael was in New York asking questions and particularly after he was seen in the company of Louis Lamy at Belmont Park and Yankee Stadium, became obsessed about his motive for being there and it was clear that, for some still unaccountable reason, they too were afraid of him.

Rice and Cheney invited him to the White House in order to test him and Cheney remained entirely unconvinced when he protested the innocent truth of his identity and yet even after the luncheon, at which Michael became certain Ms. Rice had actually been the interpreter in

Juarez despite her unassailably poker face, and now more than eight years since Amado Portillo's first mention of the accursed name, he was not one jot closer to an answer.

§

By purest happenstance, the birthdays of the two Michaels fall exactly five hundred years apart. The medieval Michael was born on October 9th, 1449, and Michael the Modern on April Fool's Day, 2005, was fifty-five years, five months and twenty-three days old. So, on the date he was let go from his at best tenuous teaching post at the then barely fledged Eton College, Michael the Medieval had managed to footle away the first forty-seven years, three months and twenty-nine days of his life and was just five and a half weeks less in age than Michael the Modern had been when he was ensnared by the Portillos.

Though separated by this yawning passage, they have much more than the oddity of timing in common.

Michael the Med made his entrance into this world at Bramhall, the second child of nine, only three of whom survived to adulthood. The youngest was Elaine, ten years, three months and eight days Michael's junior but despite the difference in their ages, and no doubt partly due to the mean competitive nature of his older brother William and ongoing disappointment at the almost annual demise of his less hearty siblings, Michael and Elaine grew very close. Though Michael was a dreamer and Elaine of a fierce, independent spirit their antics were a constant dismay to both William and their kindly but somewhat humorless parents.

Michael was also very bright when he wanted to be and it both enraged his dull-witted brother and pleasantly surprised his mother and father that he came out top of his class at the local chantry, the rather haphazard precursor of Stockport grammar school, and after his well-to-do father had pulled a few financial strings he was accepted at Cambridge. He was already fluent in Latin composition and translation since except for that very little was taught at the chantry and most of the hours were spent in religious devotion. There was no breath in rural Cheshire of the fresh winds then buffeting the wider world.

At Cambridge, however, things were different. Here at least one in ten of the masters was not a rigid ecclesiast and the curriculum included mathematics, logic, rhetoric, music, geometry and astronomy.

When Michael returned to Bramhall in the autumn of 1473 he was just twenty-four and a thoroughgoing skeptic though he kept his opinions hidden from everyone except his beloved sister and, despite it being quite impossible to predict that the accident of gender would continue to save her sex from the corruptive influence of education until the latter half of the 19th century, he set about teaching her all he had learned.

His parents were anxious he should now find some clear direction in his life and were hopeful he might consider the priesthood. They had an eldest son to take over the estate, a position William lost no opportunity in lording over his younger brother, and, given the day and age, it was a natural enough desire but it was certainly not to be.

Many male members of the extended Davenport family had lost either life or limb during the Wars of the Roses, a particularly absurd squabble between the so-called Houses of Lancaster and York over who in the lineage of Edward III had the most right to be sitting on the English throne. They were all of the same French surname Plantagenet, descended from Henry II, the feisty chap Peter O'Toole played in The Lion in Winter and Becket, who had been born in Le Mans and spent his childhood in Anjou and whose claim to kingship was that his mother was the granddaughter of William the Conqueror. But if one believed those carrying the blood of Edward's third son had more right then one was on the side of the Red Rose of Lancaster, if the second or fourth son then the White Rose of York.

The Davenports were by and large Lancastrians and Michael's youth was filled with talk of great battles won and lost, Mortimer's Cross, Ludford, Blore Heath, Wakefield, Hedgeley Moor, Hexham, Edgecote, Saint Alban's, Towton and Tewkesbury. The last took place on May 4th, 1471, while Michael was at Cambridge and the Yorkists were victorious but it consolidated the power of Edward IV and ushered in a decade of relative tranquility.

The effect of the whole protracted debacle on Michael, unlike William who found it thrilling and an endless opportunity for much purple-faced table-thumping, was a rejection of aggressive activity of almost any sort. A mildness which had not excluded siring an illegitimate daughter named Jane during his last summer at Cambridge, the existence of whom he did not become aware until after his dismissal from Eton.

What progressively ripened within him as the meandering years flowed by was sympathy. Not soppy sentiment for small furry helpless things but a deep compassion for all the wayward wanderings of lost humanity.

On January 20th, 1486, his mother died unexpectedly, just two days after the marriage of the Welsh Henry Tudor, the 2nd Earl of Richmond who had a flimsy connection to the Lancastrian side, to Elizabeth of York which had occasioned considerable joy in the household. Five months previously Henry defeated the hunchbacked and malignant Richard Plantagenet at the Battle of Bosworth Field, though both the kyphosis and Shakespeare's unsympathetic characterization are open to doubt, and upon news of his rival's death instantly proclaimed himself Henry VII and now the marriage heralded a hopeful end to all hostility. Nonetheless, hard upon his mother's sadly departed heels, his father succumbed to an infection of the kidneys and the immediate upshot was that William threw both Michael and Elaine out.

Michael was thirty-six and Elaine twenty-six and both stubbornly unwed and though they had happily dabbled in a variety of creative and vaguely helpful endeavors neither had ever been troubled by the plaguey necessity of turning such pursuits into hard cash.

William was adamant so they bade farewell to the familiar surroundings of Bramhall and traveled south stopping for a time in Stoke but hurrying on to avoid the last gasp of the Yorkists in June 1487, the ill-fated rebellion of the pretender Lambert Simnel.

Eventually they found their feet beneath the shadow of the great castle at Windsor where Edward III had been born on November 13th, 1312. Michael gained employment as a tutor of Latin at Eton College while Elaine became an assistant in the shop of a purveyor of artworks, exotic and otherwise, whose services were sometimes called upon by members of the royal court. Despite the gentleman's rather evident effeminacy they were soon sharing the same bed when fancy took them.

Michael and Elaine were thus able to maintain a frugal but increasingly satisfactory living for several years until a new headmaster, Nicholas Bradbryg, summoned Michael to his office and informed him, without warning, that the college would no longer be keeping him in its employ. When Michael asked the reason for the abrupt dismissal Bradbryg replied it was a financial matter and he was simply following the dictates of the Provost.

Michael had been taken on in the autumn of 1493 by William Horman. He was succeeded in 1496 by Edward Powell, an ambitious cleric who departed within a year and eventually met his end on the scaffold in 1540 for refusing to acknowledge the supremacy of Henry VIII. Powell was replaced by Bradbryg and he and Michael disliked each other on sight and, though it was true the college had struggled with money since its inception, they both knew very well Michael's meager stipend for his scattered hours of tutelage was not the issue.

William Caxton brought Gutenberg's printing press to Westminster in 1476 and there followed a rapid increase in the availability of books. Michael did not own any at all while attending Cambridge but now had at least a dozen, including Caxton's translation of Virgil's Eneydes, Trevisa's of Bartholomaeus Anglicus' proto-encyclopedia *De Proprietatibus Rerum*, The Sayings of the Philosophers by the king's brother-in-law and Chaucer's Canterbury Tales and Bradbryg was the author of a turgid tome attempting, in the long line of such tortuous apologetics, to reconjecture the works of Plato so they might conform with Christian doctrine, a pastime Michael had rashly described to a student as 'intellectual constipation'.

Evidently the wrong student. There were just over a hundred attending at that time and Michael tutored no more than a handful but it only takes one to sour a whole basket.

And on the same afternoon Michael had this last encounter with Bradbryg Elaine's employer disappeared and thus, after a few days, her livelihood as well. His name was David Justice and Elaine knew he had fallen madly in love with a seventeen-year-old page of the Spanish emissary to Henry's court, Don Pedro de Puebla. The boy was from Zaragoza, and of the same given name as the Aragonese king who married Isabella of Castile when Michael was twenty, and it soon became sadly evident both David and the amiable lad had most likely been murdered.

With no further possibilities in Windsor Michael and Elaine made their way to London and exactly one week later as they sat beneath an oak sharing an apple outside the Leper Hospital of St. James the Less in Westminster, which at the time stood alone in a hunting park west of the village of Charing but is now on Cleveland Row just off the bustle of Pall Mall, they were accosted by a not unattractive nursing sister on a stroll. The woman recognized Michael instantly and turned out to be his quondam lover from his Cambridge days, Martha Bud, the mother of his hitherto unimagined daughter Jane.

The hospital was obtained by Henry VIII in 1532 and entirely rebuilt. It became known as St. James's Palace and has been the home of Elizabeth

I, the mad George III, Prince Charles and, during their divorce proceedings, Princess Diana.

Martha did not hesitate to tell the story of her life and since she was so surprisingly good-humored Michael responded with a brief outline of his own that led by stages to an earnest discussion of their current dilemma.

Jane had come to the light under a bridge over the Cam at four o'clock on Easter Sunday morning, April 10th, 1474, and was therefore going on twenty-three. Easter Day being defined at the Council of Nicaea in 325 as the first Sunday following the first full moon after the vernal equinox.

Alas, she had been a vexatious child and unruly beyond justification and ran away from what she scornfully described as 'this humiliating little shithouse' when she was thirteen and Martha had seldom heard from her since. They were living in the village of Papworth Agnes west of Cambridge, sometimes known, in moments of optimism when the population surged over one hundred, as Great Papworth, where Martha slaved as a cook in the manor and Jane from the age of six assisted her as a scullion. It was a combination of despair and the swinge of an overly penitent conscience that led Martha to the lepers. However, she did know with reasonable surety that Jane was still alive.

For many years the wayward girl had been the companion to a notorious highwayman named George Purefoy. They maintained a sanctuary on the High Weald of West Sussex, in St. Leonard the Dragonslayer's Forest, which was very much larger then and where legend had it the last dragon in England was slain by a French hermit sometime in the sixth century.

While still only sixteen she had given Purefoy a twin son and daughter, whose names Martha didn't know, but since his betrayal by a fellow outlaw and subsequent capture by the Shire Reeve's men the previous November, and his inevitable meeting with the gibbet on the North Heath above Horsham mere days thereafter, Martha had completely lost contact. Yet she was hopeful Jane could be found with the children somewhere on the south coast.

Three hundred and thirty-eight years later, Michael's modern counterpart would have told them, Horsham was the site of England's last execution for the crime of homosexuality.

The medieval Michael was a tender man but he was not entirely overjoyed by the story and at a stroke becoming both father and grandfather and he and Elaine had a pressing need for money and accommodation so they decided to deal with present realities first and seek for his newly revealed offspring when the occasion would more conveniently serve.

Martha had the gist of their recent tribulations and was excited to tell that in 1450 Eton College had been granted perpetual custody of the Leper Hospital by Henry VI as well as five hides of land at Hendon and Chalcot purchased for it by sundry wealthy citizens of London and she knew of an unoccupied cottage at the Chalcot farm.

It was no more than three miles from where they stood and they jumped at the chance. They could help with the farm work and survive the remainder of the winter and in the spring would look for employment in the great city. Michael thought he might try the printing shop of Wynken de Worde, Caxton's successor, or his new competitors, either Robert Copland or Richard Pynson.

So it was that on June 27th as Michael was plodding disconsolately back to Chalcot from a second discouraging meeting with de Worde in the Almonry of Westminster Abbey where Caxton's original press was still in operation, and just as he was approaching the old Roman road that is now Oxford Street, he came upon a raucous crowd hastening west toward Tyburn.

The reason was immediately apparent for the noisy hubbub concerned the Cornish rebels Michael Joseph and Thomas Flamank who had been defeated by the King's forces at Deptford Bridge a week earlier. The humble blacksmith and the educated city lawyer were captured with their noble accomplice Sir James Tuchet, the 7th Baron Audley, and incarcerated in the Tower of London but that morning the two commoners had been drawn on hurdles to Tyburn and were now awaiting the executioner.

Michael was among a minority who thought the Cornish protest entirely justifiable. King Henry levied a new tax on the already overburdened people of Cornwall in order to afford an army of sufficient size to invade Scotland and punish the Scots for supporting yet another Yorkist pretender, Perkin Warbeck, and the rebels quite understandably felt so distant a conflict was nothing to do with them. Unluckily, however, they had not gathered the hoped for increase in numbers during their march to the capital.

Michael abhorred blood sports of any kind but, whether it was the names of the accused or the validity of their cause or his own recent disappointments, on this fateful occasion he found himself following the throng.

It was a few hundred yards to the crossroads at Tyburn village, whence in 1851 a famous marble arch would be for unknown reasons moved, and in the broad expanse of the junction a double gallows stood surrounded by upwards of two thousand rudely clamoring souls.

Flamank and Joseph were visible on the platform clad in loose shirts that barely covered their modesty. Their hands and feet were bound together at the back with chain. The sentence for their treason had been hanging, drawing and quartering and the king initially intended to have them returned to Cornwall for their punishment to strike greater fear among the people but, in the end, he had listened to his counselors who wisely feared so great an affront would do the reverse and dangerously fan the flames.

Flamank was shouting but Michael kept well back at the rear of the mob and couldn't hear his words above the din. The only snatch that carried to his ears was 'Truth alone will make you free!' An honorable and brave cliché but not one to which Michael gave much credence.

To be brief, the two men were hung by the neck and afterwards beheaded, for which they had enjoyed the king's mercy or else would have been cut down still alive from the rope and laid upon the hurdle where their genitals would have been sliced off, their torso opened wide from the groin to the breastbone and disemboweled of its vital organs and finally their heart torn out and waved in front of their faces, a barbarity that could sometimes be performed so rapidly and with such consummate skill the victim was heard to gasp at the sight.

Then the entrails would be cast upon the fire, the head hacked from the body and thrust on a pike for display and four horses harnessed to each limb and driven outward so the corpse would be wrenched asunder. In many cases when joints or sinews did not willingly give way this dismemberment had to be assisted by further hacking. At its cruelest, and customary if the tiniest vestige of conscious awareness in the victim was perceived to remain, the quartering preceded the beheading.

On this occasion, however, against the angry protestations of the crowd who were in a fever of arousal and wanted more, the fortunate men were dead and there was ultimately little difference, excepting the harsh manner of their transport, between their execution and that of their noble confederate, Lord Audley, who was hanged at Tower Hill the next day. All three heads decorated London Bridge despite the class distinction.

Such ghastly dealings, Michael knew very well, were all too frequent but at the moment the great axes were severing the delicate and miraculous integrity of Joseph and Flamank, he found himself screaming obscenities at the top of his lungs. Not the common or garden profanity filling the unwashed mouths of the mob but a thunderous fulmination directed specifically at the portly prelate on the scaffold serenely surveying the scene with prayer book in hand.

Only those in Michael's immediate vicinity could hear him but his tirade was so violent and contained words of such unfamiliar eloquence they stopped yelling to listen and it took no time at all for their dim parochial minds to take offence at this alien form of blasphemy. It quickly led to the threat of fisticuffs and Michael came to his senses and was lucky to back away and flee.

Nonetheless, the dudgeon of one or more of his attackers was evidently of such overweening zeal they must have followed him all the way to Chalcot for the next morning, as he and Elaine were hoeing round the beet sprouts in a far field, they heard the gruff unmistakable tone of officialdom and a loud insistent rapping on the cottage door. It was not immediately possible to ascertain the reason but both their instincts told them it must have something to do with his uncharacteristic outburst so they dropped their hoes and hid themselves in a copse until nightfall and by dawn were twelve miles south of London, passing through the hamlet of Cheam on their way to the sea.

Shuffle Two

"The conversion of native America was not alienation nor the imposition
of a foreign culture. Christ was the Savior for whom they had been
secretly longing."
- Joseph Aloisius Ratzinger (1927 -   )

§

As Michael and Helen came into Stratford's they could see Lamy
standing by the counter at the rear of the restaurant talking to the owner,
a middle-aged woman named Edna Phipps, and the first words from his
mouth as he turned to them were, "The old bugger's finally given up the
ghost."

"Who?" Michael asked with a slightly worried smile.

"Tell me you don't mean Warren," Helen said.

"Shit no," Lamy assured her, giving her a warm hug, "That particular
old bugger's in the pink. We had lunch at Arty's a couple of weeks ago."

Warren Allen Jones was a friend of Helen's. She had once been married
to an American art dealer named David Giudice and lived for a time in
New York. They had been divorced for many years but seven weeks after
9/11 he and his Cuban lover were found dead in the apartment above his
gallery. Michael was there investigating the transhuman phenomena and
spent the previous evening with them. It was clear they had been murdered
and he was appalled to realize their deaths might be connected to the belief
he was Bartolomeo Vespucci.

To Helen's complete surprise David left everything to her in his will.
It was Warren who looked after the probate and the sale of the gallery
which was heavily mortgaged and in the end netted only seventeen
hundred pounds but unlike the preceding twenty years when they more or
less lost contact she and Warren stayed in close touch afterwards.
However, he was now well over eighty so there was always cause for
concern.

"Who's given up the ghost then?" Michael repeated.

Lamy looked at him with a benign twinkle and went on talking to
Helen.

"Still tolerating this madman, I see."

"I'm afraid so," she replied.

"Come and sit. Ever been here? Maybe you know Madam Edna already. You'll have to be nice to her, she owns the place."

The woman came forward and shook their hands politely.

"No, we haven't met," Michael said.

"What are you drinking these days? Guinness?"

"Actually, I wouldn't mind one of those Manhattan cocktails."

They had downed a considerable number together at Belmont racetrack. Lamy bred racehorses and invited David there the day before he was found dead and Michael tagged along. David's twin sister Ruth was killed as Flight 175 slammed into the South Tower and Lamy had been in a relationship with her.

"I doubt Edna stocks Kentucky Straight Rye," Lamy teased, with a good-natured wink at their hostess, "How about martinis all round?"

"I'd love one," Helen said.

"Good. Vodka or gin?"

"Good lord," Michael snorted, "Gin."

"Perfect. Something exquisitely British and make them large ones, my dear," Lamy said, overstressing 'large ones' to show he knew the colloquial for 'doubles'. He seemed in such good spirits Michael thought he was going to slap Edna's departing backside.

"Who's given up the ghost?" Michael asked again.

"Wojtyła, you dope. Twenty minutes ago."

"Ah yes, silly me," Michael said and added in mock exasperation, "How is it you always know everything so fast?"

"Contacts, my friend," Lamy answered with a chuckle and a wave of his cell phone, "Connections. We've talked about that, no?"

"Make enough connections and meaning can't help but show its timorous face."

"It's all we've got to go on."

"Troubling but true."

"What brings you to London?" Helen asked.

"Nothing much. Thought I'd take a holiday."

"You told me you had a proposition," Michael ventured, raising a skeptical eyebrow.

"Don't give me that look. I promise you, you're both gonna love it."

Edna arrived with a tray of martinis and once she departed Lamy began to tell them his idea. He was pretty sure his younger brother Pascal, who had been the Trade Commissioner for the European Union, was about to be appointed Director-General of the World Trade Organization. It was his birthday in a few days and Lamy wanted to surprise him in Geneva where he was already setting up digs. On the way he was intending to visit 'Aunt Sonja', as he called her, in Beaumont. She had apparently discovered something new.

"What?" Michael asked.

"She wouldn't say. She wants to show you personally."

From Geneva Lamy thought it might be fun to drive down to Rome.

"After John Paul's funeral there'll be the circus of choosing his successor and I'd say if we're ever going to flush out Vespucci that might be as likely a moment as any."

Lamy and Warren had been with Michael and Helen at the White House. Lamy was in the top ten on Forbes' list of American billionaires, right amongst the Kochs and Waltons, and was acquainted with both the vice-president and the National Security Advisor. He had seen Cheney's bizarre behavior at their lunch and, like Michael, had since done everything conceivable to unearth who Bartolomeo Vespucci was and where he could be found and, most of all, why the powerbrokers of the world seemed to need him and yet be fearful of him at the same time but despite his enormous wealth and influence he too had come up with nothing.

"I hate like hell to admit defeat, don't you? So how about it?"

He had just purchased sight unseen a vintage wine-colored 1985 Bentley Drophead Continental Convertible from a business associate and didn't want to do all the driving himself so he was inviting them to join him and would cover any and all expense. He wanted to leave early the next morning and hoped it would be possible for them to manage it on such short notice. This was fine for Michael because he never worked anything but freelance and much preferred it that way in spite of the financial risk. He would do the usual and tell his boss he was researching a story for the magazine and anyway wild horses couldn't have held him back from such an adventure but Helen was assistant to the director of the Central St. Martin's College of Art and Design and didn't feel right about asking for another break so soon after the one she had quite recently taken with some friends in Malaga.

"That's too bad. Maybe you can join us in Rome if anything develops."

"I'll certainly try."

"I knew Mister Formula One here wouldn't be able to resist even though it's not a Maserati. Apologies for the comfort needs of my aging carcass."

Michael was already drooling at the thought of being behind the wheel of something so grand and powerful and knocked back the last of his martini with relish.

"Good god, think nothing of it," he said with a grin, "Let's have another.'

"He's never had a driving license, you know," Helen warned.

"A technicality," Lamy replied, "He knows how, doesn't he?"

"Bloody right I do. Learned on my dear old uncle's lap."

A distant relative had designed the Elva racing car in the 1950s.

"Oh, he can drive," Helen agreed, "I'm just not sure he's heard of the brake."

§

As soon as they left the environs of Cheam and continued south Michael the Med and Elaine were within the bounds of the present day London suburb of Belmont, a village that sprang up around a lunatic asylum in the last quarter of the 19th century.

From there it took another three days for them to arrive at Horsham by a roundabout route that included Banstead, Reigate and Salford, where they sat beside the mill and dined on bread and cheese under the willows, then Lowe Heath, the site of modern Gatwick airport where there truly were pastures filled with goats in those days, then westward along a narrow wooded path to Lamb's Cottage and High Rusper and, after two nights of rough sleeping, a hard but welcome cot in the Benedictine Priory.

Declining the monks' invitation to prayer, they were on their way again by five the next morning and it was an easy six mile walk down the Newdigate road to what is now called the Carfax at Horsham. Some say this odd word for the open space at the center of the town is derived from the Latin for four or five corners and it is undoubtedly the site of an ancient crossroads but others claim it goes back to pre-Roman times when this natural clearing in the forest was 'scarce of people' and is the abbreviation of *'scarfoulkes'*.

The Saturday market was in full swing when they arrived shortly after half past eight. They were thirsty and since there couldn't be a better place than an inn to start their inquiry into the whereabouts of Jane and the children, nor a more likely font of information than a local publican, they made straight for the sign, King's Head, that beckoned above the jabbering multitude.

§

There is no need to recapitulate the pathetic implosion of conscience and wilting of spine that occurred in the body politic of the entire world when faced with the brazen bullshit of the Bushite-Blairites after 9/11 and the unjustifiable aggression that began with Operation Enduring Freedom on October 7, 2001, and culminated in the invasion of Iraq by coalition forces on March 20, 2003, nor to revisit the imbecility of the boyishly clad president declaring 'mission accomplished' from the deck of the aircraft-carrier Abraham Lincoln cruising in the tranquil waters off San Diego on the following May 1st.

By April 2005 more than sixteen-hundred US soldiers had been killed and many thousands maimed for life as well as nearly half Saddam Hussein's regular army, though not his elite Republican Guard who more or less deserted him *en masse* and ran away, and, though quite apparently of least consequence to the global television audience, a quarter million innocent Iraqi bystanders.

The continuing and futile slaughter was the hardly surprising subject of an article in the New York Times Lamy was reading aloud as the body of John Paul trundled into the Clementine Room of the Apostolic Palace to await the traditional ceremony necessary to confirm and certify his death and Michael steered their Chianti chariot joyously south along the A22 around Uckfield. The weather was rainy and cold so pressing the button to lower the Bentley's beige convertible top would have to wait for more southerly climes.

Lamy insisted that Michael be at his hotel in Mayfair no later than 5AM and sent a car to fetch him from Chalk Farm which was just as well since it was impossible for Michael to travel without a significant amount of clobber.

Michael normally had a very poor sense of direction but assured his host he knew the roadways of West Sussex like the back of his hand, claiming in excited anticipation of things to come that the topography of the Saxon land of his youth was indelibly imprinted in his brain, and this less customary but more direct route, even though on Lamy's map it appeared to pass through East Grinstead where Michael demonstrated his mastery of the terrain and deftly avoided the traffic lights in the town center by nipping down a picturesque if rather windy and hair-raising shortcut, would be much faster to Newhaven and their ten o'clock ferry departure to Dieppe even at this early hour on a Sunday morning than the always choked M23/A23 combination via Gatwick, Crawley and Brighton

The Times article concerned an assault on the Abu Ghraib prison in the outskirts of Baghdad by at least forty armed insurgents which had been taking place while they enjoyed their first gin martini at Stratford's. It started with a car bomb that destroyed an outbuilding but continued with more bombs, heavy gunfire and lobbed grenades. The Times report claimed there were no fatalities but that twenty US personnel had been wounded along with a dozen inmates. The BBC broadcast on the Bentley's radio, by contrast, estimated the number of troops wounded at forty-four and stated the attack was so well coordinated that helicopters and tanks had to be called in to restore control.

"Spokesman Lieutenant-Colonel Guy Rudisill said 'US intelligence had told us something like this would happen but we really don't know why such a large scale attack should have taken place tonight'."

Lamy chuckled wryly.

"What the fuck does the timing matter? You can't blame them for being pissed."

"Isn't she about to go on trial?" Michael asked, "The girl in all the photos? Fity her name was England. The whole thing exposed the intellectual rot inside America. A total inside-out upside-down cake. Hey, we're the good guys but in our darkest hearts we're also a bunch of brutal racist pigs."

"There's no doubt they were just obeying orders."

"It's staggering that nothing at all changed after what we saw. Were we imagining it? It seems like we must have been."

In 2001 inexplicable appearances of the vice-president began beneath the ruins of the twin towers on the very day the 'shock and awe' bombardment of Afghanistan started and went on to haunt a memorial service at Ground Zero on Sunday, October 28th. A tourist's camera had even captured Cheney's visage on the granite face of Mt. Rushmore gushing blood between snarling wolverine lips. Still more unsettling were the ghostly apparitions that froze the president in time as he tossed the ceremonial pitch at Game Three of the World Series at Yankee Stadium on October 30th. Michael and Lamy and Warren were there and for a few brief seconds saw an hallucinatory horde of the world's starving and dispossessed covering the playing field and marching towards them and then again two nights later on the South Lawn of the White House joined by the shattered bodies of all those who were murdered on 9/11. Michael stood with the president on the Truman Balcony as he addressed them apologetically in the dawning light of that naively hopeful morning.

"We must have, mustn't we?" Michael went on, "I mean Cheney didn't die in the Yellow Oval Room, did he, that's obvious."

"Warren and I both heard the paramedics pronounce him dead, but no. Unless, like with Uncle Joe and Saddam, they've been using doppelgangers. Nor Kissinger. There were rumors he'd been poisoned the same day."

"What a pity none of it was true."

"Maybe they can't be killed," Lamy suggested with barely a trace of irony, "Alive or dead, it wouldn't have made much difference. There's no shortage of toads like Rumsfeld to fill any gap."

Michael remembered Lamy's anecdote about the Secretary of Defense and smiled. Shortly before Christmas in 2003, Lamy called and among much else told him Rumsfeld had purchased a property in St. Michael's, Maryland, in an area called Church Neck on Chesapeake Bay, so he and his wife could be near the Cheneys during down time in Washington. The old plantation house on the estate was nicknamed Mount Misery after the notoriously sour temperament of the original owner, the 19th century slavebreaker Edward Covey whose only claim to fame was being bested in a fistfight by Frederick Douglass. The press had a field day with the fact that the bluejay house facing the front gate came equipped with a hidden camera behind the birdhole.

"And now Bush is in his second term. Incredible."

"To be fair to our much-maligned electorate there was plenty of evidence of fraud and blatant interference with the Diebold machines. Kerry probably won by five million votes."

"And hasn't there been some motion to allow a third or even fourth?"

"Yup. Last February. A bill to repeal the 22nd amendment. Put forward by a little prick named Sensenbrenner from Wisconsin. One of the choirboys who got all sweaty about Clinton's impeachment."

Michael had turned off onto the A26 and they were passing a sign for the Bentley Wildfowl and Motor Museum.

"Fabulous combination," Lamy observed.

"Flamingoes and some magnificent cars."

"Any of your relative's?"

"Not there. Elvas aren't all that rare really. There are museums that have them in Bexhill and Worthing. You could probably pick one up for about ten thousand pounds. What did this beauty set you back?"

"Only fifteen."

"Not bad," Michael allowed.

It was more than he had ever made in a year.

"By the way, Bartolomeo, old pal," Lamy went on in a jocular tone, "Did you know that Charles Deville Wells, 'the man who broke the bank at Monte Carlo', once . . "

"Lived in Newhaven?" Michael interrupted, "Yes, I did. He was arrested for fraud, spent eight years in prison and died in poverty in Paris."

They both laughed.

"You're on my turf now."

§

Unluckily, the publican at The King's Head was taciturn and tight-lipped and either didn't know or wouldn't tell Michael and Elaine anything about the departed George Purefoy or his bereaved helpmeet or Michael's grandchildren.

§

As Lamy and Michael continued south past Lewes and the quaintly-named hamlets of Piddinghoe and Tarring Neville and on to the Transmanche ferry terminal in the sheltered channel at the mouth of the Ouse their conversation ranged to the other New Haven in Connecticut, home of Yale University, *alma mater* of both elder and junior Bush, as well as William Jefferson Clinton and Gerald Ford and many a presidential hopeful including John Kerry, and from there to Skull and Bones and then Michael's childhood in Worthing, the origin of the term Beachy Head, a place made notorious by the fact that the number of suicides taking advantage of its great height rivaled the Golden Gate bridge, the miraculous dispersal of the Spanish Armada, the unsolved disappearance of Lord Lucan, the erroneous claim that Seaford had once been one of the Cinque Ports and Winston Churchill, who had been Lord Warden of them from 1941 until his death, and the amusing fact that in ages past this honorary title had been held by William de Clinton and Sir Thomas Cheney, and from there to the horrors of war and the tragedy of Dunkirk and the failure of the Dieppe raid on August 19th, 1942, code-named Operation Jubilee, during which so many valiant Canadian lads perished and the outbreak of hemorrhagic Marburg virus that was now ravishing the town of Uige in northern Angola and the brainless clamor for John Paul's instantaneous beatification and sainthood regardless of a lifetime spent pushing mulishly narrow-minded policies and who might succeed him after the current period of *sede vacante* and The Godfather, Part 3, and the death of Roberto Calvi and the scandals at the Institute for Works of Religion, otherwise known as the Vatican Bank.

§

Five days after their unhelpful encounter at the King's Head Michael and Elaine found themselves on the seaweed-strewn shingle below the Bronze Age ramparts of Cissbury Ring, the then desolate seafront of what is now the city of Worthing. Both Oscar Wilde and Harold Pinter have called the place home but in the summer of the year of our lord 1497 the total of human souls subsisting there numbered no more than forty and every one of the males, who made up the vast majority, were engaged in the dangerous trade of mackerel fishing.

And there, on the morning of the 12th of July, Michael and Elaine came upon his daughter fast asleep in a makeshift hovel and her wild naked twins splashing and giggling in the waves.

Jane did not give immediate credence to their story though she realized at once that, whoever they were, their presence might provide some much-needed protection and ease her constant battle for survival. The twins, Jenny and Jack, on the other hand, were delighted with the sudden, unexpected companionship of a newfound aunt, who Michael well knew was more than a match for them in the headstrong department.

Michael's muscles were hardened by their wandering and the labor on the farm at Chalcot and he was welcomed as an extra mate on a mackerel boat and, no matter that they all came to reek of fish, for the next two months and nine days their life was as untroubled as they had ever known but then on Thursday, the 21st of September by the Julian calendar, a southwesterly equinoctial gale of hurricane force blew his hapless vessel all the way east-northeast to the island of Walcheren where it finally capsized and sank a mere two hundred yards from the dunes.

Shuffle Three

"The Theologians and Theologasters at the University of Paris have the most rotten brains, the most barbarous and spiteful tongues, the most stupid intellects, the most barren learning, the coarsest manners and the blackest hearts."
- Gerrit Gerritszoon, Desiderius Erasmus Roterodamus (1466 - 1536)

§

The Transmanche ferry onto which Michael the Mod and Lamy boarded the Bentley at ten o'clock that morning once plied the Baltic between Sweden and Schleswig-Holstein and before its recent purchase from the Travemünde-Trelleborg Line in Hamburg was known as the Saga Star. It had now been re-christened the Dieppe, painted yellow and navy blue and Lamy had arranged a private stateroom for the crossing.

"You're on your own for a while, old boy," he announced as they entered the surprisingly cramped and inelegant cabin, "It's going to be rough out there and I get seasick as hell."

After popping several Gravol tablets he immediately lay down on the only couch. It was a narrow ugly thing with shiny metal arms and hard greenish-gray leatherette cushioning but before they reached open water he was fast asleep.

Michael didn't wait to hear him snore. He loved fresh salt air and rolling swells and spent the next five hours between the bar and foredeck breasting the flying spume and happily observing his fellow passengers, many of whom had to make a mad dash for the railings and heave up over the side.

§

Michael the Med regained consciousness with a tuft of dune grass tickling his nose not knowing where he was. He remembered all too well the two day's nightmare of their passage and his stark horror as the boat foundered and sank but had no recollection of the manner in which he had been spared.

One of the mates who fled with him before the storm had been smacked overboard by a monster wave and lost somewhere off Cap Gris-Nez and the other, alas, was nowhere to be seen. He must have summoned the strength to swim for not a fragment of their shallop littered the shoreline.

Thankfully it was still light and, though the sky remained overcast and threatening, the ferocious gale had slacked.

A trace of milky sun over the leaden sea to the southwest told him he had not washed up on the coast of Norfolk as he first hoped. He was lying to the north of a broad inlet or estuary that stretched inland out of sight to the east. He was surely not in England.

A cold drizzle began to darken the sand as he struggled to his feet and set off with a shiver toward a distant unfamiliar spire.

§

Lamy looked refreshed and rested and took the wheel as they debarked the Bentley at Dieppe.

"And this is my turf," he said with an elfin grin.

It was half past four in the afternoon since, even though they had traveled more or less directly south, they lost an hour due to the time zone change.

"Only one stop on the tour today. We're due in Beaumont by seven-thirty. Aunt Sonja dines at seven forty-five and we better not be late. I hate driving at night anyway. Hope you had something on the ferry."

"A dry ham sandwich and a Guinness or two. I'll be fine."

Lamy took the D154 south-southeast and regaled Michael with his usual encyclopedic anecdotage of the history of the towns they whizzed past. Arques-la-Bataille, St-Aubin-le-Cauf, Torcy-le-Petit and Torcy-le-Grand between which they crossed over the main road for Paris, La Frenaye, Bellencombre. Michael was somewhat irritated by the showiness of the habit when they first became acquainted in New York but having realized Lamy truly couldn't help himself he now found it highly entertaining.

When they reached Saint-Saëns Lamy turned off to the southwest.

"Nothing to do with Camille who composed The Carnival of the Animals but we do know the lords of this fiefdom fought at the Battle of Hastings."

After another ten miles they came to the hamlet of Le Quesnay and Lamy stopped for a drink at a tiny outdoor café. He said he enjoyed the occasional Pernod and though Michael knew he wouldn't like it he was happy to concur.

"Looks peaceful now but it's been pillaged and burnt by English, French, Spanish, Burgundians, you name it, to say nothing of the wars of the twentieth century. As far as anyone knows it's the most likely birthplace of Radulphus. Somewhere around 1044. There are other Quesnays in Normandy including Le-Petit just down that road to the right but this is the best guess. Not much certainty about his death. Some say Rudham in Norfolk, others Street End . . great name . . in your native Sussex. Most agree he married Maud de Wateville in West Hoathley shortly after the battle."

Michael laughed with delight.

"Good lord. We were within a stone's throw. There was a signpost as we went round East Grinstead. Didn't you see it?"

"Sure."

"So you've just been saving it up."

"Timing is everything. Isn't that your motto?"

From Le Quesnay Lamy steered them quickly onto the E44 going west.

"You'd love Rouen but we don't have time. Fantastic place. The brothers Corneille were born there and Flaubert. Romans called it Rotomagus. Second city of *Gallia Lugdunum*. You can still see the remains of the amphitheater and baths."

"Perfect spot for an *auto-da-fé*," Michael observed wryly.

"Yup. Poor old Joan. La Pucelle, the nineteen-year-old Maid of Orleans. May 30th, 1431, in the Vieux Marche. Tied her to a stone pillar and burned her body three times so no one could collect any relics."

"Lord god almighty, is there nothing you don't know!"

"Only myself, philosopher, only that," Lamy sighed.

The sky cleared as they sped westward toward the slowly setting sun and Le Havre and decided the genealogy of the Cheney, Chaney, Cheyne, Chesney familial line was of marginal significance because tracing back forty generations to any ancient ancestor meant from the purely numerical standpoint they would only be one among billions.

"It's a silly exercise. Who was it said that no one alive today, black, yellow, white, pink or tangerine, can be further removed from some arbitrary example like Julius Caesar than his 52nd cousin?"

"Guy Murchie," Lamy answered without a pause, "Met him a couple of times. Warren knew him pretty well, I think. Worked for the Chicago Tribune as a photographer. Correspondent in England during the early years of the war. Wrote a book later called The Seven Mysteries of Life. Believer in the Baha'i faith and Pythagoras' *anima mundi*, the World Soul. Always liked to point out the obvious fact that death is necessary for evolution to exist. Smart fella."

Michael could only throw his head back and roar.

"Yes, it's all pretty simple really."

"Way too simple," Lamy concurred, "That's why people don't get it."

They covered the sixty miles to the amazing Pont de Normandie over the mouth of the Seine in what seemed a twinkling.

"Used to be the longest cable-stayed bridge in the world," Lamy informed Michael as he gawped. "Just to keep the orientation going you're now leaving Haute-Normandie and entering Basse-Normandie. Le Havre is the busiest port in France after Marseilles. When Marat was assassinated by Charlotte Corday they called it Hâvre-de-Marat for a while. To honor what they thought was his martyrdom. Didn't last long. Eighteen months. No sooner had Danton and Robespierre gone to the guillotine than they changed their minds. The city was almost totally destroyed by Allied bombardment in June '44. Honfleur on the south side was spared and the old harbor is still incredibly beautiful. Samuel de Champlain sailed from there in 1608 and founded Quebec."

"Is Honfleur the same as Harfleur?"

"No, Harfleur's right in the middle of Le Havre now. Bet you're thinking of Shakespeare's Henry the Fifth."

Michael was almost ashamed to admit he once played the small part of the Governor of Harfleur in an amateur production directed by his father when he was a ridiculously too young boy of fifteen.

"Lot of vicious jingoistic nonsense. 'Defile your shrill-shrieking daughters, father's heads dashed to the walls, infants spitted on spikes, mothers howling,' that's all I can remember of it."

"What else is there?" Lamy observed laconically.

"Larry Olivier's hideously over-pronounced set-pieces."

"I've always liked them."

"That's because you're a plebeian despite your impossible memory."

"Not so, not so, middle class through and through. 'Once more unto the breach, dear friends, or close the wall up with our English dead!'" he exclaimed in a piping nasal tone, "Ha! I love it!"

Having passed Honfleur Lamy took the back roads across the lowlands of the Touques valley and after another forty-five minutes of non-stop banter they were climbing a low hill into the village of Beaumont-en-Auge.

"You're in Calvados country now. You can see why they call it the *Pays d'Auge*. The valley is like a trough. Used to be impenetrable marsh land."

"You told me when we first met outside David's gallery that an auge was a stone trough for crushing apples."

"As well, as well."

In the town center before they came to the church that Michael had seen from the distance there was a lovely square on their left with a bronze statue set amongst some birch trees that were just coming into leaf.

"Who's that then? Mr. Beaumont?" he asked facetiously.

"Laplace," Lamy answered, "You're on his street. Pierre-Simon de Laplace was born here."

Michael looked uncharacteristically blank for a moment.

"Mathematical genius and astronomer. The Isaac Newton of France."

"Oh yes, of course. Spherical harmonics. Black holes. Born here. Really."

"Yup. Became a marquis after the Bourbon Restoration and the Battle of Waterloo. Made one of my favorite all time quips. He gave Napoleon a copy of his masterwork Celestial Mechanics. It was in five huge volumes and the little corporal asked him why, in so vast a tome, he had never made mention of God the Creator and Laplace replied haughtily, 'I had no need of that hypothesis'."

Michael smiled.

They were on the Rue du Paradis which he thought curiously apt.

§

Michael the Med had become an adept in the art of roughing it and took little time in finding sustenance in the form of fresh rainwater in an oak barrel by a deserted shed and some apples and pears and sprouts and carrots from a nearby farmer's field. He had always been fond of raw things. As it was nearly dusk he decided to rest for the night in the shed in order to at least partially dry his sodden clothes.

The next morning he woke before dawn and followed a rutted grassy lane that wound along the bank of the estuary and led to the harbor of what he did not know was the Zeeland town of Vlissingen. Nor could he have presaged that Christopher Marlowe would be arrested here for counterfeiting coins and deported back to England ninety-four years and one hundred and twenty-five days later. Michael was no spy or dissembler but his tired eyes were greeted by an alarming sight.

A carrack of Portuguese origin flying the Cross of the Order of Christ was unloading and among its cargo were fifteen or twenty half-naked young African women. They looked frail and thin and had clearly been given little protection against the elements. They were chained together in a line by their hands and the pain this caused was evident for they were whimpering piteously as three men with cudgels forced them to clamber thus encumbered onto the back of a filthy covered wagon.

Protestation at the inhuman treatment was about to burst from Michael's mouth but his experience at Tyburn made him stifle the instinct. The men had noticed him watching and sensed his disapproval and two of them were already edging threateningly toward him and, though he didn't understand the words, it was plain they meant him to mind his own business and move along.

Discretion is the better part of valor and he did so.

He had thought to enquire in the port about the possibility of a passage home but he was so unsettled by the women's plight that in no time he walked beyond the town. However, the men's strange guttural tongue gave him a clue to his location. He now knew the storm had blown him even beyond the coast of France and that he must be somewhere in Flanders or the Brabant.

By afternoon he found out he was on an island and after another night and an hour on a barge and another island and two more days of walking and then the luck to find an obliging ship's captain and a twelve-hour sail by night up the river Scheldt he disembarked in the late morning of September 28th on a bustling dockside in the great city of Antwerp and was instantly astonished by the sound of a familiar voice.

§

Five minutes later, at the end of a dusky tree-lined country lane called the Chemin du Bois Gérard, Lamy drew the Bentley up in front of Aunt Sonja's softly illuminated ivy-covered manor. As with his arrival at Lamy's Long Island estate in Mattituck Michael was utterly gobsmacked by its magnificence.

"She'd have to have an army of servants to 'maintain' this!" he observed to Lamy with an ironically raised eyebrow.

"She has what she needs."

"Don't tell me you don't pay for it."

"Did I say that? Welcome to the Seigneurie Lamy. Been in my family since 1542. Probably the land for several hundred years longer. Can't blame me for feeling some responsibility."

"Were the lords of this fiefdom at the Battle of Hastings, too?"

"No definitive proof but it's possible."

Michael would discover on a walk the next morning before breakfast that the property covered thirty hectares of mixed pasture and woodland, spacious lawns, an apple orchard and an enormous vegetable garden. The nine-bedroom manor was built of stone. Two colossal chimneys stood in opposing corners of the gabled roof and were flanked by matching hexagonal towers. There was a separate four-bedroom guest chalet with the half-timbered façade Michael had seen almost everywhere since Dieppe. He thought the style resembled English Tudor but Lamy corrected him about the many subtle differences. There were traces of an older manor house surrounded by a moat, a two-storey dovecote with a bell-turret, a caretaker's lodge and a stable. A tennis court and swimming pool still in its winter covering were tucked tastefully out of sight.

Aunt Sonja was standing at the top of the front steps. She was tiny, less than five feet, rail-thin and Michael fancied from a distance that she resembled a bird of prey. Perhaps a burrowing owl from his beloved Sonoran desert. Bony hands were clasped at her waist but despite a pronounced stoop she managed without a cane.

Lamy got out of the car and hustled up the stairs and she greeted him with tears in her eyes. They kissed and spoke together in excited French. Lamy was so completely American Michael had almost forgotten he was born in Paris, in the densely populated northwestern suburb of Levallois-Perret where his father worked as a manager for Citroën.

Lamy made the introduction and Aunt Sonja shook Michael's hand firmly and warmly and said, with a strong accent but in otherwise flawless English, "Gui has told me you are a very brave man. I like brave men. I am so sorry you will have to leave almost before you have arrived. Gui never stays anywhere for long. It must be a torture to live in his skin. Come and take some refreshment and then I will show you something interesting."

They entered the vestibule of the manor where a great staircase led to the upper floors and Aunt Sonja excused herself saying she would join them in the dining room in fifteen minutes. She gestured them to a lounge on their right before departing. Michael was dying for a beer and was soon accommodated by a casually dressed servant.

"Did I hear her call you Guy?" Michael asked, doing his best to mimic Aunt Sonja's pronunciation but it came out more like 'gooey'.

Lamy grinned.

"Bernard Gui was an inquisitor in the 14th century. Spelled g, u, i. Rhymes with Louis, more or less. I was always asking questions when I was a kid. Pain in the ass then, pain in the ass now. Gui was a run-of-the-mill mad Dominican zealot who wrote a lot of vapid books. Enjoyed executing Jews, fortune-tellers, Waldensians, Manichaens, Albigensist Cathars, old women like Sonja, whoever. F. Murray Abraham played the son of a bitch in The Name of the Rose."

At supper Aunt Sonja wanted to know everything about his experiences in Juarez and the plutonium and also the appearance of the ghosts on television in New York and the apparent death of Richard Bruce Cheney in the Yellow Oval Room and Michael discovered a ribald sense of humor beneath the wrinkles and a charming woman with a twinkling eye who liked to laugh.

Her grandfather was a famous *archetier* in Paris whose bows won both the gold and silver medals at the Paris Exposition of 1889. Her mother was born in Franche-Comté and traced her lineage to the end of the 15th century when that area of Burgundy was ruled by Austria and her surname was really Lamy but she had taken the name La Franche on a whim while teaching at the Sorbonne at the time of the Anschluss. She was distantly related to Louis and Pascal but it was far too complicated and boring to explain.

When they finished eating a servant poured each of them a generous glass of the Seigneurie's own Calvados and Aunt Sonja lit up a Gauloise. She offered them round and, finding no takers, chuckled wryly.

"What I have for you, Michael, is a letter. A very old letter written in Latin that has been translated here."

She passed a thick sheaf of papers across the table to him.

"The original is locked up in the *Maison d'Érasme*, the Erasmus museum in Brussels, but I assure you the document has been authenticated. It was written by the famous Dutch humanist to a young Englishman named Thomas Grey. It is dated quite exactly. September 28th. We can assume the year is 1497 because of the subject matter. Grey and a friend of his named Robert Fisher and two brothers from Lübeck, Christian and Heinrich Northoff, had been students of Erasmus in Paris and there is cause to believe Grey was probably his lover. You will see why I say that when you read it.

"In the early autumn of that year Erasmus had traveled to Dordrecht near his birthplace Rotterdam to visit two aging uncles who were the brothers of his deceased mother Margareta. As you may know, Erasmus' parents were never married. I believe the uncles' names were Florent and Antonius Boeckel. His companions on the journey were Robert Fisher and an Italian named Francesco da Crema. They were obviously having a rather rakish time in Dordrecht and reluctant to depart. However, on the 28th of September the trio were on their way back to Paris and stopped at the port of Antwerp where Fisher secured a passage home.

"Thomas Grey returned to England two months earlier after his guardian began to realize the nature of his relationship with his Dutch master and forced Erasmus to vacate the house they were sharing. The main body of the letter is a diatribe about this old man who was apparently a Scottish noble of some sort. It is eloquent and quite amusing but the postscript is what I would like you to read."

Michael had been scanning the first page as she spoke and came across a choice passage.

"This is great stuff," he said and quoted dramatically, "'Did ever the poets, spite their usual perspicacity in describing human nature, venture to portray a pimp that equaled this dastard in perfidy, a braggart soldier in vainglory, an old man in peevishness, or create such a monster of sour and envious ingratitude as this elderly humbug.' Marvelous. I had no idea."

"That is the barest beginning. It rushes from height to height. As they say, it 'doth protest too much'. But turn to the last page and read there."

§

The familiar voice Michael the Med heard on the dock belonged to Robert Fisher. He and Thomas Grey had been students at Eton four years previously. They were then eighteen and left the college the following spring but Michael tutored them both.

They spoke in Latin and once Fisher heard Michael's story and Erasmus, who was at the time going on thirty-one, became aware of Michael's original and challenging cast of mind, it was decided, instead of returning immediately to England with Fisher, Michael should accompany Erasmus and da Crema to Paris. He had never been there and why not avail himself of so God-given an opportunity.

Thus it was that Erasmus penned an addendum to the letter Robert was already carrying to Thomas in London.

§

"' . . If you could ever love a monster of that kind,'" Michael began, "'You would be the most frivolous person alive; if from the heart, you would be a complete fool; if from servility, a contemptible sycophant. It is as insane to hug an enemy to your bosom as it is to neglect a friend . . '

"Ah yes, yes, sorry, here it is, I think. Good lord. ' . . And now there is an unexpected thing I must ask of you, my most dear Thomas. Today we have had the pleasure of meeting a fine-spoken gentleman of your acquaintance here in Antwerp. His name is Michael Davenport . . '"

Michael stopped and looked at Aunt Sonja and Lamy in amazement.

"Good lord," he said again.

"Go on," Lamy urged with a smile.

"'Michael Davenport . . with whom both you and Robert were familiar at Eton.' Good lord, quite extraordinary. Eton. 'A man whose qualities shine in starkest opposition to that hobgoblin pest the land of the Goth recently spewed upon us. I shall not reveal the story of how he came to be here, Robert will tell you all. However, since Robert must make no delay in traveling to the bedside of his ailing father in Peterborough and since I know that once you understand the reason you will certainly wish to do so, I ask that you journey in his stead to the south coast where you will find Michael's sister Elaine in the company of his daughter and grandchildren at a place called Wyrthyng . . '"

Michael paused, staring incredulously at the word.

"It's quite impossible," he said, chuckling with delight and glancing at both of them again before going on, "' . . Michael has made Robert cognizant of its location. You will tell them the happy news that Michael is alive and is coming to visit with us for a short while in Paris. He has written a separate letter which you are to give to them. It says, I believe, that he intends to find his way back within the month but I appeal to you in private, my most dear Thomas, do not stint in making whatever contribution you are able as to their welfare.'"

There the document ended and Michael looked it over again.

"Astonishing. Quite unbelievable," he said, "I don't suppose you have the letter my namesake wrote."

"Unfortunately not," Aunt Sonja replied sympathetically, "It is one of the frustrations of this kind of research. Each new discovery leads deeper into the unknown and always creates more questions than it answers."

"Is there any other letter of Erasmus' that mentions Michael Davenport?"

"Not that my colleagues have yet found."

"So all we know about him is that he was once in Eton. It sounded as if he might have been a teacher at the college. I think it had been founded by that time."

"1440," Lamy said laconically, "Henry the Sixth."

Michael looked at him with a teasing glare.

"He was clearly older than the two boys," Michael went on puzzling, "He already had grandchildren and the letter compares him to the hated old Scottish guardian. It's the first time I've heard Scotland called the land of the Goths. But who was he and how can we know he's anything whatever to do with me? How the devil did he get to Antwerp? Why would he need to tell them he was alive? Had he been kidnapped? What were they doing in Worthing at so early a date? As far as I knew an actual town didn't exist there until the 1700s."

Aunt Sonja took a final puff on her Gauloise and said with a Gallic shrug, "It is most unlikely we shall ever find out."

Shuffle Four

"They have neither king, nor lord, nor church, nor religion. They yield
no obedience to anyone and each is his own master. They use no trade
and neither buy nor sell, for they live in their own liberty and are
contented with that which nature gives them."
- Amerigo Vespucci (1454 - 1512)

§

Michael's clothes were considerably disheveled after his near drowning
but as they chatted Erasmus easily convinced the always agreeable da
Crema that he couldn't wait to provide money for a new set. After a fond
farewell to Robert at the dockside it took less than half the afternoon to
visit a variety of shops that sold quality second-hand merchandise and for
Michael's metamorphosis from Bedlam escapee to vaguely professorial
nondescript to be complete. Despite da Crema's suggesting he leave his
original sea-soaked apparel behind Michael had learned the importance of
thrift since William dismissed them from Bramhall and asked the last
shopkeeper to make him a bundle of it.

Erasmus was impatient to get away and immediately set off at a brisk
pace toward a place beneath the surrounding city wall where he knew they
could hire cheap horses. It was a week's ride to Paris and he had pressing
duties there.

They had a brief discussion about weaponry, both Fisher and da Crema
were draped with sword and buckler, and Michael noticed a slight cooling
in Erasmus' demeanor when he explained he had long ago chosen never
to bear arms and was unskilled in the art and it only fully dawned on him
several days later that Erasmus both hated and feared traveling and that
he had been invited primarily for added protection and only secondarily
for the diversion of his company.

By contrast Francesco da Crema, or Franciscus Cremensis in Latin,
was an expert swordsman, energetic, handsome, erudite and easy in
conversation. He had been born in Cividale in the Friuli province of
northeastern Italy and was a scion of the noble de' Bulgari dynasty and
though still a mere twenty-seven had occupied the chair of poetry at the

University of Louvain for nearly five years. The previous holder of the post had been Cornelio Vitelli whom Michael had, by chance, heard lecture on the Eclogues of the Roman poets Titus Calpurnius Siculus, who was contemporaneous with the emperor Nero, and the 3rd century Marcus Aurelius Nemesianus, who was Carthaginian but spent his adulthood in the Eternal City, at Exeter College in Oxford during he and Elaine's stay there in the freezing winter of 1492.

Francesco was amused by this and asked Michael if he could recall Vitelli mentioning the name Fausto Andrelini and Michael had a vague memory of it though he could not remember the precise context. Francesco then explained that Vitelli had publicly accused Andrelini of plagiarizing the two Romans in his own work. The ugly controversy had not served Vitelli well. Andrelini was now professor of humanity at the University of Paris and a favorite of Charles VIII, as well as an intimate friend of Erasmus, and Vitelli had virtually disappeared.

Michael could not find much interest in the anecdote and told da Crema about the women he had seen being debarked in Vlissingen, he now knew that was the name of the little port because Erasmus informed him so after his tale of the storm and shipwreck, and Francesco was not surprised. Even in England almost everyone had heard the names Ferdinand and Isabella and was at least vestigially aware of the voyages of Cristoforo Colombo but Michael was greatly astonished to learn from da Crema the extent of Portuguese exploration down the west coast of Africa.

He described the ship and the flag and da Crema spoke of a friend of his, a Portuguese nobleman named Velascus de Lucena, who told him it was really the emblem of the Knights Templar. Though the order was abolished by Pope Clement V in 1312, under pressure from King Philip IV of France because he owed them a crusade load of money, in Portugal they had merely changed their name to the Order of Christ's Cross and the new king, Dom Manuel I, had adopted their standard while expelling all the Jews and Moors from his country who refused conversion to Christianity. Not that Manuel himself was all that keen but it was a non-negotiable pre-condition the aforementioned rulers of Spain demanded before they would consent to his marriage with their daughter, the widowed Infanta Isabela of Aragon, since her doting and devout parents had already succeeded in ridding their vast realm of the same infidel scourge.

Kidnap and slavery and intolerance, Michael and Francesco agreed, were as old as human history and these were but further examples of their cruel and continuous manifestation.

§

Lamy insisted they take their leave of Aunt Sonja by half-past seven the next morning because he wanted to be in Geneva no later than lunchtime the following day. He said he preferred secondary roads rather than belting along the freeway on the more direct route via Auxerre and Beaune which would, in any case, necessitate an unpredictable spell through the southern outskirts of Paris and he thought Michael would enjoy his planned itinerary though typically enough he didn't divulge what it was going to be.

Michael took the wheel for the first leg and, accepting Lamy's challenge to do so, found their way back to Beaumont-en-Auge without help.

They came to the central square with the statue of the great astronomer in the distance to their right and a vine-smothered hostelry called the Auberge de l'Abbaye to their left and Lamy indicated with his finger for Michael to turn onto the road for Drubec and Bonnebosq.

Lamy told him the square was named Place de Verdun in commemoration of the 1916 bloodbath that took nine months and forty million artillery shells to kill two hundred and fifty thousand soldiers and ruin the lives of twice as many more with crippling wounds.

As Michael made the corner onto the Rue de la Libération Lamy pointed to the second doorway on the right.

"Bet you can't guess what goes on in there," he said.

"I shudder to think," Michael replied.

"One of the last kaleidoscope manufacturers in Europe."

The lower floor of the house was unmarked by a sign and painted entirely black except for three rows of alternating black and white tiles laid horizontally along the bottom of the wall. Newly planted flower-boxes adorned the upper windows.

"Good lord, really."

"That's why I like road trips."

"I fail to see any immediate connection."

"One little shift of position and you've got a whole new ball game," Lamy explained and burst out laughing.

As they continued on Lamy answered some questions Michael had about the Seigneurie. Gérard Lamy, for whom the Chemin du Bois leading to the manor was named, could be traced back to 1314 as the owner of the woodland. The great house had been built near the ruin of an older structure by a wealthy landowner, Dumain Lamy, in the mid-16th century and for two hundred and forty years the property was simply a farm but the family were unsympathetic toward both the egalitarian ideals and summary methods of the revolutionaries and in the 1790s, though none were unfortunate enough to meet their maker on the guillotine, they were booted off the land and lost most of their fortune. The entirety of the 19th century became a maddening sequence of legal battles to regain title to the many separate holdings that made up the original and was finally achieved by Lamy's great-great-uncle in 1893.

The estate escaped much of the horror of the Great War but during the last phase of WWII it had been occupied by *Generalleutnant* Josef Reichert, the commander of the 711th Infantry Division, who used it as his headquarters and in the aftermath of the Allied invasion it had fallen into disrepair. When Aunt Sonja and Lamy's parents returned in the autumn of 1946 they found a broken empty shell. Lamy was seven and his mother was pregnant with Pascal and he remembered the visit because she cried. They spent every holiday doing what they could with small fixes but it was not until he started to make real money from his South American construction projects in the late '70s and particularly after he sold his companies and became an overnight billionaire in 1996 that he had been able to finance a complete restoration.

"We only finished three years ago. Tried to keep everything authentic but who the hell knows."

A strange and uncharacteristically sad expression flickered across Lamy's face and made Michael think of his Peruvian housekeepers in Mattituck and ask about their health.

"Charlie's dead," Lamy answered quietly, "Last January. Night after what he figured was his ninetieth birthday. Drifted away in his sleep. Wonderful old bastard. I loved him. Camilla was still OK but she'd been having problems with the veins in her legs. She wanted to bury his ashes in Lima so we went together and found a nice place where she can put her feet up and be comfortable."

"Good lord. You mean she's there now?"

Lamy nodded.

"How on earth have you managed without them?"

"It's only been a month or so. I'm leaving the place for Pascal if he wants to use it. If not, my daughters can sell it."

"Where are you going to live? The apartment on Washington Square?"

"I'll keep it. That's where I've been bunking but by next fall I'll be moved here."

"Really," Michael said with a sly anticipatory smile.

No need to elaborate. He knew Lamy could read his mind.

By the time they reached Le Haie Tondue and crossed over the Autoroute de Normandie, with its countless frantic transport lorries hurtling toward some secret assignation, and turned onto the D45 for Lisieux at Valsemé, the subject had changed to the great tapestry at Bayeux.

"Yes, I'm aware it isn't a true tapestry!" Michael said, almost shouting.

He could recount even more details than Lamy for once. The wife of an old school chum had just written a play about its creation.

They passed through Saint-Eugene and Saint-Sauveur.

"I find it quite extraordinary," Michael commented, "That so many towns in this area are named after some local patron saint."

"In all of France," Lamy answered, "And Italy. And Spain. Half the damn world," and, as though on cue, the colossal hulk of a basilica loomed up on the horizon.

"Good lord," Michael said, "What the devil's that? Just look at the size of the wretched thing. It's like it's holding down the whole bloody landscape."

"In more ways than one. The Basilica of Lisieux. Sanctuary of the blessed Sainte Thérèse. Ha! Bet you don't know a damn thing about it."

"Bet I will now."

"Hey, not if you don't want."

"Yeah, yeah, yeah. Go for it. I don't want to get covered in globs of your exploding brain."

Lamy chuckled.

"Biggest shrine in France after Lourdes. Two million pilgrims a year. All because a little ten-year-old girl got understandably fucked up about being sick all the time. Imagined she saw a statue of the Virgin smile at her and got better. May 13th, 1883. Became a Carmelite nun at fifteen. Died of TB at twenty-four. Wrote some disjointed sentimental rambles that were published posthumously. 'I wanted to find an elevator that would take me to Jesus.' That sort of shit. But hey, they canonized her within thirty years. Took Joan of Arc four hundred and thirty. Good old John Paul II even declared her parents venerable and eligible for sainthood. Made Thérèse a Doctor of the Church. Only two other women in history have that honor. Teresa of Avila and Catherine of Siena."

It was Michael's turn to laugh.

"I've never known such an irremediably catholic heathen!"

"It's all just bits and pieces. Bullshit bits and pieces," Lamy replied almost tragically and then joined Michael's mirth, "Lisieux was flattened in '44 but the locals still believe it was Thérèse's hotline to God that spared the basilica. What can you do with minds like that?"

§

Erasmus, Michael the Med and da Crema didn't have further occasion to speak before Erasmus decided they should stop for the night half way between Dendermonde and Aalst at a grubby little inn beneath the walls of the castle at Gijzegem. They had traveled well over twenty miles in three hours because he pressed the horses to a canter for most of the way.

However, Michael was treated to an example of the Dutchman's humor as he waited impatiently for a truculent and greedy bargee to ferry them across the Scheldt where it meanders westward at Dendermonde.

They were talking about the Devil and comparing the benign demonology of the ancient Greeks and Romans with the rabidity of the Inquisition. It had been rekindled in the 1480s by the crazed religiosity of Ferdinand and Isabella and thanks to her Dominican confessor, the hammer of heretics, the Inquisitor General Tomás de Torquemada, was now blazing across the continent anew. Erasmus observed wryly, "They preach the Anti-Christ is so clever he could be born of a monk and a nun. If such be true their rant is entirely justified since it follows our poor world must be very well populated with Him."

Latin was the only language in which the three were able to communicate and one might be forgiven for thinking this couldn't have been much of a knee-slapper but it was.

§

The signs went on without let up, Saint-Martin-de-La-Lieue, Saint-

43

Martin-de-Mailloc, Saint-Julien-de-Mailloc, Saint-Pierre-de-Mailloc, La Chapelle-Yvon, Saint-Martin-de-Bienfaite-la-Cressonière, La Vespière, Saint-Mards-de-Fresne, Saint-Germain-la-Campagne, Saint-Aubin-du-Thenney, Saint-Jean-du-Thenney, La-Chapelle-Gauthier, Friardel, until they reached the A28 autoroute and Lamy instructed Michael to take it south toward Le Mans.

"Oh ho," Michael chortled, adopting a horribly overdone French accent, "Zee site of zee *fameuse* endurance race. Zee *vingt-quatre heures du Mans*. I sink I begeen to persever *un peu de méthode* in zee madness."

"Pure coincidence, *mon ami*," Lamy replied coolly, "We have to pick up time somewhere or we'll never make it."

"Hokay, you aire zee boss."

There was a sign off the autoroute for Broglie which sparked another wild ride through the history of the Ducs de Broglie and their intimate alliance with the Rothschilds, their occasionally liberal and anticlerical views, the villa in Dieppe where the most famous of the tribe was born, he of the wave-particle duality, Louis the seventh duke, 1929 Nobel winner for Physics and great-great-grandson of Madame de Staël, their chateau at Sainte-Amadour in Anjou, the Bois de Broglie and their manor in the nearby village, the library of which was said to contain not only all the books that had belonged to her but over forty thousand others and to be the second largest private collection in France.

"De Broglie got his prize six weeks to the day after Black Tuesday. Stock market lost thirty billion. More than twice the national debt. Funny, huh?"

"Are you hinting that bankers like the Rothschilds were behind it?"

"Noooo, would I do that?"

Lamy said he was going to take a nap and told Michael to ignore the speed cameras and put his foot down.

"Like I say, yo is zee bossman," he agreed merrily.

In less than half an hour Michael clocked fifty miles and, as they passed the sign for Alençon, Lamy opened his eyes long enough to look at his watch and said, "Good going."

It was still only ten after nine.

Lamy closed his eyes again and licked his lips and mumbled, "William the conquering hero laid siege to Alençon long before he set his greedy sights on your tight little island. He was a bastard, you know. Old ma was an embalmer's kid from Falaise and when the burghers of Alençon taunted him about it he cut off their hands," and then went back to sleep.

§

Michael the Med and his companions set off from Gijzegem at dawn and went via Aalst to Geraardsbergen where they finally stopped to eat. The horses were tired from their first afternoon's exertion and they were forced to a slower pace which made Erasmus grumpy despite the glorious autumn weather.

Da Crema walked into the old town to purchase some refreshment and came back with a dozen *mattentaart*. They were simple cheese curd pasties and perhaps because he was famished Michael found them quite delicious washed down with several bowlfuls of the local beer. They sat and ate in silence by the Dender as the horses drank on the very spot where three hundred and eighteen years later the duke of Wellington and von Blücher would review their cavalry and parade six thousand marching men before proceeding to meet Napoleon at Waterloo.

Two hours more riding and it was quite dark. Erasmus would not travel at night and cursed himself for having avoided Brussels because they were still several miles from Ath and since no accommodation presented itself they had to sleep under the trees.

§

As the A28 bypassed Le Mans to the east Michael was beginning to think Lamy had missed it when he suddenly opened his eyes again and spoke.

"Take the exit for the Technoparc," he said, "You can drive part of the circuit. We'll get back on the freeway in a few miles."

Michael was thrilled and jabbered on excitedly about the history of racing on the Circuit de la Sarthe, the great Bentley-Bugatti rivalry of the '20s and '30s and how drivers Woolf Barnato and Bernard Rubin set the course record in 1928 in a Bentley nicknamed 'Old Mother Gun' and covered one hundred and fifty-four laps or two thousand six-hundred and sixty-nine kilometers in just over eight hours and before he knew it they were on the Chemin aux Boeufs and right in the midst of the eight and a half mile track with the shorter Bugatti Circuit and the start of the Porsche Curves on their right and Lamy instructed him to take a left at the roundabout and go back across the grounds and then a right onto the Route du Tours.

"This is it, babe," he said, "AKA the Mulsanne Straightaway. Go on. Blow your mind."

Michael grinned and floored it and swerved out into the oncoming lane to hurtle past a dozen astonished motorists barely missing a head-on collision with a honking cursing lorry driver but, alas, his joy was only moments long because he had to come to a screeching halt at a traffic light.

"Wow," he said, breathing hard despite the experience's brevity, "What a car. We touched a hundred and sixty-five miles an hour."

"You missed your calling."

Lamy told him to carry on through Trois Bras and Écommoy and as they rejoined the freeway at Marigné-Laillé Michael commented on something in the rearview mirror.

"It's peculiar," he said, "I'm sure it's the same car. Why would it follow us off the autoroute and still be behind us now."

"Are you telling me you've only just seen them? That ol' blue '73 Mustang got on the damn ferry with us."

"You're joking. Why didn't you tell me?"

Lamy didn't reply.

"Christ Almighty," Michael said, "The car looks the same as the one that followed me in New York."

"Then maybe it is."

"How is that possible?"

"Beats me. You gave the little fuckers a hell of a scare back there though," Lamy said and laughed some more.

"What say I lose them," Michael offered wickedly.

"Hell no, let's invite them for lunch."

§

On the third day they arrived at Valenciennes which was then still located in the county of Hainault. Virtually all of what is now the Netherlands was once part of Burgundy but came under the rule of the Holy Roman Empire in 1477 through the marriage of Maximilian, the son of Frederick III and Eleanor of Portugal, and Charles the Bold's daughter Mary. This united the so-called cadet House of Valois with the Habsburg dynasty, a result which was not to the liking of King Louis XI of the royal French Valois line and though Maximilian was to defeat him at the Battle of Guinegate in 1479 everything was only finally settled by the Treaty of Arras in 1482 in which Maximilian, perhaps because he was confused or still mourning the recent loss of his wife or just plain tired of it all, agreed to marry his daughter, the Archduchess Margaret of Austria, to the Dauphin, later King Charles VIII, bringing most of Burgundy with her as her dowry and thus pretty much wiping it off the map, not that it made the slightest ultimate difference to anything.

The temporary decrease in population caused by this pointless ruckus and the weeping and wailing of countless widows over yet more starving embittered fatherless children is too banal for comment.

Erasmus was much more talkative and the discussion as they rode ranged over a multitude of subjects. Erasmus and da Crema's opinion that a knowledge of classical literature and pagan philosophy was essential to civilized Christian society. Michael concurred but would have left out the word 'Christian'. The corruption rampant within the Holy Church and the evil of indulgences which aroused no conflict between them whatever. The observance of the Eucharist and the belief in transubstantiation which Michael challenged and da Crema vehemently defended and Erasmus offered mild rebuttal. Whether free will was central to human life or whether it is predestined to which all three agreed the former. The issue of gradual versus revolutionary change with Erasmus arguing eloquently and at great length against the latter and finally, but by no means least since it took up the entire afternoon, the nature of God.

Michael gained an appreciation for the gentility of the soft-spoken Dutch ecclesiast and was amazed by the depth of his erudition but his own experience had led him to a firm understanding that awareness of the miraculous inherent in all things did not require, and was richer without, the invention of either a panoply of minor and ineffectual gods or a Supreme Being lurking somewhere behind the cobweb impenetrable veil of circumstance, yet no argument he put forward could ruffle the viewpoint of either companion.

§

The freeway system in France is very well supplied with service areas and within a few miles they came upon one just beyond the exit for the delightfully named village of Dissay-sous-Courcillon. The Bentley needed a fill-up but more than that Lamy and Michael couldn't wait to confirm the identity of whoever it was in the Mustang and sure enough the car followed them in.

Michael wheeled into a stall and they watched the Mustang hesitate and then pass behind them and go all the way to the far end of the gas pumps and the restaurant and finally come to a stop beside a picnic area near the exit.

"Let's make them squirm," Lamy said.

They went into the restaurant to the section selling fast food and groceries and souvenirs and ordered a coffee and a croissant which they took their time consuming.

Lamy said he was willing to bet that not only was it the same Mustang but would turn out to be driven by the same two men. Michael had spoken to them in New York and jokingly called them both 'Nikolai', though that wasn't their real name, and they enjoyed quite a droll time of it. The assumption was they were two-bit Mafia goons who were watching his movements as a favor to the now undoubtedly dead General Larry McWhirter, most likely with the collusion of Condoleezza Rice, because of almost everyone in the tight circle around the president's idiotic belief he was Bartolomeo Vespucci. But who had hired them now? The same cabal? And how did they find out he and Lamy were going to Rome for John Paul's funeral? It was all too ridiculous.

They went back outside and it was true. Both Nikolai were standing by the Mustang doors smoking. Michael could hardly believe his eyes but their identity was unmistakable even behind the sunglasses and as soon as they saw him they made an attempt to look nonchalant and turn away.

"Unbelievable," Michael whispered, "It's them. No doubt about it. You're sure you want to confront them? Maybe we should pretend we don't know and play them along for a while."

"Ah, but *mon ami*, how can we resist?"

The two Nikolai got back into the Mustang as Michael and Lamy strolled toward them but the car didn't move. The tall bony Slavic one with the horribly nicotine-stained teeth was in the driver's seat and rolled down the window as they approached.

"Well, I don't believe," he said in what sounded like a bad actor's version of an eastern European accent, slapping his huge hands on the steering wheel and trying his best to seem surprised, "If it isn't prickyprick.

What in the name of holy fucking hell do you here?"

"You know what I'm doing, Vladimir," Michael replied with a sweet smile, "What are you doing?"

"Going to Italy like you tell me to do," Vladimir said, pounding the wheel even harder and laughing at his joke like a hiccupping donkey, "You remember how we agree? Everybody love Italy!"

There were flecks of brown saliva on his lips.

"Hey, you know my friend Ciccio," he went on, nodding at the short neatly-dressed Mediterranean one with the permanent stubble in the passenger seat, "What you think? From his heart's goodness he comes to translate."

Michael leaned down to look in.

"*Ciao*," he said, "Didn't you tell me you were Albanian?"

"I am," the swarthy little critic answered drily, "I am Ciccio Albanese and you are Enrico Caruso."

It was a tender spot. Michael, though a lover of the beauty of the human voice, was cursed with the inability to carry a tune. He had nonetheless been inspired to attempt a few bars of La Bohème outside Lincoln Center in New York and Ciccio had mocked him then as he was doing now.

"Watch it," Michael warned, "Or I'll sing the whole aria."

§

By the fourth day Michael the Med had grown tired of philosophizing and was beginning to question his sanity. Why on earth did he choose to visit Paris? What irresponsibility! How the devil did he expect Elaine and the children to cope? And despite being the spoiled offspring of wealthy parents he and Elaine had spent the last eleven and a half years fending for themselves and he was uncomfortable letting da Crema continually pay for everything. He decided to stay no more than three days in Paris and then go straight home.

Erasmus divulged as they trotted along that morning that after his parents died he was forced into the monastic life by poverty. He had taken holy orders as an Augustinian canon in Steyn in 1492 but never truly acted in the capacity of a priest since shortly thereafter he was appointed secretary to Hendrik van Bergen, the brilliant and powerful Bishop of Cambrai, a post he held for three years before becoming, with van

Bergen's blessing, a student of the ascetic Jan Standonck in the Collège de Montaigu. He explained that the direct route to Paris lay through Cambrai, which was neither part of France nor Burgundy but an independent bishopric, and though it was the seat of his benefactor he was choosing to avoid it altogether because he had discovered life at court was not conducive to study, that in fact it had come to terrify him and the relationship between them had cooled.

The bishop's brother Antoon was a Benedictine abbot and also his patron. A second brother, Dismas, was to become a master of requests to Margaret of Austria and a member of the future emperor Charles V's privy council and a third, Jan, was already chamberlain to Maximilian I and, like Hendrik, a Knight of the Order of the Golden Fleece.

Erasmus had developed a profound distaste for such a life and knew from experience Christ's teaching dwelt not in the courts of the mighty.

Thus it was they side-stepped from Valenciennes to Le Quesnoy, where Charles V rebuilt the castle ramparts which Vauban improved for Louis XIV and the 4th New Zealand Rifle Brigade scaled in November 1918 losing over two hundred men, to the ancient Roman road that ran south-southwest to Le Cateau-Cambrésis, birthplace of Henri Matisse, and stopped for the night just beyond the crossroad leading from Cambrai to Saint-Quentin, once known as Augusta Veromanduorum, after the Belgian Veromandui, site of the Christian ex-senator Quentin's cruel torture and beheading by the soldiers of the prefect Rictiovarus in the year 287.

§

Lamy was amused by the banter and at the same time quickly bored by it and told Vladimir and Ciccio they were going to stop for lunch in Amboise at a restaurant called Le Clos and they were invited if they wanted to come. Why not, he said, since it was on the way to Italy. The prospect delighted Vladimir and seemed to make Ciccio a little apprehensive but they agreed.

The conversation as they continued south was only somewhat more to do with the confusion of present possibilities than historiography.

Before they got to Tours, where in 732 Charles Martel, the grandfather of Charlemagne, finally stopped the advance of Abdul Rahman Al Ghafiqi and his Muslim horsemen allowing the rise of the Carolingian dynasty and ultimately France and the Holy Roman Empire, they turned off the A28 onto the A10 at Chanceaux-sur-Choisille.

"Tours was sacked a century later by a Viking chieftain named Haesten or Hastein or Hasting," Lamy mentioned as they passed the exit for Monnaie and a mile further pointed Michael off the freeway towards Reugny and Nazelles-Négron, "Interesting, eh? The Norman historian Dudo of Saint-Quentin hadn't much good to say about him. He got up your way too, raping and pillaging. No proof he gave his name to your south coast town but I'd put money on it."

The Mustang stuck to them like glue and as they approached the Loire crossing the magnificent Château d'Amboise became visible on the far side of the river. It was such an exquisite sight Michael nearly drove off the road and for the umpteenth time on the journey cursed Lamy for insisting he not bring his camera.

"Why? What was the harm? You get to blather on," he muttered.

Lamy told him over dessert at Stratford's how irritating the damn thing was and Helen wholeheartedly agreed. The deal was off if he had to stop every two minutes to feed Michael's habit.

"If you want me to shut up just say so," Lamy replied, "But I'm sure you'll want to know what I'm gonna tell you. This place is one of the highlights of the whole trip."

Michael gave him a baleful glance.

As Lamy directed him across the Pont du Général Leclerc and the Isle of Gold and up the Rue Victor Hugo past the famous Clos Lucé, where Leonardo da Vinci spent the last years of his life at the invitation of Francis I and where replicas of forty or more of his inventions including a formidable circular tank and a helicopter stood in the park, and down a narrow one way avenue bearing his name to Le Clos d'Amboise on Rue Rabelais, he spoke of Fulk the Black, son of Geoffrey Greymantle and Adelaide of Vermandois, ancestor of Charles Martel and the Plantagenet kings of England. Fulk was another who had been given a bad rap by the history books, perhaps because he flambéed his first wife in her wedding dress after finding her fucking a goatherd, but he did make four pilgrimages to the Holy Land and built the original chateau. It was extended by Charles VIII in the 1490s and lived in by Henry II, of France not England, and his wife Catherine de' Medici who raised their children with Mary Stuart when she was betrothed as a child to Francis II and who in 1560, during the conflict between Huguenot Bourbons and Catholic

Guises known as the French Wars of Religion, hung twelve hundred gibbeted Protestant corpses from hooks on the city walls and in 1572 instigated the Saint Bartholomew's Day Massacre in which more than twenty thousand Protestant Huguenots perished.

There was an archway to their right with a single lane entry and Michael deftly nipped through it into a spacious garden in complete contrast to the drabness of the street. There was valet parking and Lamy told him to stop. The Mustang didn't follow but Michael could see Vladimir ramming the car back and forth and squeezing it into a tiny space directly outside.

At the end of the garden there were tables and chairs set out on the lawn in the sunshine.

"Splendid," Michael said, "I wonder if they serve Huguenot for lunch."

§

The next day the weary travelers rode from twilight to twilight and made it all the way to Compiègne, where Joan of Arc was captured by the Burgundians and sold to the English and after the so-called Day of the Dupes on November the 11th, 1630, Marie de' Medici, queen consort to Louis XIII and great-great-grand-daughter of not only Maximilian I and Mary but Ferdinand and Isabella as well, was exiled by Cardinal Richelieu and her double-crossing son. Where two hundred and eighty-eight years later, on the eleventh hour of the eleventh day of the eleventh month, the armistice for 'the war to end all wars' would be signed.

By the following afternoon they came to the Latin Quarter and the house Erasmus was now sharing with his student Heinrich Northoff, whose brother Christian had returned to Lübeck, and Northoff's friend Augustin Vincent, or Augustinus Vincentius Caminadus, a publicist for the latest books to be found in the new *librairies*, who hailed from Viersen near Cologne.

§

"You could have parked in here," Lamy said as Vladimir and Ciccio came through the arch, checking furtively to either side as they did so.

"Who knows," Vladimir answered with a toothy grin, "Maybe you plan for assassination. We cannot be too much uncareful."

They were seated by a waiter who managed not to sniff at Vladimir's less than appropriate attire, faded jeans, worn sandals and a frayed sweatshirt with no sleeves, and they ordered drinks. Lamy told Michael he would drive in the afternoon and to feel free to indulge. Michael and Vladimir both wanted a beer and were inclined to the Kronenbourg 1664 since they didn't recognize any of the other brands but Lamy suggested the Trois Monts.

"It's a good strong pale ale," he said, "I guarantee you'll like it."

He couldn't resist mentioning the name referred to three hills in Flanders near Ypres that saw ferocious combat in 1914 and 15 and the first use of both chlorine and a mustard gas called Yperite and Ciccio and Vladimir just stared at him blankly.

"He has a disease," Michael explained.

"Something we should know what?" Vladimir asked, leaning away.

"No, no," Michael answered reassuringly, "Now look, I've got a question. How is it you're driving the same car? Why would you go to all the trouble and expense of bringing it when you could have simply rented one?"

"Hey, look, my friend," Vladimir replied, "We are poor guys, him and me, yes? We need car. Was cheaper to bring than buy new. Besides I like. OK, I tell you what happen. Immigration fuckers catch us without paperwork and we get big bum's rush. I tell you true. We can no go back no more."

The beer came and Vladimir downed all but a sip before the waiter had put Lamy's mineral water and Ciccio's Coke in front of them and pointed with his forefinger into the glass for another.

"You are right," he said to Lamy, belching loudly, "Is very good."

"Did you know who he was," Lamy began, trying a different tack and nodding at Michael, "When you were tailing him in New York?"

"Sure, sure, but we knew was bullshit."

"What was bullshit?"

"He was not guy."

"What guy?"

"Guy they think."

"Who was they?"

"Come on, come on, don't fuck."

Michael nearly burst out laughing but Lamy persevered.

"General McWhirter?"

"Yes, yes, of course. Him and that black bitch Condolenza."

"Condoleezza," Ciccio corrected him.

"You said I was the guy," Michael begged to differ, "On the C train as we stopped at 72nd Street, remember? Bartolomeo Vespucci."

Ciccio squirmed a little in his seat and put a finger to his lips.

"Hey, not so loud. OK, yes, then maybe. Now we know it was shit."

"So who was your boss?" Lamy asked, "Brighton Beach?"

There was no answer and more beer came and they let Lamy order food because the menu was in French.

"Is that who you're working for now?"

"I tell you don't fuck," Vladimir said sternly, "We are going to Italy."

"For a holiday," Ciccio added laconically, "My family is from Lecce."

"An Albanian from Lecce," Michael said, giving him a dubious look.

"*Si*, and why not?"

"Well, if you're on holiday, where have you been living since they rushed your bums? And how long ago exactly was that?"

"You ask too much nothing," Vladimir snorted, waving his empty glass at the waiter, "Week, month, year, who gives? We were in London, what else? We love England too."

The conversation went round in similarly futile circles, though it became pretty clear neither Vladimir nor Ciccio had much idea what had been going on in New York nor why they were ordered to follow him, until at last, after they ate dessert and the waiter brought coffee and Vladimir inhaled his ninth Trois Monts, the bleary-eyed Uke, or whatever he was, let out yet another protracted belch and, with a witless wink, admitted, "OK, I tell you something, prickymen. Is not Brighton Beach." He snapped the last word to rhyme it with his familiar epithet for the recently-appointed Secretary of State then, shaking a finger for emphasis, repeated, "No, not. Is much much bigger." At which Ciccio jumped up and hauled him to his feet and told him they were going to wait in the car.

"Why wait," Lamy suggested, quickly scribbling an address on the back of one of his cards, "Tonight we're in Mâcon, tomorrow Geneva, third in Firenze and that's where you'll find us in Rome."

He handed Ciccio the card.

"Relax. Take a break. Why sweat it?"

The straight man and the stooge took their leave without a word of thanks but nonetheless the Mustang slavishly followed the Bentley all the way through the Forêt d'Amboise and the town of Vierzon, bypassing Bourges, though they could see the distant spires of the great Gothic cathedral of Saint-Étienne rising majestically above the afternoon haze, and then continuing east to the south of Nevers, Julius Caesar's Noviodunum, where the treacherous Aedui massacred his rearguard and burned his arsenal to the ground, and Magny-Cours and the Bardonnay racetrack, site of Michael of Hürth-Hermülheim's incredible seventh victory in the Formula One French Grand Prix the previous July. There was no time for a detour to pay pilgrim homage as Lamy had planned because they had tarried too long over lunch. The disappointment caused Michael to launch into Lear's terrifying line over the dead Cordelia, five repetitions of the word 'never', in a hideous French accent, "Zow'll't come no moire, Nevers, Nevers . . et cetera . . " Then onward via Moulins, Yzerne, Dompierre sur Besbre, Paray-le-Monial and Charolles to Mâcon-sur-Saône, the southernmost city of Burgundy, where they stopped for the night at the Hostellerie La Sarrasine in Replonges north of the Beaujolais Hills.

Shuffle Five

"God is not willing to do everything and thus take away our free will and
that share of glory which belongs to us."
- Niccolò Machiavelli (1469 - 1527)

§

Neither Michael nor Lamy were hungry that evening and they were
tired. Lamy had arranged adjoining suites at another incredibly beautiful
converted 17th century manor house and both wanted to bathe and use
the telephone and agreed to meet for a nightcap in the bar in an hour.

They decided during the afternoon the only way anyone could know
they were going to Rome was bugging his phone in Chalk Farm, Lamy
never used anything but his cell, and then by overhearing them at
Stratford's.

Michael remembered thinking it was odd that his ancient rotary, which
he had for years stubbornly refused to replace despite an ever-present
infuriating static crackle, had suddenly and miraculously ceased this
malfunction during his absence in New York in 2001. He assumed at the
time that his *bête noire*, British Telecom, must at long last have heeded his
complaints and solved the problem but they concluded with some
merriment it was much more likely an implanted device had somehow
effected a cure.

However, the thought that his private sanctum had been invaded and
that everything he said in the last three and a half years had been listened
to and analyzed wasn't funny at all but spooky and vile and intrusive and
he had to do something about it. So he called Helen on her cell, thankfully
she carried one, he never had because of some inarticulable scruple about
not kowtowing to the insistent mercantile whine of modernity, and told
her about Aunt Sonja and the Seigneurie and the amazing letter and then
asked her to disconnect his phone from its jack on the instant and put it
away in a drawer so he could examine it later and, if she had time, buy a
new one and change their number which, of course, he knew would
occasion some concerned questions in response but his farcically long-
winded attempt to explain why without any mention of Vladimir and

Ciccio ultimately failed.

"Oh my god," Helen said with a worried laugh, "How do you manage it? Every time you go anywhere you immediately land in the shit!"

"You know bloody well it's not my bloody fault! I didn't want to become Bartolomeo fucking Vespucci!"

Lamy's first call was to Edna Phipps to ask who had been seated close to them that night and after going through her credit card receipts she found the name Gerald Craven. He was an elderly man whom she had taken to be Jewish who arrived with an elegant gray-haired woman a few minutes after Helen and Michael. They didn't have a reservation but a table close to theirs happened to be vacant due to a last minute cancellation.

Lamy made two more calls and discovered that Gerald Craven's real name was Gerhardt Krasinski. He had once been an associate of the Kray twins and was now deeply involved with Semion Mogilevich, who Michael knew all too well from the ghastly events he witnessed in Amado Portillo's penthouse suite in El Paso, and a Russian-Israeli businessman and convicted arms-dealer named Arcadi Gaydamak.

"Well, jolly good," Michael said with grim sarcasm, as Lamy sipped a glass of chilled Mâcon-Pierreclos and he took a big gulp of another Trois Monts on a candle-lit patio snuggled beneath the eaves of the *hostellerie*, "But what does that tell us about our two idiot shadow men?"

Strangely enough the Mustang turned off toward Lyon as they approached Mâcon and hadn't reappeared.

"They said they know now I'm not blasted Vespucci. Clearly they weren't sent to kill us or they already would have. So . . what?"

"Krasinski must have heard me saying the name though so maybe it's still about him somehow," Lamy answered, not sounding very certain, "And what's about to happen in Rome? 'Much bigger,' he said. A bigger boss? Or something even bigger than 9/11."

"The plutonium?" Michael suggested quietly.

They looked at each other in silence for a moment.

"Too bad Ciccio pulled him away. He'd have told us after a couple more."

"They're lethal," Michael agreed, taking another swallow, "Our soap opera Slav was out cold in the passenger seat behind us."

"That's why I ordered them."

Lamy grinned briefly but fell silent again.

"The plutonium?" he repeated, looking at Michael with the same fleeting sad expression he had seen as he spoke about the restoration of the Seigneurie, "At the funeral? Vatican just announced it for Friday morning. Boy, I sure as hell hope not."

§

Something of lasting consequence happened to Michael the Med on his second full day in Paris.

The population of the city was three times that of London and on the first day he had walked until he was footsore and seen the sights, the great river and the cathedral of Notre Dame, the Sorbonne and the university, the abbeys of Saint-Germain and Sainte-Geneviève, the Place Maubert, the Rue du Fouarre, the printing houses and bookshops and in the evening met more of Erasmus' friends, the poet Fausto Andrelini from Forlì and Jakob Batt from Bergen ap Zoom, who had just resigned his post as the town secretary of Bergen and been helpful in securing Erasmus' release from Bishop Hendrik, and Pierre le Dru, a printer and Parisian born and bred, all three of whom somehow managed to live 'the literary life on slender means' without stinting a generous consumption of alcohol.

Perhaps it was his hangover the next morning or the bright autumn sun or the rapid approach of his forty-eighth birthday but when Andrelini caught up to him in the Rue Galande just as he was about to re-enter Augustin Vincent's house and breathlessly introduced him to a pale-skinned fresh-faced blue-eyed fair-haired seventeen-year-old from Montefioralle, by way of Florence and the University of Bologna where he had been studying astronomy, for some quite unfathomable reason, as Andrelini pronounced the Latinate of the boy's name, Bartolomeus Vespucius, Michael's field of vision began to spin, his inner ears began popping and hissing and reverberating with each individual phoneme as though his Eustachian tubes were clogged with catarrh and something he had never felt before took place deep within his being.

§

Lurking behind the reappearance of the Nikolai in Michael the Mod's life were many things Vladimir and Ciccio didn't know and some that Michael and Lamy would never answer completely.

The two minor Mafiosi understood very well what they had been hired to do. They were to find Bartolomeo Vespucci and, if necessary, eliminate him. Of course, they hadn't been told why and it was true no one at all, at least no one involved in the deeper machinations of the plot, believed any longer Michael was the Italian mystery man but the plotter's difficulty was that none of them knew what he really did look like nor where or how to find him.

The plutonium's source was obsolete Russian weaponry. It was smuggled out through Georgia and its ultimate possible use was so secret that Gaydamak and Mogilevich both insisted on a middle man since, quite naturally, they didn't trust people like Amado Portillo and all parties to the transaction finally agreed on the almost mythical Vespucci. Amado had never heard the name but said he would make the contact and, when he failed to do so, was daring enough to put a disguised Michael in his place. The ruse worked and lay undetected for years partly because Amado was killed by his tiger and his cartel taken over by the Arellano brothers and a berserk parade of kaleidoscopically fragmenting groups that went on terrorizing Juarez with the same heartless violence. The Arellano-Felix allowed independent witnesses when the plutonium was stashed in the Samalayuca but after the decision not to use it on 9/11 it just stayed ticking away in the desert waiting for another bidder.

The trouble began in 2003 when an identical collection of warmongering swine to those who had brought about the devastation of 2001 by other means began furrowing their brows over the election of Mahmoud Ahmadinejad as mayor of Tehran. The probable rise of a more militant government in Iran than the relatively amenable Khatami regime led them to the gloriously satisfying idea of nuking the Uranium Conversion Facility at Isfahan. A nagging boil that was rising to an ugly white head by the late winter of 2005.

The majority of this bewilderingly short-sighted boy's club were in favor of a straight-out up-front old-fashioned bald-faced military strike but a few sly dogs among them suggested it might be better, considering the rapidly growing lack of sympathy in the world for pretty much all things American or Israeli, to make it look like an unfortunate accident. 'Everyone knows towel-heads don't know dick about serious technology' was their claim and in the end that faction prevailed. The subject of the stashed plutonium was broached and before you could say hot-diggety or Hiroshima they found out the goddamned stuff had fucking well been stolen just two days before. The guards had been drugged and their truck was gone. They were found wandering a mile away like a pair of crazed hermits and were unable to give a description of their attackers because they were so dehydrated they could no longer comprehend nor speak.

Semion Mogilevich immediately realized this unexpected revelation wasn't going to do much for his longevity. He received several exceedingly uncryptic messages, not only from his normally reliable pals at Mossad and the CIA but also indirectly from the offices of the vice-president, the Secretary of State, the Justice and Homeland Security Departments and Kissinger Associates, the gist of which was 'recover the goods or die' and this had provoked a tidal wave of killings, kidnapping and torture, not only throughout Chihuahua and the rest of Mexico but the West Bank and Gaza and the cities of Medellín, Djakarta, New York, Lisbon, Paris, London, Naples, Amsterdam and Sevastopol-Balaklava as well, as the Brainy Don's henchmen frantically tried to find out what happened, a largely unreported bloodbath that went on for a full month with no success.

Speculation was rife. Depending on the particular bias it was either some ultra-fanatical splinter group of Hamas who were going to lob chunks of it into Tel Aviv or an alliance of the JDL, Kahana Chai, IRIS and EMET bent on the obliteration of the refugee camps at Jabaliyah, Shaykh Radwan and Al Shail or any one of Al Qaeda, the Kurdistan Freedom Falcons, Tamil Nadu, the Orange Volunteeers, Kanglei Yaol Kanba Lup, Shining Path, the Baluchistan Liberation Army or the National Democratic Front of Bodoland.

By the middle of March Mogilevich had run out of bodies to flay and was called to account. He and his new Russian-Israeli wife Galina Jambulskaya were forced to get down on their pudgy knees on the 16th century Tabriz medallion carpet in their fortified villa outside Budapest and lie.

"It was Vespucci," he grunted.

"Where is it?"

"I don't know but I swear on my balls no one else has it."

His interrogators appeared to accept the explanation and told him to keep looking, both for Vespucci and the contraband.

It was his connection in Whitechapel who hired the two Nikolai. The one thing they had told Lamy and Michael the truth about was their run in with the Immigration and Naturalization Service. They were in London and knew what Michael looked like at least and when Krasinski heard the name Vespucci in the restaurant it didn't take more than half an hour for arrangements to be made. It was a hell of a long shot anything would come of it but, as the saying goes, you do what you have to do.

In a world stocked with six and a half billion interlinked perceiving brains it's obvious Michael and Lamy would not be alone in their concern for nuclear security at the pope's funeral yet Vladimir and Ciccio and Krasinski and even Mogilevich were unaware the Mustang was also being followed.

§

The next morning Lamy and Michael met for breakfast on the patio of the *hostellerie* and confessed they hadn't slept well though Lamy realized during the night they were not about to be vaporized in the Piazza San Pietro as the result of a terrorist plot.

"I used the words 'flush out Vespucci', remember?" he said, biting into a brioche, "I think they hope we'll lead them to him, that's all."

"Who is?"

"I'm guessing more or less the same bunch."

"Cheney and Rice?"

"And the rest."

"Why?"

"Maybe they're as confused as we are whether he's real or not."

"That would hardly come under the heading 'much bigger'," Michael said, leaning forward and imitating Vladimir's voice and gesture.

"I'm not saying the plutonium isn't part of it. But not at the funeral. Think of all the big boys sitting in that square. Come on, there won't be anyone or anywhere in Lazio that isn't strip-searched."

"If there was a plot they'd be most of the plotters."

"My point."

They left Replonges and Michael took the wheel for the hour and a half drive to Geneva. The Mustang was still *in absentia* which was puzzling.

"I see they've had to put off Chucky and Camilla's wedding because of the funeral," Michael said.

"Yup," Lamy answered, "To Saturday. Nothing supercedes a Popeathon."

Michael smiled in appreciation of the term.

"Ain't it a shame and ain't it a pity," he added happily.

Lamy kept mostly silent and Michael reveled in the incredible stability of the Bentley as he negotiated the twists and turns of the Autoroute Blanche at maximum throttle, passing Saint-André-de-Bâgé, Saint-Cyr-sur-Menthon, Saint-Martin-du-Mont, Saint-Germain-de-Joux, Châtillon-en-Michaille, crossing the Rhône at Bellegarde-sur-Valserine and finally coming into sight of Lake Leman at Perly-Certoux.

The one thing Lamy did talk about was his suspicion that someone in his office in New York, he maintained a staff of twelve in a separate apartment on Washington Square to look after his enormous portfolio and deal with the slow divestment of his fortune, must be giving information to the CIA.

"Can you be sure?" Michael asked, "I thought they were hand-picked."

"Yup. They are. Just got a nasty feeling."

"Maybe your office phones are bugged."

"Not a chance with the software I put in. But when I spoke to Aunt Sonja this morning she said someone claiming to be my secretary from the office had called for me twice yesterday. They gave the right name, Valerie, so she said I was gone and to try my cell. Thing is, I never told anyone I was going there."

"But wouldn't they have known it was possible?"

"Sure, but Val knows to call my cell. Anyway, I told her not to unless it's an absolute emergency. You know I haven't used it. Too easy to find you."

"So what are you saying?"

"There's no tracer on the car. I had it checked. I'm guessing there's one in the Mustang and someone was wondering why Vladimir and Ciccio were so far off course."

§

Thus it was that Michael the Med found himself still in Paris long past the self-imposed deadline of his birthday.

§

It was only eleven fifteen as Michael the Mod and Lamy checked into the Beau-Rivage on the Quai du Mont Blanc where Lamy had reserved two deluxe suites with balconies overlooking the lake. Despite a natural tendency to wallow like a hog in any given environment Michael knew he would never be able to fully relax in such staggering luxury. There was something about it that could so easily devour you.

Lamy surprised him by saying that he was going to take a taxi to Cologny, an exclusive suburb visible across the water behind the famous *Jet d'Eau*, and spend the rest of the day with his brother.

"I don't want any of this to affect Pascal's appointment," he said, "You're my decoy. I'll meet you in the Atrium bar at nine if you're still up."

Lamy suggested an afternoon drive to Montreux and the Castle of Chillon at the far end of the lake but, despite its being the setting of Daisy Miller and Byron's epic poem about the imprisonment of François Bonivard by the Duke of Savoy, Michael decided he'd be better off having a good walk and that it was safer not to go anywhere in the Bentley by himself.

He set off first to the Jardin Anglais but found it noisy so he retraced his steps past the hotel and the Brunswick Monument, a mausoleum erected by the city to honor a half-mad benefactor named Charles d'Este-Guelph who wanted an exact replica of a 14th century Veronese family tomb, and walked all the way along the water and through several more parks to the World Trade HQ on the Rue de Lausanne. The building was modeled on a classical Florentine villa and Michael thought it quite spectacular. After admiring the façade he wandered on through the park until he came to the massive Palais des Nations which he had no idea housed the UN in Europe but he didn't much like it and turned around. He couldn't resist taking the Rue Rothschild and was amused to come across a gathering of scruffy backpackers lounging on some steps.

He continued along the Rue des Pâquis and the Rue Philippe Plantamour and miraculously enough, after guessing at an intersection, came straight out on the quay in front of the hotel but before he had time to congratulate himself on his navigational brilliance he saw the Mustang. No Ciccio or Vladimir though. It was parked directly outside but empty.

He wasn't in the mood for another confrontation and slunk quickly away to the Quai des Bergues, crossed the river to the Quai de la Poste, then turned left on Boulevard Georges Favon into what was evidently the banking district. He was sorely tempted by a camera shop but carried on, passing the Rue de la Bourse and Place de la Synagogue, finally stopping at the Café des Banques on the corner of Rue de Hesse because he was desperately thirsty.

After three Trois Monts he was just about to leave when he fell into casual conversation with an impeccably dressed middle-aged man who worked for the Bank Privée Edmond de Rothschild S. A., *Société Anonyme*, whose offices were close by and whose name, to Michael's delight, turned out to be Michel.

Michel guessed immediately Michael was English, which always irritated him because he truly didn't inderstand why it was so easy, and when he found out where Michael was staying he told two extraordinary stories.

The Beau-Rivage had been founded by Jean-Jacques Mayer in 1865 and was still privately owned and run by his great-grandson.

In the early afternoon of September 10th, 1898, the sixty-one-year-old Empress Elizabeth of Austria, fondly nicknamed 'Sisi', who despite her age was rather the Princess Diana of her time, expired in her suite at the hotel. She had come to Geneva only the day before to visit Baroness Julie de Rothschild and she and her companion, Countess Irma Sztáray, were on the quay waiting to board a ferry when an Italian anarchist named Luigi Lucheni, pretending to lose his balance and stumble, stabbed her in the chest with a sharpened needle file. She was unaware of the wound at first because of her bodice but collapsed on the ferry and the captain had been forced to turn around. Lucheni only sought notoriety and was quite obviously unconcerned by his almost immediate arrest in the Rue des Alpes. His intended target had been the Duke of Orléans but when the duke's itinerary changed and suddenly skipped Geneva Lucheni opted for a different victim. He committed suicide in prison in 1910.

The second tale concerned the suspicious death of the German politician and touted successor to Chancellor Helmut Kohl, Uwe Barschel, in his bathtub at the hotel on October 11th, 1987. The rising star's reputation had been ruined by the so-called Waterkant-Gate affair in which he was accused of spying on a rival candidate to get compromising information about his tax returns and the police assumption was suicide but more than ten years later, even after a ruling by both Swiss and German examining magistrates that there was absolutely no reason to suspect the involvement of any other person in his death, the rumors of foul play were undiminished.

Comparisons were made and both agreed that history provided an almost incalculable number of such cases.

Michel also reeled off an astonishing list of the world's rich and famous who had stayed there. Sarah Bernhardt, Richard Wagner, the Duke of Windsor and Wallis Warfield-Simpson, the Aga Khan and King Farouk, Mary Pickford and Clark Gable and Harold Lloyd, Cecilia Bartoli and Phil Collins, but of most interest to Michael was the playwright Václav Havel whom he met at a party in Prague many years before Havel became the last president of Czechoslovakia and the first president of the Czech Republic.

By the time they parted company it was seven twenty-five and night had fallen which Michael's slightly sozzled brain thought was good because it might allow him to sneak into the hotel unobserved. He had polished off four more Trois Monts during their chat and was pleased with himself the return trip did not become a hopeless zigzag.

He gave the area careful scrutiny before crossing the Quai du Mont Blanc but as far as he could see the Mustang was no longer there.

Shuffle Six

"Sometimes I wonder if suicides are not in fact guardians of the
meaning of life."
- Václav Havel (1936 -   )

§

Michael the Med did not suddenly reverse his sexual orientation and begin a torrid affair with a boy a third his age. That was not at all what happened. But there was a challenge in the relationship and something hypnotic. Michael still intended to return home and wasn't the kind to callously flout responsibility but two things occurred that made his dilatoriness seem more forgivable.

The first was a suggestion by Andrelini that they accompany him to the court of Charles VIII in Amboise at the end of October and the second was a letter from Elaine that arrived ten days after his birthday.

It came in a bundle of lengthy missives for Erasmus from Thomas Grey and Robert Fisher and a man called Thomas More, of whom Michael had never heard. He had, however, discovered a third motive for his original invitation. As well as their discussions in Latin Erasmus had taken every opportunity, both on the ride from Antwerp and during the last three weeks in Paris, to practice and perfect his English. He was anxious to take up the suggestion of a former pupil named William Blount, the 4th Baron Mountjoy, that he come to Oxford University and he was hoping to lecture there the following spring. Cambridge and Oxford had very early in their existence been influenced by the enlightened teaching of the Muslim scholars of Al-Andalus due primarily to the travels of Daniel of Morley to Toledo but also Gerard of Cremona and Adelard of Bath and Erasmus was greatly interested to absorb this atmosphere.

Michael, unlike his modern counterpart, had been a tutor at Eton and was a graduate of Cambridge so he was automatically well respected by the people to whom Erasmus introduced him. He was also, by and large, some fifteen or twenty years more advanced in age and his graying hair, gentle temperament and, perhaps more than anything, his broad-minded skepticism began to attract notice, not only by the students but many

66

others in the Quarter. They sought him out for instruction in the multifold peculiarities of the English tongue as well as information on the cultural and political history of the island and, always keeping himself the exception, Erasmus made sure they paid handsomely. This gave Michael an essential source of income so he was no longer dependent on da Crema and provided further justification for his delay.

The letter from Elaine was reassuring. She told him Thomas Grey and his elder brother George and an uncle named Arthur Billingsgate had found them in Worthing on the afternoon of October 6th. They were well and very relieved to hear he was alive and the family had been extremely generous. Seeing their situation Billingsgate immediately insisted they stay with him until Michael's return. He raised sheep on the downs north of Chichester so it was an exciting prospect for Jack and Jenny. The farm was an hour's walk from the town near something local people called the Trundle, the ruins of an ancient fortification similar to Cissbury Ring, and they all hoped he would rejoin them there soon.

§

Neither Vladimir nor Ciccio were in the lobby of the hotel and Michael went through to the Atrium bar. It was magnificently mirrored and hushed and calm and the soft lights bestowed a comforting anonymity so he plopped down into a lushly upholstered armchair by the grand marble fireplace and beckoned the waiter with a subtle wave and ordered another Trois Monts.

"*Un sandwich de jambon aussi,*" he added in his rather tortured French, "*Non, non, pardonnez-moi, deux sandwich de jambon. Je suis faim.*"

"Two ham sandwiches, certainly sir. Would you like those on focaccia or rye?" the waiter replied in an almost *sotto voce* American accent.

"Good lord," Michael said, "Where are you from?"

"Ohio. I'm on a Fulbright but it's really expensive here."

"I'm sure. Um, focaccia or rye. Haven't you got some local white bread?"

"Sure. Would you like mustard on that and some greens?"

"Yes, that would be splendid, thank you."

"How about scalloped potatoes on the side? They do them real good."

"Ah, no, thank you, just the sandwiches."

The young man's name was Nick and he was a post-graduate student of international relations at the University of Geneva but there was something in his fresh-faced mid-west demeanor that made Michael keep their conversation to a minimum. The sandwiches, however, were utterly delicious. He decided it would be better to enjoy them before looking at the price. He had another beer to wash them down and the tally was sixty-five Swiss francs but since he had no clue about the conversion rate and no remaining cash in the currency he just added ten to the total and rather guiltily signed the bill to his room.

He waited for Lamy until nearly eleven but the food made him sleepy and he went to bed.

§

King Charles VIII of France, not to be confused with Charles V, the Holy Roman Emperor, who was not yet born, was languishing frustrated in Amboise because the first Italian War which he had begun auspiciously in 1494 with the sack of Naples had ended with his defeat by the League of Venice at the Battle of Fornovo in 1495.

The Italian Wars lasted intermittently for sixty-five years and are not only impossibly complex to analyze but achieved nothing whatever so their mention will be as brief as possible.

Charles was enticed into the enterprise by Ludovico Sforza of Milan who wanted an ally against the Venetians and by his own daft desire to engage in a crusade against the Ottoman Turks for which, Sforza convinced him, his claim to the throne of Naples could provide the springboard. He marched his huge army through Savoy, the Duchy of Milan, Florence and the Papal States and had taken Naples with the *condottieri* offering no more than token resistance. In Florence, thanks to the collusion of Fra Savonarola and the *mediocri*, his mere approach was sufficient to send the Medici into exile. His presence within the pope's domain, however, had been entirely unwelcome but Rodrigo Borgia was patient and waited for his revenge.

Thus Charles was moping in Amboise. He had been unable to raise capital sufficient for further adventures and his mood was only marginally brightened by the arrival of Andrelini and his companions.

§

At seven o'clock Michael the Mod's telephone rang and Lamy asked him to come down to breakfast in the hotel restaurant, Le Chat-Botté, as soon as he could make himself ready and the moment he sat down at the table he told him about the reappearance of the Mustang.

"I know," Lamy said, "They're outside now."

There was a pause as the waiter took his order. Thankfully it wasn't Nick. Michael noticed Lamy looked tired.

"It seems to me . . " he began, after the waiter had gone.

"Yeah," Lamy interrupted, "There's definitely a fucking leak in my office."

"There would have to be," Michael agreed, "Unless they can smell us."

"Should have done the damn reservations myself."

"It might not have helped."

"True. Sorry I didn't make it last night. We were talking until three. Hope you're OK to take the wheel again. It's about seven hours to Florence. There's a couple of things I want to show you before it gets dark."

"That shouldn't present any difficulty."

§

The pleasant-natured but rather simple-minded Charles became fascinated by the young Florentine in much the same way as Michael though in the king's case, Michael flattered himself, Bartolomeo did not reciprocate the interest and they made their excuses and left Amboise after a mere two weeks.

§

Lamy's opinion that they were not about to become gaseous matter along with everyone attending the funeral in St. Peter's Square might have been quite different had he known of the plutonium's disappearance. There were plenty of others in the Eternal City and elsewhere who were getting exceedingly jittery.

§

A valet brought the Bentley under the covered portico by the front doors. Michael could see Vladimir and Ciccio slouched half asleep in the Mustang and he honked and beckoned them with a wave of his arm to follow.

He thought it amusingly serendipitous that Lamy directed him across the river to the Quai de la Poste and up Boulevard Georges Favon past Café des Banques and he began to tell Michel's anecdotes but Lamy stopped him saying he knew Jacques Mayer and his wife Snuggi well and had heard them dozens of times.

"Remember the little guy I was talking to when you came down?"

Michael did. A small bespectacled white-haired man with a close-cropped beard who could easily have been Lamy's gnome twin.

"You're not Jewish, are you?" he asked.

Lamy started laughing.

"You mean because I look like him? Maybe. Who the hell cares? I want to live in a world beyond tribalism. Look, it was in the news yesterday that Israel is going to dump ten thousand tons of garbage in the West Bank every month. Is it 'the Jews' doing that? No. Is it stupid callous bastards? Yes. The government of Israel has never intended to make peace with the Palestinians. They're never going to stop building settlements and ignoring treaties. Their agenda has been the same for fifty years. They want to wall and starve and pollute the Arabs into oblivion but you'd never guess that from the media who keep the bogus hope of negotiation and a two state solution alive. Netanyahu and Sharon and Begin and Peres and their kind are lying brutal racist shits but is that because they're 'Jewish'? Of course not. It's because . . "

"They're lying brutal racist shits."

"Not that the Arabs behave any better. They didn't have to become the underdogs. What a disastrous obsession Zionism is. And you can't blame it on Hitler. OK, maybe he was the catalyst that gave it the final push. Him and the expedient hypocrisy of the rest of the world. Funny that only the Arabs and the orthodox Jews were against it. Daniel Bernard was vilified when he called Israel 'that shitty little country that'll be the death of us all.' Well, if you can believe that Canadian prick Black's wife. But imagine the planet without it. 9/11 sure as hell wouldn't have happened. What's the difference between a Palestinian Arab and a Palestinian Jew? Indiscernible genetically. I can't tell them apart to look at them, can you? They've lived side by side in Palestine for three thousand years. We're all the same fucking species. I'm sick to death of people who profit from making a distinction."

'Quite a speech,' Michael thought but decided to leave it alone.

They continued in relative silence to the Route de Malagnou, re-entering France at Thônex and rejoining the Autoroute Blanche at Etrembières. It was still too cold to put down the convertible top but the weather was clear and the sun was shining and Michael delighted in vista after glorious vista on the climb up to Chamonix-Mont-Blanc and the Les Houches-Courmayeur tunnel.

Michael had never driven through it before and was surprised it was only two lanes. Lamy regained his good humor and chatted for the entire seven and a half miles about the fire of March 24th, 1999, in which thirty-nine people lost their lives and neither were too pleased when Vladimir started tail-gating them and honking during the last minutes.

"He'll get his," Lamy predicted drily.

The speed limit in the tunnel is seventy kilometers an hour and frequent signs warn drivers to keep their distance. Vehicles are only allowed to proceed from the tollbooths with an interval between and, sure enough, as they reached the Italian side they heard a siren and the Mustang was pulled over.

"Be lucky if they don't take his license," Lamy said with a satisfied grin.

"Bloody fool," Michael agreed.

He was able to make better time down the Val d'Aosta and the Mustang didn't catch up. Lamy wanted to take the coast route via Genoa despite it being a little slower than scooting on the A1 around Milan and Bologna and Michael thought he'd like that too but was disappointed that little could be seen of the city because the freeway was more tunnel than daylight.

Nonetheless they enjoyed conversing about the great age of exploration, Cristoforo Colombo and Vasco da Gama, Amerigo Vespucci, Bartolomeu Dias and Pedro Alvares Cabral and how many believed that Amerigo, Bartolomeo's uncle, was an ambitious fake whose description of his first voyage in a letter to Piero Soderini was concocted purely from imagination.

After Genoa it got warm and Lamy agreed to put the top down and they sped along the Levantine coast like movie stars passing Rapallo, where Lamy quoted Ezra Pound's wonderful line about the thought of what America would be like if the classics had a wide circulation troubling his sleep, and Carrara, where the source of Michelangelo's masterpieces was still being visibly chiseled from the mountainside, and Viareggio, where it was Michael's turn to quote. He had once been in a student production of Tennessee William's strange dramatic poem Camino Real and enacted the corpse of Kilroy among other small roles like Don Quixote's squire Sancho Panza and Lord Byron's words from the play had stuck in his brain.

"When Shelley's body was recovered from the sea," he intoned, rolling the 'r's in a thick brogue, "They burned it on the beach at Viareggio . . "

Lamy couldn't bear it and cut him off.

"He was born in Dover."

"Ah, but his mother was Scottish."

"Mary was the real genius," Lamy said, "The sickness of modern industrial society in one big metaphor."

"The whole sickness of meddling mankind," Michael added.

"Did you know she wrote Frankenstein in a villa in Cologny?"

"No, but I know Byron was with them with his friend Polidori who wrote The Vampyre at the same time. I'd love to have been a fly on the wall."

"Lord Ruthven and Aubrey traveled to Rome together, didn't they?"

Lamy tried to look vampiric without much success.

"Ha ha."

From Viareggio they skirted the bustling cities of Lucca, Pistoia and Prato and as they approached Florence through the wide valley of the Lombrone and the Stella, Lamy began to talk about the Vespucci, both the Renaissance *famiglia* and the modern phantom, and his current view of their quest.

"Going back to the start. Was it Mogilevich or Rice who wanted Vespucci at that meeting?"

"I've no idea."

"OK, let's say both. And neither of them knew what he looked like."

"I don't know, maybe she did. It was Cheney who was trying to find out at the lunch. Maybe she knew all along I wasn't him. Maybe she knows he doesn't exist."

"He has to exist. Anyway, according to our goons everyone realizes now you're not him. Not that it lets you off the hook because you know about the plutonium. You were smart not to write about it. Or all the craziness that went on after 9/11. You'd definitely be dead. What I'm trying to figure out is his function. What was in it for him if they had decided on the nuclear option?"

"Vicarious pleasure?"

"Hey, more than likely," Lamy agreed with a snort, "But why would his presence make the deal OK?"

"The Devil as a third party witness?"

"I guess something like that. OK then, why didn't he show up?"

"Maybe he never got the invitation."

"It's a possibility."

"Or he just likes to fuck with people's minds."

"That's a probability. OK, so where does he live?"

"Italy."

"A reasonable assumption. Nothing links him to anywhere else. Not New York or London. No one can hide in New York. So where can you live in Italy that nobody ever sees you or knows what you look like?"

"A graveyard?"

Lamy burst out laughing.

"Portillo and his sister believed in vampires, not me. Where else?"

"The Vatican?"

"It has to be, doesn't it? Or somewhere like it. For him to remain so secret we can't find a picture or an address or anything at all to prove he exists."

"So why do you say he has to?"

Lamy paused.

"OK, let's go back to the Renaissance."

§

Michael the Med and his newfound bosom companion did not return to Paris with Andrelini but set off by themselves on the road for Italy.

§

They exited the Autostrada del Sole and drove into Florence on the A76 passing Amerigo Vespucci airport in the industrial suburb of Peretola.

"The damn runway's probably right where the Vespucci had vineyards and olive groves," Lamy observed, "They had a huge estate out here."

Michael knew every bit as much about the history of the Vespucci family in Quattrocento and Cinquecento Florence as Lamy and they tossed the subject back and forth. Wealthy business associates who had checkered relations with the Medici, silk importing, wool mills, wine, rental properties, banking, spices, a quite normal for the time connection to the slave trade. The Borgo Ognissanti, an area that once lay outside the city walls where the majority of the clan lived and had their shops. The Chiesa di Ognissanti, All Saint's, built by a sect of Lombard monks in the 13th century, 'the mortified ones', the *Umiliati*, founders of the Florentine wool trade who constructed canals and the massive weir of Santa Rosa to harness the Arno river's hydraulic power. Simone Vespucci who rebuilt one of his houses into the Hospital Santa Maria dell'Umiliata in 1380.

Ghirlandaio's portrait of the family in the Vespucci chapel in which Amerigo is pictured as a teenager. The tombs of Sandro Botticelli and the love of his life, Simonetta Cattaneo de Vespucci, immortalized in The Birth of Venus and Primavera, who myth would have it Giuliano de' Medici, Lorenzo *Il Magnifico*'s younger brother, turned into a vampire rather than see her die of tuberculosis at twenty-two. Guido Antonio Vespucci who in the 1470s took his nephew Amerigo with him to Paris while serving as ambassador to the court of Louis XI and who was influential in the formation of a new government after the death of Savonarola. Agostino, Machiavelli's confidante, Antonio, chancellor of the public records, and, of course, Bartolomeo, a professor of astronomy in Padua, who seemed to be the least significant of the whole lot.

"Is there any point to all this?" Lamy asked with a shrug, "How the hell can we know?"

"Leave no turn unstoned the lady said."

From the airport Lamy directed Michael for the last six miles on the Via Francesco Barracca and then a quick right and left on the Lungarno Vespucci and in a matter of seconds turning left again into the spacious piazza in front of the Westin Excelsior hotel.

"This is it," Lamy said, "The heart of Vespucci territory. That's the Chiesa Ognissanti right there."

Michael had visited Florence twice before but never this part. He had seen pictures of the church, however, and recognized the 13th century bell tower.

The suites Lamy reserved on the fifth floor had huge marble balustraded balconies providing magical views of the Arno, the Ponte Vecchio, the dome of the Chiesa di San Fredino in Cestello across the river and the Ponte Amerigo Vespucci. A magical vista and an utterly different world to Chalk Farm, even Beaumont and Mâcon, and certainly to the well-ordered stuffiness of Geneva.

By the time they checked in it was twenty past five and Lamy told Michael he had less than ten minutes to make himself ready because they were going out for a stroll.

Their first stop was the French consulate directly opposite in what Lamy informed him used to be the Palazzo Lenzi. In the middle of the square they passed a marvelously chthonian statue of Hercules wrestling the Nemean Lion and as Michael paused to admire it he was given a thirty second rundown on its Florentine sculptor Romano Romanelli who had an affair with Isadora Duncan and fathered her third child which lived less than a day.

The piazza was open to the river on the southwest. Beside the consulate stood the elegant Grand Hotel, the old palazzo of another noble family called the Giuntini. The main floor of the Lenzi Palace, which had kept the essence of Brunelleschi's original façade, housed the Institut Française and an adjoining French bookshop with a leather goods store at the corner near the church and, in the doorway between, a man was waiting for them.

Lamy spoke to him in French and introduced him as Bernard and Michael understood he was the honorary consul and soon to be appointed director of the institute and they began walking briskly toward the church.

It was open until half past six but they wasted no time finding the chapel of St. Isabel of Portugal where above Ghirlandaio's fresco of the Descent from the Cross the Madonna della Misericordia spreads her protective cloak over the kneeling Vespucci. Bernard pointed out two possible depictions of Amerigo, one in the upper panel as a boy and the more likely as a young man standing at the far left in the lower panel behind his uncle and tutor, the humanist scholar Giorgio Antonio. Simonetta was evident in the upper panel and Bernard next led them to her tomb with Botticelli's immediately beneath, as rumor had it he requested, and to the choir entry with the frescoes of Augustine and St. Jerome on either side that Botticelli and Ghirlandaio had designed to face each other to capture the mystical vision Augustine experienced in Hippo as Jerome lay dying in Jerusalem. Above Augustine's head was the Vespucci crest, a blood-colored shield with three golden wasps on a diagonal azure band, and they chuckled about the open book behind him on which Botticelli intermixed an anecdote mocking the worldly appetites of the *Umiliati* amongst the scribbles.

From there they went into the Refectory, or *Cenàcolo*. Bernard arranged a key since it was not open to the public except Monday, Tuesday and Saturday mornings. Lamy wanted to have a look at Ghirlandaio's *Ùltima Cena*, though it was nothing to do with their quest, and Michael said he thought the perspective achieved by the use of the two archways was superior to da Vinci's rectangular room and liked Judas sitting in front of the table and Bernard spoke of Guido Antonio's house in Via dei Servi where the walls of one room had been painted by Piero di Cosimo with Bacchanalian scenes and the extraordinary number of artistic commissions the Vespucci had given. Not only di Cosimo, Botticelli and Ghirlandaio but Vasari, Verrocchio and Andrea Sansovino as well and they all laughed at his story about a youthful Leonardo da Vinci, with sketchbook and charcoal in hand, following Amerigo's grandfather Amerigo through the streets in order to capture his virile good looks because he was so much in admiration of them.

It was starting to get dark as they left the church but Lamy had more for them to see and they walked quickly down toward Piazza Goldoni passing Via della Porcellana and at 20 Borg'Ognissanti there was a small plaque proclaiming it was once the site of the Ospedale San Giovanni di Dio, the same hospital renamed that Simone Vespucci bequeathed to the city. Bernard had another key and led them into a grand foyer with great staircases on either side flanked at the bottom by the statues of Faith and Hope and Charity at the top and here, too, were the arms of the Vespucci.

Michael was amused to notice the Pizzeria Baccus across the street. He was ready for a drink but Lamy told him he could wait and they continued on a few more doors to a nondescript building opposite an antique shop that was, Bernard informed them, the house where Amerigo was born.

That was the end of the tour and they walked back to the piazza in front of the church. It was also a subject of inward mirth to Michael that the street was lined with dozens of parked motor-scooters which he always thought of as Vespas despite their wide range of manufacture. But what did the connection of the Vespucci to wasps have to do with anything?

Lamy thanked Bernard and invited him to join them for supper but he politely declined, saying it was good to meet them but he had other plans.

"Nice fellow," Michael said as he departed.

Lamy started off in the other direction past the church.

"Come on. We're not eating at the hotel in case our two idiots show up."

"Maybe they're in jail," Michael suggested.

"We can hope."

§

On the 22nd of November, 1497, Vasco da Gama's fleet of two carracks, a caravel and a storage ship rounded the Cape of Good Hope on their way to India and a week later, on Wednesday the 29th, as dusk cast its golden light on the Tuscan hills, Michael the Med and Bartolomeo Vespucci reached the inn of his great uncle Niccolò in Peretola, the family still owned it though Niccolò had died sixteen years previously, and found his seventy-eight-year-old great uncle Giovanni as drunk as the proverbial *moffetta*.

Michael had become conversationally fluent in Italian on the thirteen days of their journey from Amboise thanks to the very able and patient tutelage of his companion.

The Vespucci were a very large family and Bartolomeo did not occupy the lowest rung on their ladder as Michael the Mod and Lamy supposed but stood somewhere half way between the bankers and politicians and the ne'er-do-wells and jailbirds.

§

The Ristorante Il Profeta was a block beyond the church at the corner of Via Melegnano and right beside the Boom Bazaar which Michael thought didn't augur well but the meal was magnificent. Antipasti, ribollita, a tripe dish as well as rare slices of beef on a bed of *verdura* and a sweet apple pastry washed down with an excess of Brunello and Vin Santo and Kirsch. They were in Bella Italia so Michael was happily drinking wine despite the consequences.

They agreed that seeking for clues to the identity and whereabouts of the modern Bartolomeo among the activities and exploits of the Vespucci family in the Renaissance was almost certainly a waste of time. The wasps, however, had a certain intriguing *je ne sais quoi* and, of course, for Michael, so did the vampire story.

"Did they have vampires for hire?" he wondered, "How did this Giuliano chap turn Simonetta into one? The anecdote says he paid a local vampire. Did they hang about on street corners? Maybe they kept office hours."

"It's crap. It never happened."

"I read somewhere they buried vampires with a brick in their mouth. After they'd done the stake through the heart, I suppose. Just for good measure."

"They believed a lot of things. That they could turn lead into gold for a start. Paracelsus and the Hermetic tradition. Ficino's demons and music-spirit theory. Necromancy, alchemy, astrology, that's what Bartolomeo was for god's sake, an astrologer not an astronomer. His letter to Machiavelli was about the influence of the stars. He 'stoutly maintained' that life couldn't exist below the equator because what he called the 'torrid zone' was uninhabitable. There was just as much ignorant bullshit back then as there is today."

"At least they could claim an admissible excuse."

Shuffle Seven

"We are now facing the final confrontation between the Church and
the anti-Church, of the Gospel versus the anti-Gospel."
- Karol Wojtyła (1920 - 2005)

§

Mel Sembler, the American ambassador to Italy, was nearing his
seventy-fifth birthday and the likely end of his term. He was an avid reader
of trashy novels and as he and his wife Betty waited for the arrival of Air
Force One and its escort of F-16s in the military reserve of Rome's
Ciampino airport all he could think about was the plot of Dan Brown's
Angels and Demons.

It was nearly eleven o'clock at night and that morning, in preparation
for the American delegation, the Berlusconi government ordered a five-
mile radius no-fly zone around the Vatican. The Aeronautica Militare
Italiana was on hair-trigger alert to intercept violators. The area adjacent
to St. Peter's Basilica was already bristling with anti-aircraft missile
installations. Warships of the Marina Militare armed with torpedos stood
by along the coast. Gunboats patrolled the Tiber from the port of Ostia
to Fonte di Papa as well as the smaller waterways of the capital. The
Carabinieri had performed a sweep of every aqueduct and sewer with the
very latest sensing equipment. On the day of the funeral itself a thousand
marksmen would be deployed on the rooftops and the surrounding streets
surveyed by every helicopter the task force could muster. Ciampino and
the commuter airports would be shut down and only Leonardo da Vinci
left open and it had even been arranged for the president to sit as close as
possible to Khatami of Iran just in case of who knew what, yet still Mel
felt extremely uneasy. He hadn't been told about the missing plutonium
despite thinking he had bought his way into the inner circle but it made
no difference. The perfidy of evildoers was without limit.

§

Before they went to sleep Michael and Lamy sat together in Lamy's suite watching Judy Woodruff's Inside Politics on CNN.

From Ciampino waiting limousines had whisked the president and Laura and virtually their entire entourage directly to St. Peter's so they could view the corpse of John Paul lying in state. For their security, Guido Bertolaso, special commissioner for civil protection and good buddy of the Italian prime minister, ordered that this was to be complete before the millions of pilgrims still waiting outside would be informed they were out of luck and turned away.

Legions of the faithful had already filed past the open coffin and as many more snaked in an endless line beyond the Castel Sant'Angelo but they stood in patient silence as the limousines arrived and the steps were cordoned off and Cardinal Egan of New York and a bevy of Vatican officials in black cassocks and *zucchetti* and strung about the neck with pectoral crosses of varying size and distinction welcomed the delegation and led them through a separate entrance.

"No doubt," Michael said, "No cameras allowed inside though. Not much of a photo-op."

"Not tonight. We'll be plastered with it tomorrow. They'll all be kneeling respectfully with JP laid out in the foreground, dollars to donuts."

Other news of the day included the occupation of a dozen farms in Brazil by members of the Landless Worker's Movement, the naming of the Kurdish leader Jalal Talabani as president of Iraq, the death of Prince Rainier in Monaco and sixteen U.S. military personnel in a helicopter crash in Afghanistan and that the College of Cardinals had set April 18th as the date the conclave would begin to elect John Paul's successor.

§

The summer of 1497 had seen an upsurge of the plague in Florence but the arrival of cooler weather made it safe to return and so on Friday, December 1st, Michael the Med and Bartolomeo knocked on the door of a modest house in Borgo Ognissanti and were greeted by a small child with a dirty face.

A moment later a woman came and when she saw Bartolomeo burst into tears and flung her arms about his neck. Michael judged her to be thirtyish. She began speaking and sobbing at the same time, more of a drawn-out howl than a story. She barely paused for breath, holding Bartolomeo by the cheeks, stroking them and staring into his eyes, grasping him tight and weeping inconsolably on his chest.

She was his half-sister Isabella and Michael understood through the rush of words that both Bartolomeo's mother and father were dead. Something his great uncle Giovanni either didn't know or had been too drunk to recall.

She sent letters to Paris in July telling him they were sick with *la peste* and to come home but it would have been useless because the wretched disease had carried them off in less than a week.

Having seen the state of the streets in the *borgo* Michael was not surprised. They left the horses in the pleasant pastures of Peretola and traveled the rest of the way on foot but as soon as they entered the Prato Gate a nauseous stench assailed their nostrils. Bartolomeo said it came from 'Sardigna island', a colossal refuse dump by the Arno overflowing with the accumulation of centuries. The river was a foul foaming brown, darkened with dyes and heaven knew what else and the narrow muddy lanes were littered with leather and wool trimmings, fetid straw and mule dung.

The area, for all the filth and stink, Bartolomeo told him, was the center of the Vespucci's industrial and commercial wealth and it was inconvenient for most of the family to live elsewhere. There were exceptions, of course, and the grandest of them all was Guido Antonio whom he was shortly to meet.

§

At three o'clock in the morning Michael was outside on the balcony of his suite leaning with both hands on the broad marble balustrade. An empty glass stood beside him. He was waiting for the bicarbonate of soda, a large screw-top jar of which he always carried on his travels, to allay a savage heartburn. He had been known to produce prize-winning belches on occasion and one such was at the point of eruption when he heard a squeal of tires in the piazza below. It was followed by shouts and a door slamming and then loud baying or what seemed to be baying. Since his balcony encompassed that corner of the hotel he went to look.

The Mustang was in the middle of the square by the statue with the lights on and the engine running and Vladimir was pissing in a great glistening arc on Hercules' back and the tuneless yowl shattering the night air was coming from between his rotten teeth. Only if one listened very attentively was it possible to make out the cadence of 'Moscow Nights'.

" . . *Pjésna slyshýtsja i nje slyshýtsya . . vétjich tíchjije vjichirá . .* "

Before he could get his bull's pizzle of a member reinstalled in his jeans Ciccio leapt out, jammed a pistol in his mouth and threw him back in the car.

§

Several days later Bartolomeo took Michael to the house on Via dei Servi, which his great uncle had just acquired the week before, and introduced him to Guido Antonio. He was an imposing old devil in his sixties with a fine head of white hair under his cap, a Doctor of Law, fluent in Latin, French, Spanish and Greek, a master of mathematics, logic, rhetoric and poetry, a gifted artist in his own right and mellifluous of voice.

Michael was now familiar with Florentine history since he and Bartolomeo had spent hour upon hour discussing the subject. He knew about the Etruscan heritage, Roman Florentium, Radagaisas and the Gotho-Byzantine War, Queen Theodolinda and Countess Matilda, the defeat of Fiesole, the Commune, the encroachments of Frederick Barbarossa, the development of the Oltrarno, the expansion of credit, the rise of the guilds, the influence of the religious orders, Servite, Augustinian, Carmelite, Dominican and Franciscan, the Guelphs and the Ghibellines, the poetry of Dante Alighieri, the Plague, Giovanni de' Medici and the company of Calimala, Cosimo and Piero the Gouty, Lorenzo and the Pazzi conspiracy, Simonetta and Marco Vespucci, the assassination of Giuliano, the humanist philosophers, the great artists, the premature death of Lorenzo in 1492, Pierfrancesco and Semiramide d'Appiano, Piero the Unlucky, Lorenzo's son, or as Bartolomeo preferred to call him, Piero the Feeble-minded, who was still in exile due to the recent aggression of Charles VIII and the ascendancy of Savonarola, all of which knowledge was to stand him in good stead.

Guido Antonio greeted them warmly and commiserated briefly about the death of Bartolomeo's mama and papa. It had been a ghastly summer but he seemed more inclined to talk about art. The house did not yet contain a stick of furniture. A chaos of ladders and workmen and dropcloths distorted their path as he led them into what was to be his pride and joy, the Bacchanalian room.

Piero di Cosimo was perched high on some scaffolding, applying the first splotches of color to what would eventually crown the whole, The Fall of Man. The naked figures of Adam and Eve had been drawn in outline. They lay upon the ground facing each other with hands outstretched toward a central fig tree around which a thick serpent with a woman's head was coiled. Guido showed sketches for two others called The Discovery of Honey and The Misfortunes of Silenus and in them as well Michael observed that a gnarled contorted tree took central focus.

Not wishing to disturb his artist's progress further the great man led them to another room where a painting in a gilded frame was leaning against the wall. It had adorned the front of a *cassone*, a wedding casket exhibited the day before a marriage containing the bride's dowry of silverware and jewels. Bartolomeo clearly recognized it and told Michael it was the work of Alessandro di Mariano di Vanni Filipepi, familiarly called Sandro Botticelli because his older brother resembled a barrel, and that it had been done for his parent's wedding fourteen years previously. Michael didn't have time to be surprised because Bartolomeo immediately confirmed without a glimmer of embarrassment that, yes, he was born a bastard.

The width of the frame was more than twice its height and the necessity of its origin had forced the composition of the painting. It was a depiction of Venus, fully clothed in material so diaphanous she seemed almost nude, leaning on her elbow on the ground observing a sleeping Mars with his head thrown back. Their legs caressed each other and only his loins were covered. His elbow rested on a small cherubic satyr and three others were playing at war with his weapons behind them. The look on her face exuded perfect contentment and confident possession. Several wasps were in evidence buzzing round a stump.

Guido Antonio told Bartolomeo he was keeping it safe and he could have it once he had a house to put it in and he laughed because the painting made Lorenzo di Pierfrancesco, a wealthy banker and politician and distant cousin of *Il Magnifico*, so jealous he commissioned Botticelli to create two more, of Spring and the Birth of the Goddess, which now hung in his villa in the Mugello.

Lorenzo and his brother Giovanni were nicknamed *I Popolani* because they supported the Republican cause and were trying to bolster Savonarola's flagging fortunes. Rodrigo Borgia had excommunicated the fiery Dominican but he was ignoring the ban and planning to perform mass again.

Bartolomeo couldn't resist teasing and praised the monk's courage.

Guido Antonio grunted dismissively, "We'll soon be rid of him."

§

Lamy seemed refreshed as he took the wheel the next morning. Michael told him about Vladimir and Ciccio and the reappearance of the Mustang over breakfast but it was nowhere to be seen. It was another glorious day and they were able to travel with the top down as Lamy steered them out of the city. Michael was amazed he hardly ever needed to consult a map.

They passed the Firenze Circolo Golf Ugolino which Lamy informed him was the oldest course in Italy and, though Lamy's wife had once been a big fan of the sport, they were both in complete agreement with George Carlin that it was a mindless activity engaged in by white male corporate criminals solely so they could make deals. The vast acreage devoted to it should be used to house the homeless.

Lamy had been right about the photo-op. Every channel that morning had pictures of George W and Laura and Poppy and Bill Clinton and Condoleezza kneeling reverently with the corpse of JP in the foreground.

They continued south onto the Via Chiantigiana, the tourist Chianti Trail, passing Chiocchio, Spedaluzzo and Giobbole. At Greve in Chianti Lamy turned off to the west and wound up through a mile of vineyards and fig orchards to the spectacular little hillside town of Montefioralle with its fortified monastery seemingly held in perfect position by an exquisitely natural jumble of houses with sun-bleached ochre walls roofed in red tile.

"They've got some classification system for towns like this," Lamy said.

"Yes, one of the hundred most beautiful in Italy. I can see why."

"Used to be Monteficalle because of all the figs. Monastery dates from the 10th century. Vespucci are recorded among the five oldest families."

"Quite amazing."

"Must have been magnificent back in the day. The wine industry didn't really take off until Leopold started drainage projects in the next valley over in the late 1760s."

"Leopold who?"

"Grand Duke of Tuscany. Second to last Holy Roman Emperor. Brother of Marie Antoinette."

"Ah. Oh yes, that one."

Lamy parked the Bentley and they went on foot along a narrow lane to number 21, the house where the brochures tell that Amerigo was born, and on the capstone of the arched doorway was a simple V with a single wasp facing upward in the crook.

"Well," Michael said, "Good for us. No stone unwasped. Strictly a tourist thing, eh? The capstone."

"Looks pretty recent to me. Nice new mortar."

They strolled back to the car and stopped for an espresso at the Taverna del Guerrino and spoke of Castruccio Castracani, duke of Lucca, a condottiero whom Machiavelli claimed equal to Philip of Macedon or Scipio of Rome and immortalized in a somewhat tongue-in-cheek biography. His army had sacked Montefioralle in 1325 as part of his constant battle against the Florentines.

"It was the most important town in the valley. A fortified stronghold."

"Definitely worth ruining then," Michael observed.

"Betcha didn't know Mary Shelley . . "

"Wrote a novel about Castracani? Yes, I jolly well did. Valperga. Ha!"

"Good for you," Lamy teased, "Ever read it?"

"No. Have you?"

"No. But she must have been imagining this town. She called it Valperga. Ruled by the Countess Euthanasia. Castracani falls in love with her and forces her to choose between him and liberty. She sails off to her death."

"A sensible decision."

"OK, here's another one for you. What's the difference between a Guelph and a Ghibelline? You buy lunch if you get it wrong."

Lamy never bragged about his wealth and never tried to make Michael feel like a sponger. He had astonished him on the first afternoon of the journey by saying that his disposable income from investments was between two and three million dollars a day so why not help him spend it.

"All right," Michael agreed, "But I get to pick where. The Welf were the dukes of Bavaria and the Waiblingen the Hohenstaufen dukes of Swabia."

For some reason the effort of German pronunciation caused him to wildly overstress each W.

"The Welfs," he went on in the same vein, "Supported the pope, more or less, and vague republican ideas like communes and middle-class morality and the Waiblingen were all for empire and the old feudal aristocracy. In Italy this nonsense transmogrified itself into the Gs and Gs after Frederick Barbarossa, another HRE with a red beard, rode in and destroyed Milan."

Starting with the word 'transmogrified' he began pronouncing all the r's as W like an upper-class English twit and Lamy made an attempt to strangle him but Michael evaded his grasp.

"You asked for it, sweetie. Fweddie B pwoclaimed an anti-pope, named Victor I believe, but was soon defeated by the Lombard League and forced to sign the Tweety of Constance. Always liked that name. No idea why. Hated the actress I saw play her in King John. Anyway the mad factionalism that followed and became an assumed part of life pwitty much wuined Dante's, as I see it."

"OK, OK, I don't want a cheese sandwich anyway," Lamy growled.

Something odd was happening that might explain this particularly childish interlude because Michael was overcome with giddiness and nausea and had to steady himself on the back of a chair.

"Good lord," he said, "I feel like I'm going to faint. All cold and sweating and shivery. Sorry. Been having what they call a *déjà vu*."

"You better sit down. You look awful. They'll have a toilet in the back if you're gonna be sick."

"No, no, I think I'll be fine. It's very peculiar though. It started to come on when we were joking about the door."

"What?"

They were sitting now and a waiter brought the coffee.

"*Anche vorremmo una grande bottiglia d'acqua frizzante, per favore*," Lamy said to him.

"*Si Signore, subito*," the man replied and walked away, giving Michael a not very sympathetic glance.

"Fizzy water, yes, yes, thank you. Had a rather bad night. I shouldn't drink wine. Specially with anything tomatoey. Gives me the pip."

"So what's the *déjà vu*?"

"It's silly really. You know all about what happened in Juarez but I don't know whether I've told you. It was just before Chuck was killed by the sniper. There was a phone call up in Amado's suite and Cecilia Portillo found out her mother had been killed. When she put the receiver down the expression on her face was indescribable. She was very drunk already but she got to her feet and wobbled over to the bar and filled her martini glass brimful with vodka twice and downed it and then stood looking at herself in an ornate mirror that was hanging above the bottles. It might have been thirty seconds and while she was doing it I felt the whole building start to shake. It was quite quite bizarre. Like I could feel the foundations rattling. Then she went straight out onto the balcony and told Amado and I thought I saw some kind of bright light passing between them, crackling back and forth like an electric arc, and a second later she shot him point blank in the stomach. But he didn't react at all to the bullet. He just let out a terrifying howl and before anyone could move to stop him he lifted her high above his head and threw her over the edge. I watched her fall. It was almost in slow motion. She looked like a bat because of her outfit. A kind of flowing purple silk suit. Her head hit the diving board of the hotel pool ten floors below. It turned her face to jelly they said. She was stunning, I told you that. I could see her blood spreading in the water and then there was another gunshot and Chuck fell backwards. He was dead in an instant. It caught him just above his eye. Then Amado staggered inside and the police arrived and he looked at them as they came through the door and let out another howl and I felt it reverberate down through the hotel and ripple out into the city and the desert beyond. I'll never forget the sensation or the sound. Deep bass chords in my bones more than my ears. Subliminal. The same as when some idiot child has cranked up his woofers a mile away but a thousand times more. And I just felt something like it happening now."

"But nothing similar in New York?"

"No. No, not to me, funnily enough. I wonder about George though. His whole body was shaking when Cheney came in and shouted at him. When the ghosts appeared on the field at Yankee Stadium and on the White House lawn, yes, it was mind-boggling and spine-chilling and all those cliché things. Yes, it was horrifying but it didn't make me feel sick in the pit of my stomach in the same way. Just now I thought I was about to break up into tiny pieces."

"Because of the sound?"

"Not really sound. Like the world's turning in on itself and coming apart."

"Maybe this is getting to you more than you know."

"Helen says so. She keeps telling me to come home."

"We can jack it in if you want."

"No, I don't want. I'm enjoying it all immensely."

The waiter came with a bottle of carbonated water and a glass, poured it half full, then set both on the table and walked away.

"Grazie," Michael said gratefully and began sipping it.

Lamy observed him with a thoughtful smile.

"No, no, I don't want to go home. I promise you, I'm better already. Let's go get blown sky high."

§

This was going to be a busy day for the U. S. delegation despite the long day's journey and the late night. In the afternoon there would be a courtesy call to Carlo Azeglio Ciampi, the current president of Italy, at the Quirinale Palace, then George and Laura were hosting a reception for all the American cardinals, archbishops and bishops at the Villa Taverna, Melvin Floyd Sembler's Roman residence, and then they were off to Palazzo Grazioli to dine with the President of the Consiglio, Italian prime minister Silvio Berlusconi, and Laura wasn't too interested in having him pat her on the bottom and moan about the disastrous defeats he had suffered in the local elections of the past week and the inevitable forthcoming vote of non-confidence and she was planning a migraine. But first up were the intelligence briefings.

George had graciously invited his two predecessors, GHWB and WJC, to listen in on the regular one as a gesture of respect, the daily one they all had to endure concerning things like the recent terrorist attacks in Qatar, the downing of the helicopter in Ghazni, the status of the wars, the security arrangements and the protocol and seating for the funeral but they had definitely not been included in the second one about the plutonium. That could look very bad if it ever leaked out. This was only for the inner circle, Condi and her replacement as National Security Advisor, Stephen Hadley, Chief of Staff Andrew Card and CIA director Porter Goss.

Unfortunately Goss had no good news to report. It hadn't been found. He suggested they create some emergency to fly home but George said he wouldn't do that. Everything humanly possible was being done and they'd just have to tough it out.

Goss and Condoleezza had decided before the meeting there was no point informing the others about bit-players like Michael and Lamy because they, at least, were under control.

§

It was three-thirty as Lamy drove the Bentley up to the green gates of the Casale dei Cedri, a walled retreat on the Janiculum hill he had reserved for their stay, and before he could press the intercom button they opened.

"Someone's on the ball," he said.

The exclusive resort was part of the much larger Villa Doria Pamphili but enclosed in its own lush seven-acre park. From the top floor it was possible to see the dome of St. Peter's and the winged angel of Castel Sant'Angelo.

There were only three guest apartments and Lamy had booked all of them for the month. Michael asked how he managed it on such short notice since everything in Rome was surely full to bursting and Lamy just laughed. He had wired the owners a bonus of fifty thousand euros per week to cancel any other reservations.

But even before they arrived at the main house they could see something strange was going on because Ciccio was sitting in a lounge chair smoking at one end of the pool and Vladimir was carving the water with an exuberant back stroke. Two elderly gentlemen dressed in light-colored suits, wearing sunglasses and sporting straw fedoras sat together at the other.

"Good lord," Michael said, "That looks like Warren."

"It is Warren. And his friend Luigi Lazzari who picked him up at da Vinci. They're supposed to be here. What the fuck is going on?"

Lamy had stopped in astonishment and two men in dark suits strolled up to the car from the house and opened both their doors part way.

"Who the fuck are you?" Lamy demanded, yanking his door shut again.

"If you take it easy, sir, I'll tell you," the man at Lamy's window answered calmly.

"Why did you let those two goons in?"

"For the same reason we'd like to keep you here."

"What the fuck do you mean? Who are you?"

"Just step out of the car, sir. Giovanni will park it for you and take your bags to your room."

The owner, Giovanni Marrone, a robust middle-aged Sicilian with a kindly face who had hurried down the steps after the men, was standing about twenty feet in front of them. Lamy was beside himself with rage and the poor man was looking at him like a scolded dog and shrugging in deep apology.

"Before I do anything, buster," Lamy said, "You're gonna have to tell me who the fuck you are!"

"I'm not going to argue, sir," the man replied quietly and pulled a Glock 22 from inside his suit jacket.

The man on Michael's side did the same and pointed the gun at him.

"Now, now, steady on, old chap, keep your shirt on, I'm getting out."

Lamy had little choice but relent and opened his door again.

"Whoever you fuckheads are you're going to regret it," he snapped.

"I doubt that, sir. Come on inside and Giovanni'll fix you a drink."

Shuffle Eight

"There are some brutal people out there who would kill to enhance
their agenda."
- George Walker Bush (1946 -   )

§

CIA operatives Howard Rabinovitch and Ben de Groot had been
waiting to detain everyone at the Casale dei Cedri until the funeral was
over. Not that Porter Goss or Condoleezza thought the wayward
pilgrimage they had tracked day by day from London presented any
likelihood of danger but they needed to be absolutely sure.

Susanna Marrone, Giovanni's wife, served refreshments and Michael
and Lamy were now sitting comfortably in the lobby. Howard was pacing
and Ben stood looking out the window toward the pool. A glass of wine
lay untouched on the table beside Lamy but Michael was nibbling from a
plate of antipasti and happily pouring himself a second Guinness. It was
perfectly room temperature as he knew it would be. Lamy thought of
everything.

"So that's the story," Rabinovitch concluded, "No one goes in or out
until this time tomorrow afternoon. And no one uses the phone. We
found a laptop in the car. It's with your bags but you won't have Internet
capability and, sorry sir, I'll be taking your cell."

He held out his hand and Lamy gave it to him.

"Thanks. I appreciate that, sir. I promise you it's the best way. The
house phones won't give you a dial tone so don't bother and the front gate
is locked. I've mentioned to our two goodfellas if they try to go over the
wall things could get nasty. We've confiscated their weapons. I'm sure you
understand what I'm saying."

"Yeah, we've got it," Lamy said curtly, "Here's my question. There's
three suites. One for my friend, one for Mr. Jones outside and one for me.
Where are you sleeping?"

"We won't be sleeping, sir. The goons, as you call them, say they've
been spending the night in their car so that's where they'll be. Mr. Jones
said it was fine if Mr. Lazzari slept in his suite. It has a large living room,

two balconies, two bedrooms with king beds, each with their own bath and shower. I can't see that anyone should be inconvenienced."

"OK," Lamy said with a sigh and got up, taking the glass of wine and the bottle from the ice bucket, and made for the door, "Just stay the fuck out of my way."

Michael followed him, carrying the food.

"No problem, sir," Rabinovitch said to their departing backs.

As soon as they were outside Lamy confided that he never intended to go anywhere near the funeral anyway and his plan had always been to watch it on television. He just didn't like to get pushed around and he didn't know if it was a problem for Warren or Lazzari.

"Who were they?" Michael asked, "CIA or just bigger better goons?"

Rabinovitch omitted that bit of information from his spiel.

"Company," Lamy answered, "They stink of it."

"Ah yes, the 'Company'. Oh, ho."

Warren and Lazzari had seen them coming and risen from their chairs and were walking toward them.

"Michael, Michael," Warren said happily, "How good to see you."

"Yes, yes," Michael agreed, shaking his hand vigorously, "Well, well, how splendid. How absolutely splendid. I'll tell Helen she simply has to come. When we can call, that is. Our old pal here certainly loves his surprises. The miserable bastard didn't tell me a thing."

"Looks like the joke's on all of us," Lamy said, "Sorry."

Warren introduced Lazzari. It was the first time Lamy had met him and he was even more gnome-like than their billionaire host. Michael judged him to be a few years younger than Warren and somewhere in his late seventies. Five foot three or four at most, tiny hands and feet, appearing to be almost completely bald under his hat and possessing the irritating air of someone who always has more important things on his mind than listening to what other people might be saying. He was clearly extremely intelligent, however, and knew everything there was to know about Rome.

"Hey, prickyman!" Vladimir yelled.

He was now standing by the pool, bright pink and bare bollock naked.

"Where you have been so long? Why you not tell me you have prickyfuck friends!"

Michael raised his middle finger high in the air and they started back to the villa.

§

Michael the Med tarried in Florence until the spring of 1498. It was a cold winter but he and Bartolomeo spent it fruitfully. They lived together on the top floor of Bartolomeo's cousin Nastagio's house in the Borgo Ognissanti and in the course of those months Michael met most of the Vespucci family as well as many of the artists and poets of the great city. In particular he came to know and become friends with Macchiavelli who, though twenty years his junior, had a mind as convoluted and independent as his own.

It proved difficult to make ends meet for he quickly discovered there was not nearly such interest in learning English as he found among the students of the Latin Quarter and hardly any curiosity at all about the history or customs of the isles and that, coupled with two letters he received from Elaine in January and March, fastened him in the resolve to return home as soon as the weather and his purse would permit.

The first informed him that Billingsgate had fallen in love with her and the second that they were to be married on the last Saturday in June.

Michael came within sniffing distance of Savonarola on the day he began preaching again. Septuagesima Sunday, February 11th, 1498. Everyone knew the noose of his enemies was tightening around him.

"O Lord, thou hast cast me into a flood from which I have neither the power nor the will to escape. I beseech Thee, O Lord, that didst suffer death for the truth, to let me die in its defense for the salvation of my people."

Michael could appreciate such mad courage if not the message but what he noticed most of all as the monk swept past him down the aisle of St. Mark's after the sermon was his smell. Bartolomeo called it the reek of monomaniacal obsession but Michael couldn't help feeling sorry and watched in dismay as he strode headlong to his doom.

On the last day of Carnival another burning of the vanities took place.

It began with a mass during which Savonarola held the host high saying, "O Lord, if my deeds be not sincere, if my words be not inspired by Thee, strike me dead on the instant!"

Unlike the previous year there was a great deal of opposition in the streets led by the *Compagnacci*, a group of rowdies incited by a disaffected nobleman named Doffo Spini, who ran after the procession hurling insults, stripping the penitents of their cloaks, knocking the red crosses from their hands and pelting them with stones but, despite them, the chanting throng managed to reach the Piazza della Signoria where Lucifer and the Seven Deadly Sins were reduced to ashes amongst deafening, and to Michael rather shrill and desperate, shouts of exultation.

He found the ominous atmosphere that hung over the city oppressive and so on March 15th, the morning following the arrival of da Crema with Elaine's second letter, when Bartolomeo announced without warning that he would be leaving again for Amboise the next day Michael decided at once to join him.

Thus he was fortunate to miss the violence and murder in the Convent of San Marco on April 8th, the arrests of Savonarola and his associates Domenico da Pescia and Silvestro, their torture on the rack during which only Savonarola's right arm was spared so that he could sign a confession to heresy and sedition, their public denudation and deaths by fire on May 23rd as they hung on chains from a cross in the center of the piazza where they had burned the vanities and executed others in like manner during their brief reign.

§

The Marrones advertised organic cuisine of the finest 'biological' produce and they served a magnificent meal.

The four hirelings ate in a different room. Rabinovitch and de Groot were not about to let Vladimir's alcohol consumption get out of control so except for some initial bursts of obscenity everything stayed pretty quiet.

Michael was able to catch up on the news with Warren who had brought another small check for Helen from the sale of the last items in David's gallery and who Michael thought looked astonishingly healthy for a man of his age.

Luigi Lazzari was a very old friend and long ago lover. He and Warren had met quite by chance in the summer of 1944 after the 5th Army liberated Rome. Luigi had been a fledgeling interpreter attached to General Clark's HQ and was now a respected playwright, poet and dramaturge and the current president of the *Unione degli Atei e degli Agnostici Razionalisti*, the annual meeting of which had for months been scheduled for the coming weekend. Warren had agreed to be the guest speaker so when Lamy called and said he was going to meet Michael and Helen and they might be traveling to Rome as well the idea that Warren should stay at the Casale dei Cedri with them quickly fell into place.

Warren frequently wrote for the Gay and Lesbian Humanist Association magazine in London and had just reviewed a book titled The Intimate World of Abraham Lincoln which convincingly outlined several homosexual liaisons that had been of lasting importance. Joshua Fry Speed, Billy Greene and Captain David Derickson were the three main objects of the president's affection and their names resulted in some sophomoric jokes around the table. Warren was also in Rome to aid Lazzari in the creation of an Italian affiliate.

Even before they finished their first pre-prandial cocktail the conversation turned to Bartolomeo Vespucci and, of course, the reason that they were being detained and who had ordered the detention.

"It has to be the plutonium," Lamy said.

This prompted Michael to begin filling in the background of the story to Lazzari but Warren cut him off once he got to Chuck Bowman's death.

"They put it somewhere secret in the Samalayuca desert," he said, "So the only explanation for all this has to be that they can't find it. Or someone took it and they don't know who."

"Who is they?" Lazzari asked.

"The original partners. The Russian mob and the American government."

"Some prominent people in the government," Lamy added in clarification, "We know it involves Rice and Cheney and Kissinger and a bunch of their neo-con co-conspirators. I think Warren is right. As far as we can tell Vladimir and Ciccio are working for the Russians. The same two shadowed Michael when he was in New York after 9/11. We think the mob was doing it then as a favor to Rice. And now it's obvious their car is being tracked by the CIA. And for sure someone in my office is handing the CIA information."

"If you were a Mafioso," Michael observed, "You would already have had everyone in your office whacked. Isn't that the word? But you wouldn't do that. Three cheers for civilization."

"And this is all because they still think you are Vespucci?" Lazzari queried, turning to Michael with an incredulous stare.

"Not so much that," Michael replied, "Not any more. We think they think we might lead them to him."

"Because he has stolen their plutonium?"

"Yes, we think perhaps that's it."

"And intends to blow up St. Peter's Basilica?"

"We assume they think it's a possibility."

"But why would he do that? If, as you say, he very likely lives nearby."

"I agree it makes no sense. It's hard to say what goes on in their heads."

"So, if they do think what you think they think, they must be very worried about tomorrow."

"Yes, I'm sure they are."

Lazzari chuckled.

"Then it is very foolish of them to have kept you here," he observed and suddenly laughed out loud, "Unless, of course, they imagine I am he!"

Michael couldn't help finding the moment a wee bit creepy and looked at Lamy but he was clearly enjoying Lazzari's mirth.

"If they do," Lazzari went on merrily, "By tomorrow evening we will all be in jail!"

"It's unbelievably dumb," Lamy chimed in, "What? Did they think Michael and I were carrying a home-made nuke in the boot of the Bentley!"

"Terrifying though," Warren said, "The slim chance someone could be."

§

On April 8th Michael the Med arrived in Paris and found Erasmus in the hallway of Augustin Vincent's house with two large trunks packed and ready to depart for London. He was planning to stay in England until September and was expected by William Blount in Oxford before the end of the month.

He was already aware of Elaine's marriage to Thomas's uncle Arthur and confessed to be quite tickled by the news and he was also mildly curious about Bartolomeo's sudden return to Amboise, the reason for which Michael did not really know. Nor did either of them divine it when they learned that on April 7th Charles VIII had died the victim of a tragic accident. He struck his head on the lintel of a door while playing *jeu de palme*, a game similar to handball, fell into a coma and succumbed within the hour. But what did not appear in the official version of the event, and perhaps no one knew, was that Bartolomeo had been alone on the court with him.

Michael did not enjoy the journey from Amboise because, for safety, he accepted the company of three young Dutch seminarians who bored him stiff but the timing with Erasmus was marvelous and the meticulous humanist was pleased to accept Michael's suggestion they cross the channel together.

§

The Fathers of the Church, St. Paul, Chrysostom, Augustine, Aquinas and the rest, never voiced any criticism of slavery, regarding it as very much in the natural order of things. The trade in human chattels is as old as humankind but in the early 15th century most of the household slaves in Italy were Circassians, Russians or Tartars who came on Genoese ships from ports on the Black Sea. The Bosporus had been the gateway from Europe to Asia for millennia and the ancient 'silk road' that began there was vital to the wealth of Florence and the rest of Europe long before the travels of Marco Polo and when this route was cut off after the fall of Constantinople to Sultan Mehmed II and the collapse of the Byzantine empire in 1453 it resulted in a frenzied determination to find an alternate passage.

It also massively increased the value of slaves with a darker pigmentation, though the light-skinned among them were always the more highly prized, and a shift from predominantly Arab traders to Portuguese ones.

As early as 1415, no doubt because he could see this was coming, Prince Henry, known by modern schoolchildren as 'The Navigator', the third child of João I of Portugal and Philippa of Lancaster, John of Gaunt's daughter, began a serious exploration of the West African coast. In the next thirty years his ships discovered Madeira, the Canary Islands and the Azores and dared to go beyond Cape Bojador as far south as modern day Nigeria where they built a settlement on Lago de Curamo, a once pristine lagoon now despoiled by runoff from the unstoppable sprawl of Lagos.

Someone had the bright idea of kidnapping a local African nobleman and telling him he could trade freedom for an equal worth of slaves and in August, 1444, a tax-collector named Lanzarote de Freitas shipped two hundred and thirty-five of these unfortunate souls back home.

By the 1450s men of such enterprising zeal were already using black slaves to work their sugar plantations on Madeira. They hadn't bothered to wait until June 18th, 1452, the date of Pope Nicholas V's bull, Dum Diversas, which gave them free rein as long as the slaves were not Christians, but nonetheless it must have been nice to know they weren't sinning any more.

Michael had seen many black servants during his four months in Florence. They made up fully one percent of the population. The Signoria had legalized slavery in 1364 with the same caveat regarding the victim's religious persuasion. Black faces were visible in England in those days too but he had seldom lived where he might notice them and found it strange and shocking.

Through uncle Guido Antonio he met Bartolomeo Marchionni, a wealthy Florentine living in Lisbon, a friend of Columbus and nephew Amerigo, whose family had long been associated with the transport of slaves from Kaffa on the Crimean peninsula, who told him without a trace of conscience that in 1490 he paid the Portuguese crown five thousand ducats for slaving rights in the Niger delta and was now selling as many as that in a year.

Amerigo was then living in Seville. He was sent by Lorenzo *Il Magnifico* in 1489 to sound out joint business ventures with Gianotto Berardi and by 1492 moved to Spain on a full time basis and was working for the soon-to-collapse Medici bank.

Florence was home to the largest banks in Europe during most of the 14th and 15th centuries. The Bardi, Acciaioli, Peruzzi, Alberti and Altoviti and for a time beginning in the 1420s grandfather Cosimo transformed the Medici bank into the wealthiest of them all. When Lorenzo became ruler in 1469 it had branches in London, Venice, Rome, Bruges, Geneva, Lyons, Avignon, Lübeck, Valencia, Barcelona, Pisa and Milan and agents and partners throughout the known world but its decline was already in progress.

The huge sums the bank unwisely loaned to both sides in the Wars of the Roses that neither had repaid and the unsuccessful conspiracy of 1478 in which the Pazzi, Pope Sixtus IV and the Salviati, who were his bankers, attempted to murder and displace the Medici and the appalling savagery of the revenge that followed were two of the many things that hastened its demise and it was also true Lorenzo had no interest in nor understanding of the bank's affairs. In the years before his mysterious death in 1492 he had embezzled from it to pay his debts but broader problems in the European economy were the overlying cause and more or less in the same moment that Savonarola came to power the bank completely collapsed.

Thus from 1492 onwards, because he had no desire to return to Florence, Amerigo had sought alternative employment and was now making a living as a middle man supplier to the Indies' fleets.

Michael too was on an errand for the Vespucci that would prove lucrative enough to provide for future wanderings.

§

After the phone call from the Hostellerie Sarrasine, during which Michael the Mod admitted that he was once again being followed by two minor Mafiosi, Helen insisted he contact her every evening and by midnight, one o'clock in the morning in Rome, she had dialed the Casale dei Cedri seven times and heard only the same annoying busy signal so she spoke with an operator who spoke with the exchange in Rome. The conversation between the two was not audible but she was eventually informed the line was not busy but out of order.

She also woke up Marta, Michael's wife, to see if she had talked to him in the last few hours and Marta said she hadn't, not even in the last few weeks.

She felt anxious enough to call Aunt Sonja in Beaumont-en-Auge but was too considerate at such a late hour.

At last she went to sleep, fearing the worst, and by six o'clock the next morning, as preparations for what was likely to be the most watched funeral in the history of humanity were reaching fever pitch, she was trying again with the same lack of success.

At seven she called the Seigneurie in Beaumont and was given a number at the university in Rouen where Aunt Sonja would be at nine but when they spoke it only served to worry the old lady. She remembered Lamy's cell but there was no joy there either and by three in the afternoon, four in Rome, when Michael was at last allowed to call, Helen's flight was already nearing cruising altitude above Ripe and Upper Dicker on the South Sussex Downs.

Shuffle Nine

"If I don't enter politics I'm going to jail and into bankruptcy."
- Silvio Berlusconi (1936 -   )

§

Michael the Mod was considerably hung over but nonetheless came down to breakfast with the others at seven forty-five. Lamy had the television in the dining room tuned to RAI Uno. St. Peter's Square was packed to capacity with standing mourners and the gathering crowd stretched along the gaudy breadth of Via della Conciliazione, Mussolini's ugly, unpopular 'grand thoroughfare'. A trickle of foreign dignitaries and clergy was beginning to ooze through the great doors of the basilica and were slowly being led to their seats.

"What an insane thing to try and organize," Michael said in greeting.

Lamy was chuckling.

"We just had it on the BBC. Some journalists smuggled a fake bomb into the grounds of Windsor Castle in a delivery van. No authorization but they said they were waved straight through. Had a package in the back marked 'bomb' in big black letters. No problem at all."

"Our security services are notoriously hopeless," Michael replied.

"Ours too," Lazzari said, "Despite this man Bertolaso."

"Who is he?" Michael asked.

"A playboy like Berlusconi. That's him talking now. Special Commissioner for Civil Protection."

"What's he saying?"

"That everything is under control, what else?"

"I suspect it is," Warren observed wryly, "If the CIA had time to bother themselves about us."

"Could they have frisked a million onlookers?" Lamy added dubiously.

Michael became aware of a rasping snore coming from a room nearby, the unmistakable sound of Vladimir.

"I thought they were sleeping in the car."

"The *signora* took pity on them," Lazzari said, "The Italian one is outside by the pool. I think perhaps he did not rest so well."

Susanna Marrone came in with fresh coffee and a plate of magnificently yellow scrambled eggs and wished Michael *buongiorno* and he repeated the word twice rather hammily and said he was madly in love with her which provoked a jocular spate of scolding Italian he didn't understand as she patted him on the cheek and went away again all briskness and good humor.

"What did she say?"

"That you are too old to be a fool," Warren answered without looking up from his newspaper.

"Oh well, God loves me anyway," Michael replied and started in on the eggs. "Look, I was wondering in the night if any of you saw Edge of Darkness? On the BBC something like twenty years ago. A mini-series to do with nuclear skullduggery. It wasn't too bad actually so perhaps it's not a very good example of what I'm trying to get at but haven't we been bombarded with plots like this to the point of saturation. Mostly horribly trite and repetitive. My life has been one long episode ever since I was lucky enough to escape Juarez. Rabinovitch and de Groot . . lordy, the names alone make me want to laugh . . and our two goons are in some sort of movie in their heads, don't you think? I mean the ridiculousness is impossible to credit, isn't it? It can't really be happening."

"You know damn well it is," Lamy answered, "These people are deadly serious even if they live in Cuckooville. Everyone said they couldn't believe the falling towers were real but they were."

"The magic of television," Warren added, "Far more than movies, is that it is the perfect medium for spreading bullshit. Orwell's vision has come to pass. Slavery is freedom and truth is a lie."

"And nowhere is it more obvious," Lazzari chimed in, "Than in charades like the one we're about to endure."

"Well, I can only apologize," Michael went on, "I can't tell you how sick it makes me feel to know I'm the one who put us all in this situation. If I hadn't been so idiotic about that tiger . . "

"Yeah, yeah, we know," Lamy said, "But, hey, you wouldn't have met me."

"I might have. But David and Fernando wouldn't have been murdered."

"You can't run back the clock," Warren told him, "Anyway, it could have happened if you hadn't ever been in New York. David might still have sounded off at the racetrack. Maybe that was all there was to it and it wasn't anything to do with you or Bartolomeo Vespucci."

"What I'm puzzling over," Lazzari said, "Is how you propose to find this person if no one else can."

There was silence for a moment and Michael looked at Lamy blankly and shrugged.

"My thought," Lamy answered, "Is make him want to find us."

Michael was a pacifist and firmly of the opinion violence only ever begets more violence yet, as they watched the funeral, he found it hard to imagine a place and time where a weapon of mass destruction might have been detonated with greater benefit to humanity.

All those dreadful old men in costume, all those incompetents puffed up with delusions of power, archbishops and bishops, archimandrites and exarchs, imams, ayatollahs, rabbis, eparchs, metropolitans, grand mufti, patriachs, kings, queens, presidents, princes and prime ministers striking pious poses and silently staring at a box containing the spiritless substance of a little man from Poland whose neurotically austere view of the world had only increased its pain. What do these self-important poobahs represent but blind alleys and dead ends on the road to equality and justice? Like intestinal blockages or clogged drains they choke the path to freedom and thought processes long out of date narrow their minds like so much arterial plaque.

What a shame some flood or pestilence or vapor or conflagration could not selectively snuff out the lives of these cheats and murderers. But, alas, what would be the point? To have structure you must have hierarchy. It wasn't really all that much to do with these particular poor slobs after all. No one can claim immunity from greed. Why should they be expected to sluff off the hardened sediment of history? They were innocent babes once and may well have been unaware of their gradual deformation. But wait a minute, he thought, let's not be too quick to forgive. They surely understood now that anyone who itches for undue wealth and power inevitably becomes an instrument of evil yet they sit there without a flicker of guilt or apology. They wallow in the unfairness of their good fortune and promote themselves as the very embodiment of altruism and public service. No, they do not deserve a flyspeck of compassion.

As the TV cameras roved among the massive crowd beyond this elevated clutch of vermin Michael could see the schizophrenia of faith plainly etched on every face. Each struggling brain as clenched as Luther's buttocks in his privy, desperate to squeeze emotion out of vacancy in the futile search for meaning in the meaningless. The terror of death hung over the square like the ghost of a malignant ancestor and an inexpressible horror lay beneath. How can any of us be 'protected from all anxiety'? Yet that was the prayerful wish on every lip. Wake up and embrace the gift of life! A miraculous universe is ours to explore! Dangerous but delightful. Why all these obsequiously bowed heads? How sad. How deeply depressing. A more hideously empty spectacle was impossible for him to conceive.

Mercifully his gloom was dispelled at the beginning of the homily because the door slammed open and Vladimir came staggering in like the Jabberwock with bloodshot eyes aflame.

"What the hell?" he groaned derisively, lurching to the table and grabbing a plate of brioche and a half empty jug of organic pear juice and downing what remained at a gulp, "Why you so smart fuck cookie-Jews sit watch fuck-diddle funeral of fuckpig prickypoop?"

The others stared in dumbstruck disbelief and, as Michael began to laugh and applaud the absurd yet magnificently inspired outburst, Vladimir's attention focused for the tiniest fraction of a second on the epicene image of Cardinal Ratzinger.

"Whaaaat?" he roared in an instantaneous kneejerk of revulsion, "Look at this fuckface cocksuck . . !"

Rabinovitch and de Groot were only a few steps behind and the obscenity was cut short by Rabinovitch who clubbed Vladimir hard across the back of the head with the butt of his Glock. They both caught him under each armpit as he slumped unconscious and, deftly wresting the jug and plate from his hands and depositing them on the table as they did so, dragged him quickly out.

"Sorry," Rabinovitch said.

§

Michael the Med at last came into sight of the little chapel in the Trundle atop St. Roke's Hill at four o'clock on the warm and sunny afternoon of May 7th, 1498. He hadn't a penny left in his pocket and had walked sixty miles since he and Erasmus parted in London. During the ramble he had plenty of time to mull why being in England again felt so strange. A mere seven months and five days lay between the September gale and landing at Tilbury on April 26th but something profound and not altogether pleasant had altered within his soul.

Language was one thing. It felt odd speaking his native tongue to Erasmus on the way. The Dutchman insisted in anticipation of his forthcoming lectures but Michael had only conversed in Latin or Italian or French since leaving Paris for Amboise with Andrelini and Bartolomeo and they very rarely spoke English together, though Bartolomeo could do so perfectly, because Michael had been so intent on mastering Italian.

However, that wasn't truly the cause of his alienation. It was more to do with a peculiar desire to travel further, to plumb the depths of the cruelty he had observed, a feeling that began at Tyburn and was reinforced on the dock in Vlissingen and, though it pained him, he knew this visit with his dearly beloved sister would not be long.

§

At four o'clock, as the presidential lovebirds aboard Air Force One passed over Le Teste-de-Buch, the Bassin d'Arcachon and the dead straight beaches of the Biscay coast on a direct flight to Bergstrom AFB in Austin, Texas, and the haven of Prairie Chapel Ranch for a few days of R&R, Rabinovitch gave Ciccio the keys to the Mustang and he and Vladimir, who was looking dark and surly and holding a bag of ice to his head, sped off through the gates without the slightest gesture of goodbye.

"Why didn't you arrest them?" Michael asked the two CIA men, "They're criminals, aren't they?"

"Not our jurisdiction, sir," Rabinovitch replied.

"Oh, but it's OK to kidnap us."

"Just doing our job."

He had already returned Lamy's cell and the keys to the Bentley and given Lazzari the key to his Panda and since Michael knew it was no use trying to get information from stones he let the matter drop.

Lamy couldn't be bothered either and the four of them just watched from the veranda as the two men got into their black Cadillac SRX and drove away.

§

As the Davenport ancestral lands were restored after the Conquest by the Venables, the Billingsgate's had been by Roger de Montgomerie.

The newly created Earl of Shrewsbury had been one of William's chief counselors and his reward comprised all of what is now West Sussex as well as substantial holdings in a dozen other counties. He built two great castles and the countryside surrounding each was called the Rape of Arundel and the Rape of Chichester.

It was at Arundel Castle on July 27th, 1380, that twelve-year-old Mary de Bohun married John of Gaunt's third son, Henry Bolingbroke, the future King Henry IV. Mary was the daughter of Joan FitzAlan and Humphrey de Bohun, the 7th Earl of Hereford, whose great-grandfather, according to Aunt Sonja at least, was a plausible direct ancestor of George W. Bush.

A hide of land was roughly thirty acres, sufficient to support a family, and the next division of a shire was a Hundred which consisted of a hundred hides and beyond the Hundreds came the Rapes, there were just six in the whole of Sussex, which generally included at least one river, one forest and a castle.

The Billingsgate manorial seat was considerably larger than a Hundred and stretched up through the Lavant valley from Binderton to West Dean and over the Downs almost to Cocking, Bepton and Didling. The manor house itself lay below the Trundle near the village of Singleton. The entirety was between five and six thousand acres, approximately half chalk grassland with a smattering of rye and barley pasture and half forest, mainly yew, oak, ash, hawthorn and holly. There were ancient stands of yew that would have been seedlings when Alexander of Macedon fought the battle of Gaugamela.

The day Michael the Med arrived the fields were full of newborn lambs and the annual sheep-shearing began the following morning and by the time he gave Elaine's hand away at the end of June all seven thousand two hundred and fifty-three ewes and eighty-eight rams were shorn, cool and happily bleating in every corner of the vast estate.

Arthur was exactly one year younger than Michael, a widower with four grown children and a man of pedigree and substance. Despite having a proud Saxon heritage like his bride-to-be he would have preferred a grand ceremony in the great Norman cathedral in Chichester but he was not at all inflexible or stubborn and his already patient nature had been ripened by love. Thus when Elaine insisted on a country wedding instead he gently acquiesced and admitted afterwards that her wish proved utterly magical.

Upwards of nine hundred guests came including the forty-three families that worked the land and lived scattered about the farm and Thomas Grey and his brother George and Robert Fisher and Martha Bud, whom Michael sought out at the Leper Hospital in Westminster on the first of three trips to London bearing Vespucci letters of exchange, and brother William even rode all the way down from Cheshire. It was more than a decade since he dismissed them from Bramhall but Elaine was curious and took the chance to invite him. Perhaps it was mostly a desire to rub his nose in her good fortune yet after an hour or two of reacquaintance it was plain beneath his still brusque manner he had come to make amends and once he put away a sufficient ballast of excellent Billingsgate ale he became almost unbearably sentimental. Michael and Elaine didn't know which was worse, the cold meanness or the blubbering heat.

Jane, too, appeared to have had a change of heart and the reunion Michael secretly orchestrated with her mother was an unqualified success.

As for Jenny and Jack, life was a paradise. Billingsgate had provided Jane with a cottage for the three of them on the southern slope of Linch Down and the children, whose ninth birthday fell on July 26th, never tired of roaming the hills and dales. An old Roman road that led to Chichester passed by the cottage and they were fond of searching for artefacts on the Trundle, shards of pottery, chalk cups, stone tools and flintwork and Jack's pride and joy, a phallus carved with exquisite accuracy from an ancient roe-deer bone.

However, even such a summer of delight did nothing to change Michael's intent and, in any case, he was not one to go back on a promise.

By mid-August he had made all necessary arrangements for the shipment of fifteen tons of fine Southdown and Ryeland wool to the Vespucci mills in Borgo Ognissanti. It didn't take Arthur many seconds to realise the profitable future of the proposal nor much persuasion to agree to the price and the cargo was now strapped, baled and ready to depart on a long line of waiting wagons for the twenty-mile trek to Portsmouth.

§

"What now?" Michael the Mod asked, "Have we seen the last of them?"

Lamy was fiddling with the keypad on his cell and not paying attention.

"We should go as soon as you're ready," Lazzari said to Warren in Italian and then turned to Michael to explain, "It is the first evening for the Unione and Warren is our guest of honor. I will return him by midnight."

"Or I turn into a prissy old pumpkin," Warren added.

As they went into the house to get their things the Marrones were holding the doors for them and came outside.

"I cannot know how to say sorry enough for this, Signor Lamy," Giovanni began with a mixture of stress and relief, "We have no warning. We make ready yesterday morning and at ten the gate bell ring and they say they are you. So we let them in and right away they show guns and start give orders. We have no thought still who they can be."

Lamy had his cell to his ear and was listening to a string of messages.

"We're not sure either," he replied, lying.

"They will come more, you think?"

"I don't know. I hope not. It's me that should apologize for bringing you trouble. I'll try and put a stop to it but if you want us to leave I'll understand."

"No, no, Signor Lamy, *sei molto gentile. Grazie, mille grazie.* Do not worry. We make everything super-perfetto from now. We make beautiful supper. Your friends do not stay?"

"No. They have an engagement this evening."

"You have the other guests maybe?"

"Yes, one, I think. *Una bella ragazza.*"

Michael looked at him questioningly.

"*Bene, bene,*" Giovanni said with a smile, "Nine o'clock, *come sempre?*"

"*Si, molto bene. Grazie.*"

Susanna came to them with tears of gratitude in her eyes and kissed them on both cheeks before returning inside and Giovanni hurried down the steps toward the pool.

"Our *giardiniere* will be here," he said, "He attend the piazza *per il papa.*"

"What young lady?" Michael asked as they watched him go.

"Wait a sec," Lamy replied, pressing some buttons on the phone, "Whole slew of messages. First Aunt Sonja. Helen called her this morning. Then Helen with a bunch. More and more worried. Last one says she's on her way."

"Blast. I thought she might do that. When?"

"Left Gatwick fifteen minutes ago. Arriving Fiumicino at six twenty."

§

Michael the Med set sail from Portsmouth on August 22nd. He felt a great rush of freedom as the Simonetta, a *caravela latina* flying the Vespucci coat-of-arms, came out of the harbor channel into the blustery winds of the Solent.

The lateen-rigged caravel had a carrying capacity only a quarter the size of the larger merchant carracks but it was able to make the twenty-three hundred mile voyage to Livorno five days faster. It had brought a cargo of Tuscan wine to the thirsty shores of England, in sixty tuns containing fifteen thousand one hundred and twenty gallons, and was now laden with sixty tons of wool, not only from Billingsgate farm but five others in Hampshire as well, and Michael was the sole agent on board shepherding their safe delivery.

The Simonetta was one of several small ships owned by the Vespucci that regularly plied the waters from Livorno to Portsmouth. Piracy was rare because the Vespucci colors proclaimed a cargo that would be more trouble than it was worth as well as powerful and dangerous allies. There were many possible ports of call along the way but in this particular case there would only be Palos de la Frontera, the tiny outpost from whence the Santa Maria, the Pinta and the Niña had sailed and the home of the captain for the first leg of the present voyage, a taciturn Castilian named Cristóbal Roldán.

The experience of open water was new and thrilling to Michael and on the fourth day, after they had passed Alderney, Guernsey and the nose of Brittany, between Ouessant and Île-Molène and were traversing the always billowy Celtic Sea, there came a moment when they were beyond sight of land and any other vessel. The full circle of the horizon and the enormity of the sky above were so overwhelming he became quite magically intoxicated.

The crew of the Simonetta were seven natives of Palos, three Portuguese and one each from Italy, Morocco, Greece and Turkey and the communication between them was carried on in an almost impenetrable mish-mosh of nautical slang and quasi-Iberian *joual* so it was not surprising they gave a wide berth to the jagged peninsulas of Galicia, named for long ago worshippers of the Celtic hag-mother Cailleach though now a self-governing province of the Kingdom of Castile, and it was only after the fifth day that Michael became aware the crusty Cristóbal was the elder brother of Bartolomé Roldán.

Bartolomé had been an apprentice pilot with Vicente Yáñez Pinzón on the Niña in 1492 and sailed again with the much larger expedition of 1493 and at the end of May had departed with Columbus for a third time and despite the horrifying massacre at La Navidad and the hardship and general disgruntlement experienced at La Isabela he was intending to remain in a new settlement on the south coast of Hispaniola called La Nueva Isabela. The name is now Santo Domingo, the first and oldest European city in the Americas.

Several of the crew from the first voyages fought in the army of Charles VIII and were thus not only responsible for the exile of the Medici and the rule of Savonarola but the introduction of the spirochete *treponema pallidum*, more familiarly known as the syphilis bacillus, into the future sex life of Italy.

By the second week Michael had gained Cristóbal's trust and learned many more astonishing things that his brother told him.

Of the daily increase in terror and ultimate near rebellion of his shipmates after leaving San Sebastian de la Gomera in the Canary Islands on September 6th, 1492, due to their widespread belief that the world was flat and they were doomed to plummet from its edge. Of the extraordinary stubbornness of their leader who even after a decade in which no royal house from whom he sought funding could be persuaded that Asia lay less than three thousand miles west of Lisbon stayed steadfast in his conviction that it did so. That only after *Los Reyes Católicos*, Ferdinand and Isabella, had defeated the Emirate of Grenada, the last Moorish stronghold in Spain, did they summon him to the *Alcazar* in Córdoba and finally agree to his proposal. That, in a typical display of English dithering, Henry VII was too late in deciding to sponsor the expedition. That Columbus was now vindicated in his 'discovery', not of Antillia nor the Islands of the Blessed nor the mythical realms of St. Brendan or Prester John but what must surely be the easternmost isles of Cippangu and Cathay.

Of the bad omen of the admiral's flagship, Santa Maria, running aground and breaking up on Christmas Day. That all forty-four who stayed behind in La Navidad had either vanished or been killed by the local savages. That, naturally, none of the twenty from Palos had been stupid enough to join them. That after the first voyage a number of kidnapped *'indios'* had been paraded at court in Madrid. That the much larger second voyage of 1493 with its seventeen ships and hopeful cargo of farmers, carpenters, stonemasons, animals and priests was intended to form the basis of a permanent colony and initiate the sacred work of bringing the indigenous population to God. That Columbus skilfully played one group against another, approving the capture of a thousand Arawak and Carib and turning them into slaves as a gift to the Taino chieftain Guacanagari so they might retain his good favor. That five hundred of these unfortunates had been transported to Portugal. That most perished but a few survivors had found their way to Spain and, despite Isabella's public avowals to the contrary, were now chained to oars in her galleys having been conveniently denied the benefit of Christian conversion. Of mountains of gold and chopped off hands, pagan rituals, rape, forced castration and many another lurid tale Michael hoped were at least partly fanciful exaggerment.

On September 3rd they turned to the east and rounded the high cliffs of Cabo de São Vicente, the southwestern extremity of the continent, the land of the Oestrimini who, according to the ancient Greeks, had been chased there by serpents and for all but a hundred years were the very limit of the known and the knowable, and on September 5th they waited two hours for high tide to lift them over the sand bar at the mouth of the Odiel and at dusk dropped anchor in the sheltered harbor at Palos.

How astonishingly admirable! What bravery! Setting off in tiny vulnerable craft on a vast sea toward they knew not what. Men from this little town made up a quarter of the entire crew on the first voyage and now one at least desired to be the permanent inhabitant of another world. What staggering potential!

Yet even at so great a distance, and having been told so little, Michael was overcome by a strange sensation. An ominous foreboding deep within that, far beyond the gloriously setting sun, some monstrous unstoppable calamity was in the first dark tremor of its birth.

§

"Of course we haven't seen the last of them," Lamy said as Michael turned the Bentley off the Via Aurelia Antica and up the on-ramp for Via Leone XIII, "But maybe they're about to change shape."

"How so?" Michael asked, "You're not suggesting something occult."

Lamy chuckled.

"No. Just visitations from higher up the food chain."

"Ah. And why would that happen?"

"Don't know. But I feel like giving them a shove."

"I feel like banging them on the head with a mallet but what if they shove back?"

Lamy didn't reply.

Giovanni had offered to drive them but they said no. The directions were simple. Follow Leone XIII through Villa Pamphili and keep straight on Viale dei Colli Portuense to Viale Isacco Newton and the autostrada for Leonardo da Vinci. Lamy said he would have no problem finding their way home.

Vincenzo Gioacchino Raffaele Luigi Pecci, Leo XIII, was the third longest serving pope, after his immediate predecessor Pius IX and Karol Wojtyła, and the oldest, dying still shod in the shoes of the fisherman at ninety-three.

The traffic was unbelievable and dusk was starting to make Michael's task a bit tricky.

"So how do we make Signor Mythicus Vespucius want to find us?"

Lamy considered the question for a moment.

"I went over the car and it's clean but no doubt Rabinovitch has bugged my cell. I was going to toss it and get another but I decided it'll be better to do nothing. I haven't been using it but now I think I will. I'm not going to let my office know I'm onto them. CIA'll be tracing Helen's as well. And they'll have a bug on the hotel line. We can use it to our advantage. Maybe we should drop some hints that their collective disbelief is a mistake."

"Disbelief?"

"I called Aunt Sonja to say we're OK. We spoke in French naturally and I told her we'd been kidnapped by the CIA and that everyone's running round us in circles like a pack of barking hounds below a pair of treed wildcats."

"Yeah, so, what will that do?"

"Make them try and figure out what I meant."

"I wish them luck. So . . disbelief in what?"

Lamy grinned wickedly.

"What Vladimir said. That 'you are this guy'."

Michael turned to look at him in horror and the Bentley swerved slightly. He opened his mouth to scream in protest but an instantaneous barrage of irate honking forced his eyes to jump back to the road.

§

Roldán and four of the crew who had wives in Palos were to debark there and be replaced and great haste was being made since the Simonetta needed to set sail again with the next tide. Two skiffs were rowing toward them before the anchor dropped. There looked to be ten more besides the oarsmen and Michael could make out Bartolomeo Marchionni standing upright in the lead vessel with another man who he did not recognize. There were men standing in the second dinghy as well and as the two boats drew alongside Michael was appalled to see four naked copper-skinned *'indios'*, two males and two females, crouched in the stern.

Marchionni was first up the ladder followed by the other man and they both shook Roldán's hand and Marchionni greeted Michael warmly and it took only a moment for the crew to switch and the first skiff to row away.

Boarding the *'indios'* was more complex because they were bound together to prevent them from leaping into the water but it was accomplished without a shout or shove and they were taken below. Michael found it hard to bear but Marchionni took him aside and introduced him to the new captain who he was surprised and ultimately delighted to discover was Bartolomeo's uncle Amerigo. Before Michael could question either of them about the captives Amerigo went quickly to his duties and Marchionni clambered down into the second rowboat and waved 'God speed' in departure.

Once they reached open water Amerigo told him the *'indios'* were a gift from Guido Antonio to Frederick IV, the king of Naples, and the guards would prefer he did not try to make any kind of contact. He could hear their strange murmurs from his tiny cabin during the night and sleep was hard.

It was not until late morning of the next day, as they sighted Cadiz off the port bow, that Amerigo and Michael conversed further. Amerigo was pleased with Michael's excellent Florentine Italian for though he was fluent in Spanish, Portuguese and French he spoke not a word of English. It would have been possible for them to communicate in Latin but it was stiff in comparison and rapidly going out of fashion. The language of Dante was much more amenable and expressive.

In the afternoon they passed through the Strait of Gibraltar, derived from Jebel Tariq, Tariq's mountain, known to the ancients as the Pillars of Hercules, beyond which Plato proclaimed that nothing lay but the isle of Atlantis, from whence eleven millennia ago great armies came to conquer western Europe and then vanished beneath the waves one mysterious night.

Amerigo was a soft-spoken and highly efficient man and meticulous in his duty. Michael already knew quite a lot about him. Five years his junior but with somewhat wider experience of the world. Not much given to humor though on the seventh day as they skirted north of Majorca, the greatest of the archipelago on whose shores nude warriors armed with slings once repelled the conquering consul Quintus Caecilius Metellus, he did betray a tiny smile when they touched on the youthful siring of illegitimate daughters.

Michael was relieved that the *'indios'* were allowed on deck during the day. They remained loosely bound together but appeared well fed and were treated with relative civility by their guards. Their dark eyes revealed little of what must have been great inner turmoil. They were all young, Michael judged them to be no more than twenty, lightly muscled with scant body hair and taller by a hand than most Mediterranean Europeans. The weather was hot and humid and they seemed perfectly comfortable wearing nothing but a loincloth and the women made no effort to cover their bare breasts despite the crew's constant staring. Michael was aghast to imagine the fate awaiting them in Naples.

Amerigo was able to fill in many of the blanks in Roldán's rambling tales of Columbus. Of how he and Gianetto Berardi arranged the financing of the voyages since *Los Reyes Católicos* were virtually penniless because of a surprising generosity to the vanquished Moors of Grenada who they allowed to keep their faith and customs and even the Emir to remain as the head of a vassal state but almost immediately thereafter drove every Jew who refused conversion out of Spain with the result they were rather foolishly bereft of moneylenders.

Of how Columbus had been lionized in all quarters on his first return and demonized in like degree after the second. Of the shocking change wrought in the man between the conquering hero of 1493 and the half-mad, demoralized penitent of 1496 with his leadership mired in controversy. Amerigo spent a year and a half working to reinstate him in the fickle princes' good favor and now he was off again in an attempt to repair his tarnished reputation.

The primary problem had been slaves and their value and some abstruse niggling over the legality of their enslavement. Not that anyone really cared but for Columbus they were a quick source of profit since gold had not been found in abundance, savages who deserved nothing better, and he could not accept that he was suddenly being vilified for so commonplace an opinion as well as being denied essential and deserved income.

More amazing to Michael was the story of Giovanni Chabotte, a Venetian citizen of Genoese origin, once known for selling slaves in Crete. A trader in spices and silks, familiar with the countries of the Middle East and a self-styled civil engineer, who had been chased from Venice by insolvency. Amerigo made his acquaintance in Seville where, while fleeing his creditors, he was contracted to build a bridge over the Guadalquivir. The great river was easily navigable to Seville, fifty miles from the sea, and as far as Córdoba in Roman times.

Caboto, as some called him, was possessed of one brilliant idea, to take a more northerly route than Columbus and, by virtue of the narrower degrees of longitude, make the trip to the Indies shorter.

This simple notion found favor, quite understandably, in England where on the 5th of March, 1496, the dilatory Henry VII granted him royal patent and 'free authority to discover and investigate whatsoever islands, countries, regions or provinces of heathens and infidels, in whatsoever part of the world placed, which before this time were unknown to all Christians.'

But, as is so often the case, fine words were accompanied with insufficient funds for the task. However, Chabotto was fortunate to make the acquaintance of a wealthy Augustinian friar named Giovanni Antonio de Carbonariis who desired to sail with him and build a church and who also happened to be the London-based deputy of the papal tax collector, Adriano Castellesi, and since the Holy See owned nearly a third of the land in England and received one tenth of that land's revenue everything fell quickly into place.

Cabot was forced to turn back after encountering fierce Atlantic storms in the summer of 1496 but departed again from Bristol on a single ship named the Mathew, of similar size to the Simonetta, on May 2nd, 1497. He reached 'new found land' on the day of St. John the Baptist, June 24th, went ashore only long enough to plant the Venetian and Papal banners, take on fresh water and claim the land for the king of England, then spent a fortnight exploring the rugged coast without spotting a single Cathay or Cippangoid and was back in Bristol by August 6th having very satisfactorily proved his point.

At that time Michael was catching mackerel but, even in the six weeks before his shipwreck and despite Cabot's having ridden straight to London to meet the king and crowds of people running after him agog and paying him honor, he had heard not a whisper of it in Worthing.

Though he seldom expressed emotion, Amerigo clearly relished telling the story and before they arrived in Livorno let slip that he was planning a voyage of his own within the year.

Shuffle Ten

"Father Birmingham assured me that there is absolutely no factual basis regarding your concerns for his relationship with your son and I believe he is speaking the truth in this matter."
- Cardinal Bernard Francis Law (1931 -   )

§

Leonardo da Vinci was jammed with the departing faithful, recharged and ready to continue promulgating their dismal vision in every corner of the globe. The autostrada was at a virtual standstill and Michael had inched along the last two miles. They were within seconds of being late but Lamy said not to worry he would deal with the car. He told Michael to make a dash for it and was now sitting in the Bentley directly outside the terminal doors. Simply done if you can afford to palm the traffic co-ordinator five hundred euros.

By some miracle Helen's flight was on time. She had only packed a carry-on bag and almost as soon as she entered the arrivals area she bumped straight into Michael wading frantically toward her through the crush and the surprise combined with the flood of relief made her want to hit him.

"What are you . . ? How the . . ? Why in hell didn't you . . ?"

He covered her mouth.

"Ssh, it wasn't possible. We were held captive."

"Whaaat . . ?"

"Just shut up and I'll explain."

They were half way back to the Casale before she calmed down. It wasn't Michael and Lamy's explanation but the news Warren was in Rome that did the trick. It would at least make the expense of the flight worth it.

Lamy wanted to know about the customs check. If the officer questioned her in any way she thought peculiar but the woman hadn't asked anything at all, just put her passport in the scanner and returned it.

"Why? You think because my name is Davenport . . ?"

"Could have been. You don't use Giudice, do you?"

Giudice was the surname of her murdered ex-husband.

"God no. Never did."

There was a momentary silence as Helen lit a cigarette. She was in front beside Lamy and finally started to chuckle.

"I have to hand it to you," she said through her laughter, "You lads really know how to plonk yourselves in kaka."

§

At Livorno Michael the Med was relieved of his duties as shepherd of the wool by an agent of the Vespucci and was free to ride as fast as he could to Florence where Bartolomeo was waiting to greet him with a warm embrace. It was the evening of September 18th and had been one hundred and seventy days since they said farewell in Amboise and just under a year since the equinoctial gale shipped Michael to the coast of Holland.

Bartolomeo knew about the gift of the *'indios'*. Factionalism between the *popolani* and *ottimati* had been extremely volatile throughout the province since Savonarola's execution and Guido Antonio, Bernardo Rucellai, Giovanbattista Ridolfi and others of the *ottimati* who wanted Florence to be governed by an experienced elite were trying to strengthen the relationship with Naples as well as with *'Il Moro'*, Ludovico Sforza, in Milan. The reason being that the new king of France, Louis XII, an elder distant relation to the unfortunate Charles whose four children had all died in infancy, immediately announced his own ambition toward the throne of Naples based on a similarly tenuous right of descent from yet another paternal grandmother and it was rumored that, like his predecessor, he was gathering an army to march once again on Milan.

Bartolomeo followed this news with a fatalistic smile and shrug but it was not possible for Michael to divine what lay behind the gesture.

§

The missing plutonium had been moved less than two hundred and fifty kilometers as the condor flies across the Chihuahua desert to the south and east from its hiding place in the no man's land between El Fierro and Los Lamentos and the three hundred gallon carbon steel drum containing it now lodged at the summit of a barren crag called Cerro Pastelone above the tiny town of Ejido las Lilas in the middle of the Zona del Silencio.

Its disappearance remained a conundrum that the bloodspattered hirelings of Semion Mogilevich and the combined intelligence of the CIA, Mossad, MI5, ASIS, CSIS, SISMI, AISI, DIA, INR, NSA, NGA and all the sweaty cybercaves and crannies of AUSCANNZUKUS had not been able to penetrate.

It was quite understandably part of what continued to occupy the Warrior Princess Secretary of State and Director Goss on the flight to Bolling AFB in Washington but it wasn't all work. Goss was an avid organic farmer so they also spoke about that and Condoleezza's passion for healthy living led them to the subject of Sanibel Island off the Caribbean coast of Florida where Porter had once been mayor. It was listed among the best places to own a second home in America and its glistening white sands formed a backdrop to the crime novels of Randy Wayne White. White was also an adventurer and travel guide author and Condoleezza couldn't help cracking her famous toothy grin as she recalled giving the vice-president an autographed copy of his 1991 classic, Batfishing in the Rainforest.

As to the plutonium, they agreed to keep everything in a holding pattern and put even more pressure on the Russian mob. If there were another 'code red' in Rome, and they were pretty sure there wouldn't be, they figured it would only happen after the conclave and that was another nine days off.

§

Michael the Mod and Helen were both drunk and giggly by the time they finished Susanna and Giovanni's magnificent five course supper and sampling a variety of exotic liqueurs when Luigi and Warren returned. It was five minutes to midnight.

"Ah, Cinderella!" Michael exclaimed unnecessarily loudly as Helen got to her feet and ran to Warren and hugged him.

"Marvelous are the uses of adversity," Warren said, holding her close and kissing her forehead, "Your fool of a brother predicted too long a silence would provoke your arrival. Meet the love of my life. Luigi, this is Helen."

"I am delighted, Signora," Lazzari responded with a congenial nod and, quickly sizing up the general level of inebriation, added, "And now I must go."

Lamy was in an armchair looking sleepy but suddenly came alive.

"I have two questions before you do," he said.

"Yes?"

"What's your schedule tomorrow night between six and eight and do you know Francesco Buranelli?"

"Warren is giving his main address to the *Unione* at nine and we have some smaller meetings during the day but . . why do you ask? And yes, I know of the man you mention."

"But you don't actually know him."

"No."

"Think you can squeeze in a visit to the Vatican with us for half an hour around seven?"

"Yes, it would be possible. May I ask why?"

"Because," Michael burst in, "This lunatic is planning to get me killed!"

§

Lamy's thought was an odd one and he had no idea if it would work but they all went along with it and, in truth, Michael wasn't nearly as concerned as he made out the previous evening. It wasn't going to put him in jeopardy in any obvious way. At least, not yet. It was merely a second little attempt on Lamy's part to confuse the opposition and get the attention of their impossibly elusive quarry. Something, anything, that might, even ever so slightly, provoke him into breaking his cover.

At ten minutes to seven the Bentley drew up to an unadorned metal gate in the south wall off Via della Stazione Vaticana. It had none of the grandeur of the Porta Sant'Anna and was more like a mini-version of the Petriano entrance. The darkness surrounding it was sepulchral and clandestine but the gate began to open almost before Lamy stopped and all he had to do was show one of the two Swiss Guards his passport and they were admitted.

He still hadn't told them how he managed to arrange the visit nor why he thought it might be effective, just that there were two famous frescoes in the Sistine Chapel he wanted them to see and that he hoped they would pay close attention to the game he was playing and not give anything away.

The guards closed the gate behind them and walked beside the car as they glided down the narrow roadway between St. Charles' Palace and St. Martha's House to a parking spot near the Sacristy.

Francesco Buranelli, the General Director of the Vatican Museums, was waiting for them inside.

§

The admission to Vatican City, particularly at the beginning of novemdiales, the nine days of prayer and mourning and hocus-pocus between the death and burial of one pope and the unfortunately inevitable election of another, and at night through an entrance never used for casual visitors, caused an immediate flurry of excited phone calls.

One from Ciccio to Krasinski in London who then called Mogilevich in Budapest who then called Arkadi Gaydamak, the middleman who obtained the plutonium in the first place, and then Viktor Bout, another arm's dealer and partner in the death business who had flown it to an isolated desert strip in the Samalayuca eight years before, and then called Krasinski back and told him to tell Ciccio he would be in Rome the next morning and all of this was heard and reported by Rabinovitch to Porter Goss who called the State Department and found Condi alone in her office catching up with paperwork and taking a first nibble from a Ziploc container of home-made crab salad.

"Is that so?" she said, dabbing a driplet of mayo from her lips, "Well, well. Your boys better not waste any time digging out what's going on."

"That could be tough. You know Italians love to beat around the bush."

"I hate Italy. You can never find anyone who's in charge. Well then, tell that Ukrainian pig to get his finger out."

"Why don't we let him make them disappear?"

"Because 'they' are not our problem," she replied testily, "The plutonium is. What are you smoking over there? Do you have any idea how devious that smug little prick Lamy can be? If you kill him he'll have a billion websites wired to start spilling all kinds of dangerous shit. The sonofabitch knows everything. We're safe while he's alive because he's too smart to start blabbing."

"We've got a mole at his place in Washington Square . . "

"Don't be a fucking idiot. The woman is not going to sanction you killing him! Anyway, hadn't we decided to kill her?"

"So, what do you want me to do?"

"Go ahead. We don't need her. We know where he is and what he's doing. Find someone in Italy who he knows and won't suspect to schmooze with him and see if they can guess what the hell game he's playing. And tell Rabinovitch not to let that fat slimeball do anything stupid!"

§

Francesco Buranelli was a handsome man, a world-renowned specialist in the antiquities of Etruria with a doctorate in archaeology from the University of Rome. He was wearing a dark blue business suit and sporting a striped tie and greeted them in excellent English as Lamy made the introductions.

"I thank you for your generosity," he said to Lamy.

"I thank you for taking the time to do this," Lamy replied.

Warren had made Buranelli's acquaintance many years ago in Hong Kong at an exhibition of their mutual friend Cecco Bonanotte's bronze sculpture and they reminisced for a few moments in Italian. Michael always felt insecure and envious of people fluent in a language other than their own. Like the majority of native English speakers he didn't have the gift and, as with his inability to carry a tune, it was a lifelong embarrassment and frustration.

"Don't you think he looks like Colin Firth?" Helen whispered.

"Not really," Michael muttered.

"Oh, go on, he does. You just don't like him."

"I've only just met him. How . . ?"

"Not him you fool. Colin."

"All right. It's not really Colin but, I'm sorry, I don't see why I should like relentlessly light and inconsequential movies."

Lazzari overheard them and chimed in softly.

"I have met this young man you mention. His wife is a Giuggioli. I know the family well. Livia is not inconsequential, I promise you."

Michael looked apologetic.

"I had no idea . . "

"Yes, you did," Helen objected, "You knew he married an Italian."

"I didn't. You're the one who went to school with him."

Buranelli beckoned them and led the way down some stairs explaining it was better not to pass directly across the floor of the basilica because they were preparing for tomorrow's mass. There was a special remembrance service each day until the conclave with a different eminence presiding. This morning it had been Cardinal Marchisano, archpriest of the Vatican itself, tomorrow the vicar general of the diocese of Rome, Cardinal Ruini, and so on.

As Buranelli spoke they followed along a sequence of nondescript marble corridors which somehow bypassed anything resembling a grotto or a crypt and reached an elevator that took them up three floors into another corridor and then he opened a door and drew a curtain aside and suddenly they were in the magnificent chapel of Sixtus IV. The lights were on. Two female cleaners were at work polishing the altar and looked up a trifle startled.

Buranelli spoke quietly to them in Italian and went on.

"The cardinals will attend the conclave here in eight days. That is why they were surprised to see us. The chapel was, as you may know, a restoration of the ancient Cappella Magna ordered by his holiness Sixtus IV in the 1470s and by the early 1480s it was ready for decoration. Originally there were eight frescoes depicting events in the life of Christ but Perugino's Nativity which was on the west wall above the altar was unfortunately destroyed in the process of making room for Michelangelo's Last Judgement fifty years later. The two frescoes you mentioned were of particular interest are here on the north wall."

He led them to the second in the sequence.

"After the Baptism of Perugino and Pinturicchio we have Botticelli's The Temptations and the Cleansing of the Leper. He has cleverly intertwined these themes in the painting as you see."

He turned to Michael and Helen as they looked up at it.

"Your ancestor, Guido Antonio, is the gray-haired man in purple judge's robes looking away from the scene at the lower right. Such anachronisms were extremely common in the paintings of the time."

What on earth was he talking about? Ancestor? Guido Antonio who, for heaven's sake? Vespucci? Michael turned to Lamy in disbelief but his blandly amused expression read, 'Go with it. Play along.'

"Really," Michael said, at first sharing the madness of the moment with a wide-eyed glance at Helen and then feigning interest and putting a finger to his chin, "Good lord. Quite extraordinary."

"Standing slightly below him, dressed in red and holding a walking stick is Count Girolamo Riario, one of the many nephews that Francesco della Rovere raised to offices of wealth and power during his papacy. The most well-known being Giuliano who became Pope Julius II and was, of course, Michelangelo's patron."

Giuliano della Rovere, whom Sixtus made Cardinal Priest of San Pietro in Vincoli six months after his own election and in quick succession granted him the rich episcopal sees of Carpentras, Lausanne, Catania, Coutances, Mende, Viviers, Sabina, Bologna and Ostia, was one of the principal instigators behind Charles VIII's attempt on Naples because he was miffed that he had not been elected pope instead of Rodrigo Borgia in 1492. This was primarily due to the Spaniard's more artful placement of bribes, or simony to use the biblical term, but, unlike his scholarly and notoriously homosexual uncle, Giuliano was an army man, the father of three illegitimate daughters, a builder of fortresses and not to be dissuaded from his desire at the age of sixty after the suspicious death of Pius III in 1503.

"Guido Antonio and Riario," Buranelli continued, "Could not be called friends, as you probably know, but . . "

Lamy broke in helpfully.

"Yes, yes, the Pazzi conspiracy. Rival banks, control of the alum mines at Tolfa, all that. Guido Antonio Vespucci was a great diplomat and Riario, as we understand it, was just an ambitious puppet of those, like Sixtus, who wanted to get rid of the Medici."

"He was lucky," Warren added, "Lorenzo managed to save him from the mob. Unlike Archbishop Salviati and the other conspirators who were dragged naked through the streets and hung from the walls of the Signoria."

"Leonardo made a drawing of one, did he not?" Lazzari said.

"Yes," Lamy answered, "Bernardo di Bandino Baroncelli."

"You really are impossible," Helen said laughing, "How do you remember such things?"

"Michael calls it my affliction," Lamy went on, "In any case, despite being spared, Riario didn't learn his lesson and was assassinated fifteen years later."

"Ah, the world of politics," Michael offered with an attempt at urbanity.

"*Si,*" Buranelli concurred, "It is little changed. Tell me, how did you both discover you were related?"

"Ah, yes, well, hm," Michael stammered, not having a clue what to say, "It rather just fell in my lap."

"How so?"

"Um, through, um, a cousin . . in Mexico, of all places."

Lamy came to the rescue seamlessly.

"A distant cousin named Bartolomeo Vespucci who Michael ran into by a flook in Ciudad Juarez. An amazing coincidence because Michael and Helen are not direct descendants of Guido Antonio but from the nephew of his nephew Amerigo, another Bartolomeo, who was, as far as they've been able to trace it, an obscure professor of astronomy in Padua."

"How interesting," Buranelli said, "I have not heard of this man."

"It's a fascinating story but shall we move to the next?" Lamy suggested, "Call me crazy but I'm seeing a facial resemblance."

"Yes, perhaps," Buranelli agreed and led them the few steps to a position beneath the third fresco. He was clearly beginning to find the situation a little odd but was too polite to comment. Michael gave Lamy an 'I don't believe you' glare behind his back as Helen and Lazzari shared a silent shrug of puzzlement.

"I'd say you look more like Riario," Warren whispered wickedly.

"Now we come to The Calling of the Apostles of Ghirlandaio. I'm sure you are aware of his portrait of the Vespucci in the *chiesa* of the Ognissanti."

"Of course," Michael said, though his attitude was verging on send-up.

"Yes," Lamy confirmed, "Amerigo is pictured in both the family portrait and in the Misericordia below with another uncle, Giorgio Antonio."

"Amerigo's tutor," Warren added, surprising everyone, "A liberal-minded humanist despite being a Dominican friar."

"The two things are not mutually exclusive, I hope, even today," Buranelli countered gently, "In Ghirlandaio's great fresco here you see Peter and Andrew kneeling before Christ in the foreground and James and John coming ashore in the little boat far behind. Guido Antonio again makes an appearance but as a younger man standing in full figure at the far right in a red gown and wearing a red cap. I think the familial similarity is more pronounced in this one, no?"

"Yes, decidedly," Warren said, nodding in appraisal.

"Oh, definitely," Helen concurred.

"Is Count Riario here as well?" Lazzari asked. The mockery beneath their tone was becoming noticeable and he didn't want to offend their host.

"I don't think so," Buranelli replied, "But there is a portrait by Melozza da Forlì in the Pinacoteca of Pope Sixtus and several of his nephews including . . "

"You're very gracious but we've imposed too much already," Lamy said.

"And I must get Signor Jones to an engagement," Lazzari added.

"I'm speaking to the Atheist Society," Warren continued innocently, "And since I'm also here to help Luigi create a parallel association of gay and lesbian humanists becoming reacquainted with the overpowering gayness of this room has been marvelously useful. Despite the other's brilliance it's Michelangelo's art that dominates the atmosphere."

He pointed up to Adam and Eve in the Garden and went on.

"Where else can you find an Eve with such immense biceps?"

Then gestured toward the Last Judgement above the altar.

"Or a Christ muscled like a Grecian wrestler. Yet, at the same time, as is everywhere apparent, the reduction of the penis to a trivial appendix. Evidently our glorious Buonarroti felt he needed to keep his sexual identity hidden from his audience and didn't realize these choices gave him away instead."

"Most of the nudity was painted over after the Council of Trent declared it obscene," Lamy joined in, "Stayed hidden for over four hundred years."

"That's right," Buranelli said, quite unflustered by their comments, "And even with our recent restorations more than half remains obscured."

"Why has sex always been such an issue?" Helen murmured.

"Because everyone can be made to feel guilty about it," Warren answered, "Guilt is the great weapon of the church."

"And the purity of the clergy the biggest lie," Lazzari added.

"It's interesting," Warren went on, "That Sixtus IV didn't invite Leonardo to create one of these early frescoes. It was whispered that Sixtus was fond of beautiful young men and often elevated them for sexual favors. Do you think young da Vinci's two arrests for sodomy might have had something to do with the omission? *Grazie*, Francesco. I'll add these little observations to my lecture."

"Why not?" Buranelli responded amiably and turned to view them all with a benign smile, "Are there any further questions?"

§

For the next three summers Michael the Med made the round-trip voyage from Livorno to Portsmouth to shepherd more wool and by 1502 had become a sufficiently seasoned mariner to captain the Simonetta himself. It was always a joy to see his beloved Elaine and a great relief that the whole family seemed so settled and happy at Billingsgate farm. Jane had taken up with a local swain and Jenny was blossoming and slowly his relationship with Jack grew and ripened in the way it always should be with grandson and grandfather. The boy was full of romantic notions about the wide world and Michael promised that one day he could join him.

On May 16th, 1499, Amerigo's careful planning came to fruition and he set sail from Cadiz with Alonso de Ojeda and the cosmographer, Juan de la Cosa. Michael had broken his second journey to England to wish him well and felt a pang of envy as the three tiny vessels disappeared over the westward horizon.

The expedition took a southerly course and in a bare three weeks sighted land near the mouth of the Orinoco river, then continued on to the island now called Trinidad and a bay Amerigo dubbed Venezuela because it reminded him of the great lagoon of Venice. Despite his habitual brutality to the native people Ojeda married a Guatemalan Indian and on their return sixteen months later they carried a cargo of four hundred slaves which, now the picayune legalities that frustrated Columbus were cleared away, Amerigo and Marchionni had no problem selling at a handsome profit.

Because the Vespucci were generous in payment for his services Michael was able to spend the winters in Florence with Bartolomeo as idly as he desired. They enjoyed the company of Machiavelli when he was not preoccupied with being second chancellor of the new republic and secretary to *La Guerra dei Dieci* or away on some diplomatic mission.

They watched with sadness the decline of uncle Guido Antonio, though he remained deeply involved in affairs of state to the end, and amusement the humiliation of Ludovico Sforza after Louis XII sent him packing from Milan, an unexpected and happy result of which was Leonardo's return to Florence.

Bartolomeo Marchionni, 'the Turk' as da Vinci nicknamed his childhood friend, introduced them on one of his visits from Lisbon and Michael and he became rather unlikely intellectual sparring partners, though not on the subject of slavery. The great polymath's mother was an Arab stolen from the eastern shores of the Middle Sea and delivered to the quiet Tuscan town of Vinci by a ship of the Marchionni.

But more than anyone, those turn of the century years were dominated by the man Niccolò called Duke Valentino, Cesare Borgia.

126

Shuffle Eleven

"The Vatican museums exemplify the commitment of the Roman
Pontiffs to promoting evangelization through the language of art."
- Francesco Buranelli (1955 -   )

§

The ferocious kisser from Birmingham, Alabama, was just stepping out
of the shower at five minutes past six on Sunday morning when her cell
rang. She checked the caller's ID and answered with a snarl.

"What?!"

"Don't bite my head off," Goss said, "I waited since just after
midnight."

"With what?"

"We should think again about our lady in Washington Square."

"Why?"

"Twenty-four hours ago Lamy transferred a hundred million dollars to
an account at the Vatican Bank."

"What account?"

"She didn't know. She didn't handle it. The transfer came from
Rothschild in Geneva. She said Lamy has more than a billion stashed
there."

There was a chilly silence.

"So what in fucking hell were they doing last night?"

"We still have no idea."

"Why not?"

"None of our contacts knew anything about the visit."

"Jesus. A hundred million and no one knows anything about it?!"

"The last thing they'll talk about is money."

§

As they made their way to listen to Warren's lecture, which took place
in a surprisingly large room at the rear of an antique shop on the Via
Flaminia near Piazzale Ankara and made Michael smile because it was so

reminiscent of some subterranean meeting of anarchists in a Hollywood black and white movie, they had finally broken through Lamy's sly reticence with a barrage of questions.

"OK, OK. I knew Buranelli wants a Picasso for the museum and I said I'd get one for him if he promised to keep the gift anonymous. Not that it'll stay secret for long. I'm pretty sure who the leak is in my office. I'm surprised and a bit hurt I have to admit after all these years. Anyway, I let her find out about the transfer but not the details. I can hear the phones ringing in D.C. already. But if Buranelli keeps his promise they won't be able to figure out why. No one at either bank'll ever tell them so they're bound to conclude it's something to do with Vespucci and the plutonium."

"And for this joke you are willing to spend one hundred million dollars?" Lazzari asked in the incredulous tone of a man whose intellectual passions had inevitably led him to a life of frugality.

"Sorry to tell you it's chump change. And, hey, why shouldn't the Vatican have a Picasso? They've got just about everything else."

"I can't imagine what Picasso they'd find suitable," Helen said.

"Shouldn't be a problem," Warren added wryly, glancing over his shoulder from the passenger seat beside Lamy, "Their tastes are catholic."

They shared a brief chuckle.

"OK," Helen went on, "But why the fun and games in there? Didn't you say you wanted to make them think Michael was Vespucci?"

"Well, it'll make them start to wonder again, won't it? It's a two-front deal. The money thing works better if they know we also paid a visit but the charade was for Vespucci. If he exists. Shit, I'm so damn curious now I'd give another hundred million to find out. Didn't anyone but me feel Buranelli get a bit weird inside when I brought up our pal Bartolomeo?"

"Maybe," Michael answered glumly, "But so what?"

"Come on, don't you think it'll piss him off or perk his interest at least?"

"Brilliant. Now he'll want to kill every one of us."

§

Like William the Conqueror, Leonardo and Bartolomeo, like Michael the Med's daughter and grandchildren, like Cesare's brothers, Giovanni, Goffredo and Ottaviano, his infamous sister Lucrezia, his half-sisters Isabella and Laura and half-brothers Pier Luigi and Girolamo, the lord of Imola was a bastard.

He was also known variously as Captain General and Gonfalonier of the Church, Bishop of Pamplona, Count of Dyois, Lord of Piombino, Camerino and Urbino, Prince of Andria and Venafro, Duke of Valentinois and Romagna and Cardinal of Valencia. His mother was Vannozza dei Cattanei of the House of Candia though his father was not her husband Domenico. He was the son of Rodrigo Lanzol who became Pope Alexander VI in the year Columbus sailed the ocean blue by simply outspending his Sforza and della Rovere rivals.

It is little wonder they were caught by surprise. Della Rovere's candidacy was bankrolled by Genoa and the King of France to the tune of three hundred thousand gold ducats, half the annual income of the entire Florentine republic, the contemporary equivalent of three hundred million dollars, but it had not been nearly enough. No doubt Rodrigo's rivals seconded the unsportsmanlike grouch of Giovanni di Lorenzo de' Medici, later Pope Leo X, when he warned, "We are now in the power of the most rapacious wolf the world has ever seen and if we do not flee he will devour us all."

The unexpected founder of the Borgia feast was Rodrigo's uncle Alfonso who had more or less stumbled into the papacy by a compromise vote in April, 1455. He was already seventy-seven and of a retiring disposition and did little of consequence during his two year stint in Peter's Chair except issuing the bull *Inter Caetera* which following *Dum Diversas* reversed *Sicut Dudum* and reaffirmed the Portuguese in the Order of Christ and gave them the consent of the Roman Pontifex to enslave infidels and Africans.

If Cristoforo Colombo had sailed under the flag of Portugal instead of the other *Reyes Católicos* he wouldn't have suffered the hypocritical quibbling nor the financial setbacks, nor been accused of cruelty and incompetence and sent home in chains by Francisco de Bobadilla, his replacement as Governor of the Indies, in the late autumn of 1500.

Suddenly having a pope for an uncle was an irresistible stroke of luck for young Rodrigo and he immediately rechristened himself by his mother's family name. He had been in Spain idling away the time as a cadet but Alfonso was urged to send him for a brief term of law study at the university of Bologna and shortly thereafter made him Cardinal Deacon of St. Nicola *in Carcere* and Vice-Chancellor of the Roman Church. He held the position for thirty-seven years and, as chief administrator of the Papal Chancery, acquired great influence, at least eight illegitimate children, countless archbishoprics, bishoprics, abbacies and other dignities and, through them, enormous wealth.

Modern historians give Rodrigo Borgia almost uniformly bad marks but the citizens of the Eternal City welcomed him. During his progress from St. Peter's to St. John Lateran on the day of his coronation they lined the streets with garlands. He made them safer from foreign attack and cut down on crime. There had been more than two hundred assassinations in the months before his election but now the guilty were hung on the spot and their houses razed to the ground. His reputation for financial liberality attracted the finest architects, musicians and artists. He was a skilful negotiator, a survivor who ably changed course with the wind and thereby kept himself and his offspring alive and the general carnage to a minimum during the incursions of Charles VIII and Louis XII, and he was even tolerant toward the Jews.

Like his father, Cesare was an attractive child and grew to be a handsome, athletic and charismatic man. He was born in Rome on September 13th, 1475, and was released from the necessity of proving his birth by a bull of Sixtus IV five years later. He was made a bishop at fifteen by Pope Innocent VIII and as soon as Rodrigo took the office he was elevated to cardinal.

Until 1497, however, he was frustrated in the shadow of his elder brother Giovanni, the dashing captain general of the papal army, but then on June 15th fortune stepped in and the latter's body was fished from the Tiber with multiple stab wounds and throat slashed wide.

Shortly thereafter Cesare renounced his cardinalship and really got down to business. He had accompanied Charles VIII to Milan along with his enemy Giuliano della Rovere and was also with Louis XII when he entered the city in the first week of October, 1499, on the heels of the successful campaign of his hireling *condottiero*, Gian Giacomo Trivulzio. Charles had appointed this grizzled traitor governor of Asti and the French continued to pay him an annual retainer equivalent to ten million dollars.

The news of the conquest reached Florence on the evening of Michael the Med's fiftieth birthday and added to the jollity of he and Bartolomeo's already too fevered celebration.

It was well known that since Giovanni Borgia's tragic demise Cesare and his father, who had been genuinely overcome with grief and even threatened to abdicate, were attempting to create a new power in Middle

Italy. Until then the Papal States, an area covering most of what is now Lazio, Umbria, Le Marche and Emilia Romagna, were not much more than a muddle of small competing fiefdoms centered on individual cities that had good reason to be fearful of the Borgia's ambitions and looked to Louis for protection.

However, Louis was greatly in Rodrigo's debt for having interceded in his failing lawsuit to divorce Joan, the daughter of his second cousin Louis XI, on the untruthful ground that she was physically deformed and far too ugly to bed. There was some justification because their bloodlines were consanguineous but that had been disallowed as ultimately unprovable. Louis wanted to marry Anne of Brittany, Charles VIII's widow, to unite the Duchy with the French throne but the proceedings became a melodrama of allegations, charges and counter-charges until Rodrigo stepped in and granted the king's wish for annulment.

Not only that but Louis was very fond of Cesare. He had recently married Charlotte d'Albret, a sister of the king of Navarre and a lady-in-waiting at the court in Amboise, and in gratitude for Rodrigo's help Louis made him the duke of Valentinois, a large province on the southern border of Burgundy, now the department of Rhône-Alpes.

Instead of being sensible, something which Niccolò later wrote about and predicted to an inebriate Michael and Bartolomeo on the very day they received the news, Louis did not consolidate his victory but, since his main ambition was to rule the Kingdom of Naples, allowed Rodrigo and Cesare to quickly overrun Mantua, Bologna, Forlì, Faenza, Pesaro, Rimini, Camerino, Urbino and Imola and to dispossess, murder, banish or co-opt their dynastic families. In Ferrara things went peacefully because the son of Duke Alfonso d'Este was induced to marry Lucrezia.

While this bloodthirsty landgrab ravaged the countryside to the north and east, Florence was left alone despite Rodrigo's former enmity. This was not due to the diplomatic efforts of people like Niccolò and uncle Guido nor Rodrigo's awareness of the kaleidoscopically unreliable treaties and alliances between the great powers, France, Spain, Venice, Naples and the Ottoman and Holy Roman empires and lesser ones of Pisa, Lucca, Genoa, Siena and Milan. It was because of something quite simple and mundane. Something Michael and Bartolomeo knew very well though Francesco Guicciardini omitted it from his history. The fact was Cesare liked to party there.

§

When Semion Mogilevich's luxuriously appointed, jet black Sikorsky S92A helicopter touched down on an isolated pad at Rome-Urbe it was a few minutes before noon on Sunday morning. Through the window he could see a tall man in sunglasses who he did not recognize standing beside Vladimir in front of the rented Mercedes limousine. The flight began in the peace and seclusion of his estate in the Buda hills and was careful to avoid Bosnian airspace by traversing a path just to the south of Zagreb and Ancona but it had taken three tedious hours and encountered uncomfortably turbulent air over the Adriatic so he was craving a substantial liquid lunch and the sight of the stranger only added to his irritation.

The co-pilot opened the rear exit and four dark-suited bodyguards came out of the chopper into the bright sunshine. They scanned the area for anything suspicious and a few seconds later the don's obese bulk appeared in the shadow of the doorway. He was casually dressed in a capacious dark leather sport jacket and puffing on a cigarette.

"Who the fuck is that?" he growled in Russian as Vladimir hurried to the bottom of the access ladder.

"One of same CIA pricks we tell you about from hotel," Vladimir replied with uncharacteristic deference, "They follow us for the last two days."

"What does he want?"

Vladimir stooped to whisper in his ear.

"He says he has message from Signor dell'Utri."

Mogilevich tossed the butt aside on the tarmac and strolled up to the car.

"OK, what?" he demanded in strongly accented, guttural English.

Rabinovitch's muscular enormity towered above him.

"Signor Marcello won't see you," he answered, "The senator has returned to Milan and says no one in Italy believes that what you are looking for is here. He suggests you go home too. He thinks it will not be safe for you to stay."

"Who the fuck is Signor Marcello?"

Rabinovitch didn't bother responding to such an obvious bluff.

"For what it's worth, I don't think so either," he said, "But suit yourself."

The Ukrainian bear let out a malignant half-choking chuckle.

"And who the fuck are you?"

His bloated reflection in Rabinovitch's sunglasses was the only reply as the big man looked down at him for a calculated moment and then walked away.

§

The same warm spring sun had been streaming through the windows of the dining room at the Casale dei Cedri during breakfast when Lamy suggested a ride in the country to the Alban hills. Warren and Luigi were attending a final luncheon with the *Unione* so Warren was reluctantly obliged to decline.

Helen said she ought to get back to London since Barbara, her boss at the college, was expecting her to be at work in the morning but Michael said, "Oh, bugger Barbara, she's an absolute cunt," and Lamy assured her that she needn't worry about the cost. Even Warren told her she should stay. He had postponed his return to New York indefinitely because he was too curious to know how things would turn out.

They shared a laugh at his comparison of the Sistine Chapel to a daycare center decorated with fairy stories and nursery rhymes and Michael couldn't resist adding, "Or gay-care center," and that led to the imminent conclave and the gathering of the cardinals.

"When does the whole nonsense start?" Michael asked.

"A week today I'm guessing," Warren answered.

After breakfast Helen left a message at the school saying Michael was ill and she might have to stay in Rome for up to a week and then called Marta and asked her to please keep looking in on the apartment and feeding the cat. Lamy got Michael to tell Marta everything was going well and they probably wouldn't even need to stay that long for the benefit of any eavesdroppers.

He admitted he had no real plan about going to Castelgandolfo and Nemi other than continuing the game. The first was a fairly obvious choice since it was the pope's summer residence and coupled with their visit to the Vatican it ought to deepen the confusion but the lake of Caligula was more obscure.

"It's just a hunch," Lamy said, "You can tell me what you think later."

They put the Bentley's top down and all sat in the front seat with

Michael driving and Helen between him and Lamy. The traffic wasn't too bad once they passed Ciampino airport and the perfect line of the Via Appia Nuova ushered them headlong toward the beckoning green of the Colli Albani via Poggio delle Mole and Fratocchie, Santo Spirito and the Castelgandolfo Golf Club.

They saw the blue Mustang as they left the Casale and waved in greeting but didn't look carefully enough to notice the passenger wasn't Vladimir but de Groot and by now their constant shadow was almost forgotten.

"Women used to walk to Nemi from Rome," Lamy said, nearly shouting to be heard above the bluster of air billowing over the car, "Only fifteen miles but you can see it's a climb."

"Utterly glorious though," Michael yelled in reply.

Lamy wanted to go to Nemi and the lake first and then retrace their steps to Castelgandolfo for lunch and told Michael to bypass Ariccia and Genzano di Roma and follow the sign for Via Nemorense.

He looked at Helen in apology, sensing her desire to stop and explore, and said, "Sorry, I know these towns are stunningly beautiful."

"Hey man, no problem," Michael brayed in his best Yankee tourist twang, "If ya seen one, ya seen 'em all."

§

The Borgia conquest of the Romagna began with Rodrigo's dismissal of his vicars there. They were such a vile lot that Cesare was initially welcomed as a vast improvement but it wasn't entirely plain sailing. Louis provided him with three hundred cavalry and four thousand foot soldiers which, coupled with the ragtag papal army, was easily sufficient to thrust Caterina Sforza from Forlì and Imola and when Louis asked for his troops Cesare simply hired mercenaries to replace them.

His next victim was Giovanni Sforza of Pesaro and Gradara, like Cesare a bastard and sister Lucrezia's first husband. This Borgia-Sforza alliance began in 1492 with a proxy marriage when Lucrezia was thirteen, solemnized at a lavish ceremony in the Vatican a year later. But Rodrigo found out Giovanni was a spy for the Milanese and he and Cesare plotted his assassination. When the attempt failed they sued for an annulment claiming impotence to which Sforza countered with an accusation of fraternal and paternal incest. Eventually he was forced by his relatives to submit and signed a paper agreeing that Lucrezia was a virgin despite her very obvious pregnancy. In 1500 Rodrigo excommunicated him and some of his own citizens tried to kill him so it wasn't particularly difficult for Cesare to boot him out.

Then Pandolfo Malatesta was deprived of Rimini and Faenza surrendered after their teenage ruler Manfredi was captured, taken to Rome and shut up in the Castel Sant'Angelo. He was eventually murdered on Cesare's orders and his corpse tossed from Hadrian's bridge into the Tiber.

In May 1501 Rodrigo created his beloved son the Duke of Romagna and, on June 24th, Cesare stormed into Naples at the head of the French army thus causing the temporary collapse of Aragonese rule. Even the Florentine Signoria was so much in admiration of his successes that they hired him to complete the conquest of Piombino and granted him lordship thereof.

On October 30th, the Borgias, father and son, held a party in the Apostolic Palace now known as the Banquet of Chestnuts. It was a thoroughly distasteful affair, drunkenness, gluttony, naked clerics slobbering over fleshy courtesans, blowjob contests, gang rape, competitive ejaculations, but nothing really out of the ordinary, an orgy is an orgy, modern or medieval, and boringly predictable. Niccolò had been married to Marietta Corsini for just two months and declined the invitation but Michael was back from his annual voyage to England for the wool and Bartolomeo persuaded him to attend and shameful to relate, having convinced themselves it was only sensible to savor everything life has to offer, they both joined in.

By the summer of 1502 Cesare had Camerino and Urbino in his grasp and was planning his campaign against the Bentivogli in Bologna, a city which he intended to make the capital of his new Romagnan duchy, when, after a secret meeting in the castle of the Kings of Malta at Magione, some of his heretofore faithful *condottieri*, who had become nervous of his growing power, deserted and pinned him down at Imola. He was lucky they did not attack at once but sent instead to Florence in hope of obtaining approval for his destruction. It was poor judgement because the Florentines despised the Vitelli and Orsini who were the main conspirators and sent Niccolò as their envoy to offer the bereft duke shelter and assistance.

Thus it was that on October 7th Bartolomeo and Michael, once again newly arrived from England, entered Imola in their friend's company and were delighted to find Leonardo there with Salai, a young and handsome acolyte who had been part of the Vinci household for a dozen years regardless of his general loutishness and reputation for thievery.

Cesare had employed Leonardo as a military architect to improve the city's fortifications and he was in the process of measuring and mapping it. Salai had done little but complain during the month they had been there and Michael was quick to volunteer in his place. They made an eccentric sight. Michael sweating and wheeling Leonardo's cumbersome hodometer through the streets while the latter read its turning dials and made notes at every stop. It's a common device now for finding the length of a road but much lighter and more manageable.

The development of Leonardo's astonishing aerial view of the city allowed plenty of time for discussion and argument between them and, in the course of it, Michael became aware of a remarkable thing. The great man possessed not a shred of concern for the conventional morality of his fellows nor was he in any way deterred by the good or bad that might result from his ceaseless invention. The sole focus of his genius was to challenge the limits of the possible. Neither god nor man mattered beyond that.

In November he received an ambassador of Sultan Bajezid II, the ruler of the Ottoman Empire and thus the archenemy of Christendom. Bajezid wanted to know if Leonardo could design a bridge to span the Golden Horn and it took no more than a week for him to draw the plan for a magnificent structure. It would have been the longest bridge in the world and most certainly given the sultan a tremendous advantage in his desire to conquer the republic of Venice yet Leonardo's Olympian detachment was such that he submitted two plans for defending it at the same time, a movable dam to flood the Isonzo river and bar the way of the sultan's army and submersible vessels to attack the Turkish fleet from below.

Michael was in awe and admiration of such total impartiality, though well aware Leonardo's was a special case that could not be compared to the callous profiteering of moneylenders and armament manufacturers.

While all this was going on Niccolò, Bartolomeo and Cesare were plotting the downfall of his rebellious former allies. Their chosen method was guile.

Cesare was a master dissembler and promised the insurgents he would not march on Bologna and if they allowed him to retain his title of *principe* he would withdraw again to Rome and they could keep the individual principalities they had acquired. Behind their backs he wrote to Louis for assistance and bought a new army that he cleverly dispersed throughout the Romagna. To their cost the fools believed him and by the end of December he reversed the situation and cornered them at Senigallia.

Leonardo and Michael had completed the survey and returned to Florence in the middle of December but when Bartolomeo rejoined them at the end of January he described in gruesome detail the manner in which the conspirators met their demise.

Vitellozzo Vitelli and Oliveretto da Fermo were strangled on New Year's Eve, the first begging he might crave Rodrigo's pardon for his sins, the second blaming the first for the injuries he had committed. They were bound back to back with their necks wound by a single cord through which an iron bar was slowly turned tighter and tighter. Cesare put their bugle-eyed cadavers on show in the main square for three days to impress the population.

He then waited until January 18th for word from his father that Cardinal Giambattista Orsini, the archbishop of Florence at whose castle the conspiracy had been hatched, was locked up in the Castel Sant'Angelo where he was later poisoned, before putting his kinsmen Francesco Orsini, the duke of Gravina, and Pagolo Orsini, the lord of Palombara, snickeringly known as 'my lady', to death in the same ghastly way.

Michael never thought to question Bartolomeo whether he took any active part in these hideous events because he described Cesare himself standing to one side but, more than that, he assumed the gentility of his young friend could never have permitted it. Many years were to pass before suspicion crept into his mind.

§

They didn't stop in the center of Nemi because the *belvedere* was overrun with two busloads of Japanese tourists but as they began their descent to the lake on Via del Tempio di Diana they found a much better viewpoint and got out of the Bentley to have a look. The road was narrow and winding and Ciccio nearly rear-ended them as he came around the corner. He quickly put the car in reverse and backed out of sight but they noticed de Groot in the passenger seat and it made them laugh though they couldn't agree whether the incongruity was more silly than sinister.

"Incredible," Michael moaned, taking in the vista, "Where, oh where, is my fucking camera!"

"You can certainly see it's a crater," Helen observed.

"The whole area is one big volcano," Lamy told her, "But don't worry, it hasn't blown its stack for seven thousand years. Still emits sulfurous fumes and carbon monoxide though. Gas gets concentrated in depressions and kills a few cows and sheep from time to time."

"Great," Michael said, "Let's get on down there."

"Caligula knew it was a place of power. The navel of the world. Wanted to be the Rex Nemorensis. Thought he could get in touch with the life force here and become a god. Like all crass shits he ruined the place. Built two enormous pleasure ships to sail on it. Platforms for bloodsports and orgies, I'd guess. The idea of anything genuinely tranquil is ludicrous. The boats were a twentieth as long as the whole lake. It's not much more than a mile. Imagine him disturbing the peace with stupid little races or floating in circles indulging his nasty whims. Thankfully they couldn't wait to get rid of him."

"Well, he was mad, wasn't he," Helen added.

"They were all mad," Michael snorted, "They still are. Bush, Cheney, Blair, every one of those smug useless bastards sitting in the square on Friday. We're all mad. Mad, mad, mad."

"I'm starting to wish I'd let him bring the damn thing," Lamy said.

Helen laughed and Michael eyed them scornfully.

"It's marvelous in a pointless sort of way, don't you think?" he said, "That Caligula was Julius Caesar's great-great-great-nephew and the conspirators who stabbed him thirty times were led by another Cassius."

"Now how did I know you'd know that?" Lamy chuckled.

"Ha! On that occasion republican zeal was crushed in half a day."

"So what was the Rex Nemo whosamajiggy?" Helen asked, feeling a vague need to keep things calm.

Lamy gestured to Michael with a smile, 'Be my guest.'

"All right," Michael said, accepting the challenge, "Where would you like me to start? The cult of Isis? Or Orestes and Iphigenia? Or perhaps their flight from the Black Sea with the statue of Artemis hidden in a faggot of sticks? Or Diana the Huntress? Or plucking the Golden Bough? Or . . "

"Oh god," Helen groaned, "Whatever you do make it short."

"History can't be made short and stay accurate, my dear. Very well.

Diana was a goddess for women. Fertility, easy childbirth, bountiful harvests. If any guy came across her in the forest hunting in the nude she got pissed and turned him into an animal that couldn't speak about it like a stag or a pig or whatever. Her temples were sanctuaries for slaves which I think was the big deal. The Rex Nemorensis, which means king of the woods, was a runaway slave who had to break a golden bough off a tree in her sacred grove and then manage to kill the previous Rex, presumably a chap who was once a slave too, which allowed him to take over the privilege of screwing the high priestess but, of course, the rub was he too had to fight off any eligible rivals once a year. And so on and so on. How was that?"

"Wonderful. I'm impressed. Let's go."

They drove to the bottom of the hill where at the north end of the caldera the land rises above the level of the water and is primarily given over to farms and vineyards and stopped outside the boat museum where the bare bones of a replica stretched for seventy meters along the roadside.

"No need to go in," Lamy said, "Just wanted you to see how big the ships were. When they began constructing da Vinci airport they found an even more colossal barge at Ostia. It's how the obelisk in front of St. Peter's got here from Egypt. Insanity. Some pharaoh has it erected in his honor at Heliopolis around 2500 BC, then Augustus has it moved to the forum in Alexandria, then Caligula ships it to Italy where it stands in the middle of Nero's Circus witnessing a lot of Christian martyrs including old Pete getting crucified and finally in 1586 Pope Sixtus V decides it needs shifting the few hundred feet to where it is now. Took his engineers more than a year."

Michael grunted in disgust.

"Obelisks, steeples, the Trade Center Towers, all just stone cocks, pathetic symbols of impotent male power. My name is Ozymandias, king of kings. Bah! This isn't the navel of the world, it's the vagina. Caligula just wanted to defile it with his fucking boats."

"Ah," Helen said, "And what's your feeling about the telephoto lens?"

"Oh, haha, hoho, hohee."

It was several degrees hotter than up in the town. They were all sweating and Michael and Helen found the atmosphere claustrophobic. They were silent for a moment and then Lamy went on.

"The Romans dug a channel to drain the lake. Don't know why or if they ever did it but in the twenties, after they discovered the boats were lying on the bottom, Mussolini ordered it done and the surviving hulls were reconstructed on shore. The laugh is they were destroyed by fire near the end of the war. No one knows who did it but I'd bet on some local farmer. Same with the temple of Diana. Nothing much to see except a bit of crumbling wall and some two foot pillar nubbles, even though the ruins were excavated and exposed at the turn of the last century, because the owner of the land has let it all grow over."

"Can't blame him wanting to have it back," Michael muttered.

The words were a bit indistinct and Lamy leaned forward in his seat to get a good look at him.

"Feeling all right?" he asked, "About to have one of your turns? I thought you might."

"No, no, I'm fine. Just hot. Don't much like it down here."

"There's no air," Helen concurred.

"Time for lunch," Lamy said.

Michael didn't need coaxing and swung the Bentley around in the parking lot in front of the museum and they all cocked a snoot at the Mustang as they roared past it up the hill.

Shuffle Twelve

"Those trees in whose dim shadow the ghastly priest doth reign, the
priest who slew the slayer and shall himself be slain."
- Thomas Babington Macaulay (1800 - 1859)

§

In the summer of 1503 the Borgias were planning to engulf Tuscany
and poised to become the greatest power in Italy when fortune turned its
wheel.

Michael only heard about it later. He was in England on his fifth and
last errand for the Vespucci and enjoying the cool sunny days and the
company of his family. Jack and Jenny turned fourteen and their beauty
and innocence were pure enchantment.

On the evening of August 6th Cesare and Rodrigo went to dine at
Palazzo Torlonia on Via della Conciliazione a few hundred yards from the
Vatican, the recently completed and excessively lavish home of their
wealthy crony Adriano Castellesi, now Cardinal Adriano da Corneto, and
after the meal all three fell grievously ill.

The cause of their sudden sickness was hotly disputed. Some claimed
it was an ague brought on by incautious exposure to the night air, some
malaria, some a stray *fungo velenoso*, others an arsenic concoction called
'Cantarella' in the wine. With reason perhaps because the Borgias had used
the fatal distilment on many previous occasions and fondly dubbed it 'the
liquor of succession'.

It was more or less certain the wine for the dinner was a gift from
Cesare but unlikely he wished to poison himself. If he and Rodrigo were
plotting the murder of Castellesi to take his money they were being rather
careless at best. Though hard to believe it was an attempt by Cesare to
murder his father it was not impossible. Whatever the theory, Cesare and
Adriano eventually recovered but Rodrigo died after twelve days of agony,
his body so swollen it was as wide as it was long, his peeling skin covered
in mulberry-colored bruises, convulsed with fever and bleeding profusely
from the bowels.

The papal chronicler Johann Burckard, a German who bought the office of Master of Ceremonies from Sixtus IV for four hundred and fifty ducats and on whose description of such events as the Banquet of the Chestnuts modern historians rely, reported the Venetian ambassador's words, "It was the ugliest, most monstrous and horrible dead body that was ever seen, without any form or likeness to humanity." The corpse emitted foul sulfurous gases from every orifice and they had to jump up and down on it to cram it into its coffin.

The dinner marked the beginning of the end for the Borgias. The new pope, Pius III, Francesco Todeschini-Piccolomini, forbade the customary mass for the repose of Rodrigo's soul claiming it was blasphemous to pray for the damned and, immediately upon election, arrested Cesare who was conveniently convalescing in the Castel Sant'Angelo.

Like Rodrigo's uncle Alfonso, Piccolomini was a compromise candidate. Both he and his own uncle Pius II were scions of the great Sienese banking family but he was ravaged by gout and old before his time and wore the crown of Peter a scant eleven days before being succeeded by Giuliano della Rovere who named himself Julius II and was almost certainly involved in the Petrucci plot to poison him.

Pandolfo Petrucci was ruler of Siena and had been invited by Cesare to Senigallia where he would have been murdered with the Vitelli but something told him not to go.

Despite Giuliano being a tireless foe of the Borgias, in the confusion that followed Piccolomini's death Cesare managed to escape Castel Sant'Angelo and flee to the Romagna where he hoped to regroup his army. However, fortune deserted him and he was captured by one of the conspirators at Magione who had not fallen to his wrath, the tyrant of Perugia, Gian Paolo Baglioni, and his lands were confiscated and quickly subsumed within the Papal States.

In 1504 he was exiled to Spain. Ferdinand and Isabella imprisoned him in the dungeon of their stronghold at Medina del Campo. He escaped again and joined forces with his brother-in-law, King John III of Navarre, and was just thirty-one when he died fighting at the Siege of Viana in 1507.

But what has been missed by all is that Cesare had entrusted the delivery of the suspect wine to a third guest at Castellesi's supper and it was he who related the story to Michael.

§

On the way to Castelgandolfo Lamy entertained Michael and Helen with his customary monologue. Albano's surface area was nearly four times that of Nemi though their volumes were similar due to the latter's far greater depth. Albano was formed by two conjoined craters with an underwater ridge down the middle. Above was the site of the ancient city of Alba Longa, founded by Ascanius, the son of Aeneas, and destroyed by the Romans in 656 B.C. Many a patrician built a villa there in republican times and in the 1st century A.D. the emperor Domitian outdid them all with a gargantuan citadel much larger than the entirety of the modern town. It faced west toward the sea and some of it still underpinned the pope's summer residence.

Lamy had arranged lunch at the Antico Ristorante Pagnanelli since it was not in the *centro storico* which would most certainly be a zoo and lay at the north end of the residence gardens, slightly lower down but no more than a hundred meters from the gated rear entrance on Via Palazzo Pontificio.

They were shown to a terrace table with a spectacular view of the lake and two and a half hours later sat back in a state of perfect satisfaction having dined sumptuously and gratefully on seven different courses not noticing that in the process they had consumed fully five bottles of the local Colle Picchione wine. Michael was responsible for more than half the excess and so overwhelmed by the location, the view and magnificent food that he chose once again to ignore what it was inevitably going to do to his stomach.

At twenty minutes to three a gray-haired, quite ordinary-looking man who Michael judged to be a robust seventy came onto the terrace and looked about questioningly. Lamy caught his eye and stood up and the man walked over to their table and introduced himself very politely as Saverio Petrillo. Lamy asked if he would like to sit down for a glass of wine but Petrillo said that if they were ready he would prefer to go.

"Signor Petrillo is director of the Pontifical Villas," Lamy explained with a sly smile, "He has kindly offered us a brief tour."

§

Semion Mogilevich had also just finished lunch at the Russky Klub on Via Sicilia off the Via Veneto. He ordered Vladimir to wait outside with two of his henchmen where they had been served food but nothing hard to drink despite Vladimir's repeated attempts to cajole a bottle from the waitress, while perhaps not so wisely he and his other two bodyguards had knocked back a dozen Birra Moretti with an equal number of large Polish rye vodka chasers.

§

In the Mustang, De Groot nudged Ciccio awake and they both watched as Petrillo led Michael and Helen and Lamy from the wisteria-covered portico and gestured them to a waiting golf cart. Lamy sat beside him with Michael and Helen facing backwards and they whizzed up the deserted tree-lined avenue to the wrought-iron gate of the papal sanctum which was opened by two Swiss guards and they passed through without Petrillo having to slow down. Michael and Helen could see the Mustang awkwardly parked on a parallel street behind a low stone wall and both waved merrily.

De Groot saw Petrillo's arrival and assumed it would be something to do with Lamy so he had taken his picture and took more as they came out of the restaurant and he was already dialing Rabinovitch.

§

Hamas leader Sheikh Hassan Yousef travelled from Ramallah to the Al-Aqsa Mosque in Jerusalem that morning to deliver an illegal sermon and Israeli security was arresting him at that very moment. They had cleared two Zionist protest rallies against the proposed pullout from Gaza and a roadblock during rush hour in Tel Aviv and another on the Haram al-Sharif, otherwise known as the Temple Mount.

At the same time Palestinian militants from Islamic Jihad were once again lobbing mortars into two contested settlements in reaction to the death of three teenagers the day before.

§

The Alban villa had been built by Julius Caesar's rival Gnaeus Pompeius Magnus. Domitian acquired it during the reign of his father Vespasian and expanded it into a colossal palazzo as large as the dynasty's Domus Flavia in Rome with a three hundred meter long, thirty foot high cryptoporticus beneath it on the lake side, three gigantic terraces facing the sea, aqueducts, reservoirs, baths, nymphaea, a theater and a racing circus.

According to Juvenal he was fond of bizarre practical jokes. For example, at a funeral banquet to commemorate the dead of the Dacian campaign, an area of conquest that is roughly equivalent to modern day Transylvania, he had the room painted entirely black, tombstones for place-tags, naked boys dancing in black greasepaint, special dishes for the spirits of the slain, only he was allowed to speak and spoke of nothing but death and slaughter, then sent the terrified senators home with unfamiliar slaves so that they were certain they were about to have their throats cut but were instead showered with expensive gifts.

Petrillo was showing his guests the ruins of the theater where Domitian, a stickler for the letter of religious law, had condemned the Vestal Cornelia to be buried alive for promiscuity and her lovers hung upside down from crosses and beaten to death with iron rods and Lamy was just describing his assassination, Stephanus' clumsy stab wound in his groin, the frantic wrestling match on the floor, the final hacking, when Michael suddenly broke into a cold sweat, began to reel and collapsed to the ground. Petrillo had no initial intention of violating the sanctity of the papal residence itself during their visit but honest kindness forced him, with Lamy and Helen's help, to lift Michael back onto the golf cart and half carry him inside to a clinic where a nursing sister took his pulse, blood pressure and temperature and gave him a glass of water.

Michael had almost fully recovered in the theater but was sly enough not to reveal it and as Petrillo showed them out again through the gilt and marble hallways a tall thin man in the simple black robe of a Jesuit passed them walking quickly in the opposite direction. He didn't slow his pace but nodded courteously and as his pale blue eyes met Michael's for the briefest fraction of a second Michael felt a weird but unmistakeable shudder of recognition.

§

Michael the Med saw much less of Bartolomeo on his return to Florence in the autumn of 1503 because his young friend, perhaps not so young now at twenty-four though Michael often marveled that he didn't seem to age, having completed his course of study despite the many distractions of the six years in which they had known each other, took a position as doctor of astronomy at the University of Padua.

§

As soon as the golf cart reappeared through the gates on Via Palazzo Pontificio Lamy saw the Mustang take off with a squeal of tires and a second or two later his cell phone rang. It was Warren and Lamy told him to wait while they said goodbye to Petrillo and thanked him for sparing them so much of his time. Michael was itching to ask about the Jesuit but he could tell from Lamy's face that Warren's call was urgent.

"Where are you?" Lamy asked as Petrillo drove away.

"At the Casale. You need to get back. All hell's broken loose here. We've got Rabinovitch and a dozen CIA, the Carabinieri, Vladimir and Michael's old pal Mogilevich drunk as a skunk with four ugly henchmen. Luigi and I are fine but Mogilevich says he's not leaving until he talks to you."

Lamy smiled at Michael.

"We're on our way."

§

On October 24th, 1503, having nothing better to do, Michael the Med left Florence to accompany his now very good friend Niccolò to Rome where the Signoria hoped he might persuade a number of influential cardinals to cast their vote for a new pope sympathetic to the city. Francesco Piccolomini had given up the ghost on the 18th. They arrived on the 27th and the conclave began and ended on the 31st. Niccolò's artful tongue probably had little or no effect on the outcome but in those four short days the lies, bribery, ruthlessness and venality Michael witnessed were shocking even to him.

The man who would become known as *il pontefice terribile*, Giuliano della Rovere, readily agreed to such tight restrictions on his temporal power that only an idiot among the Sacred College could imagine him tolerating for one second after his coronation and the conclave itself lasted a mere three hours.

§

Michael the Mod did his best to explain his collapse as Lamy wheeled the Bentley back into Rome.

"Yup. Same as in Montewhatzit and . . "

"Montefioralle."

"Yes, yes, all right, all right. And the same as El Paso but this time it was as if the whole earth was inside one of Quasimodo's bells. I was literally shaken off my feet onto the grass."

"Do we see some common denominator here, I wonder?" Helen ventured sarcastically, "Any connection, do we think, with an insane overconsumption of alcoholic beverages?"

"Oh, fuck off," Michael replied, "I don't fall down in a faint every day."

"And you don't drink five gallons of white fucking wine every day."

"You drank a bit of wine in Florence too," Lamy reminded him.

"OK, OK, but not in El Paso. I'd only had a couple of beers. I was tired that's all. Portillo's sister Cecilia had fed me some green muck the night before and . . "

"Mescal?" Lamy asked.

Michael didn't answer.

"Ah ha!" Helen exclaimed triumphantly, "Case closed!"

§

Word of the ructions at the Casale dei Cedri were rapidly spreading by the time the Bentley purred through the gate and had already penetrated the office of the vice-president in the West Wing as well as the 26th floor of the tower block at 350 Park Avenue where Heinz Alfred Kissinger was enjoying a mid-morning massage.

"So?" he grunted into the phone.

He dismissed his teenage Balinese masseuse from the room and rolled to sit on the edge of the table with hairy pudge aflop and varicose legs dangling.

"Dick wants them all killed," the Warrior Princess replied, "He's pacing up and down the hall in his undies and stocking feet right now repeating the word 'kill' over and over."

"So lock him in his office and cut off his phone. Slip him a double dose of his meds. We have to be invisible in this, *Leibchen*."

"Being brain-damaged has made him slyer in an eerie kind of way."

"You're a fool for letting them revive him."

"I've told you a hundred times it wasn't my fault. George was speaking to the ghosts. I had to know what he was saying. I was by the balcony doors and my back was turned so I didn't see them come in with the gurney. They rushed Dick to the infirmary and by the time Andrew and I could get down there the ambulance was already pulling away."

"You should have stopped them somehow."

"Don't I know it."

There was a regretful pause and they both sighed.

"You're the lucky one for not swallowing that capsule," she added.

"Luck had nothing to do with it. It was instinct. The smell of cyanide is in my blood."

She couldn't help but chuckle.

"OK, look," he went on, "You say where they are is a private compound more or less. So keep the *paparazzi* out if you can and let whatever happens happens. I'm fed up with the whole thing."

"Warren Allen Jones is there as well and . . "

"Who?"

"You know, the atheist faggot."

"Oh, *ja*. I'm not interested in your hang-ups, *Liebling*. It's his brain I don't like. Christ, he's as old as me. Why isn't he dead?"

"He's with an Italian national."

"So what?"

"And there are the two owners of the hotel."

"Aren't they from Sicily? They won't invite trouble."

"What about our missing item?"

"To hell with it. We'll get more. It was a bad idea anyway."

"And what if this idiot really is Vespucci?"

"Don't be stupid," he snorted, absentmindedly fondling the folds of loose skin that hid his virtually ingrown member.

"It could get out of hand."

"Let it."

"And if there's an inquiry?"

"Who are you talking to? My whole fucking life has become an inquiry. As long as it doesn't lead to us, who cares? Look, their government's in crisis and they're electing a new pope. No one who matters will notice."

§

The garden of the Casale was a jumble of cars. Mogilevich's limousine had obviously skidded to a stop at the steps and Rabinovitch's Cadillac SRX was touching its rear bumper with two black vans behind it. A deep seaweed green Alfa Romeo that carried Achille Serra, the Rome Prefect, to the scene and nine assorted vehicles of the Carabinieri and Polizia lined both sides of the drive. Lazzari's Panda and the Mustang were parked on the lawn near the gate.

The Marrones were nowhere in sight and neither was Mogilevich or Serra or Rabinovitch but Vladimir was cavorting in the pool with the four henchmen, two still drunk and all stark naked. Warren and Lazzari lounged in deckchairs admiring the view, Ciccio was crouched against a cedar as far away as possible from their antics smoking by himself and fifteen men in uniform had taken up strategic positions around the villa, three with FN Minimi light machine-guns at the ready.

"What the fuck .. ?" Michael murmured as he took it all in.

"We're going to die," Helen said and smacked him hard on the shoulder.

"Sssh, children."

Lamy, obeying the curt gestures of one of the policemen, followed slowly up to the steps and on his order stopped beside the limousine. The grim-faced little man opened the driver's door and said brusquely, "*Andare all'interno.*"

"Good lord," Michael teased, "Doesn't he know who you are?"

Helen hit him again.

"Shut up, you fool. We're going to die, I can feel it."

At that moment de Groot came out of the Casale and waved them in.

Mogilevich was snoring flat out on a couch in the lobby with Rabinovitch and Serra standing apart both talking on cell phones and as Lamy and Michael and Helen entered they quickly terminated their conversations and Serra came forward to introduce himself. He could almost have served as the doppelganger of Saverio Petrillo. Their manner revealed a similar inner tension though Serra's job had led to a toughness and cynicism not evident in the papal functionary.

"I am sorry for this," he said in a cultured, slightly gravelly voice, holding his head to one side in a way that reminded Michael of Albert Finney playing Hercule Poirot, "We thought it would be better to get it over with. We will try to keep the meeting brief. Please do not worry. You are in no danger."

"Why haven't you arrested him?" Helen demanded bluntly.

There were six men in light gray suits and sunglasses ringing the walls with their hands identically folded at the crotch.

Serra looked at her with a mixture of apology and amused condescension.

"It is not so simple, Signora."

"Could we get something to drink?" Michael asked, "And I need to pee."

"Of course. Please visit your rooms if you wish."

By the time they came back down to the lobby the Marrones had brought in several trays of antipasti and a variety of liquid refreshments including three bottles of what Michael most desired, Guinness, and he quickly helped himself.

"Good lord," he said, "I love that woman."

"You should be having water," Helen reprimanded him while she poured a large glass of white wine.

Mogilevich was now sitting up bleary-eyed and staring at them blankly but when Michael turned so that he could see his face the obese don let out a gasp, rose unsteadily to his feet, staggered a few paces toward him and then stopped with his mouth agape as if he had stumbled unwittingly into the presence of the devil.

"Bessmertnaja smert' nash vladelec!" he yelled, saluting with arms held high.

Michael thought, 'Lord in heaven, please tell me he doesn't expect another vampiric ritual,' but the great bear let out a roar of tubercular laughter. The waft of stale booze, rotten bile acids and tobacco juice was quite overpowering even at three yards distance.

"You are joker, yes?" Mogilevich went on loudly after a dismaying struggle to recover his breath, "You kill Amado Portillo and now you steal from me. Is not good, not good. Why you are doing this? What do I do to you that you do this? You make everyone mad at you. Why?"

He paused to light a cigarette and Michael observed a pressure behind and beneath the muscles of his face and eyes that was truly terrifying. It seemed as if his blood carried the burden of his gruesome deeds and the heavy pulse of it was in imminent danger of bursting him wide open.

"I am not who you think," Michael said, finding his voice.

Mogilevich cackled contemptuously.

"Whaaat? You think I think you are Vespucci? Fuck no. But what you are doing at Vatican? And why you go Castelgandolfo?"

"*Sì*, Signore, we also would like to know this," Serra added.

Michael shouldn't have been surprised by the remark but he was.

"I'm a benefactor of the museums," Lamy told him simply, "Buranelli and Petrillo were just showing their gratitude by giving my friends a private tour."

"Of what, may I ask?"

"Some frescoes in the Sistine Chapel and the ruins of Domitian's villa."

The reply seemed to satisfy the *prefetto*, it was undeniably true after all and would be easy to confirm, but Mogilevich turned on Lamy with a nasty smile.

"You are as big bullshit artist as me only I have more money," he said and the vanity of the boast made him cackle even louder, "More than Berlusconi or Portillo or anyone. Why you make part in this? I am doing favor only but what you do? Why you want fuck with us? Solution is simple. Say where is what you steal and I leave you alone."

"Why don't you tell everyone what you're talking about?" Lamy responded calmly.

The don's manner suddenly cooled and hardened.

"Because is not their business," he snapped, "You know and he know and she. I promise is better for all if stop playing game."

"He's threatening us," Helen broke in forcefully, confronting Rabinovitch and Serra together, "You heard it. Why don't you arrest him?"

"*Prego*, Signora, they are nothing but words," Serra replied and then turned to Mogilevich who was still facing Lamy aggressively, "But it is time to make an end. I think you must believe them. I think they do not have what you seek."

There was an ominous silence as Mogilevich stubbed his butt on the tiled floor, lit another cigarette and dragged on it deeply.

"OK, OK," he said, raising his pulpy palms in mock compliance, "I go but is no finish. I warning you. Never be finish until. Maybe no even then."

He let his message sink in with a menacing leer and then lumbered out the door and as he went down the steps he roared at his henchmen that they were leaving. He took the wheel of the limousine, spun it around and the men hadn't a second to dry themselves or put on their clothes but were forced to sprint for the car and leap in as Warren and Luigi whistled and applauded.

Shuffle Thirteen

"No mask like open truth to cover lies as to go naked is the best
disguise."
- William Congreve (1670 - 1729)

§

For as long as anyone could remember, and for reasons as lost to
memory as one's second birthday, the Florentines and the Pisans had been
enemies but neither ever amassed power sufficient to prevail in any
permanent way over the other. The Arno flowed through both cities, their
effluent washed into it, the river was the *sine qua non* of both existences but
Pisa, which lay forty-three miles south-west of the Tuscan capital, was only
five miles from the Ligurian sea and the ease with which the Pisans were
able to conduct their trade and commerce was a constant source of envy.

In his *Commedia*, which Boccaccio dubbed divine, the father of the
Italian language, Dante Alighieri, dreamed of destroying Pisa by moving
two islands in the Arno to drown it. A century later the architect
Brunelleschi convinced the Florentine government to try something
similar by damming the river Serchio to flood the nearby city of Lucca and
though the attempt did not succeed the idea stayed dormant and
blossomed again in the winter of 1504. Leonardo had been mulling over
the viability of such a project for more than twenty years.

In the summer of 1503 Pisa was under siege for the umpteenth time
by the Florentine army and because the troops were too few for a full scale
assault they opted for the age-old strategy of laying waste the surrounding
countryside and in the process of this mindless destruction managed to
take the towns of Vernica and Vico yet still by the autumn the situation
remained at stalemate.

Thus it was that upon Niccolò and Michael the Med's return to
Florence from Rome on December 22nd they met with Leonardo to
consider his plan to divert the Arno away from Pisa entirely and forever.
He had designed siege engines capable of smashing through the upper
ramparts and mortars to rain stones on the hapless defenders as the army
rushed in but a captured Pisan had recently revealed what the citizens of

the beleaguered city most feared. It was losing their outlet to the sea, the only viable supply route for the aid they were receiving from the Genoese.

Leonardo's minutely imagined network of tunnels and canals was intended to achieve far more than the obliteration of a hated rival. The ultimate aim was to make the Arno navigable all the way from the Mediterranean and so greatly reduce Florence's vulnerability to the territorial ambitions of the French or the Spanish or any of its neighbors and to prevent the return of the Medici. Beyond that was a fervent desire for the riches of the New World.

Amerigo's letters describing his voyages south of the equator in 1499 and 1501, though Michael knew the first was little more than creative fiction he was generous enough not to let on, had been absorbed by many in his native city. His observation of the pattern of stars in the southern sky made it certain the earth was a globe and larger than Cristoforo Colombo thought and that what had been discovered was not Cathay or Cippangu but a whole new continent or even continents. Despite a few passages Michael coined quite 'un-Amerigan', to wit, 'the native women encourage venomous insects to bite their husband's private parts which causes them to swell to such a size they appear deformed and on occasion, if left unattended, break off completely and render them eunuchs,' most of the information they contained was entirely revelatory.

Michael and Niccolò sent them to Padua and Bartolomeo replied praising the utility of astronomy in human affairs, though appending the caveat that 'of the stars' influences themselves no change can happen through eternity,' and all, including Leonardo most particularly, took delight in Amerigo's statement that he had seen things 'incompatible with the opinions of philosophers.'

§

The moment the limousine disappeared the police closed in on Vladimir and Ciccio. Ciccio tried to run for it but was stopped before he could get to the Mustang. Vladimir was still sopping wet and naked and not immediately aware of his fate.

"Hey, Italy boy, wait for me!" he yelled but then saw that Ciccio was being handcuffed and turned and, without bothering to retrieve his clothes, made his own mad barefoot dash across the lawn in the other direction intending to leap over the wall. He was just a yard or two from temporary escape before he was tackled by one *carabiniere* and knocked out cold with the butt of a machine-gun by another as he started to struggle. Warren and Lazzari were hoping he would make it knowing that, had he succeeded in his vault, on the far side was a street snarled with rush hour traffic and that he wouldn't have cared.

The police car with the two of them bundled inside was the first to leave followed by the Mustang with the grim-faced officer seated stiffly at the wheel. Then the rest left at staggered intervals so as not to draw attention. As that was happening Serra came from the Casale, strolled over to Warren and Lazzari and spoke to them for several minutes. The CIA men were next and the six walked briskly to the vans and departed but Rabinovitch and de Groot waited in the SRX with its engine running until Serra finished his conversation and returned to his Alfa Romeo and as his chauffeur drove out they went after and the gate closed.

Warren and Lazzari watched them go and then walked up the steps into the Casale. Lamy had gone to apologize yet again to the Marrones but Michael and Helen were still in the lobby sitting in armchairs at opposite ends of the couch and they all stared at each other in bemused silence for a moment.

"Have a drink," Michael suggested finally, raising his glass of Guinness.

"The prefect thinks you should leave," Warren said.

"Yes, yes, we know. He says he can't protect us."

"Or won't," Helen added.

"Rabinovitch said the same. Fuckers. Making Ciccio and Vladimir the fall guys. They were harmless. Something Mogilevich definitely is not."

"Serra is a good man," Lazzari said, "He took them into custody to show he is serious. That this Mogilevich chap should back off and stay out of it."

"In that case he should have shot him on the spot," Michael countered.

"Do you think he knew what there is to back off from?" Helen asked.

"Probably. But he is still a good man. He was a student of mine for two years during the nineteen fifties at the Liceo Augusto. I was teaching English to pay my rent. He has made a distinguished career."

"He must have handled the situation quite well," Warren chimed in, "You certainly didn't have to suffer the don's charms for very long. What did he say?"

Michael leapt to his feet and roared in a terrible imitation, "Vhaarrr iss vot yoo haff stollon vrom mee! Gifff mee bacch maya plootonskium!"

"Shut up, shut up, shut up, shut up!" Helen screamed, slapping her palms on the serving table in front of her so ferociously that her glass of wine nearly toppled over and several bits of antipasto jumped off their plates to the floor.

Michael stuck out his lower lip as if he were a chastised two-year-old and sat down again.

"Did he actually say plutonium?" Warren asked doubtfully.

"No, of course not," Helen replied, "The whole thing was totally pointless and silly if you disregard the fact that he threatened to kill us."

"That was nothing but bluster," Michael demurred, "He had to save face. He's gone. They've all gone. It's over and we've got nowhere. Where the hell is Lou? I agree with you, you obnoxious savage. Why you need to trample on my modest theatrical offerings I don't know, but you're right. I can't see what there is to hang about for now. It's been a total failure."

The door from the kitchen suddenly flew open and Lamy came through it chuckling.

"What failure?" he said, "We're not dead yet. All is forgiven. Susanna and Giovanni say we can stay. They'll have supper ready in a couple of hours. And I'll give you three guesses where we're invited Tuesday night. A little shindig at Palazzo Grazioli."

Michael and Helen looked puzzled but Lazzari smiled.

"The residence of our glorious prime minister."

§

The first phase of the Arno diversion began on August 20th, 1504, with Michael acting as Niccolò and Leonardo's on site eyes and ears since they were both too busy to be in daily attendance at a project more than forty miles away, Niccolò with affairs of state and Leonardo because of mounting pressure from the Signoria to complete a gigantic patriotic mural in the Grand Council Hall of the Palazzo Vecchio. It was to be a depiction of the Battle of Anghiari in which the Italian League, a coalition of powers including Venice and the Papal States but led by Florence, defeated the Milanese on June 29th, 1440, by far the largest painting he had ever attempted at eight by twenty meters.

Leonardo's plan, which he had drawn in meticulous detail, was therefore entrusted to a well-respected hydraulic engineer named Colombino. It involved digging two deep channels a mile in length starting at the Stagno di Livorno, a brackish marsh near the sea south of Pisa, converging into a single broader one that would join with the Arno a mile upriver from the city where it had to be eighty feet wide. The two outlets into the Stagno would be sixty each and all at a depth of thirty feet over the entire distance. Leonardo reckoned a million tons of earth would have to be moved which would take the two thousand laborers the special tax levy could afford twenty-seven days.

The immense project started to go wrong almost immediately. The Grand Council wanted to keep the cost as low as possible, as civic committees always do, and Colombino, to stay in their good books and thinking he knew better anyway, began cutting fatal corners in Leonardo's carefully worked out scheme. Instead of converging the channels into one he recharted them as two, one sixty feet wide and the other forty, and both ditches were dug to a depth of only fourteen feet with the result that when the last earth was removed and the waters of the Arno diverted into them, since instead of being much deeper they were much, much shallower than the river, the banks collapsed and it didn't take more than a few minutes for the original course to be restored. The absurd fiasco lasted six and a half weeks. Michael and Biagio Buonaccorsi, Niccolò's assistant, sent countless warnings about the alterations and Colombino's poor judgement and the impending catastrophe but despite their and Niccolò's best efforts everything came to naught.

Michael involved himself because Machiavelli asked him to do so and he felt the need to repay his remarkable generosity in some fashion but it made him realize how lucky he was never to have been forced to take part in a war and he vowed to try and keep it that way.

§

The sexual molestation of children is the most repugnant and degraded of all the human species' many atrocities, unless it be to kill from a safe distance as was the case on August 6th, 1945, the day the dream of America began to wither and die.

Bernard Francis Law was an ambitious man who Karol Wojtyła appointed Archbishop of Boston in January 1984 and elevated to cardinal sixteen months later, at the same time making him titular Cardinal-Priest of Santa Susanna, the American Catholic Church in Rome, and if priests were not equally subject to the temptations of the flesh as anyone else he would probably be remembered for his good deeds. As it stands, however, he will only be remembered as a man who, during eighteen years in office, covered up the abusive predations of his colleagues upon thousands of innocent boys and girls.

The facts of this appalling betrayal of trust are well documented but what has been given too little attention is that his decisions had the direct approval of his boss. He had to wait a trifling five hundred and thirty-one days after his resignation to be appointed by the same devious hypocrite to an even more prestigious position, Archpriest of the Basilica of Santa Maria Maggiore, 'the most important monument to the Virgin Mary in all of Christendom.'

And the unforgivable toady was still archbishop *'emeritus'* in Boston as well as being a member of the Institutes of Consecrated Life, the Congregations for the Oriental Churches, Clergy, Divine Worship, Discipline of the Sacraments and the Evangelization of Peoples, the Bishops and Pontifical Councils for the Family and the Societies of Apostolic Life and Catholic Education and many other organizations dedicated to the wholesale marketing of spiritually vacant nonsense.

He was chosen to celebrate the third of the *novemdiale* masses at St. Peter's on Monday, the 11th of April, 2005, and Barbara Blaine and another member of SNAP, the Survivor's Network of those Abused by Priests, flew to Rome to protest but when they tried to hand out leaflets to the worshippers waiting to enter the basilica that morning they were prevented from doing so by the police and moved aside.

§

"I do hate that!" Michael exclaimed.

He and Helen and Lamy took a taxi to Piazza Colonna because there was very little in the way of convenient parking and he was pointing up at the statue of St. Paul that Sixtus V ordered stuck on top of the victory column of Marcus Aurelius in place of the original of the meditative emperor in 1589. It matched a statue of St. Peter he had plonked on Trajan's column near the forum two years earlier.

"It's medieval. An insult to their own history. Why doesn't someone have the damn saints taken down and the emperors put back where they should be?"

"You've got to be kidding," Lamy said.

"It's a Catholic country, you fool," Helen added.

"Oh, I'd say paganism is alive and well," Michael countered and woggled his eyes and fingers at her like a ghoul, "Whaat luurrkks beneeaatth!"

"I think it's kind of funny," Lamy went on, "Ironic that the whole column is decorated with images of misery, suffering, death and defeat."

"That's what Caesars do."

"And missionaries?"

"You can't come home in triumph if you don't go out and vanquish some barbarians by ransacking their minds."

"On this occasion proto-Germans on the Danube," Lamy told them, "Old Marcus may have wanted to be a philosopher king but he knew it was a dog eat dog world."

"Maybe St. Paul is meant as an apology," Helen ventured.

"Whaat?" Michael responded, almost shouting with incredulity, "They put him up there to show that their stupid vision is superior! They're not too big on apology in case you hadn't noticed."

"Sorry sweetie, just a thought."

They were on their way to La Rinascente, Italy's premier department store, to buy some clothes for the evening do. Unlike four years ago when Helen had been thrown for a loop by the surprise invitation to lunch at the White House and they managed to convince her the outfits she brought from England would be fine, mainly because it was so sudden that finding something else would have been impossible, this time she insisted and to their collective astonishment even Michael agreed he ought to try and spruce up a bit. His old sports jacket with academic patches at the elbows that he had worn to meet Cheney and Rice somehow didn't seem right on this occasion. Lord knows why, he said, since they were all crooks, but apparently it wasn't just going to be an informal bite with Silvio and Veronica but a larger gathering with dozens of guests.

"I thought he lived over there," Michael said, nodding to the north side of the square where several gun-toting carabinieri were wandering about in front of the doors of Palazzo Chigi.

"That's the official residence," Lamy answered, "I don't know. Maybe the other's the party house."

"Who were the Chigi?" Helen asked.

"Sienese bankers. Good pals of Julius II, Giuliano della Rovere, the pope who hired Michelangelo to bedaub the ceiling. Families intermarried.

Influential to this day. Latest one to inherit calls himself Prince Flavio Chigi Albani della Rovere. How's that for a fancy handle. Maybe thirtyish now I'd guess."

"You remember that awful fucking movie," Michael added, "Charlton and Rex. Ninety-nine percent agony, no ecstasy at all."

"You're in a foul mood."

"Sorry sweetie."

"Why Albani?" Helen asked.

"Don't know," Lamy replied.

Michael burst out laughing.

"Good lord, that's twice in two minutes he's said 'I don't know.' Are we about to be hit by an asteroid?"

§

The olive branch is a traditional symbol of peace and good will. For Noah, when the dove returned to the ark with one, it signified that his god's wrath was at an end. Jeremiah praised the blessings of grain, wine and olive oil, the Psalms sing of 'wine to cheer man's heart, oil to make him glad and bread to strengthen him' and blind Homer tells that harming an olive tree was punishable by death.

The many crimes perpetrated by Israeli settlers on Palestinian farmers and their crops are well known to the United Nations Office for the Co-ordination of Humanitarian Affairs. The aggression has been continuous since 1948 but in the first five years of the current century alone it is estimated by the Palestinian Authority's Minister of Agriculture that 1,355,000 trees were illegally destroyed in the West Bank and Gaza and roughly 446,000 of those were olives and that, in the majority of cases, the destruction was accomplished with the complicity of the Israeli army.

§

Michael the Med traveled to Padua in the second week of November with the hope Bartolomeo might be sufficiently well established to secure him some tutorial work teaching English to tide him over the winter with the intent of sailing to England on the Simonetta in the spring. He missed the annual voyage the previous summer because of his involvement in the Arno debacle and he was regretting it. In fact, he was not sure he would return to Italy afterward and his unannounced arrival at his young friend's lodgings did little to change this feeling.

To his surprise Bartolomeo was living with a young woman named Elena Lupesca. She was probably not more than sixteen but had a sophistication and allure beyond her years. She seemed completely Italian and so, since neither she nor Bartolomeo ever mentioned it, Michael never found out her family had fled their native Turnu in Wallachia at dawn on the day Mehmet I took control of the city in 1415 and her birth name had been Lupescu.

Michael sensed that she was pregnant and their accommodations were too cramped and the air too filled with tension to stay so he spent three nights at an inn that he could ill afford and, after an evening together in which they avoided the subject and both got horridly drunk, kissed Bartolomeo farewell.

§

Helen was now in her middle-forties, admittedly half a stone heavier than she had been when she leapt on the vice-president's back to prevent him from shooting Michael and set off his regretfully not quite fatal heart attack, but still what people like to call a handsome woman, reasonably well put together with typically English stovepipe legs, and she had chosen a claret-colored full-length evening gown with matching shawl that revealed a tantalizing glimpse of gently blossoming cleavage and a pair of black Roberto Botticelli knee-length leather boots. She had spent the afternoon at a *parrucchiera* and her naturally ash-blonde hair was freshly styled and shining.

Lamy suggested to Michael that he replicate as closely as possible the look of the fateful occasion when Amado Portillo dressed him up as Vespucci and though Michael was at first adamant in refusal he finally gave in and, following his grudging description, Helen and Lamy found a virtually identical Egyptian blue double-breasted suit, a pearl shirt and silver cufflinks and lapis lazuli tie and, instead of his scuffed Hush Puppies, a pair of elegant highly-polished slip-on loafers.

Lamy brought a blazer and slacks from New York which looked just fine after Susanna pressed them and Warren and Lazzari said they were too old and lazy to care and came decked out in the same slightly rumpled suits they wore to the opening dinner of the *Unione.*

160

Lamy had no idea why they had been invited. He had only met Berlusconi once and though he was approached in the late sixties to invest in Milano 2, the huge apartment city that was the foundation of the prime minister's wealth, he was warned off because of suspected Mafia involvement. So at twenty past nine that evening, as they stopped at the front entrance on Via Plebiscito to make their identity known and the guards waved the Bentley through into the inner courtyard of the palazzo that Lamy informed them belonged to the Gottifredi family in the mid-seventeenth century, one of whom became the ninth Superior General of the Society of Jesus, and was called the Palace of the Cat because of a statue found in a nearby Temple of Isis that was now set above the rear door that resembled one but was more than likely a monkey, none of them had the slightest notion what to expect.

"*Un scimmiotto*," Lazzari said, "Our pet name for him."

"What's it mean?" Helen asked.

"Little monkey. Silly man," he told her and they all shared a chuckle at the coincidence.

§

Given the time of year Michael the Med decided to return to Florence and was grateful that Niccolò employed him in translating a number of diplomatic dispatches to the English court regarding Catherine of Aragon's tricky situation. He was as usual playing both ends against the middle since, due to Louis XII's blundering, Spain was again in full control of the Kingdom of Naples and her mother Isabella had died on November 26th throwing the throne of Castile to her half-mad sister Joanna. This caused Henry VII to rethink her betrothal to his second son and he was holding her hostage in Durham House because the value of her dowry was now uncertain.

Catherine's first husband Arthur, the future Henry VIII's older brother, succumbed to the 'sweating sickness' on April 2nd, 1502, a devastating form of haemorraghic fever that swept through England on numerous occasions during the sixteenth century. She too had taken ill with it but recovered. And, strange as it may seem, on the day of Berlusconi's party at Palazzo Grazioli the World Health Organization announced the death toll from the outbreak of Marburg virus in Angola had reached two hundred and three.

Whether it is more tenable to be optimistic or pessimistic about the future of the recklessly burgeoning human species in its ongoing contest with rapidly mutating microscopic organisms, Michael the Med's heart was filled with happy expectation as he boarded the Simonetta at Livorno on April 2nd, 1505. He nearly arrived too late because the Pisans cut off the main road and the wheat caravan with which he was traveling was forced to detour through the hills but even had he known ten years would pass before he would see Bartolomeo or Italy again it could not much have dampened his spirits.

Shuffle Fourteen

"We must never forget that we are dealing with a semi-savage people
with extremely primitive concepts."
- Moshe Smilansky (1874 - 1953)

§

There were only about twenty people in the grand living room as
Michael and the others were ushered in. They all had their backs turned to
the door and faced a colossal television and were groaning in
disappointment because Paolo Maldini had just missed a goal and it was
another four minutes until the referee blew his whistle for half time before
anyone noticed they were there. Lazzari explained it was the second leg of
the Champions League quarter final between Berlusconi's AC Milan and
their perennial rivals Internazionale and the prime minister ought to be
pleased because with only forty-five minutes left to play his team,
familiarly known as *I Rossoneri*, were ahead on aggregate 3-0.

Lamy told them the names of those he recognized. Berlusconi, of
course, and his wife Veronica Lario, a former low-budget film actress
twenty years his junior, his lawyer Niccolò Ghedini who maintained a
lucrative practice in Padua and who Michael observed would make good
casting for Lucifer, Cardinal Law in mufti, friend and advisor Marcello
dell'Utri who despite convictions for tax fraud and conspiring with the
Mafia was now a senator from Lombardy, Mel and Betty Sembler, a frail-
looking white-haired man sitting alone on a crimson 17th century chaise
in a gold lamé jumpsuit who Lamy was surprised to see but Lazzari
confirmed as Dean of the College of Cardinals and odds-on favorite to be
the next pope Joseph Ratzinger and, standing behind the chaise with a
hand protectively placed on the old buzzard's shoulder, his astonishingly
handsome tanned blond fiftyish lover and private secretary Georg
Gänswein.

"What the fuck are we doing here?" Michael whispered.

Helen was wide-eyed and ready to bolt.

"Smile, children, and stand your ground," Warren added softly as Mel
and Betty Sembler broke from the chatter and made their way towards

them.

"I hate this prick," Lamy mumbled under his breath.

"Lou, Lou, well, well," Sembler began with an empty chuckle and without offering his hand, "Slumming as usual, I see."

"You should have told us you were in Rome," Betty admonished.

At first sight one might have thought them innocuous enough. A pair of benign septuagenarian lovebirds yet Michael knew instantly they were the kind of Jews who give Jews a bad name.

"My god, yes, I remember you," Sembler said, scrutinizing him from head to toe after Lamy did the introductions, "Christ yes. You remember, hon, don't you? We saw it all on TV."

"I sure do. He was wearing the same suit."

A slight twang betrayed her middle-class Tennessee childhood.

"Damn, that was a fine thing you did," Mel continued.

"Um, what exactly?" Michael asked, sensing the worst.

"Killing Amado Portillo."

"Ah, yes, hm, well, I didn't actually . . "

Michael's peripheral vision could feel the others slinking away.

"Come on now, don't be so damn modest, it was a fine, fine thing. Too bad about that DEA agent Borden."

"Um, Bowman. Chuck Bowman."

"Yes, that's right. The man was a damn hero."

Michael gritted his teeth assuming he would now have to endure a rehash of the whole demoralizing experience but he was wrong because the Semblers immediately started talking about themselves. How they had been the founders of a revolutionary adolescent drug treatment program called Straight which had run into problems as many things do if they're before their time but they hadn't let that stop them and were now channeling their passion into something called Drug Free America and for her untiring efforts Governor Jeb Bush, who liked to call her 'ambassadorable', had created a special Betty Sembler Day and she was sure she would soon be inducted into the Florida Women's Hall of Fame. For some unfathomable reason Mel pulled out his wallet and flipped through a sequence of photographs of himself with Ronald Reagan and George Bush Sr., with Dick Cheney and his daughter, Donald Rumsfeld and Colin Powell, of he and Betty with George Jr., Laura and the Netanyahus and, which Michael could scarcely believe, with Nancy Reagan and Princess Diana in the same shot, but mercifully their self-serving twaddle was cut short by Berlusconi shouting for everyone to come and watch the second half of the game.

"Oh-oh, the master calls," Mel said with an insider's indulgent wink, "We'll talk later. I forgot to ask what brings you to Rome."

Lamy and Warren filled Michael in about the Semblers on the drive back to the Casale.

Mel, or 'Buddy' as he was better known, was born in St. Joseph, Missouri, the son of a barkeeper bookie. He and Betty were sweethearts at university and afterward returned to Dyersburg, Tennessee, where her father ran a 'style shop' for ladies. A bit of a comedown for a gal whose great-grandfather had owned a plantation in Greenville, Mississippi, but Mel took a job there and convinced the elder Schlesinger to expand. By 1970 they were able to move to Florida and did so well building vast shopping malls in ecologically sensitive areas that they now lived in an exclusive enclave constructed entirely on tongues of reclaimed land in the shallow waters of Tampa Bay appropriately called Treasure Island.

From the beginning they knew the high career value of fundraising for the Republican Party and had personally contributed huge sums to the presidential campaigns of both Poppy Bush and his wayward seed for which they had been rewarded with prestigious ambassadorial stints in Australia and Italy. An annex to the embassy in Rome had been recently purchased and refurbished courtesy of the American taxpayer to the tune of well over a hundred million dollars and was now christened the Mel Sembler Building, an honor never before bestowed on a sitting diplomat not even Benjamin Franklin.

Following a family row in which one of their sons had thrown Mel down a flight of stairs in a drug-aggravated rage, or so was the claim, they decided to get into rehabilitation and made a fortune with a countrywide chain of so-called treatment centers before they were shut down by a landslide of allegations of abuse including savage beatings, rape, torture, starvation, sleep deprivation and inmates being locked up in their own excrement. The hands-on sadist in charge of this operation was a megalomaniac named Virgil Miller Newton who styled himself Father Cassian after the 4th century Scythian ascetic. Tragically, by 1993, when the Sembler's licence was finally revoked for 'cruel and inhuman attempts at behavior modification,' twelve thousand teens and pre-teens had 'graduated' from these medieval horror chambers but a network of corrupt and powerful friends assured the owners never faced prosecution.

To Michael it was no surprise that cold phony social-climbing sycophants such as these, whose sole interest in life was money and the influence it could buy, were implacable defenders of the State of Israel right or wrong and on the board of the Florida Holocaust Museum. He found it utterly depressing that a bunch of Zionist thugs had been allowed to transform the terrifyingly common atrocity of genocide into 'holocaust' and by tarring any dissenting voice with the brush of anti-semitism forever hogged the pain of it for themselves as if this particular instance were somehow a special case. Their mendacious PR-job had irremediably deformed the polity of the world.

Michael noticed Lamy talking with Berlusconi out of the corner of his eye and Helen with his wife Veronica but as the second half began everyone turned their attention to it. The five drifted together again and Lamy whispered in his ear, "He's got an ongoing court case with a guy who stole a penis pump from his garbage and is trying to sell it on eBay."

Michael barely managed to control a guffaw.

"Berlusconi?"

"No. Mel."

§

As the whitewashed walls of Cadiz made their appearance four miles off the starboard bow of the Simonetta on April 13th Michael the Med stood on the rolling deck and thought of Amerigo but not because he was in Seville getting married. The smell of the open ocean and its ever more alluring majesty as they sailed on toward Cape St. Vincent stirred old longings within him, desires that were not to abate even in the bosom of his beloved family.

He arrived at Billingsgate farm not only on the very day and very hour but at the very minute that Jane gave birth to a second set of twins, also a boy and a girl, whom she named Billy and Bess to please Bryan, her aforementioned local swain and lover, who had himself been born in that very cottage.

The little miracles entered the world at twenty-two and twenty-six minutes after eight on the evening of April 29th which naturally meant that Michael and Bryan and Arthur and Jack had to toast their good health and fortune until well into the morning leaving Elaine and Jenny and a hired nursemaid to tend.

At the end of June Elaine and Arthur celebrated their seventh anniversary and in July Jack and Jenny turned sixteen. Arthur and Michael became fifty-five and fifty-six respectively in October and on January 17th of the new year Elaine was forty-six, yet no one would have guessed. Her marriage had proved a great blessing and given her volatile spirit a mature stability and peace and Arthur too was marvelously hale and hearty and full of the joy of simple things and though Michael was also his experiences had unsettled his inner life and imbued it with a searching restlessness that was not easy to ignore.

On February 2nd news came that Martha Bud was ill and he and Jack went up to London and were in time for Jack to hold his grandmother's hand as she died. They stayed for a week afterward with Robert Fisher and were able to see Thomas again and Erasmus and their mutual friend Thomas More. One dreary afternoon Erasmus and More took them to Durham House to meet Catalina de Trastámara y Trastámara and Cuthbert Tunstall, who was to become bishop of the great city, Master of the Rolls and Lord Keeper of the Privy Seal despite his illegitimacy. Like Thomas Grey and Robert, Tunstall was a student of Michael's at Eton and a recently graduated Doctor of Laws from the university of Padua where he had made the acquaintance of Bartolomeo and Elena Lupesca.

The house was entered through a private courtyard on the Strand. Michael and Jack thought it more like a palace with its chapel and lush gardens running down to the Thames but its episcopal opulence had clearly failed to impress the prim Spanish widow. Notwithstanding her unrevoked betrothal to the younger brother of her dead husband and the future king, the necessary dispensation for which had been one of the first acts of Giuliano della Rovere on his accession after years of malicious dithering by Rodrigo Borgia, she did little but complain about money and her lack of it. She had just turned twenty and though she was well educated and spoke four languages and had a reputation for intelligent and scholarly discourse on humanistic matters Michael found her opinions rigid and humorless.

There was discussion of the voyages to the New World, in particular More wanted Michael to tell him everything he had heard from Amerigo, and after tea the sky cleared enough for a stroll to the river. More took the occasion for a virtual soliloquy on his ideas for a book about an imaginary ideal society set on an Atlantic island he called Utopia. It was partly to be a satire on contemporary English life which was all very well and interesting but then they came to the subject of slavery and More said without a qualm that every household would have two and Michael was appalled that no one else in the company seemed to find the slightest objection. Luckily Jack had gone ahead and did not overhear the discussion. Michael knew he would not have remained silent.

Worse still was More's proposal for citizens who did not believe in God. Though religious tolerance would be central, and even various forms of pagan worship allowed, monotheism, and Christianity most of all, would be preferred. Atheists, by contrast, would be considered a danger to the state and forced to attend remedial classes until brought to an understanding of their error. It was the only time the princess betrayed any animation and as she said, "Hear, hear, Master More, hear, hear!" in a startlingly shrill, unpleasant voice, Michael saw such a cruel expression come into her eyes it made him shiver.

§

It had been obvious during the first half of the game that the home fans at Stadio Giuseppe Meazza were in the mood for blood and in the twenty-eighth minute of the second half things erupted. Internazionale had scored but it was disallowed for a foul and a moment later some yahoo in the stands behind AC Milan's goalkeeper threw a flare that hit him on the shoulder, burning him quite badly and causing him to collapse. The referee had little choice but to stop play and order the teams to leave the field.

Berlusconi was screaming obscenities at the screen as a flunkey came into the room and whispered in his ear. He excused himself brusquely saying he was wanted on the telephone.

Ratzinger broke the ensuing silence.

"We were expecting violence last week," he said softly in rather difficult to understand, strongly-accented English, "In Liverpool. Not here. But it is what happens in any society without faith."

"It is so true, Eminence," Law agreed.

Even Michael knew the first leg of one of the other quarter-finals was the first time Juventus and Liverpool had played each other since the 1985 final in Brussels when thirty-nine people were crushed to death in a riot started by Liverpool supporters.

"What must we do to bring the young to Jesus?" Ratzinger sighed, raising his slender white hands in a gesture of despair and then carefully taking another small liqueur glass of green liquid from an offered tray. Two very pretty girls in slightly naughty outfits had been circulating all the while with drinks and hors-d'oeuvres. Michael opted for brandy, since they'd never heard of Guinness, and Helen white wine and they had already consumed several.

"My god," Michael whispered to her, "Look, he's guzzling absinthe."

"You don't know that," she replied, "It could be anything."

"True. Maybe it's peppermint schnapps."

Berlusconi came back looking calmer and suddenly the teams were on the field again and play resumed but it only lasted a few moments because the fans started flinging flares again as well as other debris and the referee stopped the game for good. There were fires in the stands and parts of the field looked like a war zone and Berlusconi snapped the television off with a remote.

"Quale feccia!" he shouted and then went on in a combination of stumbling horribly-pronounced English and rapid-fire Italian, "I'd like to line them up in front of a fucking firing squad! Now I am forced to speak to the press and the television. In the morning they will demand it. I will promise drastic measures. What fucking drastic measures? My hands are tied. Mussolini was such a lucky bastard. He could do any fucking thing he wanted! I hate democracy."

He burst out laughing and took a glass of white wine from one of the girls while at the same time fondling her half-exposed buttock.

"You wouldn't look so good upside down," dell'Utri observed wryly.

"That guy looks like *Il Duce*," Michael muttered to Helen behind his hand, "Don't you think so?"

"I think we should go," she hissed.

"Perhaps it is time to rekindle our glory days," Ratzinger suggested with a tiny sideways smile and a Hadean gleam in his eyes, "They would not behave so badly if they had seen a real *auto-da-fé*."

Everyone laughed appreciatively.

"Nothing works without teeth."

He stretched out a set of soft limp fingers and Gänswein took them and helped him to his feet and as the others regrouped into different conversational knots he turned toward Michael and Helen with Georg at his elbow to steady him and began shuffling slowly towards them. Blood-red suede slippers peeked from beneath the flared legs of his jumpsuit and a line from The Rime of the Ancient Mariner flashed through Michael's mind as they stood transfixed, 'He holds them with his glittering eye, they cannot choose but hear . . '

"They tell me you come from the Vespucci," Ratzinger said, taking Helen by one hand and holding it gently in both of his. His finger ends were slightly flattened and reminded Michael of his grandmother's. He wondered if it could be from playing the piano but didn't know if Ratzinger also had that talent. He was an eerie amalgam of the long deceased old lady and Count Orlok.

"Yeees," Helen replied uncommittally, drawing her hand away, "It was all rather a long time ago."

"So we're only very little from," Michael added clumsily.

He could feel his cheeks getting red. He looked over at Lamy chatting to Berlusconi and dell'Utri and wanted to strangle him.

"*Un petit, petit peu,*" he went on and then corrected himself, "No, silly me, not *peu,* only a tiny *po, un piccolo po,* no, no, sorry, *eine kleine, kleine, kleine.*"

Ratzinger gazed at him with a milky expression of benign amusement.

"Might it not be traced much farther?" he asked with what appeared to be genuine curiosity, "You went to Castelgandolfo and were shown the Alban villa of Domitian. Have you found some connection? I am fascinated."

"No, no. No connections where none intended," Michael answered with a silly giggle and then realized he was paraphrasing Samuel Beckett, god knows the situation was absurd, "Or is it puns? No, no, of course not, it's symbols. No symbols where none intended, that's it."

Ratzinger went on as if he hadn't been listening.

"There is a Vespucci who might be willing to shed light on what you seek. Would you like to meet him?"

Michael nearly fell over.

"Oh, ah, yes, well, yes, we would, wouldn't we, um, sweetie?"

Helen stared at him as if he had finally lost his last remaining marble.

"Good lord, yes," he burbled, "Come on, sweetie, you know it would. Be, oh yes, quite absolutely marvelous."

Ratzinger looked at him oddly but there was nothing malicious in it.

"Then I will see what can be done," he said and turned away.

Gänswein gave them a winning George Clooney smile as they departed.

"What's wrong with you?!" Helen demanded once the Tennessee Williams' twosome were out of earshot, covering her fury with a party face, "Why do you become such a brown-noser? Don't you have even a vestige of spine? He's just some dreadful old ponce. What on earth does he matter to you?"

"He doesn't," Michael replied and then dropped his head on her shoulder in mock despair, "Oh god, kill me, it's altogether too awful. Never been able to stop it. Like everyone else, I suppose. Going to jelly in front of celebrities. But didn't you hear what he said?!"

"Oh, shut up. Lou's coming this way with Berlusconi."

"It's a Barnum and Bailey world," Michael croaked tunelessly.

§

By the end of March the cherry trees at Billingsgate were coming into bud and Michael the Med was growing impatient. He and Jack had spent many days and hours together over the course of the winter dreaming up a secret plan and on April 1st they sprang it on the others. Michael knew if Jane hadn't had the new twins she would never have given her consent but in the end she relented and on April 3rd, after an emotional farewell, he and his beloved grandson set off on the road for Portsmouth.

§

Unlike the almost neurasthenic cardinal, Berlusconi was charming and full of energy. His ribald good humor and engagingly toothy smile might not be to everyone's taste but Michael was pleased that he immediately asked to be called Silvio and addressed him in the same manner.

"No, no, is not for you, Michele," he divulged with a peninsula-engulfing grin, "We spikka da Inglish for Mel and Betty. Only America has the chutzpah to send *ambasciatore* who no spikka Italiano!"

"*Straordinario*," Michael concurred.

Helen shot him a warning glance but it didn't take more than a minute for Michael and the media magnate to 'hit it off,' as they say, and by the end of the evening they were both absolutely pie-eyed and sworn bosom buddies and the same went for Warren and Luigi and Ratzinger and Gänswein who spent the whole time on the couch swapping gay jokes in seven different languages and laughing until they cried. Lamy got stuck into a discussion on the politics of the two Italys, north and south, with dell'Utri and Ghedini and off somewhere in another room Veronica and Helen and three women who Michael had assumed were wives but may not have been snorted cocaine. Only Mel and Betty seemed left out because no one was bothering to speak English any more and stayed most of the time beside Cardinal Law. Michael didn't notice when they left but the three of them were gone long before the festivities broke up and thankfully Helen didn't find the moment to start in on child molestation with the cardinal and Mel never did get a chance to ask his question.

Berlusconi took Michael into his private office and after a dozen brandies he had blabbed pretty much everything there was to know about the plutonium and Amado Portillo. It wasn't that he was being careless or stupid, not at all. In his drunken mind he was the one playing the fox.

They each spoke their native tongue throughout the unlikely colloquy and it worked surprisingly well because though neither was any good in the other's language they were both natural histrionics and as they proceeded to get more and more blotto they talked slower and slower and, as sometimes can happen on such occasions, began to communicate almost telepathically.

Silvio became helpless with hysterical laughter at Michael's re-enaction of the vampire ritual in Amado's penthouse in El Paso and Condoleezza taking it stoically in the behind from a hairy Russian mobster. He confided he had never liked her and always wanted to prick her façade.

The subject led to 9/11 and the prime minister agreed completely that the official version was bullshit. The whole world knew it but, after all, such nasty dealings weren't unusual. The general public were sheep. Fools who were easily made to believe anything. Mindless slaves to be whipped and moulded into any shape the ruling class desired. It was the way human society worked best. Keep them docile with bread and circuses and as soon as they get out of line bring in the centurions. He was no different than the Caesars. He cared for his people's welfare but understood they had no real desire, or indeed use, for the truth.

Michael asked if he wasn't concerned about his political future in light of the recent election losses but he chuckled and said he would survive. He would resign if necessary and then reshuffle and go on with a minority if it had to be so but he would survive.

"What about all the court cases?"

"Ha!" Berlusconi scoffed, "The tip of an iceberg! You can't be in politics, here or anywhere, if you want to avoid scandal. Look at Prodi, Romano Prodi, my nemesis, my rival. He's the KGB's man in Europe. I can't prove it any more because the Russian colonel who says so got shot on Saturday. I'd like to have fucked him in the ear just like he wants to fuck me with all this Mafia shit. Now I have to kill the guy who was our connection to the colonel because he knows it was us who wanted the information. It's a dirty business. That little bastard Sembler is putting the screws on me right now to hush up an investigation into the death of one of our secret service agents. American troops opened fire on his car near Baghdad airport. By mistake, they claim. Bush called me to say how sorry they were but it's me that has to deal with our magistrates. I'm telling you, Michele, sometimes I wonder why I bother. I have to dance so fucking fast for the shit not to stick to me it makes my head spin."

Michael, of course, wondered who his ebullient and ever more inebriated host thought he was. Berlusconi didn't ask and Michael could only assume that he must know everything about him. An impoverished and powerless nobody to whom it was quite safe to confess but just after one o'clock in the morning he burst out laughing all over again and said, "*Incredibile!* The idiots had it stolen from under their noses! And they're the ones who bitch about nuclear security! Come on, Michele, tell me where it is. You and your Frenchy billionaire who's even richer than I am, come on, you're just fucking with them, no? If you need I can help you move it. You have to keep moving it if you don't want them to find you. Who are you working for, the Jews? Come on, it must be the Jews."

'Aha,' Michael thought, 'It finally comes out. The reason for the invite and the old pal routine.'

"*Mi dispiace,*" he said, "I haven't got a clue."

§

Michael the Med took Jack on his new adventure to introduce him to the wider world and broaden his outlook but the ugliness of the scene that greeted them as they arrived in the port of Lisbon on April 19th was something far, far beyond his intent.

King Manuel I of Portugal ordered the Jews in his realm to convert to Christianity in 1496 so he could marry the Infanta of Spain. Unfortunately this Isabella, eldest child of Ferdinand and Isabella, elder sister of Joanna the Mad, Catherine and Maria, died giving birth to their son Miguel in

1498, and Miguel, christened *La Paz*, would have become the ruler of a united Portugal and Spain had he not snuffed it before his second birthday.

Many of the Jews who chose expulsion rather than deny their ancient faith were stopped by soldiers as they tried to leave and forcibly baptized by zealous priests. These 'new Christians', or *marranos* or *conversos* as they were called, were granted a period of thirty years in which their beliefs would not be too closely examined but they remained a suspect minority to say the very least.

The plague had ravaged Lisbon during the month of March and naturally, in a society steeped in the superstitions of the Catholic church, the populace of the city were looking for a scapegoat to blame for their loss and when, two days before Michael and Jack debarked, some *conversos* were found to be celebrating Passover in the traditional manner all hell broke loose.

On the morning of the 19th, in a Dominican church where an 'unearthly light' was emanating from a crucifix and a reliquary in glass on display in a side-chapel, some *marranos* foolishly attempted to show that the 'miracle' was due to quite natural causes and one of their number was dragged from the church by an enraged female worshipper and killed.

As Michael and Jack came ashore two Dominican friars with crucifixes in hands raised high were screaming 'Heresy!' at the top of their lungs. They were followed by a frenzied mob, swelled by Dutch and Flemish lascars attracted by the outcry, that stormed through the streets murdering not only *marrano* men, women and children but any Christian known to be associated with them. The insanity went on for forty-eight hours and resulted in the death of over four thousand people.

Michael was familiar with Lisbon and led Jack to the house of Bartolomeo Marchionni where they found sanctuary. Several times on the way he had to hold Jack's passions in check, an admirable instinct to intervene in the butchery which would have brought the boy's own life to a certain end.

Marchionni was himself of one quarter Jewish ancestry though a baptized Catholic. His magnificent *palacio* had been turned into an armed fortress and he was harboring many of his Jewish business partners and associates in the slave trade with their families inside its walls. One of the wealthiest of them all, João Rodrigo Mascarenhas, had been slaughtered with his wife and children and his house completely demolished.

They could only wait for the manic explosion of viciousness to burn itself out and while they did Michael and Marchionni caught up on many things and Jack listened. Of course, they spoke of Amerigo, of his marriage and his letters, three to Lorenzo di Pierfranceso de' Medici concerning his two actual voyages to Brazil and one to Piero Soderini describing four voyages, the first and last of which were pure fiction. Imaginary or not they had become known as far away as Germany where Marchionni heard a great world map was in the process of completion naming the new continent or continents, if such they proved to be, after Amerigo. Columbus, according to a recent letter Marchionni had received from him, was languishing in Valladolid and near death but apparently bore no resentment. They talked of the amazing rapidity with which the once daunting expanse of the great ocean had become a commonplace thoroughfare for trade and that just in the previous year Marchionni had been able to develop a sugar plantation on Santo Domingo. He was intending to have it worked by African slaves and had several serving in his household. Only Jack's still vestigial grasp of Italian kept him quiet.

Dom Manuel was deeply religious and not without a sense of fair play and ordered the Dominican friars garroted and burned and the other ringleaders of the massacre quartered and hanged as well as anyone found guilty of murder or pillage and their property confiscated.

The foreign sailors, however, who had so lustily taken part, were allowed to leave unpunished on their ships.

Marchionni, acting on the request Michael sent from Billingsgate farm on February 12th, had made the necessary arrangements and on April 30th, eight days after Easter Sunday, Michael the Med and a sadder, wiser, brooding Jack boarded the Lagrima de Cristo, one of nine caravels under the command of a crippled gnarl-knuckled seventy-four-year-old named Diogo de Azambuja and, with Michael as captain at the helm, set sail for the island of Mogador on the Moroccan coast of Africa.

Shuffle Fifteen

"Monotheism is easily the greatest disaster ever to befall the human race."
- Eugene Louis 'Gore' Vidal (1925 - 2012)

§

"Christ, I remember now!" Michael exclaimed at breakfast, "It's all coming back to me!"

"We're surprised you're alive," Helen said dourly.

"You're a fine one to talk after the tonnage you stuffed up your nose. OK, maybe I dreampt it but I don't think so. At one point Berlusconi asked me if I believed in vampires, which I didn't find odd because I imagine most Italians do, but when I replied that for me the jury was out on the subject he smirked and said I ought to because Ratzinger was one!"

"I wouldn't call it vampirism exactly," Warren chuckled, "But you missed quite a treat. At midnight two very well-endowed young black men came in and proceeded to perform a striptease and sex show and at the culmination of it our next pope gave the last few strokes to one of their beautifully swollen members and with an expression of elfin delight ejaculated it into the other one's waiting mouth."

"Yuuccch!" Helen exclaimed and put down her knife and fork, "Warren! Did you have to? God, what awful people! Do you know what you missed out on, sweetie? Or maybe you didn't. Maybe you were both at it in there."

"At what?" Michael said, feigning offence.

"You could have availed yourself of any one of those young girls."

"Really? What a shame."

"At least two of the gentlemen I was chatting with did," Lamy told them, "What did you and *Il Cavaliere* talk about for so damn long? I nearly came in to rescue you."

"I was being my usual brilliant self," Michael answered.

Helen snorted in disbelief.

"Now, now, don't be nasty. I found out why we were invited."

"Anything we hadn't thought of before?" Lamy asked.

"He wanted to know about the plutonium. He offered to help us move it. I think he really might have enjoyed messing with our American friend's minds. But no, I guess not. Someone definitely put him up to it."

"No need to wonder who," Lamy said wryly.

"He insisted we must be working for the Jews," Michael added and Lamy laughed out loud.

"How utterly ridiculous," Helen said.

"Not really," Lamy demurred.

"I wondered how his wife could tolerate it," Helen went on, "But then I got stuck talking with her and those other dreadful cows."

"There, there," Michael teased, patting her hand, "You managed."

"Oh, shut your cake-hole."

"They got together after he saw her topless in a play," Lazzari chimed in.

He had stayed overnight because of the lateness of their return.

"Called *Il magnifico cornuto*, The Magnificent Cuckold, if you can believe it. She's no angel. She's had plenty of affairs herself."

"With Cacciari, no?" Warren mentioned rhetorically.

"So they say. You would know better than I."

"And who's Cacciari?" Helen asked.

"A friend of Warren's. One of our notable communist philosophers. Also famous for his good looks."

"Ow, that must hurt," Michael observed to everyone's amusement.

"He's running again this month for mayor of Venice."

"I asked Silvio if he was worried about his political career but he didn't seem to be at all."

Lazzari chuckled.

"Would you be if your chief rival was a man we call La Mortadella because he's so bland he almost lacks a personality?"

"You mean, um, Baloney?" Michael asked.

"Si, mortadella. His name is Prodi. Romano Prodi."

"Yes, that's it, sorry. Berlusconi told me he's a Russian spy."

"They've been trying to pin that on him for years."

"Is it true?"

"Maybe. I don't know. They don't care if it's true or not. Once such things are established in the public mind it doesn't matter."

§

As they spoke Walter Dröge, a fifty-five year old Ku Klux Klan member and leader of the white supremacist Heritage Front, was shot to death in an east side apartment in Toronto, Canada. Likeminded dimwits immediately layed the blame on ZOG, or the Zionist Occupation Government, but as it turned out Dröge was also a drug dealer and his murderer just a crazed addict.

Dröge and nine other gung-ho good old boys once plotted to overthrow the government of Dominica but were arrested by FBI agents in New Orleans on April 27, 1981, before their chartered boat left the dock. It was loaded with automatic weapons, shotguns, rifles, handguns, dynamite, boxes of ammunition and a black and white Nazi flag. Their intent was to return the former prime minister of the tiny island to power and create a white supremacist country, a brainless plan whose timely thwarting is better known as The Bayou of Pigs.

§

Lamy as usual regaled them with tidbits of the day's news. A panicky recall by the College of American Pathologists of test-kits they had distributed world-wide containing the strain of Asian flu that killed millions in 1957 and to which no one born after 1969 would be resistant. The National Geographic Society and IBM's joint plan to collect DNA samples from people on every continent to track *homo sapiens* migration out of Africa. The homosexual cannibal Armin Meiwes, who sought a willing victim on the Internet and, having received more than a hundred replies from his native Germany alone, chose Bernd Jürgen Brandes, a young man who wanted to have his penis bitten off and to consume a chunk of it himself before being killed and eaten, had lodged an appeal to reduce his eight year sentence to five claiming the murder was an act of mercy. And a group of Indigenous Australian's were threatening to disrupt next year's Commonwealth Games if prime minister John Howard, among others, was not charged with genocide.

But, of course, the main excitement around the table was Ratzinger's hint that he knew a Vespucci and would see what he could do, presumably to set up a meeting.

Despite this, Helen announced that the Mogilevich incident coupled with Berlusconi's soirée had frightened and disgusted her and, because she was still feeling guilty about her absence from the school, she had definitely decided to return to London on the three o'clock flight.

§

Lamy and Warren went with Michael and Helen to Leonardo da Vinci and as they were saying farewell the Warrior Princess was pacing back and forth in her office in Foggy Bottom mulling over the meaning, if any, contained in two very similar yet altogether different messages.

The first was in the form of a brief telephone call from Mel Sembler about the goings-on at Palazzo Grazioli.

"The man is a nebbish," Sembler said, "There's no way he'd be capable of pulling off a major terrorist act."

"What about Lamy?"

"Lou's nothing but a blowhard. Anyhow, he's far too lazy."

"Do they know where our missing item is?"

"I'd say they don't even know it's gone."

She cut their conversation short because either Mel was stupid, which she knew not to be the case, or he had not done as instructed and incompetence and dereliction of duty made her feel nauseous.

The second was a message from Berlusconi, read to her verbatim by a rather embarrassed Sergio Vento, the Italian ambassador in Washington.

"*Cara mia*," it began, "This man is one sly dog. He knows exactly where is what you want but never will you make him say it. He is working for the Jews, I am sure. Have done my best but am up to my neck in my own problems. How goes your love life? I hear great things. *Baci*, Silvio. Bunga, bunga!"

"Did you say 'bunga, bunga'?"

"Yes, I am sorry. He told me I must not omit it."

There was an uncomfortable silence.

"Please thank him for the subtlety of his opinions," Condoleezza said with a tired sigh, "And remind him that, in this matter, we are the Jews."

§

The Lagrima de Cristo had a cargo of hides and finished leather goods for trade. Of the other caravels in the convoy, one carried a hundred soldiers of the king, another an equal number of mercenaries, five more were laden with food, water and supplies, tools and building materials and the cooks, tailors, armorers and artisans who were to put them to use and in the lead vessel of commander de Azambuja, which thus far unknown to Michael was captained by Cristóbal Roldán despite his being a Spaniard, were two dozen women brought along for the obvious purpose and Diogo's own private guard.

Bartolomeo Marchionni was the richest man in Lisbon and an intimate of Dom Manuel and their joint venture was the construction of a fortress on the island of Mogador at Essaouira to protect Portuguese ships carrying gold, ivory and slaves from West Africa and silk and spices from the Far East from piracy. Bartolomeu Dias reached the Cape of Good Hope in 1488 and Vasco da Gama the Calicut coast of India a decade later and since then the sheikhs, sultans and zamorins of Mozambique, Mombasa, Malindi, Zanzibar, Anjediva, Cannanore, Cochin and Quilon had become all too familiar with the duplicity and greed of the white-skinned adventurers and in the last few years had been suffering the caprices of Manuel's newly-appointed viceroy, Dom Francisco de Almeida.

A quarter century earlier de Azambuja was chosen by João II to oversee a similar exploit in the Gulf of Guinea in an area known for centuries to be rich in gold. He brought all the necessary building materials with him and succeeded in erecting the first tower of the notorious Elmina Castle in an astonishing twenty days despite heavy resistance from the native population.

It was hoped on this occasion the local Berbers could be bought off with gifts but it did not turn out to be realistic and de Azambuja first had to take and occupy the town of Azafi which lay on the coast some fifty miles to the north of Essaouira. This was more difficult than anticipated, though it was carried out with the utmost brutality, and it delayed their arrival at the island by two and a half months.

§

When Helen entered the flat in Chalk Farm it was nearly half past nine because, after boarding, the plane had to wait on the tarmac at Fiumicino for an hour and twenty minutes and no sooner had she dropped her bags, turned on the hallway light and kicked her shoes off through the bedroom door than she was grabbed roughly from behind by someone with an unwelcome but familiar boozy breath, a large hand was clamped over her mouth to stop her screaming and she was hefted bodily into the sitting room where a table-lamp switched on revealing Ciccio lounging on Michael's favorite stuffed armchair.

Unfortunately she had already called Lamy's cell in the taxi on the way in from Gatwick to let them know the flight was late and so there was no reason for anyone in Rome to worry.

"If you promise to be quiet he will let you go," Ciccio said calmly and lit a cigarette, "If you don't keep he will break your neck."

Helen was trying to kick Vladimir in the shins with her heels but without her shoes it wasn't having much effect and she acquiesced.

"How did you fuckers get in?! Aren't you supposed to be in jail?"

"They only deport," Vladimir said, "Always deport. We drive for two days like hell."

"How did you know I was coming back?"

"Not know. They call few hours ago while we still on ferry. Christ channel was fucking rough. I get sick all over the place."

"Who called? How did they know when?"

Ciccio didn't answer but got to his feet.

"Don't bother to unpack," he said, "We are leaving in five minutes. Please give me your *telefonino*. Use the bathroom if you wish but don't lock the door or cry out or . . "

Vladimir looked at her apologetically.

"Got it. He'll break my neck."

§

Eight of the nine caravels anchored in the shallow bay at the north end of Mogador on Jack's seventeenth birthday. De Azambuja left one at Azafi with supplies for a garrison of a hundred soldiers. The island was deserted or at least had been vacated at their approach and construction of the Castelo Real began apace and went on unhindered for two weeks.

There had been few takers for the leather goods at the ports they stopped in before Azafi even though the Wattasid Sultan Abu Abd Allah al-Burtuqali Muhammad ibn Muhammad, who maintained a loose control over the vast area from his desert stronghold at Fez, favored appeasement rather than aggression. The Sufi order that ruled Essaouira were of exactly the opposite mind and well aware of the recent carnage and Michael and Jack were met with murderous looks whenever they ventured ashore.

And so, on August 12th, since the Lagrima was not needed either for battle or to build the fortress, de Azambuja agreed to let them join a merchant fleet that happened to be passing and they set sail southward for the Gulf of Guinea in its company.

§

Ciccio and Vladimir weren't driving the Mustang and escorted Helen into the back seat of a dark green Jaguar S-Type sedan with tinted windows.

"Ooooh, fancy," she mocked.

"We are come up in world, yes?" Vladimir agreed with a goofy grin.

It was parked ten yards from the front door of their two-storey apartment building but she hadn't taken any notice. The flat was on the second floor and no lights were on to warn her and she just hurried inside.

Vladimir had not completely sobered up from the eleven pints of draught bitter he downed on the ferry before being sick so he got in beside Helen and Ciccio took the wheel. The Russian's enormous hands fumbled to bring forth a woman's shiny black satin sleeping mask from his jacket pocket and he told her to put it on.

"Best you could do?" she said with a smirk.

"Please," he replied, "Is not easy for us too."

"Well, let's go to the pub then."

"Ugh, no, I would be sick all over again."

Then, with a sheepish expression, he handcuffed their wrists together. She was afraid she might have to listen to the story of his life but instead he went almost immediately into a hop-saturated coma and since Ciccio wasn't naturally talkative and was unwilling or unable to answer any of her questions all she had to contend with during their approximately two hour journey was the stink of bile and beer permeating the car as Vladimir snored.

§

At seven o'clock the next morning Lamy's phone rang. He was still in bed enjoying an adolescent dream but rolled over to sit before he answered.

"I tell you is no finish, not so rich man," an unmistakable gravel voice said and burst into a choking cackle.

"Good morning, Semion," Lamy replied, "To what do I owe the pleasure? Looking for bail money?"

"You joke but I have sister. You tell me where is what I want now, yes?"

Lamy suddenly felt cold. He knew they shouldn't have let her go alone. "Where is she?"

"You make big trouble for me, you know."

"Not me. Your friends in Washington."

"Friends?! Such friends I would wish on God!" Mogilevich rasped and his attempt at humor made him start to cough.

Lamy threw on a dressing gown and went out into the hall.

"OK, OK," the don gasped, "I be *velikoduzhnyi*. You know what means?"

Lamy knocked on the door of Michael's suite.

"No."

"I give one whole day but no call and tell . . tomorrow night *ist kaputt*."

"Where? Call where?"

"Viktor at Russky Klub."

Lamy knocked again.

"Is that in Rome? Are you still in Rome?"

"*Tak*, Russky Klub in Rome."

The line went dead and Lamy had to knock a third time before there was any response.

"Whaaat? Who? What is it?"

"It's me. Open up. We've got a problem."

It took another fifteen seconds for a naked bleary-eyed Michael to appear and Lamy pushed past him into the room.

"Close the door."

"Pity you aren't Susanna," Michael said.

Lamy ignored the comment.

"Mogilevich says he has Helen."

Michael was shocked instantly alert.

"What?! What do you mean 'has'?"

"He's had her kidnapped."

"When?"

"He didn't say. Sometime after she called."

"By who?"

"I don't know."

"Why?"

"You know why. He thinks we stole his plutonium."

"Where is she?"

Lamy was dialing.

"I'm calling her right now."

"Shit! I knew it. Why does she have to be so damn stubborn?"

Helen's voice answered and said to please leave a message.

"Helen, it's Lou. Mogilevich called. We understand and we're onto it."

There was a second of silence.

"How can we be onto it?" Michael blurted, "Where is she? We don't have the fucking plutonium! What the fuck are we going to do?"

There was a knock on the door. It was Warren.

"Has something happened?" he asked.

§

By ten o'clock the London police had traced Helen's cell phone to where Ciccio left it under the lamp in the sitting room at the flat. No calls had been sent or received in the last five days that could not be accounted for. The police found no sign of a struggle. The only evidence of intrusion was a cigarette butt stubbed out on the hallway floor.

"Cheeky little prick," Michael said.

They knew in all likelihood who had done the kidnapping because Lamy wasted no time calling Achille Serra and the *prefetto* freely admitted that he gave Ciccio and Vladimir forty-eight hours to leave Italy or face a minimum five year jail sentence and also said that as far as he was aware Mogilevich had returned to Budapest.

"Great. What now?" Michael muttered.

Lazzari arrived with Warren having told him the story and because it was raining heavily the four of them were in the foyer of the Casale. Giovanni had just brought another tray of coffee and a selection of fresh brioches.

"Scotland Yard found no other clues?" Lazzari asked.

"They found their car."

"The blue one?"

"The Mustang. The CIA had a tracer in it. In the National Theater parking lot in Waterloo."

"Which is weird and helps us not one fucking iota," Michael groaned.

184

"They searched the car but there was nothing useful. They're looking for a mobster called Gerald Craven. Real name Gerhardt Krasinski. He's connected to Mogilevich and hired our two thugs but so far no success."

"What time was it when they took her?"

"Around half past nine we think. No way to know for sure."

"She rang us in the cab from the airport. They could have been waiting for her or it could have been the middle of the night," Michael added.

"And no one in the area saw them?"

"No."

Michael was pacing and turned to Lamy.

"Going back may not be as pointless as you think. I might find something. I'm jumping out of my skin."

Lamy shrugged as if to say 'go ahead if you want.'

"Isn't there some method of finding where Mogilevich's call came from?" Lazzari asked.

"Not here, I tried."

"So you're not totally sure he's gone."

"Not totally. His chopper took off from Rome-Urbe less than two hours after he peeled out in the limo but that doesn't prove anything."

"What about calling the State Department?"

"I left a message. It's four in the morning in D.C."

"Ah yes, of course. But really, the Americans can't possibly believe you're involved, can they?"

"They've been tracking us from the start. They sicked Mogilevich on us. They bugged my phone. They had a mole in my office and now no one knows where she is. They told Sembler and Berlusconi to suck up. Even Ratzinger seems to be part of it. I'd say there's a serious doubt in someone's tiny mind."

"*Incredibile.*"

§

The Jaguar was now safely stowed out of sight in a quadruple garage that had once been a stable adjoining a lavishly renovated farmhouse on a dead end off Singledge Lane, a narrow hedge-lined seldom-used road between Coldred and Whitfield running parallel to the A2 motorway just five miles from Dover. The hideaway was the property of Gerald Craven but unfortunately for Helen it had been purchased by a corporate entity unknown to Scotland Yard.

§

By noon Michael was still dithering about whether to go back to London or not when Giovanni hurried into the foyer with a written message.

"They would not wait for me to call you to the phone," he said, handing a piece of notepaper to Michael, "I am sorry but it is in Italian."

Lazzari got up from his chair and put on his spectacles.

"*Prego*," he said and Michael gave him the note.

They waited for a moment as Lazzari scanned it and looked up at Michael with wide questioning eyes.

"It says, 'If you will meet by the Temple of Fortune in Largo Argentina at ten tomorrow I will tell you what I can. We will know each other. Come alone or bring your sister if you wish. No one else please.'"

Lazzari paused.

"Is from *il tuo cugino*," Giovanni added helpfully.

"*Si,*" Lazzari confirmed, "From *'il tuo cugino'*. Your cousin."

Shuffle Sixteen

"I have no worries about American pressure on Israel. The Jewish
people control America and the Americans know it."
- Ariel 'Sharon' Scheinermann (1928 - 2014)

§

The captains of the now nineteen vessel merchant fleet were two sons
of Pedro de Cintra named Silvestre and Ricardo. Both were out-and-out
shits and made the three thousand mile voyage to Elmina pure misery.
Everything they could do to stymie and hinder the sale of the leather goods
on the Lagrima they did and also made it as difficult as possible for
Michael and Jack and their small crew to take on necessary food and water
or the Melegueta pepper, salt fish and gum arabic that they sought to
return to Portugal.

Their first stop was the trading post at Santa Cruz do Cabo de Gué,
now the great city of Agadir, with its magnificent curve of white sand
beach, then on past Capes Chaunar and Bojador which less than eighty
years before had been thought the absolute southern limit of the world,
then Ras Nouadhibou and the island of Arguin where the tiny settlement
run by Captain Gonzalo da Fonseca could only be approached at high tide
because of the encircling reefs and sand banks and though just forty-one
people dwelt there they managed the purchase and transport of eight
hundred slaves each year to their native lands. Cristóbal Roldán asked
Michael to greet Captain Fonseca for him because his cousin Luis was
once married to his sister.

The bullying of the de Cintra brothers was mercifully halved at this
point because Ricardo split off with seven ships on a nine hundred mile
side trip west to the slave-gathering center of Ribeira Grande on Santiagu
in the arid brown cluster of the Cape Verde islands, called verdant only
because of their adjacent position to Cap-Vert on the African mainland,
the site of modern Dakar.

After Cap-Vert came another forlorn incongruous outpost on a
peninsula at the southern side of the mouth of a great river now known as
the Gambia. The native Libou fishermen of Serrekunda had cast their nets

into these waters for countless generations and Michael observed with a smile to Jack how joyful and carefree they seemed in comparison with the sullen sweating shipmates of Silvestre de Cintra, almost as if one group were real and the other were not.

Next they sighted the hills of Serra Lyoa, the lion mountains so named by Silvestre and Ricardo's father because of their imposing shape. Pedro had been the first European to see and explore the huge natural harbor that lay beneath them and the further prominences of Cabo do Monte and Montserrado but he never could have imagined the astonishing futures that lay in store for Freeport, Sierra Leone, nor Robertsport nor Monrovia in the free state of Liberia.

At Cape Palmas the convoy turned due east and then east-north-east and for four hundred miles made no stop, hugging a sandy coastline without natural harbors, backed by lagoons and with a continuous high rolling surf that would have made any approach too risky, and even if that were not sufficient reason the crew were superstitious and fearful of the whale sharks which frequented their company, but beyond the Ankobra river everything changed and Silvestre put ashore in a single skiff to the half-finished fort of São Antonio at Axim. He returned within the hour and after another two sweltering days and a hundred more miles, on the morning of December 1st, 1506, Michael and Jack watched a white stone turret amid waving palm tree tops and the flag of a castle emerging from the hilly horizon of the pale green sea.

§

Lamy spent much of the afternoon trying to tease, wheedle, browbeat and cajole several of the head honchos at Telecom Italia, including chairman Marco Tronchetti Provera, CEO Carlo Buora, General Counsel and Director of Legal Affairs Francesco Chiappetta and Security Chief Adamo Bove, into bypassing normal channels and allowing access to the number of *'il cugino'*.

Bove at first seemed willing but after they had talked for a minute or two a strange fearful quaver came into his voice and he denied the request. Sixteen months later his car would be found at the top of a freeway overpass in Naples and his shattered body on the concrete a hundred feet below though his death was, in all probability, unconnected.

Lamy then tried Serra who also said he could do nothing and Gänswein and Buranelli at the Vatican and even Berlusconi at Montecitorio but Buranelli was in Singapore and Gänswein and Berlusconi were continuously unavailable. He even tried Rabinovitch but the door was firmly closed there too.

At four-fifteen he did get a return call from Foggy Bottom. Not from the Secretary of State herself but Richard Boucher, her smooth-talking spokesman and Assistant for Public Affairs.

"She apologizes that she isn't able to speak with you personally," Boucher said, "She's going to Moscow in a few days. Prep for the Bush-Putin summit in May. The Middle East's top of the agenda and she knows you appreciate how delicate and important that is. She wanted me to tell you she understands your present concern but doesn't think there's much she can do beyond what you've done already. She asked me to get Ambassador Sembler to look into it and he is. Otherwise she thinks it's best left to the Italian and English authorities."

§

At eight o'clock Washington time that morning, however, some two and a quarter hours previously, an owly Warrior Princess had torn a strip off Porter Goss and he in turn had done the same to Rabinovitch in Rome who was now doing everything in his power to track the 'stupid fat Russian sonofabitch' and 'the fucking little sister' and stop what was happening. The trouble was he had made zero headway finding either. All he knew for certain was that Mogilevich was not in Budapest and 'Viktor' was not at the Russky Klub nor would anyone there admit to knowing him so when Lamy called for help he bluntly refused to cover the embarrassing fact that he had none to give.

§

Since they couldn't think of any more stones to overturn and the meeting with *'il cugino'* wasn't until ten the following day Michael and Lamy and Warren and Lazzari went round in endless discursive circles about who *'il cugino'* might be. Was he a joke cooked up by Buranelli, Gänswein and Ratzinger because of their phony charade in the Sistine Chapel, or some long lost Sussex relative, a scion of the Romantic poets who ventured abroad in ages past and stayed, who had stumbled upon

Michael's presence in the Eternal City purely by chance but, no, they always came back to the certainty that the coincidence was too unlikely to be coincidental and surely must be connected to what Ratzinger had said and his blasted Vespucci alter ego. They hoped it might also have something to do with Helen's disappearance, the terrifying possibilities of which and the horror of not knowing how nor where she was caused Michael to become more and more desperate and upset and by the end of the evening, shame to say, he was once again quite drunk.

At five that afternoon they had all taken a taxi to Largo di Torre Argentina and Michael had been introduced to the cats. Hundreds of them, everywhere he looked, sweet homeless moggies of every hue and shape and size, free to roam as they pleased among the ruins of four ancient temples sunk in a deep stone rectangular sanctuary in the middle of the square.

The site had been unearthed in 1926 during demolition work and thrilled the archaeological world. The Area Sacra dates from the 4th to 2nd centuries and what remains of the temples are renovations made by Domitian. The complex was once a part of the Campus Martius and included the Baths of Agrippa and the Theater of Pompey in the *porticus* of which, lying just behind and between the *Aedes Fortunae Huiusce Diei*, the Temple of the Fortune of the Present Day, and the altar of the Temple of Feronia, Julius Caesar was cut down on the Ides of March in the year 44 B.C. The temples of Juturna and Lares Permarini flank the other two.

"Staggering," Michael said, "But how shall I bear it until tomorrow?"

In answer to his question why the 'Largo' was 'di Torre Argentina', Lazzari shepherded them across the tram lines past an 18th century opera house, where he told them the premiere of Rossini's *Il barbiere di Siviglia* had taken place in 1816 and Verdi's *I due Foscari*, based on Byron's play, in 1844, and then along Via del Sudario to number 44 where a splendid theater museum, *La Casa del Burcardo*, is annexed to a tower erected in 1503 by Papal Master of Ceremonies, Johann Burckard, who named it for his native Strasbourg which the Romans called Argentoratum.

§

The situation at São Jorge da Mina was not at all what Michael and Jack were anticipating. The fortress was far more impressive than any other they had seen and the village of the Fante surrounding it was much more substantial. As they came into full view of the lagoon dozens of pirogues were paddling from the town to greet them.

There was no sense that the Portuguese had taken control over the native population. They were merely tolerated guests who would be allowed to stay as long as they supplied the cloth, leather, copperware and brass jewelry the kings and chieftains wanted but it was clear they held no real power yet.

Gold had been finding its way to Europe and Asia across the vast Sahara desert for more than a thousand years, at first by donkey or horse-drawn wagon and then as the climate grew drier by camel, and now the vessels of Bartolomeo Marchionni and his partners were bringing nearly a ton of the pleasing metal to the treasuries of Lisbon every year but still the bulk of the trade went north via Djenné and Timbuktu. The Europeans never quite believed the Malinke kings that the source was alluvial, coming mostly from the forested headwaters of the Niger and the Senegal, and had been harvested since time immemorial by the Bambuk and Bure as supplemental income for their agriculturalist way of life.

Problems began immediately. Marchionni had guaranteed Michael that the return cargo of the Lagrima would not include slaves and there was no shortage of interest in the leather and plenty of alternatives for barter but Silvestre was violently insistent that his orders were to the contrary and if Michael were not willing to carry one hundred and twelve back to Lisbon he would be happy to relieve him of his command.

Michael and Jack had visited the dungeons of the fortress where the slaves were kept before shipment and the cruelty and viciousness of their handling by both black and white masters alike was unspeakable. It would have been quite impossible for them to be party to it. They wished they could have found some way to release the poor devils but they were too well guarded so instead they decided to try and slip out of the harbor in the middle of the night and risk sailing alone to rejoin Diogo and his fleet at Mogador.

Unfortunately, as they were preparing to weigh anchor with three other likeminded members of the crew they were prevented from doing so by the rest and the following morning they were put ashore where an enraged Silvestre had them paraded in chains to the castle and thrown in with the other slaves. Their situation might well have been hopeless had it not been for a wily Arab trader named Faroc al Jannesh who forestalled their transport to the Portuguese sugar plantations on the island of Fernando

Pó by purchasing them himself.

§

Fernando Pó is now called Bioko and as Michael the Mod was receiving his invitation from *'il cugino'* Amnesty International was exposing the fact that political detainees held without charge or trial at Black Beach prison in the capital Malabo were suffering torture, chronic illness and starvation.

§

Despite yet another thick head and a virtually sleepless night Michael was once again looking down at the cats by half past nine, his nervous state akin to a doubleboiler of bubbling porridge, and at ten o'clock precisely a young man appeared at his side. He was feeling faint again and trying to steady himself and hadn't noticed him approach. The boy was unmistakably Italian, no more than twenty, innocent of face, casually and at the same time elegantly dressed and, to Michael's throbbing eye, utterly beautiful.

"Good morning, Signor Davenport. I am sorry if I startle you. I hope you are well," he said with concern in very mildly accented English.

Michael wondered if his hangover was that evident.

"Quite well, yes, um, ah, are you . . ?"

"No, I apologize but I am not. I bring you a message."

"From, um . . ?"

"From your cousin, *si*."

"Is he, um, is his name Ves . . ?"

"His name is Guido."

"Ah. And would that be, um, Guido Vespu . . ?"

"I know him only as Guido. He asks you to forgive him that he could not come today but he has heard the news about your sister and he is busy making arrangements for her release. He says not to worry and that she will be calling you by eight o'clock this evening."

Michael was too astonished and relieved to speak.

"Further, he hopes that you will remain in Rome and meet with him on Monday instead. If your sister is able he would like her to be there also. He will contact you as to the place and time."

The young man began walking away.

"What is your name?" Michael blurted.

"Benedetto."

"Benedetto . . Vespucci?"

"No, Signore," the young man replied with a smile, "Benedetto Solario."

§

"The boy's name was, um, Benevento Soldado, at least I think that's what he said," Michael answered, still trying to catch his breath.

Warren and Lamy were sitting in the shade by the pool and Michael had screamed the great news about Helen's release as soon as he came through the gates of the Casale and ran towards them.

"Let's see if we can find out anything about him," Lamy replied, getting to his feet, "And Guido Vespucci, if that's your cousin's name."

"Soldado sounds Spanish," Warren said, "Soldier is *soldato* in Italian."

"Well, it could have been that. It's very noisy there and you know me."

"Sure it wasn't Benito?" Lamy asked wryly.

"No, no, four syllables, then three, I'm positive."

Unsurprisingly they found nothing whatever about either and so all they could do was wait but at four twenty-six in the afternoon, as they lingered over another delicious lunch in the dining room, Lamy got a call from Mogilevich.

"Ha ha, rich man," the growl began, "So? So?! Was not so hard, *tak*?"

Lamy looked at the others but the voice was so loud he didn't have to tell them who it was. There was the drone of an engine in the background and a lot of static on the line. Lamy put a finger to his ear and, in contrast to his normal sloppy enunciation, spoke as clearly as possible in reply.

"What wasn't?"

"Giving back what you steal!"

Even Lamy was temporarily at a loss for words but mouthed, "I think he's got the plutonium."

"So you have it OK?" he said.

"*Tak, tak*, I have it. Associates have it."

Lamy wanted to ask, 'And what associates would they be?' but bided his time.

"Good. That's good," he said, bluffing his way through.

"Good for fucking Michael Davenport's fucking little sister!"

Lamy gave Michael a hopeful thumbs up and changed the subject.

"I never understood why you needed the old product. You could have got more, no?"

"Sure, sure, easy, but Americans get nervous. Have to know where is. Why you want do and make trouble? Why you hate Jews so bad?"

Lamy was silent for a second. Here, at last, was a clue.

"What makes you think I hate Jews?"

"Why else you steal?"

"So you think I'm an Al Qaeda sympathizer, some kind of terrorist?"

There was a cackle of laughter that nearly got out of control.

"Ha! What is terrorist? Everyone is terrorist! But why take side of Arabs? They even worse than fucking Jews!"

"OK, I won't argue who's worse. Have you let the sister go?"

"Maybe will, maybe no. Maybe don't like your fucker Vespucci."

Lamy whispered to the others, "He's been in touch with Vespucci."

"Oh, I think you will," Lamy answered, "Signor Vespucci trusts that you're a man of your word."

"Trust?" Mogilevich bellowed in derision, "Are you some stupid rich man? He not trust me like I don't trust him, like you no trust me and I no trust you!"

"OK, OK, you're right. So, good, you have what you want and now we get what we want, yes? It's over."

"Ha! I not tell for sure nothing! Is only finish when fat bitch sing!"

There was another nasty peal of mirth followed by uncontrollable hacking and wheezing and then sudden panicked voices speaking in Ukrainian bleeding into the mix and what sounded like the beginning roar of an explosion coupled with a throttled gasp from Mogilevich and the line went stone dead.

§

A similar cat-and-mouse scenario was taking place in the West Bank city of Nablus after a raid on the Balata refugee camp by Israeli Defence Forces in which a young member of the Al Aqsa Martyrs Brigade named Ibrahim Smeri had been shot and killed in violation of an informal month-long ceasefire.

The Israelis were claiming Smeri was a 'ticking time bomb' who had fired on them first. Palestinian witnesses, on the other hand, said the Israelis were a special unit disguised as Arabs who shot him without warning and then tossed his body into the back of a van and drove away.

It is not entirely unconnected that, at the very same moment, the police in Shanghai arrested fifteen people for selling blood containing the AIDS virus.

§

The words Lamy used to describe the roaring noise were eerily similar to the 'most unearthly howling' that David Giudice heard as he lost phone contact with his sister Ruth in her office on the 81st floor of the South Tower when United flight 175 slammed into it at 9:03 on the morning of 9/11.

"So let's see," Warren said, "If Mogilevich thinks you stole the plutonium to help the Arabs by somehow thwarting the Jews, then maybe the Israelis and our neo-con thugs in Washington were planning to use it and make whatever pea-brained skullduggery it was going to be look as though it was the work of Al Qaeda or Fatah or some other terrorist group."

"Could be," Lamy replied, "And they needed their bomb made from that particular material so if the site were examined by the IAEA it would lead them back to the point of origin which is very probably Russia."

"Obviously 'Guido' my *cugino*, whoever in hell he is, must have had the plutonium stolen and has now 'arranged', as the boy said, to give it back. But why did he want it in the first place? And why is Helen important enough for him to return it? Where is it and who the devil are Mogilevich's 'associates'?"

§

It was now just after five o'clock in Rome and thus ten in the morning in Ciudad Juarez and a battered white delivery van was parked by the fountain in the center of the turning circle outside the palatial front doors of what used to be Amado Portillo's villa. It had been retrieved by the present occupant's men from a rubbish-strewn no-man's-land on the southern outskirts of the city at eight fifteen. The key was in the ignition and it had been stripped bare except for two torn vinyl bucket seats and a three hundred gallon carbon steel drum bolted to the floor in the rear cargo compartment which the men had examined carefully and reported the serial numbers to their superiors. After waiting half an hour to be given the OK they had driven it up the hill.

The van stood peacefully by the fountain for nearly an hour while the men smoked and swapped rude stories with their companions and then two older better-dressed men suddenly rushed from the doors to the top of the steps and began screaming for them to take it away and as they shouted the van exploded into a billion pieces, creating a shock wave that killed them all instantly, blew out every window in the building, cracked the façade wide open and sent up a gigantic plume of smoke and debris that could be seen rising from as far away as Rim Road scenic drive underneath Comanche Peak to the north of El Paso.

§

Michael and Jack spent the next six and a half years in Jannesh's company and he turned out to be an extraordinary gentleman. They were essentially his slaves but he never treated them as such. He had been born in Granada in 1440 and for fifty years led a happy and prosperous life as a trader in gold, salt, ivory, pepper and slaves, fathering seventeen children in the process, but the winds of the *Reconquista* were blowing and in 1490, two years before the soldiers of *Los Reyes Católicos* swarmed into the Alhambra, he fled with his family to Tlemcen and then, as the Spanish and Portuguese began penetrating North Africa, to the oasis of Sijilmasa and finally to Timbuktu and Gao where, by virtue of astute business acumen, he continued to thrive and was now a trusted intimate of the Songhai emperor Askia Muhammad mostly because he once accompanied him on a *hajj* to Mecca, arguably the most important of the Five Pillars of Islam, though the thirty camel-loads of gold he brought with them in honor of the Prophet, peace be upon him, may not have been entirely peripheral.

The relationship between Jannesh and Michael became rather like it had been with the Vespucci and their wool. Both Michael and Jack crisscrossed the great desert, the Sahel and Maghreb for him, leading his caravans as far east as Cairo and north to the shores of the Mediterranean at Tunis and Kairouan. He respected what he called their 'sensitivity' and never forced them to carry slaves though they knew countless, even many captive Europeans, were being worked to death in the grain fields and threshing floors of the Songhai empire.

They never tried to escape Jannesh's service, though they talked about it many times, partly because he never made threats or put any pressure on them to stay and since he was their saviour at Elmina they felt it would be ungrateful. Besides, they found a great deal of wonder and delight as well as horror in their travels to Ghat, Agadez, Zaria, Djenné, Mopti, Oulata and Nione, which by the late spring of 1513, when Faroc decided it was time for them to go home and gave them his blessing, rivalled the legendary journeys of Ibn Battuta.

§

A heavy silence hung over the foyer of the Casale. Lazzari had arrived at seven-fifteen. Lamy spent the last two hours trying to get hold of Rabinovitch and Mel Sembler without success but he didn't want to tie up the line any more in hope of Helen's call. Michael was pacing impatiently back and forth and the others sat with untouched drinks and watched him.

At seven thirty-five the phone rang and Michael leapt for it. It was Helen. They had not expected her call to come until eight, if it came at all, because of the message the boy brought from *'il cugino'* but she was back in the flat in Chalk Farm and ringing from her cell.

Her story was muddled because they were both overflowing with emotion but, in essence, as Michael relayed bits of their conversation, she first told him about the kidnapping and the ride with Vladimir snoring beside her to she had no idea where, then the nearly two days of her incarceration which, surprisingly, hadn't been that unpleasant despite being locked in a windowless room without a television or reading matter or anyone to talk to. The room was comfortably furnished with twin beds, a sofa and recliner, had an expensively-accoutred *en suite* bathroom with a spacious shower and the food and drink that descended at regular intervals on a dumb-waiter were perfectly sufficient and of reasonable quality. She had been left completely alone and other than a distant barking dog and an insistent car horn once or twice she heard nothing.

Then, at approximately half past three, there were several gunshots, maybe six or seven, perhaps more, and after another minute her door was opened by two men wearing stocking masks and she was sure she was going to be killed. She knew they weren't Ciccio and Vladimir because they were the wrong shape and size but instead they blindfolded her, took her outside and helped her into a car without being rough in any way.

They drove for two hours during which neither man spoke a word and then stopped outside the flat and her purse was placed in her lap. One of them told her she could remove the blindfold and get out and to please do it without looking at them. She did as they instructed and the car drove away. She thought it was a green Jaguar but hadn't clocked the plate number because she was still dazed and her legs were shaking.

Ciccio allowed her to bring the purse but took her cell phone. He had also taken her keys but now she found both in the purse again. The phone was shut down but fully charged and she hurried upstairs, took a moment to catch her breath and called.

Through tears of relief Michael told her all that had been happening on their end and that he would come straight back to London if she needed but to everyone's surprise she said she would rather return to Rome. She wasn't in the least bit tired because there hadn't been anything to do during her captivity but sleep so Lamy booked a first class ticket on the seven AM flight from Gatwick and a hotel so she could spend the night there since she was too nervous to stay in the flat. She said she wanted to see *'il cugino'* on Monday if the meeting materialized and thank him for saving her life.

Shuffle Seventeen

"The splitting of the atom changed everything except our way of
thinking, thus we drift toward unparalleled catastrophe."
- Albert Einstein (1879 - 1955)

§

From Gao and then Timbuktu Michael and Jack made their way down
the Senegal river to Awlil where by chance they ran into Gonzalo da
Fonseca who took them as far as Arguin and after a week was able to add
them to the crew of a caravel of Marchionni's carrying sugar from
Fernando Pó to Lisbon.

In Lisbon, Marchionni, who was just Michael's age but looked much
older being overweight and ashen-skinned from indulgence, listened to
their amazing tale with sympathy and in a moment of rare generosity
reimbursed them each a thousand gold florins, six times the amount an
unskilled laborer might have earned during the years of their enslavement
to Jannesh.

There was some satisfaction in the news that the de Cintra brothers
were both dead, apprehended at Elmina and flayed of their skin in the
sacred grove of the Eguafo by a Fante king who found they had been
screwing him.

Marchionni also told them of Amerigo's death from malaria in Seville
on February 22nd the previous year, honored now forever by
Waldseemüller's map and still bearing the title bestowed on him by *Los
Reyes Católicos* of *Piloto Mayor*, of Leonardo being again in Milan and the
Medici's return to Florence in August aided by Spanish troops and the
machinations of Giuliano della Rovere. It was no surprise that Marchionni
cared little for the death of the republic and didn't seem the least troubled
by Niccolò's false arrest for conspiracy, nor his torture and dislocated
shoulders, nor his banishment to Sant'Andrea in Percussina, all of which
cut Michael to the core.

But the corpulent Croesus could offer no information about
Bartolomeo and Elena Lupesca other than that they were most likely still
in Padua and had a daughter named Daniela or Donatella or Delfina who

would now be almost eight.

§

By nine o'clock Lamy and Michael and Warren were having supper in the Casale dining room. Lazzari had a longstanding ticket for the opera and after Helen's call he decided to go. They were watching a brief report on CNN about the explosion in Ciudad Juarez. There was nothing yet about the gunshots at Singledge Lane, nor the fate of Mogilevich.

"It must be connected," Michael supposed, "But how?"

"It certainly wasn't a nuclear device," Warren opined.

"How do you know?" Lamy asked, "What does it look like when a suitcase nuke goes off?"

"I think even the smallest would make some sort of mushroom cloud but, you're right, I don't really know."

"It could just have been that rival gang, whatever they were called, getting even," Michael suggested, "The Alamo-Helix, wasn't it?"

"Arellano-Felix," Lamy replied, "Jorge Arellano killed Amado's mother."

"Ah, yes, yes," Michael said a little blearily, he had been allowing himself a glass or two of wine to celebrate, "It didn't take long after Amado had his head torn off by the tiger for the Portillos to take control in Juarez again."

"What about the gunshots?" Warren went on, "Six or seven or more she said. And who were her rescuers? Scotland Yard had her cell phone so it must have been them."

"Or MI-5."

"Or even 6," Michael added with an inane giggle.

"Or the CIA."

"Or Mossad."

"Or Cosa Nostra."

"Or Klingons."

"Or Jack and Jill the Ripper."

"But why?" they exclaimed in unison.

"Clearly one or all of them do my cousin's bidding," Michael concluded with an absurd air of vanity, "And maybe for him it's just because we're family."

Warren and Lamy looked at each other and raised their eyes to heaven.

"And we don't know if anything especially dire happened to Mogilevich," Warren said, "Maybe his phone just died."

The speculation went round and round into the wee hours but, in the end, there were just two things they ever established for certain. The first was that Eduardo Portillo, Amado's youngest brother, and Ricardo Garcia Leyva, his son, had been blown to smithereens on the front steps of the villa along with forty-seven others. There were only fragments to make the identification but the forensic lab at Military Camp #1 in Mexico City finally completed the work six months later by comparing the two men's dental records with the eye teeth still lodged in a few charred splinters of jawbone.

The second, which began causing a furore in the Italian news media by the following Monday but became overshadowed by the papal election and quickly forgotten, was that a large black helicopter had crashed into the Tyrrhenian sea fifteen kilometers south-south-west of Monte Argentario on the Tuscan coast at approximately four-thirty in the afternoon of Friday, April 15th. It was not on an authorized flight path and had been flying low to the water. The wreck appeared to have sunk to the bottom intact because nothing was found floating on the surface by the fishing boats that sped to the scene but though the depth in that area is less than one thousand five hundred meters the Guardia Costiera cautioned that the irregularity of the sea floor would make salvage and retrieval extremely difficult if not impossible. There were no survivors and a flyover by the Marina Militare reported several white sharks circling near the crash site.

The scandal began because witnesses in Porto Rotondo, Sardinia, claimed a similar helicopter, which one knowledgable resident identified as a Sikorsky S92A, took off from the pad at the luxury holiday home of the prime minister shortly after four on the same afternoon but his spokesman, Paolo Bonaiuti, ridiculed the suggestion as 'more smear tactics by the left.'

They discovered a third intriguing bit of news the next morning as they were driving out to Leonardo da Vinci in the Bentley to fetch Helen. Lamy was trying to get hold of Rabinovitch again at the CIA station in the embassy when Mel Sembler suddenly came on the line and, after inquiring about her release and not very subtly hinting he was responsible for it, told him Rabinovitch and de Groot had been ordered to return and were already on their way back to Washington. When Lamy asked why he said he wasn't at liberty to say.

So, putting two and two together, they decided Mogilevich had perished at sea, which was indeed the case though it was never definitively proved, and that *'il cugino'* orchestrated Helen's rescue at the same time and Rabinovitch and de Groot had been replaced because they knew too much, which had to mean that Porter Goss *et al* must somehow have been in on the mystery man's plot, but what 'clown prince' Silvio may have had to do with anything and whether the explosion in Ciudad Juarez was connected remained forever obscure.

"You know," Warren said as Michael sped along the freeway to Fiumicino at a hundred and forty kilometers an hour, "I'll bet those idiots were thinking of planting a nuke made from that plutonium somewhere in Iraq to prove Saddam had WMD."

"Makes sense to me," Lamy replied.

"And I bet Vespucci got rid of it in Ciudad Juarez."

"I thought you said it wasn't nuclear."

"Got rid of as in incinerated the stuff in the explosion."

"OK, possible, but why? Why would he want to stop them from using it? It never made sense that they thought he took it in the first place. Weren't they hoping we'd lead them to him so they could kill him for doing that? I'm pretty sure Mogilevich was. If they were too, why would they agree to go along with Helen's release?"

"Comedy of errors?" Michael suggested, "Overwhelming stupidity? Maybe he's just quicker and better at the game than they are. Perhaps he made them an offer they couldn't refuse. My god, I hope we really do get to meet him."

§

When Michael and Jack strode up the hill from Chichester on August 12th, 1513, they were accosted by Arthur and another three men on horseback who had been for a ride to the top of the Trundle and, having spied the approach of what appeared to be undesirable riffraff, galloped down to chase them away.

The assumption was quite understandable because, though they had done their best to preserve their familiar attire and purchased some additional items in Lisbon, they were unkempt to Arthur's eye and bathed in a distinctly foreign aura. They were both deeply tanned and despite the fact that Michael had taken the opportunity in Lisbon to trim his beard and hair, which were now a stark and grizzled white, he still looked more African than English with a pale cream Kufi cap on his head, a worn leather bag slung over one shoulder and a *jellabiya* over the other.

Jack, to the contrary, being now just twenty-four, was proud of his manly beard and wildly curling knotted locks that dangled half way down his back and were bleached an extraordinary golden yellow by the desert sun. He also carried a satchel and *jellabiya* but since it was late afternoon on a roasting summer day he had stripped to the waist exposing a tough, lean, dark brown and very un-English torso. They might have been a pair of displaced Bedouin in stocking hose and codpiece and Arthur nearly fell off his horse when, after rearing up and shouting, "Clear off, you, if you know what's good for you!" Jack laughed out loud and Michael shouted back, "Oh, for god's sake, Billingsgate, it's us!"

Though they wrote dozens of letters over the years only two ever reached the farm, the last arriving in November, 1510, and the family had more or less lost hope of seeing them again. Only Elaine remained staunch in her conviction they would return and when she saw them fell to the ground and kissed it, then hugged Jack hard and looked at him in wonder for a full minute before landing Michael such a blow that it sent him reeling into Arthur's arms.

He knew he deserved it and forgave her with a gentle kiss and the reunion proceeded with tears and embraces, unbridled joy and laughter and stories and more stories, long, short, tall, funny, vomitous, horrific and just plain incredible and, of course, whiskey galore.

§

It is quite sad, in a way, and another thing Michael and Lamy and Helen and Warren never found out for certain, that Vladimir and Ciccio were killed in the gunfire at Singledge Lane, along with Gerhardt Krasinski and his wife and three bodyguards though the kitchen staff and servants were spared.

There is also no reason to keep hidden which, if any, of their surmises and cogitations were on the money and which were not.

Though it was a good guess, Warren was wrong about the intended use of the plutonium and that *'il cugino'* had disposed of it in Juarez. The ingredients in the bomb at the villa were almost identical, in fact, to those used on April 19th, 1995, at the Alfred P. Murrah Building in Oklahoma City by Timothy McVeigh. The carbon steel drum in the van was a mock-up, though the serial numbers on the identification plate were correct, containing twenty-five hundred pounds of racing fuel and ammonium nitrate that had been sparked by remote control.

However, they were right about why Rabinovitch and de Groot had been replaced, but probably didn't imagine them meeting the same fate as Ciccio and Vladimir, and right in their assumption that the Washington cabal must be in on the plot, as were several trusted associates of *Il Cavaliere* who, for a variety of reasons, felt it safer to keep him in the dark.

The truth was the plotters were not any closer to finding the plutonium, not even *'il cugino'* who never had anything to do with its theft in the first place and certainly had no motive for stealing it now. He had secured Helen's release merely by suggesting it was high time for everyone to cover their tracks, forget it and move on. Most didn't take much convincing because they were all pretty damn tired of the problem and no one seemed very concerned with making it a clean sweep by getting rid of Michael and the others except the vice-president who went on stalking the halls of the West Wing in his underwear, cornering the unwary and urging them in a low voice to 'kill, kill, kill, kill, kill.'

§

A great deal had changed in the world since Michael the Med and Jack disappeared into the desert excepting the incomprehensible muddle of alliances in what is now Italy which remained exactly that. One minute Pope Julius' Holy League was allied with France to defeat Venice, the next allied with Venice and Aragon to defeat France with the Holy Roman Empire always sticking their oar in somewhere, everyone calculating the odds and playing both ends against the middle, but Michelangelo plugged away by himself and finished his ceiling and there was nothing holy about any of it.

The Fuggers of Augsburg became the indisputable leaders of the banking racket through loans to Maximilian I, the Holy Roman Emperor, among many others, which bought shares and eventual control of copper, silver and mercury mines, the spice, wool and silk trades and the global monopoly on Guajacum, a Bahamian salve for the French pox, and now Jakob Fugger was the richest man in the world, not least because the bank cut a sweet deal on remittances to the papal court for the sale of indulgences, those handy little chits that could buy even the vilest scumbag into Paradise, which were now freely available because Giuliano della Rovere, aka *il papa terribile*, wanted to bribe posterity by at last completing the construction of St. Peter's. Praise Jesus, Fugger brother Markus even leased the Roman Mint.

On a collision course with della Rovere's desire was an insufferable young neurotic named Martin Luther who chucked in law school after being stupid enough to go out in a thunderstorm and nearly getting struck by lightning and instead became an Augustinian monk. He was ordained in 1507 largely because his superiors got tired of his endless self-reproach and the quibbling niceties of his biblical interpretation and rather naïvely thought he might shut up.

It might have brought a smile to Michael's lips to learn that, on June 11th, 1509, the Florentines, under Niccolò's ever-diligent stewardship, finally overran Pisa.

Earlier that year the Portuguese, commanded by Francisco de Almeida, crushed the Egyptian and Gujarat fleets at Diu on the Kathiawar peninsula in northwestern India thus contributing greatly to the mess that has been going on there ever since.

Sadomasochism was, as always, alive and well. On July 19th, 1510, Joachim the Elector of Berlin ordered thirty-eight Jews burned at the stake. They were falsely accused of stealing church property and desecrating the host, however that is accomplished, and two who accepted Christianity were given mercy and beheaded.

In that same year Bartolomeo Marchionni loaned Ferdinand the Catholic, the King of Aragon, Sicily, Naples, Valencia, Sardinia and Navarre, Count of Barcelona, *jure uxoris* King of Castile and now regent of the same because of his daughter's unstable mind, sufficient money for the first shipments of African slaves to the island of Santo Domingo and the sugar plantations of Brazil.

On August 31st, 1512, Giuliano de' Medici, the youngest son of Lorenzo *Il Magnifico*, became the governor of Florence and many claimed God's Hand was at work after Giuliano della Rovere died with little discernible lamentation on February 20th, 1513, and the other Giuliano's older brother Giovanni de' Medici was elected Pope Leo X.

Michael the Mod was fond of a bit of toilet humor about people who run theaters but it applies equally to popes and presidents, "Flushing merely causes the shit to rise to the top and rotate."

On April 21st, 1509, Henry VII, the Tudor King of England, died and though Henry Junior had gone along with his father's increasing lack of interest in a Spanish Alliance, and been quite rude in rejecting the legitimacy of his arranged betrothal to Catherine of Aragon, he suddenly had a turnabout and married her on June 11th and they were crowned in Westminster Abbey on June 24th. Henry felt he had a claim to the French throne and wanted to extend his holdings there and so, by a pledge of mutual aid with Ferdinand, threw in his lot with the Holy League.

Four days after Michael the Med was clocked in the chops by Elaine, the twenty-two-year-old king and the hired forces of Emperor Max, to whom he was giving a hundred ducats a day to furnish his table, defeated the French cavalry at Guinegatte not far from Calais in a debacle that became known as The Battle of the Spurs because of the speed with which the ambushed and outnumbered French turned their horses' tails and galloped away.

The English army at Guinegatte was made up of cavalry, artillery, infantry and longbows and had been financed by Thomas Wolsey, a butcher's boy soon to become Lord Chancellor and Cardinal Archbishop of York, with substantial assistance from Giuliano della Rovere, and it was just as well because the Scots were taking advantage and crossing the border into Northumberland but luckily there were enough men left over for Thomas Howard, Earl of Surrey, 2nd Duke of Norfolk and Earl Marshal of England, to defeat them at Flodden Field three weeks later. James IV was killed along with more than ten thousand other poor sods and Catherine immediately sent his bloodied coat to Henry in France to keep him in good cheer. In gratitude the Howard family were allowed to add an escutcheon to their shield, the lion of Scotland pierced through the mouth with an arrow.

While this was happening Michael and Jack dallied in the warmth of their beloved family and, on September 29th, as the Portuguese were spilling into the western Pacific and putting their mark on the eighteen thousand, three hundred and six islands of what is now called Indonesia, a Spanish conquistador named Vasco Núñez de Balboa completed his crossing of the Isthmus of Panama.

§

Helen's flight arrived twenty minutes late and as Michael embraced her a cantankerous cardinal from Marktl am Inn, marketably born on Holy Saturday though it had fallen three weeks earlier this year, was lying naked on a massage table in the Vatican clinic and cursing as his lover lathered a mentholated cream over the loose wrinkled flesh of his back because, *"Gottverdammt, du arschgefickter Hurensohn!"* it was his seventy-eighth birthday and, of all the fucking times for it to happen, he was coming down with a cold and it was Georg's fault for letting him stay so late at that imbecile bagman of a prime minister's *Fussball* party!

"You should take better care of me!" he snapped in German.

Georg, his partner, advisor and masseuse of the moment and a man even more rabidly narrow-minded than he, gave an instantaneous stinging smack to his dimpled ghost-white buttock in response.

"Don't blame me, you old pervert," he said quietly, "You were having way too much fun. You'll get what you want, *Liebchen*, cold or no cold."

The cardinal knew it was true and calmed down. No one would have the guts to oppose him with anything more than fleeting tokenism. For twenty-five years had he not been prefect of the Congregation for the Doctrine of the Faith and for the last three, as Dean of the College of Cardinals, *primus inter pares*? If they so much as tried he would have their reputations on the toast-rack.

§

It was a normal Saturday in Iraq. The one hundred and ninth of the totally unnecessary war, so cynically dubbed Operation Iraqi Freedom, which at that time was averaging 1.3 suicide bombings and 2.46 coalition, 8.9 insurgent and 41.2 civilian deaths per day.

In Baquba thirteen people, including three policemen, were killed and five seriously wounded in an explosion at a restaurant.

In Baghdad two Philipino airport workers were wounded when insurgents fired on their minibus, a Kurdish television reporter, Shamal Abdallad Assad, was killed by unknown gunmen, Pvt. Aaron Hudson, 20, of Highland Village, Texas, died from wounds sustained the day before in Camp Taji when an IED, an improvised explosive device, detonated near his patrol and a member of the Ministry of the Interior commando team was shot dead behind the wheel of his car.

In Baiji a Turkish truck driver was killed and his rig burnt to a crisp by a roadside bomb.

In Kirkuk a pipeline security guard was killed by rebels, an Iraqi soldier and a policeman were shot dead *en route* to join a general's escort and another policeman was shot dead as he left work to return home.

In Touz another policeman was blown to smithereens by a bomb placed outside his house.

In Samarra one Iraqi soldier was killed and another wounded by a bomb.

In Moatassem four civilians were wounded by a booby-trapped car.

In Mosul a suicide car-bomber drove into a US military convoy wounding another civilian.

In Latifiyah Iraqi security forces claimed they killed Abu Bakr Mohammed Nayef al-Janabi, a leader of Ansar al-Sunna.

In Ar Ramadi rockets and mortar fire were directed at the US base and in the ensuing combat Sgt. Angelo Lozada, Jr., 36, of Brooklyn, New York, Spc. Randy Stevens, 21, of Swartz Creek, Michigan, and Sgt. Tromaine Toy Sr., 24, of Eastville, Virginia, lost their lives.

It was easier to find the American names than the others and very difficult to ascertain the number of people they themselves had killed but Senator Carl Levin of Michigan chose Rupert Murdoch's Sydney-based paper The Australian that Saturday to release formerly classified CIA documents that proved George Bush was lying when he said in October, 2002, "We've learned Iraq has trained Al Qaeda members in bomb-making and poisons and deadly gases," and that Dick Cheney's statement, "Muhammad Atta's meeting with an Iraqi intelligence officer in Prague is pretty well confirmed," in December, 2001, was bullshit.

Not that anyone with a vestige of brain would ever have let either of these two fine specimens of humanity sell them a used car.

At about the same time the contents of something that has gone down in the history books as the 'Downing Street Memo' were coming to the awareness of US Representative John Conyers, also of Michigan, and within a few weeks he and a hundred and thirty-one other members of Congress were demanding explanations. In a nutshell the memo, written by the head of MI-6, records a meeting at the prime minister's residence on July 23, 2002, between senior members of the Labour government and defence and intelligence officials in which the Blair-Bush decision 'to create a justification for war with Iraq by connecting Saddam with 9/11 coupled with manufactured information about his stockpiles of weapons of mass destruction' had been openly discussed.

It was then four and a half years since the twin towers plummeted to the ground at free fall speed so inexplicably. Why was unearthing these documents even remotely important? To their credit, Conyers and Levin voted against the war but is it conceivable they didn't understand the real question?

Everyone knows that to solve a crime it's essential to ask, 'Who benefits?' In the case of war the taxpayers pay with their hard-earned cash and the lives of their sons and daughters and the suppliers of everything else, bandages, splints, stretchers, gurneys, ambulances, surgeons, artificial limbs, boots, belts, helmets, body armor, bullets, guns, tanks, battleships, aircraft carriers and the bricks and mortar to rebuild, reap massive rewards and often without supplying anything whatever find a way to suck billions directly from the attendant budget.

Who benefitted from the evil charade of 9/11 and the pointless wars in Afghanistan and Iraq? Big Oil, Big Money, Raytheon *et al*, Halliburton *et al* and the government of Israel. Beside the neo-cons' insane desire for a world under the control of Washington and Wall Street, it was all about loot and *Lebensraum* and Michael did not have his tongue in his cheek when he quoted the old song and said "ain't it all a bleedin' shame."

Shuffle Eighteen

"This should not be allowed to fall down the memory hole during wall-to-wall coverage of the Michael Jackson trial and a runaway bride."
- John James Conyers Jr. (1929 -   )

§

"Is someone out there still waiting to kill us?" Helen asked.

Michael and she were walking arm-in-arm toward the terminal doors.

"I don't know but I've got a funny feeling not. We think Mogilevich might be dead. I told you something odd happened while Lou was talking to him. It sounded like he was on a plane of some sort and we just heard on the news that a helicopter crashed into the sea yesterday afternoon off the Italian coast. It's possible it could have been his and that dreadful man Sembler told Lou on the phone as we were on our way here that our CIA lads Rabinovitch and de Groot have gone back to Washington. You said there were gunshots before you were rescued. Could that mean Ciccio and Vladimir are dead too?"

"I suppose so. It's crazy but I rather hope not."

"Yes, I was quite fond of them as well."

Michael squeezed her close to him and kissed her on the temple.

"The point is, we don't think anyone's following us at the moment."

"But you don't know."

"No. Not for certain."

"When people get murdered someone always wants revenge."

"True," Michael admitted reluctantly.

"Has our cousin phoned again?"

"The boy called him 'Guido'. No, not yet."

They arrived at the car and Warren embraced Helen and held her tight for a long moment.

"We're relieved to see you," Lamy said with a smile, opening the rear door and patting her warmly on the shoulder as she got in.

"I'll drive," he said to Michael.

"I was asking Michael if anyone might still be out there waiting to kill us," Helen said as Lamy steered the Bentley into the slowly moving traffic.

210

"Well, if they are, at least it'll be someone different," he answered with a chuckle.

"How comforting."

"Assuming our Ukrainian friend is dead," Warren cautioned.

"Given what we think may have happened," Lamy went on, "I'd say it's your cousin who'd be the prime target."

"Wasn't he before?"

"It looked like it. Maybe he erased the opposition."

"Weren't Rice and Cheney and Kissinger part of that?"

"We thought so but it seems not. We're pretty sure they must have given their OK to your rescue."

"What is it they say about fair-weather friends?" Warren added wryly.

Helen sighed.

"Why people want to live in a world like that is beyond me. Thank god for my straightforward little school."

"Oh come now," Michael demurred with a smirk, "The place is absolutely awash in conspiracy."

§

Jack had long since lost his virginity in the cool moonlit oases of the great desert and the excitement of those illicit moments of passion, when as well as the obvious appendages life itself was at risk, made casual encounters with even the lustiest Sussex wench tame in comparison. The quiet country life had been spoiled for him by adventure exactly as it had been for his grandfather so it is no surprise that within less than two years of their return both were once again dreaming of distant lands.

At the end of July, 1515, after Michael was forced to get down on bended knee and swear to Elaine that Jack would be home by the following spring, they set off for Portsmouth and easily persuaded the new captain of the Simonetta, none other than Cristóbal Roldán's son Alonso, to carry them to Italy.

They set sail on August 9th and, after barely weathering a savage summer storm in the Bay of Biscay and a ten-day delay in the tiny Galician port of Vigo to make repairs but with no other stops along the way, disembarked in Livorno on September 15th, the day the newly crowned twenty-one-year-old François I, was victorious over the Swiss at Melegnano. Then, after another two weeks on the road during which the talk was of little else but the French re-taking Milan and once again dispatching the Sforza, on the late evening of September 29th they found themselves knocking at Bartolomeo's door in Padua.

He didn't seem at all surprised but greeted them warmly and proudly introduced his ten-year-old daughter Destina, a taciturn pre-pubescent lump who he was caring for by himself in a spacious, elegantly furnished house that was the property of the university. He informed them without any evident sadness that Elena Lupesca, her mother, had succumbed to a wasting disease when the girl was seven.

Jack was amazed how young his grandfather's old friend looked for a man he had been told was already pushing forty and yet seemed hardly of sufficient years to be a father. 'Ah well,' he thought, 'He's led a cultured life.'

They stayed in Padua until October 10th, the day after Michael's sixty-sixth birthday, during which time Jack and Destina, who had initially taken an instant dislike to each other, developed a grudging, hectoring sort of friendship. There was much reminiscence of Niccolò, of course, and Bartolomeo was particularly fascinated by their experiences in Africa and he and Michael and Jack laughed at the foolishness of the ancient belief that life below the equator was a physical impossibility because all one's blood would run to one's head. It was the kind of arrant nonsense, Bartolomeo lamented, that he was still occasionally forced to espouse in order to keep his job.

From Padua they went to Venice and, having visited Pisa, Pistoia, Bologna and Ferrara on their first passage over the mountains, came down the Adriatic coast to Chioggia and Ravenna before traversing them once again from Forlì to Florence. Michael, who spoke Italian like a native, was careful they joined with merchant caravans whenever it was possible because the roads were frequently blocked by belligerent soldiers. Jack had mastered Spanish and several Arabic dialects on their travels and was quick to a reasonable fluency here too.

They tarried in Florence for only an afternoon, just long enough for Jack to gain an impression of the great city, before continuing to San Casciano in the Val di Pesa and Niccolò's modest estate outside the hamlet of Sant'Andrea in Percussina. They arrived on Thursday, November 3rd, and spent a joyous week.

Niccolò seemed content enough in exile surrounded by his family and fields and orchards. Marietta provided two daughters and four sons, the eldest of whom was now thirteen. She was a woman of great ability and intelligence and, though a novella that was absorbing his attention, *Belfagor arcidiavolo*, could be interpreted as a denunciation of marriage, they were obviously happy in each other's company. He was also writing a vast work on the Roman historian Titus Livius and a second on the art of war, as well as several plays, but was, as ever, generous in entertaining his friends.

What a difference Michael thought, and said so to Jack, from the two days he once spent in London with Erasmus and Thomas More, one translating the New Testament, the other penning his stultifying treatise about an ideal society. Their concerns seemed pitiful and humorless, mere child's play in comparison.

On November 11th they left for Rome. Bartolomeo said they would find Leonardo there. In July, 1513, as Michael and Jack were in Lisbon receiving the reward from Marchionni that was paying for their present adventure, the Holy League threw Louis XII's troops out of Milan and Leonardo's patronage ended. Fortunately his friend Giuliano de' Medici, the new pope's brother, had given him sanctuary and a studio within his own household at the Belvedere Palace in the Vatican and when Michael and Jack came upon him on the morning of November 17th they were witness to an extraordinary scene.

Leonardo, whose hair and beard were now a bright blond white, was in a state of extreme agitation. He had torn most of the clothes from his body and was running in circles screaming a repeated phrase at the top of his lungs. His words were almost incomprehensible because he was virtually frothing at the mouth but it sounded to Michael like, 'So is nothing worth anything after all?' An unfinished portrait of a naked Salai as John the Baptist with right forefinger pointed to heaven hung on an easel and he and Leonardo's new apprentice, the much younger and, if possible, even prettier Count Francesco Melzi, were both frantically imploring him to calm himself. None of them noticed Michael and Jack standing at the portal for several minutes.

What had propelled the greatest genius of his or any other age into such a frenzied tizzy? They at last discovered the immediate issue was his dissection of the corpse of a child and a pregnant woman but there were a myriad of other things like his left-handed mirror writing to prick the envy and malice of tiny minds and, despite Giuliano's protection, his howls of outrage were in response to an accusation of witchcraft and necromancy delivered by a snot-nosed papal emissary who they had noticed bustling prissily away down the hall just seconds prior to their appearance at the door.

§

'Il cugino' had by no means allayed the security fears of either the Italians or Americans regarding the plutonium because there was the small matter of next week's papal election and the eventual investiture. The conclave was to begin in two days and, since the funeral, multitudes of the faithful and merely curious had been milling about in St. Peter's square with an ever-present contingent of international media. The expectation was that in forty-eight hours two million yearning souls would be jammed into the piazza to welcome their new *papa*.

§

Lazzari's Panda whizzed through the gates into the Casale garden at ten past three and he found them under the pines by the pool digesting an *al fresco* lunch. The Marrones had yet to clear the table. He was overjoyed to see Helen and gave her an uncharacteristic hug and kiss from behind her chair.

"Have you heard anything?" he asked.

"No," Michael answered a little tipsily, once again he had consumed too much wine, "Just sitting here waiting to be blown up as usual."

"Surely you no longer think that will happen. It seems to me you are now under the protection of an extraordinary power."

Michael snorted in agreement.

"Pawns, that's all we are. That's all I've ever been. A sucker and a fool."

"Oh, do stop drivelling, Michael," Helen said, tapping a spoon impatiently on her half empty plate, "You should be thankful. I am."

"It's true that pawns generally play a defensive and sacrifical role," Warren observed, "But they can also attack and very occasionally they get lucky enough to be queens."

At which everyone except Michael chuckled.

"But who is this man?" Lamy queried Lazzari, "That's what we can't figure out. Where does he get this power? In four years we haven't been able to find out anything about him. We know Portillo, Rice, Cheney, Mogilevich, maybe even Berlusconi, had or have no idea what he looks like. Only Ratzinger hinted that he might and he only said he knew 'a Vespucci' not a 'Bartolomeo'. We're assuming *'il cugino'* is him or has something to do with him but it's just a guess. Whoever he is he was powerful enough to get Helen released in a hurry and possibly order Mogilevich's death. Is he 'Guido' Vespucci? If he is I can't find a Guido Vespucci anywhere in Italy who fits the bill. There's a guy by the name in Big Piney, Wyoming. Probably goes fly-fishing with Cheney. Hey, why not? And there's a character in some Canadian movie about over-priced gas .. "

"Americans never stop bitching about that," Warren interjected, "Their heads are a very long way up their collective behind."

" .. but we're basically totally stumped."

"Ah well," Lazzari answered, "Perhaps all will be revealed on Monday."

"How was the opera?" Warren asked him.

"Magnificent."

He had been to the last night of *Estaba la Madre* at the Teatro dell'Opera di Roma, modeled on the 13th century *Stabat Mater*, The Mother was There, a new work by Luis Bacalov, the Argentinian expatriate film composer who won an Oscar for *Il Postino*, dedicated to the thirty thousand *desaparecidas* of the Dirty War and the Mothers of the Plaza de Mayo.

"Beautiful. A very moving and imaginative staging. Three levels, the upper occupied by the military and clergy, the middle by the victims and the torturers and the mothers telling their stories on the ground. The original was a hymn by a Franciscan monk describing the lamentations of Mary before the body of her crucified son. A huge screen was used to great effect and eerie images of water. As you know, many political prisoners were drugged and dropped from planes into the ocean. The chorus sang, 'Who would not weep, torn apart by so much agony?' Bacalov has lived here for more than forty years. You would recognize his music instantly. He has worked with everyone. Pasolini, Scola, Wertmüller, Fellini, even Quentin Tarantino. I wish you could all have seen it. But, if you are not too exhausted, I can arrange tickets for a play this evening."

Michael gave a barely audible groan.

"Come on, Michael," Helen sighed, "If I can you can. Have a nap."

"What play?" Michael asked in mock horror.

"*Chi ha paura di Virginia Woolf?* At Teatro Argentina. Starring Mariangela Melato."

"Now that name rings a bell," Michael said, slightly more interested, "Wait a minute, wasn't she in . . ?"

"What?"

"That film with Gia . . Giacomo . . Gianni . . "

"Giancarlo Giannini?"

"Yes, that's it. They were on a beach."

"Swept Away."

"Yes, yes! Swept Away. Ages ago. In the sixties. I loved it."

"Seventies, I'd say," Lamy cut in, "Early seventies. The full title was Swept Away by an Unusual Destiny in the Blue Sea of August."

Michael shot him a sour look and then smiled.

"Yes, I remember. Great stuff. Well hell, bugger it, why not, let's go."

§

Giuliano ordered Leonardo to give up his anatomical studies and thereby he avoided the clutches of the Inquisition but the fact that he was continually at the mercy of such utterly puddingheaded nitwits preyed upon his mind and put him into a state of understandable distraction and their few visits with him were brief. Jack marveled at his sketches and models of automata, a humanoid robot, a self-propelling cart and a nearly completed mechanical lion that could walk forward to present a bouquet of lilies and one afternoon Leonardo let slip a peculiar observation about *Belfagor arcidiavolo* which obsessed Michael for the rest of his life.

He knew the novella quite well, calling it instead *Il demonio che prese moglie*, The Devil takes a Wife, and said that Niccolò must have been thinking of Bartolomeo as he wrote but when Michael questioned why he gave a look that seemed to mean, 'Well, isn't it obvious?' and changed the subject.

Michael and Jack stayed in Rome for less than a week and by the end of the month were again at Livorno and lucky enough to obtain passage on a ship of Marchionni's named the Anunciada. It had been to Brazil with Cabral fifteen years earlier and just delivered forty Guinea slaves, three tons of sugar and a dozen gargantuan wooden crates packed with carved ivory trinkets from Sierra Leone, spoons, forks, salt-cellars, pyxes and oliphants, and was now laden with fine Tuscan wine and raw copper from the Fugger mines in Hungary destined for Seville.

They sailed up the Guadalquivir on December 19th and, on the very same day, Leonardo, having found the butcher-faced pope's favor once more, was in attendance in Bologna at Giovanni's hush-hush meeting with François I, which presumably had some clandestine purpose though none has ever been divined, at which the lion was presented as a gift and after which his fortunes changed permanently for the better. He departed Bologna in the young king's company, settled in France and never saw Italy again.

In Seville, quite by chance, they made the acquaintance of the Dominican friar Antonio de Montesinos and a young priest named Bartolomé de las Casas recently returned from Cuba who had run afoul of Thomas Cajetan, the Master of the Dominicans, for openly denouncing the cruelty they witnessed against the native Indians. Horror, as they described it to Michael and Jack, on a scale never before seen. However, in Cajetan's opinion their attitude was damaging to the affairs of the colony and, more importantly, getting in the way of the essential and painstaking process of native conversion, not to mention the daily enrichment of their overlords, and so they and several others had been shipped back to Spain on the order of the king as dangerous troublemakers. Cajetan had convinced Ferdinand about the necessity of the action but they had obtained a letter of introduction to the ailing monarch from the archbishop of Seville and were off to Plasencia that very afternoon in hope of persuading him to reverse his position and get him to do something.

Michael found it hard to convince himself that a *forza del destino* is at work below the surface of people's lives but eventually came close to conceding that what followed was an example.

Michael and Jack went with Montesinos and las Casas to Plasencia and on January 3rd, 1516, met an Englishman there named Sir Hugh Willoughby from Risley in Derbyshire who turned out to be the son of Thomas Willoughby who had attended Cambridge two years ahead of Michael. They were both of Saxon heritage and in late May, 1471, shortly after the Battle of Tewkesbury, they had journeyed north together for the summer holidays since Risley was more or less directly on the way from Cambridge to Bramhall. Michael even spent a night at Risley Manor and visited Thomas again in 1485 when Hugh was a boy of three. Many years later Hugh would be discovered frozen to death with the crew of his ship the *Bona Esperanza* on the White Sea by Russian fishermen yet at that moment in Plasencia when Michael realized his identity, and they hugged each other with joy, he was travelling with Sebastiano Caboto, the son of

Giovanni, whom Ferdinand had just created a Captain of Spain.

§

Michael the Mod didn't have a nap and to his shame dropped off during the second act of *Chi ha paura di Virginia Woolf?* Nonetheless he found it to be an enthralling production, far more imaginative with its chthonian set design of tilted, skewed and half-buried furniture than any he had seen or been involved in and the performances, particularly Mariangela Melato's, were marvelous.

He once acted in some excerpts at the Rose Bruford Academy. His wildly alcoholic Canadian flatmate essayed George and he had played Nick which he called a thankless part. He had never been much good with accents, other than his native south coast, and smarted at his friend's unfair advantage because, for obvious reasons, he was comfortably at home with the 'Americanness' of it all.

Warren knew Edward Albee well and at the interval they spoke about his vehement denial that the play was originally written for two gay couples.

"He won't let anyone have the rights if they want to perform it that way."

"I think it might be really interesting," Helen said.

"Well, I can't blame him," Warren went on, "Even though he's openly gay he can't stand being called an 'American gay playwright'. Would you call Arthur Miller an 'American straight playwright'? It's silly."

They got onto the subject of Albee's first play The Zoo Story and Lamy mentioned an anecdote of Salman Rushdie's about a production he had been in on Pakistani television. The producers had been forced to cut his line, 'God's a colored queen who wears a kimono and plucks his eyebrows while indifferently paring his nails.'

"Fatwa-loving jihadists aren't famous for self-deprecating humor," Lazzari observed.

"An accurate depiction of Ratzinger though," Michael added.

After the curtain they went backstage and met the cast and the director of the theater, Giorgio Albertazzi, and Michael complimented him on the season of plays he was presenting which included Marlowe's Edward II, Shakespeare's Coriolanus, Jonson's The Alchemist, Ibsen's Ghosts and works by Peter Weiss, Marguerite Yourcenar, Isaac Babel, Joseph Kajetan

Tyl and Pippo Delbono in a freely adapted version of Allen Ginsberg's 1956 poem entitled *Urlo*.

"Ah yes," Warren quoted with tongue-in-cheek wistful reminiscence, "The best minds of my generation getting fucked in the ass by saintly motorcyclists and screaming with joy."

"Don't be disgusting," Helen admonished him.

Albertazzi invited them to a party after the closing performance the next day which they tentatively accepted but, more than anything, after the madness of the past two weeks it was wonderful to be in a tiny haven of sanity.

When they arrived at the theater they had enjoyed the poster announcing Albert Camus' *Caligola* as the coming attraction.

§

Ferdinand died on January 23rd, 1516, before Montesinos and las Casas were able to convince him of their case but they were not easily dissuaded and continued on to Madrid where Ximénez Cisneros, the guardian of Ferdinand's underage grandson Charles whose rule would eventually unite the Holy Roman Empire with the Kingdom of Spain and upon whose realm it was to be said the sun never set, agreed to send a contingent of Hieronymite friars to examine the situation and provide a more just governance for the troublesome islands.

Caboto, on the other hand, grew impatient and a few days after the king's death set sail for England with Sir Hugh and Jack and Michael in tow. It might have put him in better humor had he known that his immediate superior Juan Díaz de Solís, appointed *Piloto Mayor* after Amerigo's death and who had set off to explore the southern shores of the new continent the previous October, was just then being eaten by Charrùa indians at the mouth of the Rio de la Plata.

However, once back in England Caboto quickly persuaded Henry VIII's vice-admiral Sir Thomas Pert to join with him in his own expedition to Brazil and on April 23rd, the date of the passing of the *Reinheitsgebot* law in Bavaria which forbade the use of preservatives such as fly agaric mushrooms, stinging nettles, henbane or soot in the brewing process and limited the constituents of beer to barley malt, hops and water, arguably the only truly important event of that year for the future of world civilization, they set sail from Plymouth in two of the king's ships and Michael and Jack went with them.

Shuffle Nineteen

"What shall we Christians do with this rejected and condemned people?
Set fire to their synagogues and bury in the dirt whatever will not burn so
that no man will ever again see a stone or cinder of them."
- Martin Luther (1483 - 1546)

§

At four o'clock on Sunday afternoon Benedetto Solario rang the buzzer
at the front gate of the Casale. A sudden shower was in progress and he
hurried along the driveway under a tiny umbrella trying to avoid the
gathering puddles and getting muddy water-spots on his polished leather
shoes.

Michael and Helen were in the foyer enjoying a cup of tea and some
small very English-looking sandwiches that Susanna had prepared as a
good-natured joke and he informed them that Signor Guido would be on
Hadrian's bridge, now known as Ponte Sant'Angelo, beneath the angel that
holds Veronica's Veil at ten the next morning and this time would not fail
to keep the appointment.

"He asks that you dress comfortably," the young man went on, adding
with a hint of a smile, "And to please be prepared for our always
unpredictable spring weather. He hopes also that you will leave yourselves
free to join him in a little *passeggio*. There is much he wants to show you."

"Of course," Michael replied, "We're all his. We love a good walk."

Helen offered their intermediary some refreshment or at least to wait
until the downpour had abated but he declined and before Michael had a
chance to frame the first of the many questions that were on his mind the
boy nodded politely and was gone.

§

One might reasonably ask what on earth could propel a rather shy,
gentle-natured sixty-seven-year-old, albeit one whose constitution had
been toughened by experience, to cross so vast an ocean in a tiny ship
even if a quarter century of traffic over those waters had made the novelty

of the passage an almost daily occurrence.

For Jack it was simply adventure but for Michael it was something deeper. Not just the urgent smell of his own mortality but a need to witness for himself the calamity he had sensed those many years ago as the sun set over the harbor at Palos. The horrific tales of Montesinos and las Casas were too compelling to ignore but from the very beginning the voyage did not go as planned.

Michael and Jack were both aboard Caboto's vessel, Michael as a kind of second mate and auxiliary pilot, Jack as an ordinary deckhand, and though the captain himself was of a gruff unpleasant disposition he was certainly a skilled mariner and untroubled by any thought of danger. He was clearly in command and the crew respected him but, unfortunately for all, the opposite was true of Sir Thomas who had heretofore only sailed his royal majesty up and down the Thames.

Since Caboto kept the lead and the ships rarely came closer to each other than a mile it was not until they sighted land that Caboto was told Sir Thomas had been keeping more and more to his cabin and given over his duties almost completely to his first mate. When they dropped anchor near the site of present day Georgetown at the mouth of the Demarara river he went to see for himself and it didn't take more than a second for him to realize a feverish and morbid paranoia had overtaken his partner's mind.

It was something Michael understood very well. How the endless circle of the horizon, the enormity of firmament overhead and the devouring vacuum of the dark could bring a man to madness. He had felt it many times on starless nights when no light penetrated the enshrouding gloom, a nausea in the guts as though one's very being was about to be wrenched away and existence itself on the verge of disappearing into a vast formless indifferent infinity. Some people cannot help becoming sickened by such terrors and it was abundantly clear to Caboto that Sir Thomas was one and so, after a day's consideration in which he most probably thought of shooting Pert and tossing him overboard, he decided it would be better for his future favor with the king to turn northwest to the port of Santo Domingo and abandon for the moment his desire of voyaging further south into the unknown.

As Caboto's continuing bad luck would have it the governor of the castle at Santo Domingo, Francisco de Tapia, took them for rovers and fired cannon at them from the shore and they were forced to flee onward to the island of St. John de Puerto Rico where they at last were admitted to the harbor of the tiny settlement of St. Germaine and able to take on much needed provision.

§

Not more than a minute after Benedetto Solario's abrupt departure Lamy came down from his suite with what looked like a small leather travel kit in his hands, something no billionaire should leave home without, but it contained an array of miniaturized transmitting and receiving equipment.

"I saw someone leaving," he said.

"We're on for ten o'clock tomorrow morning."

"Thought it might be your boy. Did you catch his name this time?"

Michael looked at Helen irritably as if it was her fault he hadn't asked.

"Ah well, what's in a name," Lamy teased.

"He was in a hurry."

"So where's it to be? Same place?"

"No, on the Ponte Sant'Angelo," Michael replied, pronouncing the Italian rather awkwardly.

"By the statue of the angel holding Veronica's Veil," Helen finished.

"Hm, mysterious change of venue but maybe we shouldn't read too much into it."

"The boy said we should be prepared for a walk."

"It seems like he wants to spend quite a time."

"Good. That's good. Why not? You've waited long enough."

Lamy sat down and opened the little case and began laying bits and pieces on the coffee table in front of them.

"We should try this out," he said, "Knowing you, you'll want to have some record of your conversation."

Michael started to laugh.

"What, you mean 'carry a wire'?"

He couldn't resist saying the phrase in a cod American cop show accent.

"Don't you think that's dangerous?" Helen asked, a little alarmed, "What if he finds out somehow? What if it starts to make noises?"

"Trust me, it won't," Lamy assured her, holding up a minute transmitter, "What does this look like?"

"A lipstick."

"Exactly. It's wireless and I can pick up what you're saying from over eight hundred feet away even if it's buried in your purse."

"Oh, so I'm the one that's going to carry it?"

"Don't you think it'll be better that way?" Lamy said with an impish grin.

"What if he's got some kind of anti-surveillance device?" Michael asked, overriding him and ignoring the slight, "Something that can sense the signal?"

"I doubt it. There's only one bug-detector out there that could. I'd say it's worth the chance."

Michael was silent for a moment and then laughed again.

"Where the devil did you get this stuff?" he asked incredulously, "Did you just go down to the local spook shop or have you had it all along?"

Lamy smiled.

"You know I'm a boy scout at heart."

Michael looked at him with a combination of amazement and dismay.

"Good lord. So what's your plan? Are you going to follow us on foot or do you have one of those spy vans? Only pedestrians are allowed on that bridge as I recall. Anyway, it's not necessary. Helen's got a mind like a steel trap. She'll remember everything."

"I think you'll appreciate it later. When you're penning your masterpiece. And who the hell knows what to expect. You might need help."

§

Caboto made all possible haste in St. Germaine and after less than forty-eight hours set sail for England but Michael and Jack and two others did not go with him despite the handful of Spanish colonists in the town being strangely sullen and the atmosphere charged with an unhealthy energy. Michael found it hard to define, a sickness of spirit that threatened at every moment to spin out of control.

Columbus put a landing party ashore at what is now Salt River Bay on the north coast of the island on November 14th, 1493, and they immediately ran into trouble. Finding a group of Taino natives held captive in a deserted Carib village they decided to take them aboard but were intercepted by a war canoe as they made for the ship and one of their party was killed with an arrow through his eye. The Spaniards, however, were able to overturn the canoe and capture their attackers and transported both sets of *'indios'* back to Spain.

Little happened for the next fifteen years until on August 8th, 1508, Juan Ponce de León, who had been Columbus's lieutenant, returned and established a settlement named Caparra and the indigenous Taino, who lived more or less peacefully on the island for a thousand years and developed a complex culture, began to be enslaved, brutalized and exploited.

They also began to die mysteriously and by the time of their unsuccessful uprising three years later measles and smallpox as well as outright murder had reduced the original sixty thousand by half. When Michael and Jack arrived in October, 1516, most of those working the fields and digging the mines had been replaced with blacks from West Africa.

At first it was astonishing and then heartbreaking that no more than one hundred and ninety Spaniards were on the island and yet had so easily subdued so many. Armor, cannon, crossbows and arquebuses, coupled with prodigious ease in lying and deceit had evidently won the day.

But it was not without cost. Everywhere Michael and Jack went they were greeted by the sight and stench of corpses in varying stages of decay. Some just bones, some bloated and flyblown or emaciated with disease. They found four naked women who had been raped and their breasts and vaginas hacked away, a male with no genitals, another headless, the body of a small child with blood-black eye-sockets and others missing hips or arms or feet. It was clear that the viciousness unleashed during the subjugation of these gentle people now ran rampant and had eaten its way into the Spaniards' very soul.

There was a Franciscan friar whom they witnessed presiding over an odd cruelty of his own invention. Thirteen wretchedly enfeebled natives, no doubt in this madman's mind as some perverse honor to Christ his Saviour and the twelve apostles, whose flesh was already ripped raw by lashing, were hung by the neck on a long gibbet resembling a modern football goal so that their toes just touched the ground to prevent strangling and, as a small crowd of colonists laughed at their frantic dance, this demented man of God ordered bundles of straw tied round their bodies and, while vehemently exhorting everyone present to pray for their salvation and making the sign of the cross before each victim, slowly went down the row with a brand lighting the straw until one by one they were burned alive.

On another occasion they saw forty whipped and bleeding natives penned in a corral and torn to pieces by the Spaniards' dogs.

§

By nine o'clock Sunday evening Michael and Helen were sitting blearily in front of the television in their suite. The plan was agreed for tomorrow and the equipment tested and Lamy and Warren and Lazzari decided to put in a brief appearance at the party at Teatro Argentina but Helen was too exhausted and Michael too on edge to join them.

They were watching a report on CNN about the one hundred and fifteen eligible cardinal electors who were now gathered in the Vatican City hotel called St. Martha's House, *Domus Sanctae Marthae*, and enjoying supper together before the conclave. They had driven past the west wall to meet Buranelli. The design was intended to reflect a monastic simplicity, though sixty-five percent of the twenty million dollar cost had been bankrolled by a Philadelphia casino owner, and Cardinal Ratzinger was said to be occupying a sparely furnished room.

The Pittsburgh architect of the adjoining Chapel of the Holy Spirit where the cardinals said their prayers before the meal claimed he felt like 'a pencil in God's hands' as he worked on the drawings.

The report was only verbal but despite that, and being perfectly sober for a change, when Michael at last fell asleep after tossing and turning for hours his mind was shaken by a vivid and appalling sequence of dream images. Whatever the connections may have been between them they were all he could recollect when he described them to the others at breakfast.

It began with Berlusconi dressed in rural peasant garb herding a flock of geese in front of him that suddenly turned into children. Then several peasant women were behind him carrying babies. Then breasts and the babies suckling. Then Berlusconi became Ratzinger shooing the children impatiently into a huge refectory with immensely long tables where the cardinals sat in their blood-red robes and golden mitres. Then Berlusconi was brought into the hall on a trolley under an enormous glass cover. He was nude and pink as a baby and evidently the main course. He lay on a gargantuan silver platter surrounded by cooked vegetables and fruit and there was even an apple in his mouth but he spat it out and his eyes opened and he began to scream and tear at his flesh and it came away in fat-soaked chunks like pork crackling. Then Ratzinger was beside him in a soiled wet nightgown gobbling the pieces ravenously as Berlusconi cursed him. Then the Jesuit they saw in the hall outside the infirmary at Castelgandolfo was exhorting the cardinals to eat and they all had massive bibs around their necks stained with the juices that dribbled from their lips and Michael became aware the blackened shapes in their greasy hands were the roasted corpses of the unborn.

Helen got up and left the room when he finished, holding a napkin to her mouth.

"You mean that's all?" Warren said drily.

§

By January, 1517, Michael and Jack had departed St. Germaine, named for Germaine of Foix who Ferdinand took to wife after the death of Isabella, and found passage back to Santo Domingo. Bartolomé was there again despite the censure and they joined him in his crusade to end the cruelty and corruption of the encomienda system.

The word comes from the verb *encomendar* which means 'to entrust' and in theory it meant that any colonist granted land by the Spanish crown would take responsibility for the safety of the natives under their control and teach them Spanish and convert them to the Catholic faith but in reality it was just another excuse for stripping the conquered of their property and enslaving them. It had been the same with the Moors during the *Reconquista*.

Las Casas had not always been so virtuous. As a young chaplain, he was involved in atrocity and bloodshed and rewarded with an *encomienda* of his own, rich in gold and slaves, but now he worked and wrote tirelessly for reform and was thus hated and in constant danger and Michael and Jack and he were often forced to take refuge in the Dominican monastery. He became so frustrated by the delays and accommodating attitude of the Hieronymite commissioners that by May he left again for Spain and finding themselves vilified in every quarter Michael and Jack decided to leave as well and made their way by stages to the grubby port town of Santiago on the southeast corner of Cuba.

Here they quickly realized the wisest course was discretion and kept their activities on Santo Domingo secret. Michael hit upon the bold idea of posing as a chronicler and made the acquaintance of the governor, Diego Velázquez, who introduced them to Fernando Cortés, both of whom had taken a leading role in the conquest of the islands and were now so desensitized to the pain of others they held contests to see who would be first to bisect a living native through the midriff with one pass of their sword. A fresh victim was used for each cut and quartered portions of their bodies were hung from hooks on Cortés' porch to feed his dogs. It was reported on one occasion, after the mother had been killed in like fashion, he threw them her baby.

Nonetheless, this syphilitic monster was Chief Magistrate of the island and married to Velázquez' sister-in-law, Catalina Juárez.

Strangely enough it never became known to Michael, though they were to spend several years in each other's company, that when Cortés was thirteen he had been at one oar of the skiff that brought Marchionni and Amerigo aboard the Simonetta in the harbor at Palos on September 5th, 1498.

By this time, despite the Spaniards' skill in playing one tribe off against the other, the *'indios'* were fighting back with greater and greater frequency and life for the massively outnumbered colonists was a constant battle for survival and the stress of watching their backs day and night was further unhinging their minds. Santiago burned to the ground the previous year, the fire most probably set by a group of rebellious African slaves, and it was still being rebuilt.

Yet in the darkness of this chaos Velázquez and Cortés could talk of little else but gold and silver and the recent settlement of Velázquez' emissary, Juan de Grijalva, on the mainland where he had come upon boatloads of both. They were delighted with the notion that their god-like exploits should be chronicled and in Latin to boot, and so, since they were considering a new expedition that would attempt to go inland beyond Grijalva and find the fabled capital of gold which the coastal indigenes had hinted at with such awe and envy, it didn't take Michael long to convince the two barking mad egomaniacs that he should join them with Jack as his assistant.

But, unfortunately, due to Cortés' philandering and the infantile quarrels that erupted daily between the two men, not to mention the brutal suppression of several native uprisings, it took until February, 1519, for anything to happen, and he and Jack often dreamed of the peaceful fields at Billingsgate farm and more than once considered giving up and returning home.

Shuffle Twenty

"The entire system of capitalism is essentially a criminal enterprise and
the people running it know that very well."
- Eric Ross Green (1941 -   )

§

Five minutes before a slightly dizzy with decongestant yet still
infuriatingly stuffed up Joseph Alois Ratzinger carefully lifted his robes to
ascend the high altar above St. Peter's tomb under Bernini's colossal
baldacchino, the columns of which were copies of the Temple of Solomon
in Jerusalem and decorated with bees and laurel leaves, the heraldic
emblems of the Barberini, Florentine wool merchants like the Vespucci,
the bronze for which had been pilfered from the ceiling of the Pantheon
and inspired the saying *'Quod non fecerunt barbari, fecerunt Barberini'*, 'What
the barbarians did not do, the Barberini did', and attempted to
surreptitiously clear his throat to begin the *Pro Eligendo Papa*, the mass for
the election of the Supreme Pontiff, a very nervous Michael and an
expectant but already somewhat 'wishing she were elsewhere' Helen got
out of a taxi on the Lungotevere degli Altoviti where it bleeds into
Lungotevere Tor di Nona at the south end of the Pons Aelius or Ponte
Sant'Angelo.

It was a pleasant morning with intermittent sun and scudding cloud
and Warren and Lazzari were in position sitting on the steps below the
statue of St. Paul. They both knew it was Paul because he always had a
book or scroll in his hands and often the sword of his martyrdom as well.
They had purchased an espresso from the 'Bibite-Gelati-Panini-Pizza' van
directly in front of them and were pretending to be tourists examining a
street map of the city and neither turned to look as Helen paid the driver
and Michael took several deep breaths and they walked together onto the
bridge.

Lamy was stationed at the far end camouflaged amongst the crowd at
the entrance to Hadrian's cylindrical mausoleum and, half a minute before
Michael and Helen arrived in the cab, he and Warren had spoken to each
other via the microtransmitter-receivers nestled like hearing-aids in their

228

ears.

"They're coming toward you now," Warren had whispered, "I'm guessing it's the young man who came to the Casale pushing him in the wheelchair with the canopy over it."

"Yeah, I see them. Panama hat, big sunglasses and a blue suit pretty much the same as Michael's. How bizarre is that. Did he finally decide to wear it?"

"I don't know. I hope not. He was still dithering when we left."

"What's with the guy's nose? It looks weird."

"As far as we could tell he's wearing some kind of protective guard over it attached to the glasses. Like skiers do but flesh-colored."

"Are those gloves on his hands?"

"Yes. Light beige. Luigi says his socks are beige too."

"Hey, a definite fashion statement. Yup, it's them. They've stopped under the angel. How old was he, could you tell?"

"I think I glimpsed white hair under the hat. You're about to see Michael and Helen. Their cab pulled up a moment ago and he did put the suit on."

"Are you kidding me?"

"I'm afraid not."

"Shit. What a comedy."

Michael was sweating heavily despite the mild weather. They were on the walkway on the west side of the bridge and by the time they reached the angel with the scourge he had to support himself on the stone balustrade beneath it.

"What's wrong?" Helen asked.

"I think I'm going to faint."

"Christ, he's having one of his turns," Lamy whispered.

"You can take it back about the drink," Michael muttered, "I didn't touch a drop last night. Good lord, it's the same as Juarez only much, much stronger. The whole bridge is moving. Is the water in the river about to wash over us?"

"No," Helen answered lightly despite the frightening look on his face, "I can't feel anything."

"Oh god. I can barely stay on my feet. Help me!"

Michael forced himself to keep moving with Helen in support at his elbow but before they got to the angel with the crown of thorns, opposite the statue of the angel with the humble cloth beneath which *'il cugino'* sat watching them, he thrust himself away from her, let out a gasp and crumpled to his knees on the cobbled pavement.

"He's fallen over," Lamy said quietly, "The boy is pushing the wheelchair over to him."

"Michael," the mystery man said in a friendly sympathetic tone.

The voice was pleasant and reminded him of the Italian actor Raf Vallone, who he happened to have watched the day before Lamy's call in a rerun of The Godfather, Part 3, and only a few days before that in a rare screening at the Hampstead Everyman of 1949's splendid *Riso Amaro*, though it carried no trace of an accent.

"I am sorry you are not well," he went on, offering a gloved hand to help Michael to his feet, "I am your cousin Guido. Could it be something you ate?"

Michael was looking straight into his face under the shadow of the canopy and his own brightly lit double reflection in the sunglasses. He was trying to decide if the man behind them was the Jesuit in his dream but he couldn't see his eyes and the noseguard was disconcerting.

"Can you get up?" Guido asked, touching Michael gently on the shoulder.

A group of elderly American tourists had stopped to stare.

"Benedetto, help him."

The young man came around the chair and with Helen lifting at one arm they got Michael to his feet. In the midst of the dizziness he noticed the angel holding the veil was missing most of the pinkie and the last knuckle of the ring finger on the right hand. Its visage was almost androgynous and a bare leg was exposed in a way Michael found very sexy and what did the inscription on the pedestal say? *Respicie in faciem Christi tui*. What the hell did that mean?

He could see Guido's lips were moving and heard his disconnected voice saying, "*Buongiorno*, Helen, it is a great honor to meet you," and then their hands shaking politely out of the corner of his eye.

"And you," Helen replied, "I want to thank you."

The sound was muted as though his Eustachian tubes were clogged shut.

"For what?"

"For rescuing me."

"It was nothing," the voice said warmly, "Forgive my odd appearance but the explanation is simple. There is a little café a few meters beyond the piazza. We will take some refreshment. Then we can talk."

The face was looking at him again. The skin was pale like the Jesuit's and wholly without blemish or visible wrinkle.

"Are you able to walk?" the voice asked.

Michael nodded. The overwhelming nausea had miraculously vanished but he was still too wobbly inside to speak.

"It's happened several times lately," Helen said, "I've no idea why. Are you sure you'll be all right?"

"Yes, yes," Michael managed finally, "Sorry. What does it mean?"

"What does what mean?" she asked.

"The inscription."

"Ah," Guido said with an almost imperceptible smile, "It says, 'Look upon the face of your Christ'. From Psalm 83."

They began making their way slowly down the slope of the bridge toward the piazza where Michael and Helen alighted from the cab.

"I think someone just took a photo of them," Warren whispered.

"Where from?" Lamy asked.

"From behind the statue of St. Peter."

"Anyone you recognize?"

"No. But I'm sure that's what he was doing. He had that clandestine look. Now he's walking away across the street."

"Keep an eye on him. I'm following them now. Be with you in a minute."

Michael's mind was awash with questions.

"Does that have some significance to why we met here?" he asked.

Guido chuckled.

"Not particularly," he replied, "Veronica, so the story goes, came out of a house on the Via Dolorosa and wiped the sweat from Jesus' face with the cloth and his image remained on it. If you'll believe that you'll believe anything."

Helen smiled and nodded at the sarcasm but Michael was still struggling to focus. Who was this man?

"Is your last name Vespucci?" he blurted.

"It doesn't matter what my last name is but, you are right, our connection goes back to the Vespucci."

"How far back?"

"Just over five hundred years."

Michael and Helen looked at each other in astonishment.

"To Bartolomeo Vespucci?" Michael asked.

"Yes."

"The professor of astronomy at Padua who knew Machiavelli?"

"Yes. I see you have done your homework."

"Incredible," Warren whispered to Lamy, "The bullshit you told Buranelli turns out to be true."

"Unless this guy heard about it," Lamy answered, "And is bullshitting the bullshitters."

"And that's not your name too by any chance?" Michael prodded.

"I have told you my name is Guido."

"Well then, do you happen to know anyone . . ?"

"Called Bartolomeo Vespucci? In Italy today? I don't think so."

Michael's collapse had made him irritable and he tried another tack, albeit rather silly.

"OK, don't you find it strange that we're wearing virtually identical suits?"

Guido gazed at him for a moment as if he was slightly unhinged.

"Yes, it is a peculiar coincidence."

"Nothing more?"

"Why? Is there something more?"

"I think you both have very good taste," Helen came in with an attempt to lighten the tone, "It must run in the family."

They were crossing the Lungotevere in full view of Warren and Lazzari.

"Beatrice Cenci was beheaded in this piazza on September the 11th, 1599," Guido told them, "Legend has it she walks here holding her head every year on the eve of her execution rather like your Anne Boleyn. The bridge has a bloody history. It was not always the pretty picture you see today."

An old girlfriend of Michael's named Leonie had played the tragic heroine in a revival of Shelley's play at the Almeida twenty years ago.

"Yes," he said, "Her father forced her into an incestuous relationship and she was convicted of murdering him. He was known to be a brutal man and there was a lot of sympathy for her among the common people."

"Exactly so," Guido replied, turning to look at Michael in mild surprise.

"But the pope . . I can't remember which one . . "

"Ippolito Aldobrandini. Clement VIII."

"Ah, yes, of course. Ironic choice of name, haha. Yes, well, um,

Clement was fearful of offending the aristocracy and condemned her to death anyway."

"Popes are no better than anyone else," Guido said, smiling again, "Their first thought is always self-preservation."

"Who were the Altoviti?" Helen asked, changing the subject and referring to the street sign on the corner wall.

"Florentine bankers. The most famous was a beautiful young man named Bindo who our mutual ancestor knew well. Raphael painted him exquisitely. He lived in a gorgeous palace just over there to the right. It is gone now."

There was something in the way he spoke of it that seemed beyond mere historical knowledge and Michael decided to stop interrupting.

"You can see we are entering Via del Banco di Santo Spirito. Five hundred years ago this part of Ponte was the banking district. Every other building was a church or bank or palazzo. In case you are interested that is now an English Methodist church on the left. The name of Garibaldi's chaplain, Alessandro Gavazzi, an Evangelical Protestant, is there on the plaque. Of course it is much more recent but a few paces further on we will find another dedicated to St. Celsus and St. Julian that dates from the 5th century. The original structure was demolished by Giuliano della Rovere to make the avenue wider. Pope Julius II. You will know him as Michelangelo's patron. The replacement was abandoned when he died and was not completed for two hundred years. Which Celsus and which Julian? You can take your pick. There was a boy Celsus martyred by Nero and another killed by Diocletian and as for Julians there are so many why should we care. The façade of the palazzo that housed the Banco di Santo Spirito is visible in the distance. It used to serve as the Roman Mint under della Rovere and then Camillo Borghese changed its function in 1605. Since it was the bank of the Papal States it can claim to be the oldest national bank in Europe."

They arrived outside the Antico Caffé di Marte and Benedetto pushed the wheelchair to one of several tables shaded by blue umbrellas on a side street called Vicolo del Curato.

Lamy joined Warren and Lazzari at the steps.

"Christ, this guy's as much of a windbag as I am," he said.

"Our camera man's in there," Warren told him, pointing to an antiquary shop across from the Methodist church, and just as he spoke the man came out and started down toward the café.

"The building we are looking at," Guido went on, "Is the Palazzo Alberini. Giulio Alberini was an ally of Cesare Borgia. The archway on the other side of Via del Banco di Santo Spirito, not very surprisingly called Arco dei Banchi, once led to the counting house of Agostino Chigi, the richest man in Rome and the money behind Giuliano della Rovere's election."

The waiter came and Guido ordered a cappuccino for himself and another for Benedetto, who was now sitting quietly beside him, and a large pot of tea for Michael and Helen.

"Of course, that is all beside the point," Guido admitted as the waiter left, "Let me begin at the beginning."

§

The sniffling prelate known as 'God's Rottweiler' because of his tooth and claw defence of church doctrine no matter how mindless or obscure was now in the middle of his homily quoting St. Paul's letter to the Galatians, chapter 3, verses 13 and 14.

"Christ ransomed us from the curse of the law by becoming a curse for us, for it is written, 'Cursed be everyone who hangs on a tree', that the blessing of Abraham might be extended to the Gentiles through Christ Jesus, so that we might receive the promise of the Spirit through faith."

He followed with a clarification in his own words.

"The mercy of Christ is not a cheap grace. It does not presume a trivialization of evil. Christ carries in His body and soul all the weight of evil and all its destructive force. He burns and transforms evil through suffering in the fire of His suffering love."

Elsewhere in the Eternal City the prime minister and his cronies were sowing an artfully constructed confusion. They began by announcing that, after the disastrous regional election results earlier in the month and the apparent defection of the Union of Christian Democrats from the cabinet the previous Friday, Signor Berlusconi would offer his resignation and attempt to form a new government with a fresh platform. They denied the accusation that it was a sly manoeuver to avoid an election which his coalition was very likely to lose, dismissing such double-dealing as 'a remnant of Italy's messy political past', but they knew the afternoon meeting with President Ciampi to ask his permission was a mere formality.

Next came the letter to the Ephesians, chapter 4, verse 14.

"What does it mean to be an infant in faith? Saint Paul answers, 'tossed by waves and swept along by every wind of teaching arising from human trickery.' This description is very relevant today! How many winds of doctrine we have known in recent decades, how many ideological currents, how many ways of thinking. The small boat of thought of many Christians has been tossed about by these waves and thrown from one extreme to the other. From Marxism to liberalism, even to libertinism. From collectivism to radical individualism. From atheism to a vague religious mysticism. From agnosticism to syncretism and so forth. Every day new sects are created and what Saint Paul says about trickery comes true with cunning that tries to draw those into error! Having a clear faith based on the Creed of the Church is often labeled today as fundamentalism. Whereas relativism, which is letting oneself be tossed and swept along by every wind of teaching, looks like the only attitude acceptable to today's standards. We are moving towards a dictatorship of relativism which recognizes nothing as certain and has as its highest goal one's own ego and one's own desires."

§

"First let me explain my appearance," Guido began, "For many reasons it is convenient for me to remain, as they say, *incognito*. You probably did not see the man taking pictures of us on the bridge. He has just gone into the tobacco shop by the archway. I don't need to protect my nose from the sun. The guard simply prevents my enemies from obtaining a clear image. They could force a direct physical confrontation but both Benedetto and I are armed and I assure you anyone trying it would not survive the encounter. There is certainly always a risk when I venture out in public, which these days is very seldom, that they could stage . . what do the American papers call it . . a 'drive-by shooting'? . . but I think by now they realize such an action would not produce the desired result. A kidnapping is also quite pointless as my friends will deny knowledge of my existence. I am not going to tell you precisely who I am nor how I was able to effect Helen's release so please do not waste our precious time by asking."

The waiter arrived and no one spoke as he set their drinks and a selection of sweet biscuits on the table.

"What I have," Guido continued, "Are some snippets of a history you will both find interesting. I believe you have already discovered you had an ancestor five hundred years ago named Michael Davenport?"

Michael and Helen looked at each other thinking, 'Yes, but how did you?' and then Michael said, "Yes, just recently. There was a letter written by a Dutch humanist . . "

"Desiderius Erasmus, yes."

Christ, had everyone on the planet been bugging their phones! Were there secret microphones everywhere? Were they all in on it together?

"But we know very little beyond that," Helen added quickly.

Guido smiled.

"Well, by pure happenstance, I will be able to fill in some of the blanks for you. Again, I would prefer that you do not question too closely how."

"We're all ears," Michael said.

Guido spent the next hour and a half telling them Michael the Med's story up to Michael and Jack's departure for America with Sebastiano Caboto.

Warren and Lazzari and Lamy were still sitting on the steps and Lamy was chewing on a *porchetta* sandwich and sipping an orange soda. Like Michael and Helen, they were all too fascinated to speak.

"I am sorry that most of what I know occurred in the years between 1497 and 1515 because the records were kept by Bartolomeo during Michael's many visits to Italy. However, he did come one last time in the spring of 1527 and I can tell you about that in some detail but first I want you to read a letter he sent from England in 1524. He and Jack had just returned from seven years in the Caribbean and Mexico. Between 1518 and 1521 Michael was employed by the Spanish conquistador Hernán Cortés to chronicle his exploits against the Aztec empire. The letter is written in Italian but mentions that the story filled eight volumes and was composed entirely in Latin. It's a great pity it has never been found. Clearly Michael had a talent for languages. He was fluent in Spanish and Portuguese as well and several North African and Mesoamerican tongues."

"I hate him already," Michael said.

Guido smiled again.

"Benedetto has translated and typed it for you since the letter itself is too fragile to be moved."

"Where is it?" Helen asked.

"In my private collection."

"And Bartolomeo's 'records', as you call them?"

"Yes, also."

"Would you allow us to see them?"

"If you wish. A photocopy of the letter is attached to the transcript."

Benedetto got up and unzipped a deep flap pocket hanging from the back of the wheelchair, took out a thin file and handed it to Michael.

"Shall we have lunch while you read?" Guido suggested, "Then go on with our perambulations?"

§

Lamy was pissed off that Michael didn't read the damn thing out loud and they had to sit and listen to Guido ordering lunch amid silence but this is what the letter said. It was addressed from 'Billingsgate Farm' and dated 'October 9th, 1524'.

"My dearest Bartolomeo, Today is my seventy-fifth birthday though I am sure you must assume I have already departed this earth! The truth is Jack and I have only recently returned from seven long years in those lands that will now forever bear your esteemed uncle's name.

"Why we ventured there is too complex a tale for a letter. It will have to wait until we again meet face to face. Something I have promised myself must happen.

"You will remember me speaking of an afternoon in Palos when I sensed, it was almost as if I was hearing the sound of it, a strange unfathomable darkness welling up on the western horizon. You know how much I was affected by the sensation so when I tell you that not more than a few weeks after we left Padua the opportunity arose to voyage there you will understand that it was irresistible. All I will say for the moment is that the darkness we experienced was deeper than even you could have imagined.

"For four years of the seven we accompanied a brute named Fernando Cortés to the very heart of the new continent where he came upon and eventually destroyed a flourishing empire called Mexica. Its center was a vast and beautiful city built upon a lake called Tenochtitlan with volcanoes higher than any mountain you have seen rising majestically above it. The first sight was quite beyond belief. I estimate that more than a quarter million people were living there amid huge and graceful pyramids of stone, the temples of their gods, courtyards, gardens, palaces with baths in every room and fresh water running along two great aqueducts from the distant hills.

"Cortés was a man of overwhelming greed and vanity but blessed by blind luck. Early on in the adventure he made a fortuitous alliance with a rival and envious people named the Tlaxcaltec whose warriors enlarged his army tenfold and helped him spread

terror throughout the land. In one of the lesser cities during our four-month march to the capital he tricked and treacherously massacred five thousand unarmed members of the local Mexica nobility and then burned it to the ground. Rampant slaughter was the stuff of every day. Jack and I became so accustomed to it that we felt our faces too could not be those of anything called human.

"The 'indios' were capable of equal barbarity in response. They customarily sought the favor of their gods with human sacrifice and in our final assault they took seventy assailants prisoner and cut out their still beating hearts on the steps of their Temple to the Sun.

"What has happened throughout the many islands discovered since Cristoforo Colombo set his foot on San Salvador and continues unabated on the two great landmasses north and south is nothing less than the complete extermination of the original inhabitants and the total destruction of their way of life. I doubt that on the islands more than one in ten that were alive in 1492 remain. More than anything their numbers have been decimated by smallpox. A fact which has allowed the colonists to claim that God himself has given them clear title here.

"Everywhere there is evidence of religiosity gone mad. Cortés, who is as profane a man as ever existed, was obsessed with converting the 'savages' and spoke continually of the glory of Christianity to them. In Veracruz, a primitive outpost where we put ashore on the mainland, he baptized four of the Tlaxcaltec leaders though I am sure they had not the faintest notion of the significance of the act. Thus Maxixcatzin, Xicotencatl, Citalpopocatzin and Temiloltecutl became Don Lorenzo, Don Vicente, Don Bartolomé and Don Gonzalo. In Tenochtitlan he forced the emperor Moctezuma to remove two statues of their gods from the Sun Temple altar and replace them with shrines to the Virgin and Saint Christopher. Such absurdity has, alas, gone hand in hand with the utmost cruelty.

"It is as though the freedom from constraint that ordinary men experienced there instead of fulfilling the great promise of a new world, bringing happiness, contentment and encouraging good order, was condemned from the start to produce a hellish chaos of unspeakable depravity, unleashing the darkest beasts of our nature. But why am I telling you this of all people? I can see your secret smile. Of course you can imagine it. It is no different here.

"With Jack's assistance I penned an eight volume history of the ruination caused by this most crude and ignorant of men. I suggested it so that we might join the expedition without the requirement of bearing arms and he was flattered by the thought, particularly that it would be set down in Latin but though he could not read the language he was continually suspicious of what we were writing and would give sections to the Jesuits who came with us to overlook and we were forced to create two versions. The first I left with

him, we could not have escaped his clutches without doing so, and now that we are home I shall attempt to have the truer story printed, perhaps in less tiresome and more manageable form, and will bring you a copy.

"It was a great joy to find the family all in good health on our return. As I trust and hope this letter will find you and your dear daughter.

"Expect me soon, Michael."

§

In the Uffici Giudiziari near Piazzale Clodio north of Vatican City and less than a mile from where Michael the Mod sat digesting and rereading the letter, Judge Orlando Villoni had come to a decision about the evidence prosecutors Maria Monteleone and Luca Tescaroli had presented over the last two years and whether it was now sufficient to indict four suspects named Pippo Calo, Ernesto Diotallevi, Flavio Carboni and Manuela Kleinszig for the 1982 murder of Roberto Calvi.

Calvi was nicknamed 'God's banker' because of his close association with the papacy but had fled Italy after being convicted of corruption. It was widely believed he had been laundering Mafia profits through the Vatican Bank.

He was found hanging beneath Blackfriars Bridge in London on June 18th. His pockets were filled with bricks and large amounts of cash in three different currencies but the London inquest concluded he committed suicide which was obviously idiotic and the result of collusion behind the scenes.

Everyone knew he could reveal some extremely damaging links between the Mafia and certain very well known members of Italy's power elite which is presumably why Tescaroli said to the press outside the courthouse, "This is just the end of the beginning. The judge has agreed to send the four to trial but the real task starts today."

Shuffle Twenty-one

"Our Lord gave so much strength to His own that we drove them back into the water of the lake and our Indian allies, when they saw the victory God had given us, had no other thought but to kill right and left."
- Hernán Cortés (1485 - 1547)

§

"Good lord," Michael said, "We even have the same birthday."

"And not just that," Helen added, "If he was seventy-five in 1524 it means he was born in 1449 which is exactly five hundred years before you."

"Good lord, that's true. It's too ridiculous."

"It is a remarkable coincidence," Guido agreed, "But perhaps not worth dwelling on any more than the color of our suits."

The waiter brought a carafe of red wine and a big plateful of pizza squares with a tantalizing array of assorted toppings.

"Tell me this," Michael began, "I've got a million questions . . "

"I may not have the answers but feel free to ask."

"OK, um, first of all, are you Italian? You don't have an accent."

"I've had many years to practice but, yes, I am Italian."

"Were you born here?"

"Yes, in Florence."

"Not Montefioralle?"

"No, Florence. Peretola, to be exact."

"And you swear you're not a Vespucci."

"As I've said, like you, I am related to the Vespucci."

"Like me?"

"Like both of you."

Michael looked at Helen in wide-eyed amazement.

"To the Vespucci?"

"Yes."

"To Bartolomeo Vespucci in particular?"

"Yes."

"How, in heaven's name? How are we related to him?"

"I will tell you but first taste some pizza. It is the best in Rome."

Michael took a swallow of wine and caught Helen's look.

"Oh, for god's sake, I'm not going to get drunk!" he exclaimed.

"Suit yourself, ducky. It wasn't me that fell over."

"A little wine is good for the digestion," Guido chimed in, taking a sip and pouring oil on the friction. He held the stem of his glass with a napkin to avoid soiling his gloves and Helen noticed that Benedetto had cut two sections of the pizza into small pieces and put them on a plate in front of him.

"Before we go on with our walk," Guido continued, "I must tell you the next to last chapters of Michael's story. He writes at the end of the letter of his joy in finding the family well when he and Jack returned from America but it didn't last. A few months later his daughter, Jack's mother, was killed in a riding accident and it broke something inside him. He was still a kind and gentle man despite having chosen a harder and harder path. Shortly thereafter came news of his brother's death and though they were never close there followed years of distressing litigation over the family estate at Bramhall. It bothered Elaine more than he and when finally they were awarded nothing she couldn't get over the unfairness and it affected her health. She developed a chronic fever and, though it caught everyone by surprise because of the toughness of her nature, she died too on January 14th, 1427, three days short of her sixty-eighth birthday."

"What?!" Helen shrieked, having done the sum in her head, "She can't be exactly five hundred years older than me as well!"

"Sounding more and more like bullshit," Lamy muttered.

"Again," Guido cautioned, "I wouldn't read too much into it."

"What about the others?" Michael asked, "The children and Arthur."

"Arthur was so devastated by Elaine's unexpected death that he went into a rapid and shocking mental decline. His sons refused to have him committed to an asylum but he was never the same again."

Michael considered for a moment and then asked pointedly, "When did he die?"

Guido looked at him and smiled.

"That I can't tell you. The record ends in the spring of 1527."

"Then how do you know he was never the same again?"

"I don't. It was an assumption. An embellishment. Bartolomeo wrote that Michael was sure he wouldn't be, that's all."

"So you don't know what happened to Jenny and the younger twins."

"No."

"But none of that tells us how we're related to the Vespucci."

"Have patience. I am coming to it."

"What do you think?" Lamy asked, "Is he just making it all up, or what?"

"Seems to me like he probably knows a lot more than he's saying," Warren answered.

"I have that feeling too," Lazzari agreed, "I sensed that he stopped himself when Michael was going on about the husband and the younger twins."

Michael took another sip of wine and decided to change tack.

"OK then, what do you know about the stolen plutonium?"

Guido gazed at him calmly.

"Only that it was stolen and people were worried."

"What people?"

"I'm sure you can guess."

"And you don't know who took it."

"I wish I did. It would have made things a great deal simpler."

"But clearly you have some pretty top level connections."

Guido put a bite of pizza in his mouth with his fork and chewed on it but didn't answer.

"I mean in Washington and London and here and Mexico and just about everywhere I'd guess. Did you order the explosion in Juarez?"

"Michael, stop it," Helen said, "He told you he wouldn't answer questions like that. We should be grateful to him for telling us anything."

"But how do we know any of it's true? How do we know it isn't just some mad invention?"

"Don't be insulting! Did Lamy's aunt invent the Erasmus letter then?"

"Well, she could have, couldn't she?"

There was an awkward silence.

"What reason could I have to lie?" Guido asked in the same calm tone, "I am telling you the truth as far as telling truth is possible. Are you not finding it interesting?"

Michael's face flushed with embarrassment.

"No, no, it's too interesting! Too fantastic! It's hard not to ask. I'm dying to know who you are and how you do what you do and how you know these things. I'm utterly blown away, overwhelmed and gobsmacked. Forgive me. I'll shut up and listen, I promise."

"He has a tendency to dramatize," Helen interjected wryly.

"There is no need for apology. Relax. Have another glass of wine. There is much more if you wish to hear it."

"Of course I want to hear it!" Michael went on, "I've been trying to find out about Bartolomeo Vespucci since I was kidnapped in Juarez! But there was nothing, just a few tiny references and some obscure papers at Yale University. And now to find out we're somehow distantly related to the man? Well, I ask you, is it any wonder I'm acting a bit peculiar?"

"You need to tell him about Juarez," Helen said, "And what happened in Washington and New York. Do it now so he'll understand. Just please try and make it brief."

"Oh Jesus," Lamy said, "Here we go again."

Michael hesitated but only for a moment and managed to regurgitate the gist of it in less than three quarters of an hour. Guido didn't say a word but when Michael got to the sexual ritual of blood in Juarez he began to laugh and more and more as the tale of Dick Cheney unfolded and little by little Michael joined him and by the end they were both in stitches at the hopeless frustration of it all.

"So you can appreciate why I'm crazy," Michael concluded, "Our only real evidence the plutonium was stolen until you confirmed it was that Mogilevich thought he could force us to tell him where it was by kidnapping Helen but we couldn't be certain even from that it was true. In fact, I was never sure if there ever actually was any. And as for my modern day Shirt of Nessus, my 'identity napalm' as I call him, this effing light blue suit of the reincarnate Bartolomeo Vespucci, just because Mogilevich and Portillo and the devious monsters in Washington either at one point believed I was him or at least believed in him even if I wasn't and Ratzinger hinted he might know him, I still don't have a shred of proof he exists!"

They had been laughing so hard it took a long time to recover.

"What a painful story. What an unjust burden to bear," Guido said at last, pulling the sunglasses slightly forward from his eyes and dabbing his tears with the napkin, "But you must admit it has a comical side."

"No kidding," Lamy grunted.

§

When Albert Einstein, a self-described 'deeply religious non-believer', died in the wee hours of April 18th, 1955, Thomas Stoltz Harvey was forty-two and a staff pathologist at Princeton Hospital and thus on the fiftieth anniversary of the day he walked into Princeton morgue and cut out the great physicist's brain and stole it he was ninety-two. He hadn't been originally scheduled to perform the autopsy and was a last minute replacement for a New York neuroanatomist named Harry Zimmerman.

It wasn't required that Harvey look inside the skull since it was apparent Einstein had died of internal bleeding due to the rupture of an abdominal aortic aneurysm that had already been treated surgically seven years before. However, the thought that the mysterious organ enclosed in it might yield up the secret of Einstein's intelligence to future neuroscientists was too tempting for the good doctor and so he quietly went to work with buzz saw, scalpel and snippers.

He sectioned some of the twelve hundred and thirty grams of gray matter he coaxed out of its protective shell of meninges, blood vessels and nerves that morning into hundreds of slices and kept them and the remaining chunk in jars of formaldehyde for forty-three years, never letting anyone see them or know where they were and only occasionally doling out small portions to researchers.

He had no permission from Einstein's family or the university to make the theft and, needless to say, he was fired from Princeton immediately afterward.

When interviewed on the anniversary at his home in Titusville, New Jersey, and asked why he had finally turned his specimen jars over to Doctor Elliot Krauss in 1998 he replied, "I got tired of the responsibility."

The only difference that was ever discovered between the treasured object and those of ordinary mortals was a slightly higher proportion of glial cells than average in certain areas and, in the opinion of those future neuroscientists, that didn't signify a whole hell of a lot.

But, whether it was the glial cells or not, when David Ben-Gurion offered Einstein the presidency of Israel in 1952 he refused the honor because he felt he 'would have to say things to the people of Israel that they would not like to hear,' such as 'the most important aspect of Israel's policy must be to institute complete equality with the Arab citizens living within its borders . . the attitude the government adopts will provide the real test of their moral standards.'

244

§

It was nearly half-past two as Guido put down his napkin and said, "Well, I will be interested to hear when we've finished our conversation whether you still feel you have no proof of his existence. Now we must continue our walk. I will have to introduce the final chapter with a little more Italian history."

Before getting up from the table Michael and Helen offered to pay for the lunch but Benedetto told them he had already done so.

Upon hearing this Lamy and Warren and Lazzari crossed the Lungotevere to the Methodist church at the beginning of Via del Banco di Spirito Santo and saw the man who had taken the photo on the bridge coming out of the *tabacchi*. They watched him nonchalantly disappearing under the Arco dei Banchi as the procession of Benedetto and the wheelchair with Michael and Helen at either side came into view and carried on toward Largo Ottavio Tassoni.

Beyond the archway the building on their right was covered by scaffolding so they took the left hand side by Palazzo Alberini which was closed with huge metal doors and being refurbished, Guido told them, into a Gucci fashion and design headquarters.

"Giulio di Giuliano de' Medici was born a bastard a month after his father was assassinated in the Pazzi conspiracy but his uncle Lorenzo made sure that he was considered legitimate through a loophole in canon law. He was made a cardinal and when his cousin Giovanni, Leo X, died he fully expected to be the next pope. However, a Dutchman named Adriaan Floriszoon Boeyens, who had been a tutor to the future emperor Charles V, was chosen as a compromise candidate in his place. Boeyens was the last non-Italian pope until John Paul II. He had never been to Rome and was viewed as a naive pedant, a dogmatist and a barbarian. Charles had appointed him Inquisitor General of Aragon and then General of the Reunited Inquisitions of Castile and Aragon and he brought the madness back to Italy in full force. Bartolomeo was sure when he died eighteen months later that he had been murdered. As you are probably aware there were similar suspicions about the death of Karol Wojtyła's predecessor. In any case, on November 19th, 1523, Giulio became Clement VII.

"At that time Charles was the most powerful man in Europe. He was just twenty-three but because Ferdinand of Spain was his maternal grandfather and his father Philip the Handsome was the son of Archduke Maximilian and Mary of Burgundy the royal houses of Trastámara, Habsburg and Burgundy-Valois were united in one person. When his paternal grandfather died in 1519 it was his good favor with the Fuggers and the lavish use of their money to bribe the electors that enabled him to defeat his rivals Henry Tudor, Francis of France and the Elector of Saxony who were also laying claim to the throne of the Holy Roman Empire and he was eventually given a full papal coronation in Bologna in 1530. In truth Giulio had little choice since it was a condition of his release from the Castel Sant'Angelo.

"Charles had the same dislike for Hernán Cortés as your ancestor. After the conquest of the Aztec he appointed him governor of New Spain but sent four royal overseers to observe and, if necessary, countermand his actions."

They arrived at Largo Tassoni and Benedetto stopped the wheelchair on the corner of Via dei Banchi Nuovi where they could enjoy an unimpeded view of the Palazzo d'Antica Zecca which Guido told them housed the Roman Mint under Giuliano della Rovere and later became the Bank of the Holy Spirit.

The man with the camera was following too closely and casually stepped into a wine shop as Benedetto turned to glance at him and twenty paces further behind Lazzari began playing tourist guide and gestured up at the façade of the palazzo in a pretense of explaining something to Warren and Lamy, after which they crossed the triangular square to a bus stop on the opposite side and stood looking in the other direction.

"Why is it called Bank of the Holy Spirit?" Helen asked.

"In 1605, Ottavio Tassoni was *commendatore* of the hospital Santo Spirito. We will pass by it. It was founded in 727 by the Saxon king Ina to provide for the welfare of English pilgrims. At Tassoni's urging Paul V, Camillo Borghese, formed a bank by using the enormous property holdings of the hospital as the guarantee. The stated intention was altruistic. It was to help small depositors avoid investing with unscrupulous moneylenders but behind this was a scheme to provide constant replenishment for the coffers of the hospital and the Papal Palace and ultimately to rescue the Papacy from the grip of private banks.

"Raising capital has always been the primary occupation of the church. It makes the statues of Charity and Frugality that you see up there to either side of Paul V's coat-of-arms something of a cynical joke. But banking is only part of this story although the primitive form of deficit financing brought in by our friend Giulio in 1526 was certainly an indirect cause of Michael's death. It was called, most delightfully, the *Monte della Fede*. *'Monte'* meaning both a method of tax collection and mountain and *'fede'* both faith and loyalty. 'Mountain of faith' is a delightful phrase, don't you think?"

Guido laughed out loud and though Michael could appreciate the humor of it he also caught a glimpse of Guido's very yellow teeth and suddenly found him a trifle crude.

"It created deep resentment because it was plain that it was just one more way of ripping off the rural population of the Papal States and securing a more consistent income for you-know-who."

Benedetto began pushing the wheelchair again toward the crosswalk over Via Vittorio Emanuele II and Michael was amused that they passed a Banco di Roma ATM on the way.

"I should go back to 1521 and the beginning of either the Third or Fourth Italian War depending on whether you count the war of the League of Cambrai against the Venetians as third or not but, I'm sorry, I can't be bothered. Teasing any kind of narrative sense from the savage imbecility of those years is beyond my patience."

"I'm fairly familiar with it already," Michael said, "And I know Helen is as anxious as I am to get on with Michael's story."

"Good. I'll make it simple. Michael was right when he wrote in his letter 'it is no different here.' In between a zealot emperor and a corrupt vacillating pope was a mule-headed bigot named Luther who kept stirring the shit without any thought to the consequence. Of course the Catholic Church was totally venal but no one seemed to mind all that much and was challenging its credibility worth the death of hundreds of thousands of German peasants? And look at the state of Christianity now in all its sectarian foolishness. Did the fat oaf really achieve anything significant?"

Michael and Helen exchanged a look. Their host seemed to be changing character and his narrative losing clarity and coherence.

"The 'eternal peace' that was supposed to follow the victory of Francis I at Melegnano, when he regained control of Milan from the Swiss and after which he became Leonardo's patron you remember, lasted less than the twinkling of an eye and, due to his own stupidity for invading both Navarre and Holland at the same time which caused nearly everyone to gang up on him, he lost it again when he was defeated by Charles at Pavia in 1525 and the feckless Giulio, who had been almost alone in supporting

France, promptly changed allegiance.

"But then Giulio decided he didn't want Spaniards having control in Milan and made a deal with France and Venice called the League of Cognac to try and limit Spanish rule to Naples and the southern half of Italy. Florence refused to take an official part in order to protect its merchants from reprisals but Giulio insisted that they contribute money and men. However, no sooner had the deal been struck than Charles' allies attacked Rome and forced Giulio to capitulate. Nonetheless he immediately went back on his words and to finally put the fear of god into him Charles sent twelve thousand German mercenaries who joined forces with imperial troops under another flip-flopper, the Duke of Bourbon, who had turned his back on Francis for the good reason that Francis' mother Louise had robbed him of his dead wife's estates and then had the audacity to propose marriage, and thus an unstoppable rabble of thirty thousand disorderly underpaid louts began marching south from Lombardy. It was mainly due to the diplomatic efforts of Machiavelli that Florence avoided being overrun and destroyed."

They had now crossed Via Vittorio Emanuele and were entering a narrow cobbled street named Via dei Cimatori with the usual line of cars and scooters jammed in on one side. A wisteria was just coming into bloom half way along and there was another great dome in the distance.

"Many Florentines lived in this area. The church you see is San Giovanni dei Fiorentini. The *cimatori* were cloth-cutters renowned for their fine finishing work. Most were employed by the Guild of Calimala. The Vespucci had a shop here. It has long since been pulled down but it was there at the end of the wall where the vine is hanging. The present house dates from the 17th century and is now a bed and breakfast, I believe. We will stop for a moment."

They were at the corner of Vicolo delle Palle facing an ancient stone wall. It was too high to see much but there were gaps in the mortar through which they glimpsed a beautiful shaded garden and Michael felt sure he could hear the soporific drone of bees. Several small balconies were visible looking down.

"It seems peaceful in there," Helen said.

"Yes, I'm glad of that," Guido replied, absorbing the tranquil atmosphere, "I think you will be too."

Lamy and the others were still on Via Vittorio Emanuele just out of sight behind a hair salon. The man with the camera, who had come to stand directly beside them before they crossed the street, was getting on a bus.

"Guess he got tired of the chase," Lamy said.

"Or had another appointment," Warren added.

"Ssssh," Lazzari admonished, "I think you're about to hear something very extraordinary."

Benedetto was moving the wheelchair again.

"Michael and Jack left England at the end of March, 1527, and arrived at Livorno on April 21st but found the entry to the harbor blocked and the citadel occupied by carousing *landsknechts* and the captain of their vessel had no choice but to sail south twenty miles to Cecina where they debarked on the evening of April 22nd. They hired horses and took a winding circuitous route through the hills to Volterra and Poggibonizio, where Lorenzo de' Medici's plan to build an 'ideal city' had come to nothing, and were at Machiavelli's door in Sant'Andrea in Percussina three days later. Niccolò wasn't there and Marietta warned them against going to Florence but, of course, they did so the next day intending to find him and, if possible, carry on north to Padua."

They were passing the steps of San Giovanni dei Fiorentini.

"The church was Giovanni de' Medici's idea. It replaced the older one of San Pantaleo, a mythical martyr of the 4th century whose name always brings to my mind Commedia dell'Arte's epitome of greed Pantalone, but the foundation of the nave was all that had been completed by the year of our story. This was the gold district. There on the other side of Via Acciaioli where you see the sign Café d'Oro were many Jewish stalls selling and trading in it."

"Were the Acciaioli Jews?" Helen asked.

"Hell no," Guido replied, "More Florentine bankers. Allied by marriage to the Medici. Acciaioli, Altoviti, Chigi, Piccolomini, all of them, reaped enormous profit collecting and laundering Giulio's 'mountain of faith'!"

Guido laughed again and again Michael's senses were alerted to something harsh and unpleasant and perhaps a little crazy beneath it.

§

In Foggy Bottom it wasn't yet nine in the morning but already the Warrior Princess was having a bad day. She was due to leave for Moscow in the evening to prepare the groundwork for the president's visit in May for the Victory Day Celebration of the Great Patriotic War, elsewhere known as WWII, but she had just flubbed an interview with James Rosen of Fox News. The previous week the House Senate Committee on Foreign Relations had been holding hearings on 'Nuclear Terrorism Prevention' and Russia was the focus of the discussion even more than North Korea or Iran and Rosen's brusque approach made her repeat herself clumsily and she didn't like that.

His first question was, "What percentage of Russian nuclear material does the United States consider to be safely under lock and key?"

"Well, I'm not able to go into numbers here. Let's just say . . "

"Is it fifty percent?"

"Well, James, I'm not going to go into numbers . . "

"So you can't assure me that even fifty percent of their nuclear arsenal is under lock and key?"

"I'm not going to get into numbers. I don't think people should believe we have a huge problem . . "

It was very embarrassing and her mood wasn't improved by the images on her laptop of Michael and Guido in their blue suits which couldn't help but stir memories of her humiliation in Juarez.

"What are they, the goddam fucking Bobbsey twins?" she muttered, "And what the hell is that fucking thing on his nose?" and in an uncharacteristic fit of spontaneous rage she snatched up the phone.

"OK, Porter, I've had it!" she shouted, "I don't care if Lamy spills the shit or that brother Pascal's going to run the WTO. If I have to make nice to Ras fucking Putin while we pretend it was good that Mogilevich got rubbed out and the Juarez cartel got blown sky high, no, no, no, I'm telling you, I don't give a monkey's backside if he's the king of the fucking vampires, I want those two jerks brought in right now. I'll change my flight to come back through Rome. I'm getting out the fucking thumbscrews!"

§

Benedetto turned left beyond the church and made for the river.

"But to return to Michael and Jack, their timing couldn't have been worse. April 26th is called by historians the day of the 'Friday Uprising' and chaos was in the streets of Florence. Anger against Giulio and the autocratic government boiled over. Ippolito de' Medici, the sixteen-year-old bastard son of Leonardo's earlier patron Giuliano di Lorenzo de'

Medici whom Giulio made *de facto* ruler in his stead, left the city with his tutor, the obscenely wealthy and powerful Cardinal Silvio Passerini, to consult with their army commanders and, taking advantage of their absence, a group of youthful *ottimati* shouting *'popolo e libertà'* occupied the Signory, demanding weapons and their immediate expulsion and a return to the 1512 constitution.

"The Duke of Bourbon and his out-for-plunder horde were now massed twenty miles away in San Giovanni Valdarno and Ippolito and Passerini tried to buy their way out of the disaster but the duke raised his price to an impossible three hundred thousand gold florins so they called on Venice and France to defend them. They were lucky the 'cavalry', so to speak, were on the doorstep.

"Michael and Jack bumped into a furious Machiavelli striding across the Piazza della Signoria as he was about to depart for home. He had been snubbed in the latest negotiations but welcomed them warmly saying they shouldn't stay because Ippolito was already on his way back to crush the revolt and invited them to return with him to the sanctuary of Sant'Andrea. Michael asked if it were possible to continue on to Padua and, to their surprise, Niccolò told them Bartolomeo and Destina were no longer there but had fled and were now once again in the house in Borgo Ognissanti. Michael was delighted and agreed to join Niccolò if necessary and he and Jack went immediately to find them."

They were in the middle of the Ponte Principe Amedeo Savoia Aosta on the right hand walkway and Guido gestured for Benedetto to stop.

"Both this bridge and the one between us and Castel Sant'Angelo, Ponte Vittorio Emanuele II, are modern structures. Prince Amedeo was the viceroy to Italian East Africa during the war and I'm sure you know about King Vittorio. In front of his bridge when the tide is very low you can sometimes see the ruins of the Ponte Trionfale peeking above the water line. It was demolished in the sixth century as a defensive measure against the Ostrogoths."

Guido waved his gloved hand like a cavalry captain and they set off again.

"In the twelve years since they had seen her Destina had blossomed into a stunning beauty and Jack didn't betray it but was instantly smitten. The joyous reunion lasted only ten minutes before they decided to ride together to Rome."

A stream of cars roared in and out of a tunnel fifty meters ahead of them and the noise of the ceaseless traffic made it hard to hear.

"You are looking at the highly unglamorous Piazza della Rovere and we're crossing the Lungotevere in Sassia," Guido said, raising his voice above the din, "It honors the Saxons, old boy, what what, haha."

Helen and Michael shared another worried look. Was their guide insane? Where was this leading? The implications about Jack and Destina were obvious but was the whole thing a malicious fabrication?

"Do you know what is happening to the young women in Juarez?" Guido went on, changing the subject without a pause, "I thought to mention it while you were telling your story. It goes far beyond the nastiness of the Portillos. Even their insatiable appetites couldn't have been responsible for so many. I'd call it 'murder tourism'. No one will catch the murderers because they don't live there. They fly in and are gone the next day. They hire local gangs to kidnap the women and provide a secure location where they torture them at their leisure and kill them in whatever manner they choose and then the gangs get rid of the bodies if there's anything left."

Michael and Helen were aghast and silent at the cold horror of the notion.

"I'd say he's got it in one," Warren murmured.

"Does that sound about right?" Guido added.

Michael's mind was still trying to absorb it.

"The thought never occurred to me. It's beyond awful but I suppose it could quite probably be true."

"Oh god yes," Guido concluded, "That's humankind for you."

Benedetto hadn't stopped and they turned right onto Via di Porta Santo Spirito. There was a high embankment to their left and the road led up a steep hill with a massive archway straddling it.

"Everything to our right is the hospital. So, on the ride to Rome Jack and Destina fell in love but what they didn't know was that the imperial troops were hard on their heels. The duke had decided Florence was too well defended for easy pillage whereas Rome he knew was not. The journey took a week and they arrived at the Vespucci house on Via dei Cimatori on May the 4th and on the 6th the looters poured over the Janiculum and Vatican hills.

"Michael was shot twice through the chest on the first morning. On Via Giulia where the steps are now outside San Giovanni dei Fiorentini. Jack and Bartolomeo were able to carry him back to the house but he died in their arms a few minutes later. To avoid scavengers or having his body carted away and thrown into the river or disposed of on some common bonfire they buried him in the garden. His bones lie deep beneath the wisteria. I do not think any more recent construction will have disturbed them. That's why I was glad you found it peaceful."

They were passing under the arch where the name of the street changes to Via dei Penitenzieri and there were buildings again both right and left.

"Good lord," Michael said, "We'll have to take a longer look."

"In the three weeks before the carnage abated two thirds of the people of Rome either perished or fled. No one could control the rapacity. Clement was locked up in the Castel and the only good news was that the Duke of Bourbon also died on the first day of the attack. Benvenuto Cellini claimed he fired the shot that killed him. In the end Giulio had to pay four hundred thousand ducati for his life. A punishment far worse for him, I think, than the wrath of god. He was forced to cede Civitavecchia, Piacenza, Parma and Modena to the empire. And the Venetians snapped up Cervia and Ravenna and Sigismondo Malatesta regained power in Rimini.

"The church now on our right is Santo Spirito in Sassia. It's the true site of the Schola Secorum, the King of Wessex's Saxon School. The hospital itself was an addition built by Innocent III in the 12th century though it still retains 'in Sassia' as part of its title. The church was defaced and devastated during the sack.

"It may also amuse you to know that the building on our left houses the Generalate of the Society of Jesus."

Michael was still grappling with the manner of his namesake's death and barely listening but the mention of Jesuits made him stop.

"Wait a minute," he said bluntly, "I'm almost sure but it's difficult because of your disguise. Didn't we bump into you a few days ago?"

"Where?"

"At Castleganthingummyjig. In the hallway by the infirmary. I had fainted outside and Signor Perdilio was kind enough to take us there."

"Castelgandolfo, Michael," Helen interjected, "And Petrillo. His name was Petrillo."

"What is it that makes him so hopeless?" Lamy said with a chuckle.

He was sweating from the exertion of the hill and taking a breather by the *porta*. Warren and Lazzari still looked fresh as daisies.

"And what is it with you old coots?" he went on, mopping his face with a handkerchief, "Don't you ever sweat? Where in hell is the sonofabitch going?"

"I'd guess the Vatican," Warren answered.

"I suppose it might have been," Guido said with a smile, "Did I see you? I can't recall."

"Yes, yes, we looked straight into each other's eyes."

"Really? I must be getting old."

Warren was correct. They had turned directly toward Piazza San Pietro.

"Shut up about that, Michael," Helen broke in, "I want to hear about Jack and the daughter. Did they go back to England or stay here?"

"They went to England."

"How do you know?" Michael asked sharply, "You said the record ends in the spring of 1527. The Yale papers claim that Bartolomeo died in 1527."

"That's right," Guido replied, smiling again, "The record ends there but if you had searched the Singleton parish registry, as I have done, you would have found several interesting things. The first is an entry notation of the marriage of Jack Davenport with Destina Lupesca, set down simply as an 'alien', on August 1st, 1527. It was the custom then as now for an Italian woman to keep her birth name and I suspect the reason she did not call herself Vespucci was that her mother Elena was never formally married to Bartolomeo. There are four more entries of the baptism of children in February 1528, March 1529, June 1531 and December 1533 and the bloodline of the youngest leads directly to both of you. And so, my dear Michael, I have the honor to inform you that not only have you portrayed Bartolomeo Vespucci but a minuscule fraction of your genetic inheritance actually comes from him."

Helen cast a look backwards to make sure the others were following and was relieved to see Warren and Lazzari just coming round the corner.

"Where the devil is Singleton?" Michael asked in blank dismay.

"Ah. Perhaps you don't know the geography of your native Sussex as well as you think. Billingsgate farm was partly within its boundary."

"Just north of Chichester? Good lord."

"So that explains us," Helen said, still far from accepting any of it, "But what about you? How does it make us related to you?"

The crowds in the piazza were coming into view.

"Oh dear me," Guido sighed, "That is a much, much longer story."

"I'd love to hear it."

"So would I," Lazzari said.

"No kidding," Lamy added, puffing along behind.

"Well, if you have some hours to spare this evening I will try and find the strength to tell you."

It was twenty minutes past four as they began making their way along Via Paolo VI which passes just beyond Bernini's great colonnade on the south side of the square and through it they could see tens of thousands of worshippers standing patiently or wandering about in anxious expectation. Michael noticed a group of black nuns on their knees praying.

"They're in the Hall of Blessings now," Guido said.

"Who are?" Michael asked.

"The cardinals."

§

The Warrior Princess nearly choked on a spoonful of mid-morning yogurt as she screamed into the mouthpiece.

"What do you mean you can't find them? I thought you had a tail!"

"He left after he took the photos. Sembler told him that was all he had to do."

"I'll chew the slimy little cocksucker's balls off!" she shrieked, spitting tiny white specks on her paperwork, "Where were they seen last?"

"Largo Tassoni. They went down a street beside it. Our man knew he had been seen and figured it was better to get out."

"Fucking Jesus Christly shit!"

"Hold your horses," Goss said, reading a message on his computer screen, "They've been spotted near St. Peter's. The cars are on their way. We'll be on them in five minutes."

§

Benedetto took a detour through the columns so they could look up at the façade of the basilica and the Loggia delle Benedizione.

"Ratzinger will be standing there tomorrow," Guido said.

"How do you know?" Helen asked.

"The Inquisition still lives."

"What are we supposed to make of that?" Michael scoffed.

"You'll see. They're off to the Sistine Chapel in a few minutes. If you had as sensitive ears as I do you'd hear them all singing that awful dirge *Veni Creator Spiritus*. My little chorus of vampires. I can't stand the sound of them."

The mention of vampires made Helen's blood run cold and she fell a few paces behind but Michael kept up as Benedetto began pushing the wheelchair faster and faster toward the open expanse in front of the Petriano gate.

"Where are we going?" Michael asked.

"You can come with me if you like."

"Where?"

"Inside."

"You live in Vatican City?"

"Not always."

Lamy and the others were a hundred yards behind them on Borgo Santo Spirito outside the church of the Sisters of the Sorrowful Mother.

"Did you hear what he just said?" Lamy asked.

Warren and Lazzari nodded.

"Are you thinking what I'm thinking?"

They nodded again and suddenly three black Cadillac SRX SUVs came careening around the corner from Via dei Penitenzieri. As the cars zoomed past Lamy could see Mel Sembler in the passenger seat of the first turning his head to stare in their direction and he looked at Warren and Lazzari and they started trotting in pursuit.

The wheelchair was now only fifty feet from the Swiss Guards.

"Why did you call them vampires?" Michael demanded, almost running to stay level, "Did you mean it? What are you trying to say?"

"Surely you've guessed by now," Guido answered.

"What?"

"All right, I'll tell you this much. You're a bit of a fusspot and not nearly as humble but, in every other respect, you're his identical twin."

"Whose identical twin?"

Michael stopped dead. The wheelchair was at the gate.

"Good lord," he said.

He looked back at Helen but realized she couldn't have heard because the Cadillacs were screeching round the curve into the Piazza del Sant'Uffizio. The lead car barely avoided crushing the life from an elderly trinket vendor as it came to a grinding halt two inches short of her trolley.

"Well," Guido called over his shoulder, "Are you coming or not?

There's a lot more I could show you."

Sembler was getting out of the car and Michael saw him and made a quick decision. Guido and Benedetto were past the guards who didn't look at them but moved in unison to a position of readiness.

"Don't Michael!" Helen shouted and hurried to him and grabbed his arm, "Don't. Please. I'm afraid. What if he's completely mad."

Michael shrugged. There wasn't time to explain.

"I know, I know, but . . how else will we find out if it's true?"

He kissed her and gently took her hand away and darted through the gates as the guards closed them behind him.

There were six agents out of the Caddies but Sembler knew it was too late. He stood by the car door fuming and as Warren and Lazzari came puffing into view with Lamy trailing valiantly behind he said loudly, "You haven't heard the last of this, Lou," but Lamy was so out of breath he could only respond with a finger and the three of them joined Helen and watched.

As Michael and Guido and the wheelchair reached the stone marking the position of the obelisk in the time of Caligula Benedetto stopped and Guido rose from the chair in a single fluid motion. His back was to them and he took off the fedora to reveal that the white tufts were attached and that his own hair was close-cropped and light brown. He removed the noseguard and the dark glasses and the gloves and placed them in the hat and handed it to Benedetto. They could see he was talking all the while and Michael was listening intently but they could no longer hear him because the transmitter was in Helen's purse. Then he embraced Michael and kissed him three times on the cheeks and draped an arm over his shoulders and the two blue suits walked slowly away out of sight around the Sacristy with the wheelchair following.

Helen's teeth were chattering despite the warm sunshine.

"I begged him not to go," she whispered helplessly.

Envoi

"Peace on earth would mean the end of civilization as we know it."
- Joseph Heller (1923 - 1999)

§

The Christian Socialist Francis Bellamy wrote the Pledge of Allegiance in 1892 and for many years its oration was accompanied by the so-called Bellamy Salute which turned out to be exactly the same as the one that a certain famous *Reichskanzler* subsequently made so familiar and so, after they had observed one hundred and sixty-eight seconds of silence *in memoriam* of the tenth anniversary of the Oklahoma City bombing and the one hundred and sixty-eight victims of that tragic day, a heavily-sedated Richard Bruce Cheney and a still remarkably boyish-looking William Jefferson Clinton stood next to each other with hands over precariously beating hearts in the First United Methodist Church at 131 NW 4th Street and as they mouthed the controversial phrase 'one nation, under God', the last two words of which had only been added by an Act of Congress and incorporated into the pledge in 1954 and were to that very day a source of offence and continuing litigation, the one hundred and fifteen cardinal electors in the Sistine Chapel were casting their fourth and final ballots in one of fastest papal elections in history.

§

One hour and forty-eight minutes later the ballots were burned and due to an error the entire chapel filled with smoke which would have been much to the horror of those who recently spent months and years restoring the artwork had they been there to see it and which caused temporary confusion among the gathered pilgrims in the square because what ushered from the chimney at first appeared black but gradually it changed to white and they began chanting *'Viva il papa'* and *'Habemus papam'* and when the bells finally started tolling in earnest, after an initial hiccup and a tense ten minute delay because someone inside had pushed the wrong button, they cheered at the top of their lungs.

258

Helen, Warren, Lamy and Lazzari were watching the spectacle unfold on television in the dining room of the Casale. It was more then twenty-four hours and Michael hadn't called and their concern and agitation was getting worse by the minute so when Pope Benedict XVI came onto the Balcony of Blessings to give his *Urbi et Orbi* speech, after an unaccountably plodding introduction by the Chilean Cardinal Jorge Arturo Agustín Medina Estévez who was obviously either in a huff or as anesthetized as the vice-president in Oklahoma, they did not share in the general jubilation.

"Is that a drag queen in heat or what," Lamy said.

The crowd was going wild and as Ratzinger raised his arms to salute them Warren put words to the gesture, "Wheee, look at me, suckers!"

"Do I hear the overture to Jesus Christ Superstar?" Lazzari mused.

"He looks like Dracula's bloody daughter," Helen added glumly, "Cousin Guido called them his 'little chorus of vampires'. Considering what happened at that dreadful party it's almost believable."

"And if what he kept hinting at is true," Lamy teased, "Then he's at least five hundred years old and you and Michael have vampire blood too."

"Don't joke. It's not funny."

"It would be pretty dilute by now," Warren observed in a tongue-in-cheek attempt to be comforting, "You'd be an equal amount highwayman. What do you think, Luigi? Shall we say twenty generations?"

"Two to the twentieth power? That must be, I don't know, less than one part in over a hundred thousand," Lazzari guessed.

"One part in over a million. Not even ten thousandth of a percent," Lamy confirmed, "Anyway, in a sense, everything that lives is a vampire."

"And doesn't live. Think of black holes and supernovas. Every gravitating particle in the universe," Warren concluded and then added gently, "Don't fret, my dear, it was probably all nonsense."

§

At four o'clock the next morning Helen was wide awake and staring at the ceiling of their suite with her mind in a fever of worry and the miraculous vault of a hundred billion galaxies each ablaze with the light of a hundred billion stars glittered with perfect crystal clarity over the great massif of Cerro Pastelone, the epicenter of the Vortex of Trino in the Zona del Silencio. It was nine in the evening though time had long ago lost interest for the two figures stretched on a makeshift platform topped by a straw pallet at the summit. They might have been the mummified remains of ancient Tarahumaran elders because of their native attire and dry dusty sun-blackened skin except for the slight incongruity that they were holding hands.

They were the two expatriate nonagenarian English adventurers who had been in El Paso during Michael's ill-fated visit to Juarez. They had bumped into him at Amado's hotel and witnessed the drug lord's gruesome death in the jaws of his tiger. They were fans of Coronation Street and recognized Michael from his brief unhappy appearance on the series. They, too, were eccentrics, eternal optimists who believed aliens are frequent visitors to our glorious planet. When Michael said goodbye to them eight years previously they were on their way to Mexico and they had stayed ever since, enchanted by its magic and beauty.

It wasn't until early February, however, that they found out from the local campesinos about the drum of plutonium. It was exciting that it was flown in by a Russian arms dealer at the same time they were in El Paso and stashed near the petroglyphs between El Fierro and Los Lamentos and they couldn't resist enlisting the help of some daring young men to steal it.

They knew the Chihuahua desert was part of the Sea of Thetis during the Cenozoic and the whole area possessed wondrous magnetic qualities. They had seen for themselves thousands of shooting stars seeming to burst directly above them on the many nights they had spent on the mountaintop and were certain the massive carbon steel drum, which to their eyes shimmered with a ghostly blue luminescence in the rarefied air, could only be an added attraction.

So there they lay, patiently gazing upward, cosy beneath layers of tattered woven blankets with their feet touching the drum as they had every night since the theft, waiting for the aliens to come.

"You know, Dickie, I've been wondering," the old woman said dreamily.

"No, I don't know, Ethel, what have you been wondering?"

"What do you suppose Mr. Davenport's doing now?"

www.ingramcontent.com/pod-product-compliance
Lightning Source LLC
Chambersburg PA
CBHW070444200726
48293CB00007B/2115